C000179909

Ronan S Costello was born in Dublin in 1973. At the age of nine he acquired the nickname 'Rossi' after Italian footballer Paolo Rossi. The similarities between the World Cup winning legend and the top goal scorer in the Under Tens North Wicklow and District Schoolboys League could not be denied.

After being turned down by Liverpool FC on numerous occasions, Costello reluctantly settled for a career in the financial markets. In the words of his mother, he "quit a perfectly good job to 'doss about' for a year."

'Satan's Whiskers' is his first novel and the result of some very strenuous 'dossing'.

SATAN'S WHISKERS

Rossi Costello

Satan's Whiskers

Vanguard Press

A CIP catalogue record for this title is
available from the British Library

ISBN 1 84386 188 7

*Vanguard Press is an imprint of
Pegasus Elliot MacKenzie Publishers Ltd.*
www.pegasuspublishers.com

First Published in 2005

**Vanguard Press
Sheraton House Castle Park
Cambridge England**

Printed & Bound in Great Britain

Dedicated to Maelisa

Acknowledgements

My biggest thanks must go to the reprobates who inspired the characters in this story.

The list is long but here goes…Paolo, Jimmy, Gav, Rae, Macker, Johnny, Horse, Traolach, Luke, Noel, Justin, Flash, Mick, Gar, Barry and all the other lads and lassies who spent too much time in the Horse and Hound arguing the meaning of life and occasionally more trivial matters. For the kind feedback from readers Alex, Aoibheann, Gavin and Ditchy, thank you for sparing my feelings. A special thanks to Siobhan for her support and encouragement throughout. Cheers to the Oxford Old Boys drinking committee for keeping me from going sane (yes sane). And finally, a big thank you to my family for their continued loving support.

Chapter 1

If she was ugly Macker still would have held the door open for her, but she wasn't ugly. She was a long way from ugly. If ugly was a cold wet weekend in Skegness she was a luxury cruise around the Caribbean. She smiled as she walked through the doorway and the cold January air instantly warmed up a few degrees. She looked a couple of years younger than him...twenty, maybe twenty-one, but certainly within jurisdiction for a healthy and horny twenty-four-year-old like Macker. Heck, even if she was seventeen or eighteen, he'd have to consider bending the rules a bit. He quickly followed her into the pub for a closer look. Unfortunately she was wearing a long coat so he couldn't check out her ass properly. As he was cursing the cold Dublin winters she ducked behind the bar into the staff quarters.

Holy shit! thought Macker. *She works here!*

Rory, the barman smiled when he saw Macker. He picked up a pint glass and placed it under the Guinness tap. "Howye Macker...Strawberry Daiquiri?"

"Why not, Rory."

Macker nodded towards the staff door. "Who's the new bird?"

"New bird?"

Macker threw his eyes to the heavens. "Yes Rory, the new girl who works here. She just walked past...y'know, long dark hair, brown eyes, sexy smile."

Rory frowned down at the Guinness tap. "Oh, I think I know the one yer talkin' about. She just started here."

"Thanks Rory! That's just fuckin' brilliant. I'm in here every second night. I think I'd know if she'd been workin' here for more than a week!"

Macker craned his neck to see who was working on the other side of the bar.

"Is Anto in tonight?"

Anto was the guy Macker needed to talk to. He'd know everything about the new employee down to her bra size.

Rory shook his head. "Nah, he doesn't work Fridays anymore."

Macker put his elbow on the bar and leaned over it. "Look Rory, I know you're happily married with fifteen kids and forty-nine grand kids, but you must at least know her name or where she's from. She's a babe for Christ sake!"

Rory smiled and shook his head. "Sorry Mack, all I know is she started here a couple of nights ago and she does lounge service. I think she might be a student."

Macker picked up his pint, saluted the helpful barman and made his way across the lounge to his usual table. At least if the new girl did lounge service he'd get a chance to order a round off her later. As he put down his pint and took off his coat he listened for a moment to the fascinating conversation his three best friends were having about cats.

"Of course, they have sex ye gobshite! How the fuck do you think they give birth to little cats if they don't have sex?"

"I'm not sayin' they don't have sex! I'm just sayin' that ye never see them doing it. You see dogs' doing it all the time, but never cats…Why's that?"

"Well, they're obviously a bit more bashful about it."

"D'ye reckon they do it doggy style?"

"Who? Cats? I suppose so. I saw some lions doin' it once, on the nature channel and they were doin' it doggy style…They'd look a bit silly doin' it missionary."

His three friends laughed, but Macker didn't join in. Usually he enjoyed aimless banter as much as anyone, but tonight was not the night to be wasting time talking about the sexual habits of cats or any other animal for that matter. There was important business to take care of and he knew he'd have to interrupt, before his friends started listing the other possible positions in which cats might have sex. When he arrived at the pub there was only one thing on his mind. As a result of the encounter with the new lounge girl, there were now two, but even the induction of a sexy new employee into their humble local pub took a back seat to what Macker came to *The Banner Man* to discuss.

First things first, he thought, taking a large gulp of Guinness before placing his glass firmly back on the table and rudely disrupting the ongoing chat.

"Listen lads." Macker ran the back of his sleeve across his lower lip. "Tonight's the night we need to make up our minds."

"About what?"

"About who wants a piece of this horse?"

The Banner Man pub was named by owner Sean Lyons who hailed from the Banner County of Clare. The pub didn't have much of a memory, but if it did, it still would have had difficulty remembering all the different names it had gone through since its birth in 1961. Some of the more colourful ones were *The Purple Lizard* during its hippy phase, *The 32 Counties* during its patriotic phase and *The Deep* during its cool phase in the eighties. *The Banner Man* had witnessed countless highs and lows over the years including fifteen engagements, three fires, two deaths, four robberies and even one birth back in the sixties. Although it had been refurbished in the last couple of years, it still maintained a certain quaint quality that had been lost from most suburban Dublin pubs after the booming nineties. By sticking to the old formula of plain wooden chairs around simple wooden tables in a dimly lit wooden pub, The pub had managed to build up strong loyalty from its local regulars. At the same time the "no-extras" formula managed to deter what Sean Lyons referred to as PTGs (potential trouble groups). With no loud music, no fancy lighting and no large MTV screens, the pub wasn't exactly an oasis for young groups out on loud drinking sessions. Apart from some very dubious music, which was played at low volume in the toilets and the odd occasion – usually a big match, when the three TVs were turned on, there were not many distractions from straight forward "pub talk" in *The Banner Man*. Even the furniture arrangement and the poor lighting seemed to entice the occupant of each seat into the forward-leaning, crouched position popular with chess players. Conversation, argument, retort, agreement, debate and laughter all filled the air.

In the most sparsely populated corner of the pub, four young men, who understood the essence of the *The Banner Man,* were having a discussion about the purchase of a horse. The youngest of them, Michael McCann, also known as Macker, was doing most of the talking.

"Lads, this is it. One way or the other we have to make up our minds tonight. The sales are on the twenty fifth of Jan and my uncle Liam needs to know at least a week in advance."

"Tell us about the money again?" asked Matt.

As far as Macker was concerned, Matt Cullen was the key figure in this whole debate. Matt knew plenty about horses. Not quite as much as Macker himself, but certainly a lot more than Shipsey and Dave. The other reason Macker was desperate to get Matt in on the venture was down to luck. All the lads considered Matt lucky. He had the amazing knack of landing on his feet at all times. If there was a bird in the sky actually *trying* to shit on Matt's head it could spend the whole day following him around, but it would be in vain. Lady luck would ensure that Matt would either speed up to catch a bus or stop to tie his shoelace at just the right moment. If Matt, for some reason, missed an airplane flight, bookmakers around the world should slash the odds of that plane going down. Macker wanted this sort of luck on his side, but more importantly he knew that he'd find it almost impossible to get Shipsey and Dave on board if Matt wasn't in.

"Liam expects the horse to go for fifteen to twenty grand and he's agreed that if it stays within that price range, he'll put up half the cash. So between the four of us we need ten grand max."

Matt had a big problem. He didn't have two and a half grand to spare. Well, actually that's not entirely true. He had almost five grand sitting in a savings account earning very little interest. Five grand that he'd worked hard to earn and save himself. Five grand that he should have been able to spend as he wished, but that he'd promised his long-term girlfriend, Samantha Kearns, would be going towards the deposit on a house that they would be buying together in the near future. He knew he wouldn't get away with blowing half his savings on one-eighth of a racehorse. He also knew that when he returned his no-vote that it would probably lead to the collapse of the whole venture. He was setting them up for the fall and wanted to make it as soft as possible.

"What about the cost of the upkeep?"

"I don't know exactly," Macker answered hesitantly. "It varies from summer to winter, but it's no more than ten to fifteen euro each, per month."

At this stage Shipsey butted in, in his usual brash fashion. "For fuck sake Macker, that all adds up! I thought the trainer was gonna do a deal for us 'cos he knows your uncle?"

"He is! And anyway, what's fifteen euro Shipsey? You've lost three times that waitin' for a bus!"

Shipsey sighed and sat back in his chair. "Five 46As in a row," he grumbled. A month earlier he lost fifty euro to Matt at a bus stop in Deansgrange, waiting for a 75 to go to Tallaght.

"And your uncle already owns our horses' brother, is that right?" asked Matt.

"Half brother...yeah...himself and the trainer Paddy Mulryan are joint owners."

"So why isn't the trainer goin' halves on *this* one? Is the other one no good?"

"No...sure they've hardly even run him yet. He just doesn't have the cash."

Macker didn't know whether this was true or not. He knew the other horse had run in at least one proper race, but had come nowhere.

He had no idea why Paddy Mulryan wasn't getting involved in this horse and he really didn't care. All he wanted was to own part of a racehorse himself. He knew the other lads wanted it too. They'd had this chat a dozen times. He was sure they'd dreamed as he had, about roaring their horse up the Cheltenham Hill or over Bechers Brook at Aintree or into the winners enclosure at the Christmas festival at Leopardstown.

Half an hour later the situation was getting more awkward and tense for Macker. He had already told his uncle that they were going in on the investment, so he was desperate for the three of them to say yes. Anytime they had this hypothetical chat before, they had all agreed that they wanted to be part of it, but now that they were playing for real, he was a lot less certain of the outcome and knew that he would have to tread delicately. If he started showing his desperation and using phrases like "come on" or "you know it makes sense" that would be more likely to scare them away. Nor did he want to start drawing flowery pictures of winner's enclosures and exotic racetracks, as this wouldn't be taken seriously. He decided that the best tactic was to continue answering all their queries to the best of his knowledge and when the moment was right, try to get one of them on his side.

"What about studding?" asked Matt.

Shit, thought Macker. *That is not the sort of question I wanted to be answering.*

"In all likelihood, if he hasn't already been, we'll have to have him gelded."

There was a sharp intake of breath around the table. Shipsey and Dave, who hadn't heard this terminology before, both swallowed and looked wide-eyed at each other. The look on the other one's face confirmed to each of them that their interpretations of the phrase "to have him gelded" were matching and correct.

Shipsey leaned back in his chair and threw a beer matt onto the table. "What's the point in spendin' twenty grand on something and then havin' its most valuable bits chopped off?"

"Well lads, it's like this ye see," said Macker, choosing his words carefully. "The horse that we're looking to buy, his pedigree is in jumping hurdles and fences, ok? And having your bare bollocks dragged through a stumpy bush at forty miles an hour isn't a horses' idea of fun and it wouldn't be mine either. On top of that, keeping a stallion is much harder work and costs a lot more money than keeping a gelding."

Shipsey leaned forward and picked up the beer mat. "Well that's decided then the bollocks goes. Can we keep it and sew it back on at a later date? It would be nice for him to get the odd shag in, when he's retired."

Matt groaned and stood up. "I have a sudden urge to go and check on my plums." He started walking towards the gents in the style of John Wayne.

The horse had actually been gelded when he was sixteen months old and if he had the choice he would have taken his chances hurdling bareback rather than go through the pain and humiliation of having his favourite bits lopped off. Macker decided to bring Dave into the conversation at this point. Matts questions had worn him out a bit and he figured as Dave's horse knowledge was very minimal it would be a good way to take a breather. "Davey boy, you got any questions?"

Dave shook his head slowly and shrugged. "No, I'm in."

Dave's response was short and simple and in Macker's eyes it changed everything. He now had a chance to get an affirmative response from Shipsey and have the whole thing sewn up before Matt got back from the toilet. "Excellent! Good man. You know it makes sense. What about you big man?" he asked, turning his attention to Shipsey.

"Ah yeah, what the hell," Shipsey agreed. "But you know that horse won't win a single race if Matt Cullen isn't involved. That chaps the jammiest bastard alive!"

"Don't worry," Macker assured them, "if I can tell him that the three of us are all in, there's no way he's gonna miss out on the fun."

"What fun?" enquired Matt, arriving back to the table.

"Shipsey and Dave are in, so it's just up to you to get off the potty and make up your mind and then the fun starts."

This whole conversation had developed like a big poker hand and it was now clear to Matt that Macker had all the cards and he would have to fold in one way or another. *These guys wouldn't even know each other if it wasn't for me,* he thought to himself. Matt always liked to think of himself as the central character in their four-way friendship. He'd known Shipsey since they were four. He made friends with Macker through football, and Dave and he became drinking buddies in college. Now, as a result of *them* becoming such good pals, he was at risk of being left on the outside. He played out all the possible outcomes in his mind, but didn't care much for any of them. Nightmare scenario number one was, he decided to stay out and they formed a syndicate without him. He simply couldn't face that. Number two was, he stayed out and the whole thing fell through. He knew Macker, in particular, would never let him live that down. The final option was, he goes for it and risks the wrath of his beloved Samantha. Somehow the four and a half pints he'd had so far that evening, added to the two "swifties" he'd had after work, were helping him deny exactly how ballistic Sam would go if she found out.

"Right. Fuck it," he said raising his glass to his chin and giving each of them a steely look. " I'm in." He drained the contents of the glass in two large gulps and lowered it back to the table with an audible firmness. "On one condition...Nobody is allowed tell Sam. If she finds out that I'm blowing a load of dosh on a racehorse...well...let's just say, that donkey won't be the only one gettin' his bollocks chopped off!"

Macker grinned and clapped his hands loudly. "Yesss! Ah lads, we're gonna have a good fuckin' laugh." As he was rubbing his hands together he caught sight of the sexy new lounge girl serving drinks at a nearby table. "By the way," he whispered. "Has anyone seen that new lounge girl? She's a little cracker."

Chapter 2

Almost everywhere he went Michael McCann was known as Macker. His mum and dad stuck to Michael and some of his work colleagues called him Mick, but by and large everyone knew him as Macker. He was the third and last child born to Garoid and Deirdre McCann and had lived all his life in the same four-bedroom house in Cabinteely, a suburb on the south side of Dublin. His eldest sister Eimear moved to London in 2001 shortly after getting married, leaving Macker to share the mostly pleasant, but at times unbearable company of his other sister Sinead. Macker realised, that at twenty-four it was probably time he got a place of his own, but was also aware how seriously detrimental that would be to his standard of living. His parents only charged him 300 euro per month for rent. Included in this deal were free meals, a complete laundry service and occasional lifts to a number of different drinking establishments. It's a deal that would be difficult to match out in the real world and Macker knew it. His parents knew it too, but, in truth, weren't in any rush to see the back of their two remaining children, having been quite upset when Eimear moved out. This was a true blessing for Macker, considering the crucifying property prices and rents of suburban Dublin in the year 2003.

Macker was one of those guys who seemed to have an endless supply of energy. If he were a battery he would be decked out in black with a shiny copper top. At home he was always the first to rise and the last to go to bed. In the pub he was usually the one leading the conversation and would be the first to suggest a change of venue if things were dull. Maybe the reason he always had a full tank of fuel was because his job as an I.T. consultant didn't require him to burn much of it. For three and a half years he had been a member of the I.T. support team in a large financial institution known as FND. In that time he had struggled and failed to dream up a more boring job than his. Even the librarian who works in the quietest library in the world is surrounded by books and is bound to know where the dirty ones are. Even the guy who sits in the twenty-four-hour garage from midnight to 8am is sure to come across the odd crazy drunk and have a few stories to tell his mates in the pub. Macker couldn't remember telling one funny I.T. story to the lads in *The Banner Man*. Occasionally this bothered him, but mostly he was fine with it. For Macker, working and getting paid were the means to an end. He never had the ambition to "further his I.T. career" or "climb the corporate ladder."

Macker didn't choose I.T   I.T. chose him. When deciding what college course he would take the criteria he set out were very basic. He had to be able to commute to the venue from home. The duration of the course was to be no more than two years and the total number of hours per week could be no more than twenty. At eighteen months long and fourteen hours of lectures per week, Dun Laoghaire College Certificate in Computer Technology ticked all the boxes. He passed his final exams no problem and within a month he found himself at FND spending most of his time playing minesweeper. Although he found his job neither interesting nor challenging, he was happy that it did have a number of redeeming features. For starters, the money was pretty good and he was rarely short of the funds he required to enjoy his extra curricular activities. He liked the hours too. There were two different eight-hour shifts, one running from 7am to 3pm and the other from 12pm to 8pm. Once you ran over your eight hours you were on to double pay. On Saturday and Sunday you were paid time and a half for your eight hours and triple pay for overtime. Although he wouldn't get away with it anymore, Macker could remember a couple of times in the past when he'd earned over eight hundred euro for doing two twelve hour shifts over the weekend. In addition to the good hours and generous pay, Macker had arrived at the stage in his job, where he worked under almost no pressure. For the first month or two he didn't have a clue what he was doing and managed to survive on his wits rather than his I.T. skills. When a call came through and someone had a problem with their computer that he couldn't solve (which at the start was 9 out of 10 calls), he would simply go around to that person's desk and bluff his way through it. One of his favourite tricks was highlighting an icon that people would rarely use, like "format" or "configuration" using the right-sided clicker on the mouse and then scanning down until he came to a word with a black triangular arrow beside it. This meant that another window of options would open up if he scrolled to the right of this arrow. He would continue doing this until he could go no further and the screen was full of these ever decreasing option windows. Then he would scan up and down this final small window only looking at the words that had been greyed out, meaning that they were unavailable options on this particular PC. Then he would move the cursor slowly from left to right under the option that he thought had the most ambiguous meaning, usually something like "advanced table properties" or "versions." At this point he would lock his lips tight into a wry smile and let out a long and meaningful "hmmmmmm" whilst exhaling through slightly flared nostrils. It's at this point that the worried PC owner whose shoulder he had been working over, would usually have something to say, so Macker knew he'd have to get in quick with one of his prepared responses. The line he used would depend on a few different things. How big he perceived the problem to be, how important he perceived the individual involved to be, that persons personality (were they known for kicking up a fuss), the time of day (was it close to lunchtime or end of day, when he would be able to come back with a more competent I.T. colleague) and lastly, who was around to help him out. Was it someone he liked and could trust not to tell the world that he was shit with computers?

So it was through the use of these masterful tactics and phrases like "it could be a problem with the server" or "I may need to work on this over lunch," that Macker struggled through the first couple of months as an I.T. consultant. After about six months, he had entered the comfort zone and could solve about 9 out of 10 problems without any help from his colleagues, and a lot of these without even leaving his desk. When he did get stuck, there were usually a couple of friendly faces around to help him, which is another reason Macker wasn't in a hurry to quit FND. He worked in a fairly young team and they often went for a few beers together after work. Apart from one or two, who were either a bit older or more ambitious, he got on really well with all of the I.T. support staff. The programmers were a different story. They were all "wankers" and "egg-heads" to be avoided at all costs. On Friday night, which was the only night the programmers went to the pub, it was always the mission of the support team to find out what pub they were going to and choose a different venue for their own, more jovial get-togethers.

"Can't go to Toners tonight, the "egg-heads" are there, we'll go to Maguires instead."

The last and most important thing that Macker liked about working for the bank was the quantity and quality of girls that worked there. Even on his first day, when he was being shown around the three-storey bank he'd counted at least ten stunning babes. Little did he know that things would get even better when the bank took over the fourth floor of the building to open up the headquarters of their telesales and information call centre. Of the fifty-five people who now occupied this busy area, forty-two were girls. Of these forty-two girls twenty-six were what Macker would categorize as scorable. This means they fell into the right age group and were sufficiently good looking. According to Macker's latest estimate, somewhere between twelve and fifteen of these babes were single. Macker reckoned he was in with a chance of scoring approximately twelve to fifteen of them. All of Macker's friends and colleagues knew him as a womaniser. Whether they referred to him as a charmer, a smoothie, or a rogue they had all latched on to the same thing. Macker liked girls and couldn't help turning on the charm when he was talking to one he fancied. He was aware that he had gained a bit of a reputation, but was neither proud nor ashamed of it. In fact, he didn't even stop to think about whether he deserved it or if he should do something about it. Maybe if he analysed it, he'd come to the conclusion that his childhood as the baby boy in a family of doting mother and older sisters had laid the blueprint for his future life urges, but Macker didn't care for that bullshit. All he knew was that nothing was going to stop him from striving to get to where he was happiest, in the company of women. And when a call came down to him from the fourth floor or Utopia, as he liked to call it, it was always treated as a priority and responded to with a personal visit and a smile.

Macker never had much trouble attracting the opposite sex. He had the confidence and the looks to pull the prettiest of them. At six feet tall, with a cheeky face and a flash of blond hair, he was off to a good start. In fact for some girls the hair was enough to make them weak. His blond locks were almost as fine now as when he was three years old and women seemed to find them irresistible. Sometimes when he was working on a young ladie's PC, Macker would turn around to catch the poor girl gazing longingly at his golden strands. He had always been aware of the effect of his magic hair, having grown up with two sisters and a mother, who for years couldn't keep their hands off it. Because of its fineness and maybe a little out of jealousy, the other lads predicted that he would be bald within three years. Macker didn't like that idea and was determined to cash in on his good fortune while it lasted. With this in mind he always made sure to keep his hair sweet smelling and when he was helping out one of the babes in Utopia he made a point of dangling the carrot just in front of the donkey's nose. It rarely failed to get the desired result. Next to his hair as a pulling attraction were his twinkling blue eyes. The combination of soft gold and suggestive blue gave Macker a look that was cheekily roguish and very true to his character. If he could change one thing about himself it would be his weight. At just over eleven stone he wished he could bulk up a bit, but his metabolism was as energetic as his libido. Ocassionally he found being skinny a bit of a hindrance on the football pitch, but it didn't come as much of a handicap when chasing girls. Now and then he would get a complaint. A girl would grab him and say, "look at ye, there's not a pick on ye." But Macker reckoned they only did this so they could grasp some part of his anatomy.

The new lounge girl moved slowly across the main floor of the pub carrying a tray of drinks. To the trained eye, you could tell she hadn't being doing lounge service for long, as she was quite slow and shaky with the tray. To the eight eyes straining to see her from the corner of the pub, she had everything perfectly formed and in the right place.

"Jaysis she's a fine young thing," said Macker, rubbing his hands together.

"Hmmmmm." The rest of the lads hummed their agreement.

"A face like a supermodel…a body like a Russian tennis player."

"Hmmmmm."

Macker picked up his pint glass. "Right lads, knock 'em back and I'll call her over."

Chapter 3

The following evening Matt's girlfriend, Samantha Kearns rang Shipsey's girlfriend Jane McGovern, who had been struggling with a hangover all day. In the seven hours she'd been awake that Sunday, Jane had spent half an hour eating, a quarter of an hour doing housework and the rest of the time was divided between watching TV, catnapping and cursing the after effects of Tequila. She was in no mood for Sam's call, particularly when Sam opened with the line, "So, what did you get up to today?"

Jane could tell that Sam had news of her own that she was dying to impart, but decided to stall her friend just for the hell of it. She racked her brain trying to think of the most interesting thing she had done that day. Then she remembered the wildlife programme she had watched with Shipsey about a large peculiar looking fish that lives off the east coast of Africa. Jane lasted a minute and a half before her memory of the narrator's words ran out.

"Well anyway, I can't remember the name of the fish, but scientists believe it can be dated back seventy million years and due to its highly unusual fins, could be related to the first fish that used their fins to leave the sea and crawl on land...It had a really funny name...what was it again?"

Jane smiled to herself. She knew Sam wasn't listening to a word. Maybe she could quiz her about it at a later date, but now it was time to stop teasing and find out why her friend had really phoned.

"So did you do anything nice yourself?"

Sam had finally got her chance to talk and she came out of the traps like a greyhound on speed. "Yeah, I had the most amazing day! Matt and I went for a walk on Dun Laoghaire Pier. We were walking and talking for hours. He's doing really well at work and reckons he'll get a good bonus in the summer and he's almost certain to get a promotion and a company car next year. But the big news is...we've agreed to move in together."

"Oh excellent! Congratulations! When?"

"His current lease is up in August, so we'll start looking in the early summer."

"Well done! I'm delighted for you."

"Thanks, it's great isn't it? We were holding hands and talking for hours. We even talked about marriage properly for the first time! But we both agreed that it doesn't make sense for another few years…neither of us wants a long engagement…but at least now, I know he's really thinking about it!"

"That's great. Good stuff." Jane was biggining to run out of enthusiasm and picked up the TV guide. She usually had more time for Sam, but her friend's energetic zeal was starting to bring back on the headache that she had spent so long trying to get rid of and besides, one of her top five favourite soaps was coming on in two minutes. Thankfully Shipsey had gone down to *The Banner Man*, so she had full ownership of the remote control and an evening of soap operas had been mapped out.

"So I was thinking," Sam continued, "you know the way your birthday is coming up in a couple of weeks?"

"Yeah," said Jane, a little bit worried, but pleasantly surprised that Sam had remembered.

"Why don't we all go out for a sort of joint celebration dinner?"

"That's a good idea," Jane agreed somewhat hesitantly. "Let's sort it out next week. I'll call you from work, ok?"

"Ok, talk to you then, byeee."

******

Shipsey plonked the two pints down on the table and took a long look at his best friend. Matt appeared to be concentrating on peeling the logo from his beer mat, but Shipsey could tell his mind was elsewhere.

"What the fuck's wrong with you? You look like someone shit in your soup!"

Matt looked up smiling for a split second before the frown returned. "Nah, I just had a marathon session with Sam down in Dun Laoighre today. It was fuckin' freezin' out, but she insisted on walkin' up and down the pier all day, talkin' complete shite! I totally missed the Liverpool match and everything!"

"You didn't miss much," Shipsey lied. "What's the problem?"

"Well, she caught me off guard and started asking all sorts of questions about moving in together and getting married and shit. So I agreed to move out of the flat and start looking for a place with her in the summer."

"What's wrong with that? You were gonna have to stop living like a student sooner or later."

"Yeah, I know. I just hoped it would be later."

"Look," said Shipsey, leaning forward. "You're mad about Sam,

26

right?"

"Yeah   course."

"And you've been goin' out together for what?   Three years?"

"Three and a half."

"Right, well it's probably about time you found out whether or not you two can enjoy livin' together."

"Yeah, I suppose so," Matt shrugged, "but I quite like livin' with Dave. We have a good laugh, y'know   I can come and go whenever I please, I don't have to take any crap...I'm my own man."

"So let me get this straight, you'd prefer to live with *Dave*, a fat smelly bloke who drinks and smokes too much, than Sam, a gorgeous sexy babe who you will have unlimited sexual access to?"

"Well, when you put it like that, maybe it's not the end of the world." Matt managed a half-smile and raised his glass. "Cheers."

Within half an hour they'd been joined by Macker and Dave. As the four men and their pints settled around the table, conversation started slowly.

"Dave, when's our lease up?" Matt enquired.

"I think it's March."

"Ok, well just in case Sam asks at any point, I've told her it's August. I'll explain why later."

Shipsey decided to pitch in at this point. "Did anyone see that wildlife programme today? The one about that ancient African fish?"

"Oh yeah! We were watchin' that!" said Dave.

"Did ye see the state of it?"

"Yeah, that was one ugly mother," Matt nodded.

Macker folded his arms and shook his head. He couldn't believe he'd been sitting down for a whole minute and the conversation hadn't moved on to what, as he could see it, was the only thing worth talking about. He hadn't slept a wink the previous night. He lay awake in bed for six hours conjuring up images of where their horse journey might take them. His mind's eye was glued to an imaginary 56 inch screen showing pictures of horses and jockeys flashing by, crowds roaring, and bookies wincing. As tempting as it was, he didn't fantasize about the sexy new lounge girl from *The Banner Man* whose name he had yet to learn. He fantasized about shaking hands with JP McManus, hearing the inside line from Aidan O'Brien, sharing a pint with Ted Walsh, but most of all he fantasized about roaring his horse across the finish line. Earlier in the day he watched four hours of racing on Channel Four, cheering each winner home as if it were his own. As the other lads discussed the appearance of some ancient fish, Macker had to stop himself from drifting into another horseracing trance.

"So, who's coming to the auction next Saturday?" he finally blurted out.

"You know we have a cup match," Matt reminded him.

"I couldn't give a shit if we were playing in the F.A. Cup final! There's no way I'm missin' out on this."

Matt shrugged. "Well, there's not much point in me going anyway. I wouldn't have a clue what's going on, so I'm gonna play footie."

"Yeah, I'm happy to leave it up to the experts," Dave nodded. "I may have to work anyway."

"I might come along for the craic," said Shipsey. "I'll let you know during the week."

"For fuck sake lads!" Macker groaned. "I was hopin' for a bit more enthusiasm than this! But if you want to miss out on all the fun, that's fair enough."

*****

Three nights later Macker's phonecall rudely interrupted Shipsey who was breathing heavily when he picked up the phone. "Hello?"

"Shipsey? What's wrong with you?"

"What are you talkin' about? You rang me!"

"You sound out of breath. Did you run to the phone?"

"I was…eh…upstairs."

"Ahhh! You were on the job. Well, sorry for interrupting." Macker looked at his watch. "Jaysis lad! Fair fuckin' balls to ye, its only half six! You must've jumped on her as soon as you got in from work, ye horny stoat!"

"For fuck sake McCann! What the fuck do you want?

"We've got a problem. My uncle isn't gonna be able to make it on Saturday."

"What?…Shit!…Why not?"

"He's goin' into hospital for an operation. He's been on the waitin' list for a while."

"Is he all right?"

"Yeah, it's just an ingrowing toenail, but he has to get it done."

"So what are we gonna do?"

"Well, he's still happy to commit his cash. It just means somebody else has to go and do the bidding."

"Like who?"

"Like us."

"You're jokin'! Have you ever been to one of these things before?"

"Yeah, but I don't really remember it."

"Why? Were you pissed?"

"No, I was six. I was too small to see what was going on. I just remember a lot of noise and a strong smell of horseshit. But I'm sure we can manage it. My cousin Kate will be there to help us out. She's quite into horses and has been to a few of the sales."

"I don't know about this," said Shipsey. "Have you seen how fast these things move?"

"No, have you?"

"Well no, but its pretty fuckin' fast I'm sure! Have you spoken to Matt?"

"Yeah."

"And what did he say?"

"Something like…"If you think I'm gonna let you two mad fuckers go to a horse auction on your own and bid with *my* money, you are sadly mistaken!"

"So he's coming then?"

"Yep, so is Dave. It's a full house."

"Excellent, well if nothing else, we'll have a good laugh."

"Defo. Right. I'll seeya later."

"Right, seeye"

"Oh, Ship, bye the way"

"Wha?"

"Say sorry to Janie for me." CLICK

"Wanker." CLICK

C h a p t e r   4

On the Saturday of the auction the four lads piled into Shipsey's car and hit the road for Kildare at 8am. The only advice Macker's uncle had given them was to get there early, observe what the other punters were doing, and do the same when their time came. There was an air of excitement running through the car as they sped their way down the N7. The buzz emenating from Macker's stomach was almost audible. For over ten years he had dreamt of owning a racehorse and the fact that the dream could soon be a reality had his tummy doing somersaults. To relieve the nervous tension the lads couldn't help themselves from roaring along to Shipsey's *Pogues* CD, which was being played at full blast.

> *"there was Slugger O'Toole who was drunk as a rule*
> *and fighting Bill Treacy from Do-O-Ver*
> *and yer man Mick McCann* (Macker loved that part)
> *from the banks of the Bann*
> *was the skipper on the Irish Rover."*

Suddenly Macker turned down the volume. "Lads, I've got a fuckin' great idea!"

The idea, whether great or not, was as follows. When Kate met them at the sales there would be five of them and Macker believed they could use their superior numbers to intimidate other bidders and ultimately get their horse at a cheaper price.

They would do this by dominating the bidding for their horse from the outset.

"If we spread ourselves out," Macker explained, "and all five of us bid really hard and fast from the start, we can scare everyone else away!"

The responses to this varied from an indifferent "let's see what it looks like when we get there" to a moderately positive "might work."

When they arrived Macker introduced the lads to his cousin Kate. As Dave was shaking Kate's hand he noticed how cold it was. He took it between his own chubby hands and started warming it up. Kate giggled a little bit and thanked him, her breath visible in the cold air.

Matt and Shipsey exchanged surprised glances. This was about as intimate as they'd seen Dave with a girl for a good three years.

Shortly after the auction kicked off, Macker's excitement levels started to soar. At first it wasn't clear what was going on, but after a while he'd sussed out where all the shouts were coming from and who was running the show. He was ready and eager to get stuck in. In fact he was so exhilarated he could hardly bare to wait for lot 26. He turned to the others. His eyes were the size of golf balls.

"Come on lads! Let's do a dummy run!"

"What?"

"Let's start bidding for the next lot. See if we can scare every one else away."

Matt threw his eyes to the sky. "Macker, we are not doing a dummy run."

"Come on! Spread out! We need to make sure we know what we're doing when the time comes."

"Macker, listen to me. We're bidding for lot number 26 and that's it."

"Just a few bids on the next lot...just to let everyone know we're here."

Matt turned to Kate. "Kate you're his cousin. Maybe he'll listen to you. Please explain to him the dangers involved in bidding for the wrong lot."

Kate took Macker by the shoulders and shook him theatrically. The other lads laughed. Manys the time they had imagined themselves doing exactly the same thing to their hyperactive friend.

Kate spoke dramatically, as if she was trying to convince an airline passenger that the plane could survive on one dodgy engine. "Cool your jets Michael. We have another hour to go yet. Pull yourself together man. Why don't you go for a walk? Buy yourself a cup of coffee or something, but not too much caffeine, or you'll be riding home on the wrong horse."

Dave was looking and smiling at Kate from the side. In many ways she was average. Average height, average build, average length brown hair, but her face was certainly pretty. She had a warm smile and kind eyes and smooth pale skin. To Dave she was anything but average. He found himself wandering if she was single.

"Next...is lot 26...a three-year-old gelding out of a useful looking line. In training, but unraced as yet. I'd like to start the bidding at five thousand." Macker could feel his heart pounding somewhere behind his ears. He was dying to put in a bid, but unfortunately before they spread out they agreed to go in alphabetical order until they got to fourteen thousand. At this point Kate and Dave would drop out and the three tallest would continue until either they got everyone else out or they reached their twenty thousand limit. Shipsey, whose real name was Alan Boate, was first of the gang to go. He bid six thousand. Matt Cullen followed him straight away with a bid of six and a half thousand. Dave Massey got his bid in at eight thousand and Kate McCann shortly after at nine thousand. Kate had only just finished her bid when Macker roared ten thousand over the top of her. Up until then the bids had gone up in five hundreds, but Macker couldn't help himself. Shipsey and Matt exchanged nervous glances. They could see Macker at the far side of the crowd and he looked like a man possessed. His mouth was distorted and his eyes were practically hanging out of their sockets. If scaring away the other bidders was what he was trying to do, he might just have the face to pull it off. A local accent bid ten and a half thousand, so Shipsey came back with eleven, followed by Matt with eleven and a half. Another local accent came back with twelve so Dave topped him at twelve and a half. The guy who Dave topped seemed pissed off and came straight back with a bid of thirteen thousand. Kate wasn't having any of that and got her final bid in at thirteen and a half.

"Fourteen Thousand!" screamed Macker, who was now visibly foaming at the mouth. The plan wasn't working though. There were two locals still keen on bidding. Shipsey got his last bid in at eighteen thousand, but was topped by the first local. Matt came back with a bid of nineteen thousand. The auctioneer exchanged glances with the eighteen and a half bidder who indicated that he was finished. The second local however came back and bid nineteen and a half thousand.

"Twenty thousand!" It was Macker's last throw of the dice and he sounded suitably banshee like. There were a few seconds silence. All eyes were fixed on the local bidder. Slowly but surely his bidding hand went up and he showed his numbered lollipop to the auctioneer.

"Twenty thousand five hundred."

Macker felt a painful sensation rip through the front of his body. It was as if he'd been shot in the stomach and all the blood in his body and air in his lungs were escaping out of this single bullet-hole. He could barely find the energy to stay standing. That was it. The dream was over. His eyes locked with Matt's through the crowd. Matt looked back with a tight-lipped expression while slowly shaking his head. This was half a look of compassion saying "yeah, that sucks," but it was also saying, "don't you dare bid any higher, you lunatic."

Just then, Macker heard the first thing he'd heard since the previous bid. He had been numbed to all the noise of the crowd and the auctioneer, from that point. It was as if hearing someone bid twenty thousand five hundred had pained his ears so much, that the blood in them had decided to pack up and move to a warmer climate. The voice and the accent he heard were vaguely familiar.

"Twenty-one thousand."

Macker could tell from the look in Matt's wide eyes that he had heard the same thing. Matt was now bouncing up and down on his toes, trying to confirm where the bid had come from.

The auctioneer dropped the hammer. "Sold for twenty-one thousand."

Matt was still trying to confirm where the bid had come from when all seventeen stone of Shipsey came crashing into him from behind.

"That was Mad Massey!"

"What?"

Shipsey lifted Matt into the air "That was Mad Massey!"

*****

Dave Massey was the only child born to Dundalk teachers Claire Sheehan and Steve Massey. He was always one of the brightest, if not one of the most popular kids at school. He was shy and never any good at sports, which always left him on the periphery of the action in a school full of loud, sporty children. Kids can be cruel and Dave received plenty of taunts for being a short, chubby, spectacled ten year old. But adults can be just as cruel, and Dave still found himself getting a hard time for being an overweight, spectacled, balding, smoking, twenty-six year old. Over the years however, he had developed a defence mechanism in the shape of a guillotine wit. His good friends who had witnessed it first hand rarely chose to take him on in a serious slagging match. At eighteen Dave qualified to do a Commerce degree at UCD and rented a flat in Ranelagh. His best friend on the course quickly became Matt Cullen and the two shared a few lectures and very many pints together over their four university years. After the first year, they decided to rent a two-bedroom flat in Stillorgan, that they had been in since. Like many teenagers who move away from their parents, Dave went quite wild for a few years. The extent of his drinking, was even worrying some of his heavy-drinking student friends. One of the few girlfriends he'd had in his life cited his excessive drinking as the reason for breaking up with him. If anything, that worsened his problem and

33

Dave went downhill from there, until at twenty-one he hit rock bottom.

It had been a normal Friday in April for the most part. Dave and Matt had gone to UCD together at ten that morning, attended one lecture and settled down in the bar for a couple of beers and a few frames of pool. There was nothing unusual in the fact that after a while, they decided to skip their afternoon's lectures and have a proper booze-up. There was a good crowd out, as many had decided to make *this* their last big session, before they started cramming for their exams. Between 6 and 9pm the crowd diminished quite a bit, with some people deciding to call it a day and others heading into town. Matt left at 8pm to go to the afters of a cousin's wedding. By 10pm Dave couldn't recognise another face in the bar, but this didn't alter the fact that he was still in the mood for more alcohol. He unsuccessfully attempted to play a bit more pool and then decided to prop himself up at the bar for the rest of the night, occasionally slurring a few words to the helpful barman. At 1.30am, as he was being kicked out of the closing bar, he had the clever idea of phoning his ex-girlfriend, who lived nearby.

"Helen will look after me," he said to himself. "Jaysis, I really miss her blow jobs... Come on phone...Work!"

He got through at the fourth attempt. "Howaya Hell's Bell's," he roared as soberly as he could. "D'you know –hic- what I was just thinkin'?"

"For feck sake Dave. It's half one in the morning! What do you want?"

"Will you –hic- marry me?"

"I broke up with you, you mad pisshead. I'm hardly going to turn around and marry you! Now, just go to bed!"

"Hows about –hic- a blow job then?"
CLICK

At 6am the next morning Dave woke up in his own bed. The old homing device had worked again. He was just drifting back to sleep when Matt walked in and shook him. This was unusual behaviour. There was an unwritten law that you don't shake your hungover flatmate when he's trying to sleep. Dave rolled halfway over unable to fully open his eyes. "Wha?"

"What do you mean 'Wha?' said Matt. "Do you not remember what happened last night?"

Dave rolled fully over and clamped both hands over his sore head. "Well, judging by my hangover I mixed Guinness, cider and whiskey."

"Do you not remember your car?"

"What? My car? Oh shit! Oh fuck!"

On cue, the pains all over Dave's body started screaming out as a reminder of what had happened. Slowly, his brain started to piece together the events that occurred after his phone call to Helen. His clearest recollection was of sitting into the passenger seat of his car, which was parked in the University car park. He reclined the seat and decided to have a nap. Ten minutes later, due to being too cold and uncomfortable, he was trying to convince himself that he could manage the one and a half mile drive home. He slid over to the driver's seat, put on his seat belt and slapped himself in the face a few times. Three minutes later he was wondering what all the fuss was about. He had negotiated himself out of the car park and on to the dual carriageway, with the skill and technique, if not the speed, of Michael Schumacher. This over-confidence was to be his downfall. His next difficult manoeuvre was to swing off the dual carriageway onto the old road that used to connect Stillorgan to Blackrock, but was now essentially the entrance to his estate and was only used by his neighbours. He was going too fast and started to lose control. In the process of trying to regain control, his foot pushed down even harder on the accelerator and he pulled sharply on the steering wheel, lining the car up nicely for a head-on collision with the wall. He ploughed into the wall at right angles doing thirty-eight miles per hour.

Dave was now bolt upright in bed looking at Matt with a very worried expression.

"Oh fuck! I crashed my Dad's car!" Dave had a badly sprained left wrist from the way his hand bent sharply back when it hit the steering wheel, a few bruised ribs from the impact of the seat belt and an extremely bad headache from the fourteen pints and eight whiskies he'd had. But his physical injuries were no match for the overwhelming pain of guilt and embarrassment he felt for doing something so stupid.

"What am I gonna do? How the hell did I get back here?"

Matt sat down at the end of Dave's bed. "You walked back. You'd left the keys in the ignition so you had to ring the buzzer."

Dave started to get out of bed. "Jesus, I better go and have a look!"

Matt held an arm out to stop him. "The car's fucked Dave. It's completely written-off and you would have been too if you weren't wearing your seatbelt."

Matt pointed to Dave's desk. "You're keys are over there. I've taken care of it."

"What do you mean you've taken care of it?"

"Just relax and listen will ye? When you got back you were in such a state, I sent you to bed, but I went up to the car with a little toolkit on me. It was a complete write-off, so I decided to make it look like it was stolen. I jimmied the lock and ripped out the ignition. I pulled the driver's seat right forward, so it might look like it was a kid driving and I put my fingerprints on the wheel, so yours won't be the only ones. It was really dark, but it didn't look like there were any skid marks. Do you remember if you hit the brakes?"

Dave was holding his forehead with one hand and scratching the back of his head with the other. He couldn't look Matt in the eye. "I'm not sure, but I don't think so."

"Well if there are no skid marks...the way the car hit the wall, it could have been going in to or out of the estate. You told me last night, that nobody saw you get out of the car. Are you sure about that?"

"Yeah, pretty sure."

"Ok, well all you need to remember when you ring the cops to report it missing, is that you left it outside the flat when you went to college yesterday and that it was still there when you got back. Tell them you got in at about midnight. I'll vouch for that."

"Are you serious?"

"What are your alternatives? You've only got third party insurance."

"Jesus Matt! You sure this'll work?"

"As long as you can keep a straight face."

Dave slumped back in the bed exhaling forcefully. "Fuck! I feel like such a gobshite...I don't know what to say. I owe you big time for this lad."

"Well, there is one thing you could do as a favour...to me *and* yourself."

"Name it."

"No more alcohol till after your last exam."

Four and a half months later Dave received a cheque for £5,500 for his dad's Audi, which had officially been stolen and written-off by joy-riders. Four and a half *years* later he was being hailed as the hero of the Kildare horse sales.

Macker barged his way through the crowd almost knocking over some of the other bidders. When he finally caught up with Dave, he threw his arms around him and kissed him squarely on the lips. "Jesus Dave, you're one mad bastard, but I love you!"

Matt already had his arm around Dave's shoulder. "So where's this extra grand gonna come from?"

Dave glanced at Kate. She too seemed impressed with the spontaneity of his actions. He turned to Matt and shrugged. "I don't know...I don't mind paying it...or we can all chip in," he glanced back to Kate. "Or maybe Kate wants to get involved?"

After three pints at the local pub Kate had been recruited as the sixth and final owner of their new horse. Later on, Matt's mobile phone rang. Macker and Shipsey knew it had to be Samantha phoning to find out where he was. He had obviously told her that he was playing football.

"What? Yeah, still out with the team. Yeah two nil, so we're through to the semi-final. Just having a few beers to celebrate."

Macker couldn't resist winding Matt up and started doing a pretend horserace commentary, "and it's *Cullen's Knob* down the far side, *Wrath of Sam* on the stand rail. *Cullen's Knob* and *Wrath of Sam* ready to battle this one out. *Cullen's Knob* is being ridden hard and the whip is coming out on *Wrath of Sam*. The mare responds to the whip and is beginning to get the better of the wilting *Knob*. And as they approach the line it's close, but...*YES*! *Wrath of Sam* cuts off *Cullen's Knob* at the post!"

"These are followed home by, "I've got no Bird" in third and "I'll use my Hand" in fourth."

While the other lads slagged each other off Dave tried to strike up a conversation with Kate. Unfortunately he was never at his easiest in the presence of a beautiful woman. He wanted to be charming and flirty and funny like Macker could be, but it didn't quite work out that way. The conversation wasn't exactly flowing along and there were few, if any laughs, but it was quite intimate nonetheless.

Dave had remembered that Kate's dad had gone for an operation that morning. "So, I presume that was your dad you were ringing? Is he all right?"

"My dad? Oh yeah, he's fine. 'Operation in-growing toenail' was a success. I was actually ringing to check on my mum. She's not quite as strong."

Sometimes it's easier to share things with strangers and both Kate and Dave took advantage of this opportunity. Kate told Dave about her mum's battle with a disease called lupus. Dave, in turn, delved into some of the unhappier bullying moments he endured as a schoolboy. Stuff he'd never shared with the lads. Kate's soft features and kind eyes seemed to bring out only his most genuine words and feelings. Although they'd only just met, Dave felt like he could tell her anything and she would treat it with the care it demanded. In any case, speaking intimately with a beautiful, gentle girl was a refreshing change from the loud banter that he was used to enduring in the lad's company. He knew three things for sure going to bed that night. Firstly, that this had been one of the best days of his life. Secondly, he was a much happier man than when he smashed his dad's car into a brick wall, but most importantly that he couldn't wait to meet Kate McCann again.

Chapter 5

"Oh Mackerrrrrrr, look what I've got," teased Shipsey in his best Marilyn Monroe impression. He was holding up a palm-sized rugby ball with a Guinness logo on it. This item was known to the lads as "the konch." Over the last two years it had played a big part in their lives and they had all suffered as a result of its existence. The rules of the konch were thus. The holder nominates a task and the spin of the konch decides who has to carry out that task. Whoever the tippex-stained end points at is the unlucky one. After carrying out a task successfully, that person gets to take the konch home and spin it himself at a future date of his choice, comfortable in the knowledge that he is exempt from the next task. As a result of the last spin, which was executed by Macker, Shipsey had to wear his shirt fully buttoned up, and back to front for the entire night. In addition he was not allowed to tell anybody the real reason for his curious appearance. This turned out to be a very long night for the bigfella, sitting in *The Banner Man* with his chin resting on the back of his collar, trying to explain it away as "the latest fashion" or "the way it's worn." Matt and Macker were not helping things by calling over every person who they vaguely knew, just to say hello.

Dave had been the luckiest so far, with only one forfeit. This was to walk to and from the toilet backwards every time he had to go. Through some extremely painful bladder control, he managed to keep his number of toilet visits down to one despite staying in *The Banner Man* till closing time. After this, Dave devised a particularly devilish task for the next recipient who turned out to be Matt. Every time Matt lifted his pint glass to his mouth he had to spin a coin on the table and mentally record the outcome. Before he was allowed to drink, he would have to recount all the previous results, which Dave had written down. Matt ended up reducing his average number of gulps per pint from twenty down to five, but still struggled to earn himself another mouthful, halfway through his fifth pint.

"OK here goes, head, head, head, harp, head, head, harp, head, harp, harp, head, harp, harp, head, head, head, harp, head, eh, harp, harp, head, harp, eh, head-

"Wrong"

"Fuck!"

"Ok, this is it," said Shipsey getting ready to spin, "the forfeiter has to wish for something bad to happen to our horse every time Old Qurikey walks past."

It was obvious to everyone that the task had been designed with Macker in mind and Shipsey had been practising hard on his spin. His practice paid off and half an hour later, Paddy Quirke, a sixty-eight-year-old local with a notoriously weak bladder hobbled past.

"I hope he cracks his shin getting out of the horse box," said Macker grudgingly.

It was a cruel task for him to have to carry out, as Macker was obviously overflowing with excitement and enthusiasm for their new adventure, but he soon got into it.

"So what are we gonna call this heap of crap that I hope snaps its spine?" he asked as Quirkey hobbled back up to the bar.

"What about *Second Place?* Offered Matt. "Y'know, and the winner is *Second Place, Second Place* is bringing up the rear. *Second Place* snatches third."

"Hows about *My Langer?* Countered Shipsey. "It's *My Langer* coming from behind. *My Langer's* been ridden hard. *My Langer* is struggling to get up."

This banter went on for quite a while with each suggestion getting wilder than the one before, until the entrance of their new favourite lounge girl distracted them.

"There she is lads." Macker spotted her first. "The girl of my dreams."

All eight eyes were now watching the young beauty walk across the lounge floor, carrying what looked like college books and folders.

"Even the way she's carrying those folders is giving me a hard on," whispered Macker.

"You what?"

"Well...y'know...it...eh...accentuates her femininity. You'd never see a bloke carry something up to his chest like that."

The rest of the lads were beginning to snigger. "It accentuates her femininity," mocked Shipsey.

"Seriously...it's from our ancestors...it's in our genes. Women are used to carrying babies close to their chest like that, while men are used to carrying spears and stuff down by their side."

"Or maybe, she's just trying to stop us from gawking at her amazingly pert tits."

"Hold the phone!" exclaimed Macker "Who the fuck is he?"

His dream girl had stopped to say a very friendly hello to a guy drinking on the other side of the lounge.

Matt frowned at Shipsey. "Is that who I think it is?"

Shipsey nodded. "Yep, that's Smelly Kelly."

Mark Kelly, as his parents had christened him, had been unfortunate enough to soil himself when he was a shy five year old in primary school. From that day forward, he became known to his classmates as "Smelly Kelly."

"What the hell's she doing talking to him?" Gasped Matt.

"I hope he suffocates in a pile of his own shite!" growled Macker.

"You don't even know him!"

"Not Kelly! Our horse!," said Macker, pointing at Paddy Quirke, who was slowly making his way past. Macker turned his attention back to the beautiful lounge girl. "So, do you think she's going out with him?"

"Who? Quirkey? Nah, I'd say he's a bit old for her," laughed Matt.

"Ha ha," said Macker dryly.

An hour later they were all looking up at the beautiful young girl who had come over to take their order. It was Matt's round so he took it on himself to find out a bit more about her. "Hello, you're new here. What's your name?"

"Michelle," she responded in a sweet, friendly voice.

Matt was disappointed that she hadn't given her surname. He was trying to find out if she was related to "Smelly Kelly."

"Do you live nearby?"

"Yeah, not far away," she answered slightly edgily.

Again, Matt had been hoping for a bit more detail. He knew the Kelly's lived on Glendale road. "What road?"

Michelle blinked a couple of times. "Sorry?"

Matt realised that he was beginning to sound like a potential stalker. "Eh…four pints of Guinness please?"

As she was making her way back to the bar to get the order, Matt was standing up red-faced, trying to get a twenty-euro note out of his pocket. The other three were in convulsions of laughter.

"That's smooth stuff Matt!"

"Ah fuck off!" he said, throwing the money onto the table. "Here, you pay for the round. I don't want to be here when she gets back!"

As he turned and darted for the toilet he nearly knocked over Paddy Quirke.

"I hope his bollocks falls off," laughed Macker.

Dave was laughing so hard at this point, that beer was coming out of his nose.

Michelle returned with their drinks, relieved that the potential stalker wasn't at the table.

"There you go," Macker said, handing over Matt's money. "Sorry about my friend, he gets a bit weird, when he's around a good-looking girl."

Michelle smiled down at Macker. "I see."

"I think he was trying to find out how you knew Mark Kelly."

"What? Oh. He's my brother."

"Ah I see. So I guess he's not your boyfriend then?" asked Macker, smiling and winking blatantly at her.

"No, *he's* not," she said, making sure to clearly emphasise the "*he*."

Macker winked up at her again and handed her an over-the-top tip. "I see...gotcha, well I'll pass that on to my buddy."

"Thanks very much."

"If you could just let me know, if you break up with whats' is name so I can tell my shy friend, that would be great."

Michelle showed off her sexy smile again. "You'll be the first to know."

"Right," said Macker, picking up his pint. "We'll see ya in about twenty minutes."

"Seeya." Michelle giggled and walked away.

"Smooth work McCann," said Shipsey admiringly.

Dave nodded in agreement.

They were all full of smiles, when Matt arrived back at the table.

"Where's all my change?"

"We left her a generous tip on your behalf," laughed Macker.

"Wankers."

"Don't worry about it," said Macker, patting Matt's shoulder and heading off in the direction of the gents. "We put in a good word for you."

Dave decided to take this opportunity to ask the other two about the girl who had been occupying most of his thoughts since the day of the auction.

"So what do you guys think of Macker's cousin Kate?"

"She seems genuinely nice and very easy on the eye," offered Matt.

"Nice rack too!" Shipsey chipped in.

"Yeah, a little bit of puppy fat there though," countered Matt.

"Nothing wrong with that. Gives you something to hold on to," growled Shipsey. He reached out his arms and cupped his big hands, just to help the lads understand exactly what he meant.

"So, are you in *lurve* Dave?"

"Nah. I just think she's really nice. But shut up now. Macker's on his way back."

"Listen lads," said Matt, as Macker was taking his seat. "You know we have this dinner on Saturday with the girls. Well, we have to be really careful that Sam doesn't find out about the horse. So no talking about it in front of her, all right?"

"Seriously Matt. This is a bit risky. You know Janie and her chat a lot. It's only a matter of time before it slips out. Why don't you just tell her and get it over with. It's better sooner rather than later. What's the worst that can happen?" asked Shipsey.

"Well hopefully, he'll never have sex again in his life," joked Macker, waving to Paddy Quirke on his way past again. "That...lads...is known as timing and all great comedians have it."

"Well done Macker," said Matt in a serious tone before turning back to Shipsey. "No really Ship, you have to make sure Jane says nothing to Sam, at least for a couple of weeks, while I figure something out."

"Ok, Ok, don't worry about it."

They spent the next few hours sharing their hopes and dreams for their horse and getting quite drunk in the process. They decided to find out what the name of the horse's parents were and combine them somehow to come up with a name for theirs. "Let's just hope they're not Moby Dick and Bray Head," chuckled Macker.

He'd had too much to drink and was struggling to focus by the end of the night. He had done his best to stick to the konch task, but was more interested in flirting with Michelle, than keeping a lookout for Paddy Quirke. As he was wobbling towards the door for home, attempting to put his jacket on, he burst into a verse of the *Beatles "My Michelle"*

"Meeeechelle my bell, these are words that go together well, My Michelle-

At this point he crossed paths with Paddy Quirke, who was making his twelfth and final visit to the gents.

"Ah for fuck sake Quirkey! Tie a bleedin' knot in it!"

Half an hour later, Matt and Dave were walking towards the entrance of their estate, past the site of Dave's old car crash. They were having a bit of a heart to heart about Kate.

"So, you really think she's a bit too chunky?" asked Dave.

"Honestly? Right now? I would say no. She's fine. She's probably only a few pounds overweight which is nothing. She's got a really sweet face and seems like a good laugh. I'd just be a bit worried about the weight thing…y'know…she's twenty-five now, so her metabolism will be slowing down soon and she might put on more weight over the next few years."

"I suppose so," Dave grudgingly agreed.

Matt grabbed Dave by his abundant love handles and laughed. "But hey lad, beggars can't be choosers and you're a bit of a porker yourself!"

"Cheers."

Matt stopped fooling around. He could tell Dave was smitten. "Look lad…I know you really like her, but take your time. You've only just met her. You probably don't even know if she's going out with anyone?"

"Nope."

"Ok, so relax. We'll be seeing plenty of her now that she's in the syndicate and I'll do whatever I can to help."

"Ok great," Dave nodded and then paused… "Like what?"

"Huh?"

"Whaddya gonna do to help?"

"I dunno…whatever you want me to do. I could drop the hint that you have an enormous cock and a flock of beautiful woman chasing after you."

Dave smiled and nodded. "I like the sound of that…what else?"

"Let's see…you speak six different languages and own a string of properties along the French Riviera."

"Good…any more?"

"You donate most of your eight figure salary to underpriviged kids, but you don't like to talk about it."

Dave frowned and shook his head. "She knows that I'm a glorified accountant working for a crappy insurance company. I don't think she's gonna buy all that. We need to tone it down a bit, but I liked the way it started off."

"What? The big dick thing?"

"Yeah," Dave nodded. "The big dick thing. That was good. Leave that part in."

Chapter 6

Matt Cullen and Alan Boate, also known as Shipsey, were best friends since they were four. They grew up within a stones throw of each other and went to the same primary and secondary schools. They both got interested in football at around age six and Liverpool was their team. At age twelve, they both started to kiss girls over games of spin the bottle and would swap and share girlfriends over the next couple of years. At fifteen, they shared their first flagon of cider and at sixteen they went to the Daniel O'Connell pub and enjoyed their first pint together. In all they'd been keeping each other company for twenty-two years and were more familiar than most married couples. Like all married couples they had come up with a number of different nicknames for each other over the years and at one stage they were known as Cu and U. Matt was Cu after the mythical Irish figure Cu Chulainn and Shipsey was U as in U-boat. The only nickname that really stood the test of time however, was "Shipsey," which Matt had christened him ten years earlier when at six foot four and almost sixteen stone he had become a very large sixteen-year-old Boate.

After finishing school, they both decided to take different routes. Shipsey, who absolutely detested exams, was keen to get straight out into the real world and start earning some cash. After working for a few months at a local supermarket, his dad helped him get a job at a nearby car showroom. Here, he rapidly worked his way up the ladder and within a couple of years was one of their top salespeople. The job seemed to go hand in hand with Shipsey's brash and imposing personality and he enjoyed the challenge of separating customers from their hard-earned cash. During his first summer there he started a romance with the receptionist Jane McGovern. Three years later, long after she'd moved on to be a PA to a solicitor, they bought a three-bed townhouse and moved in together.

Shipsey came from a family of four large boys and as a footballer he was always a goalkeeper, so being loud and argumentative came naturally to him. In Jane McGovern however, he'd met his match and they became quite a fiery couple. If anything, their relationship seemed to thrive rather than falter on the back of their verbal warfare.

"It keeps the sex interesting," Shipsey would always say.

One evening, shortly after they'd moved in together and not long after Matt had started seeing Samantha, they invited their friends over for dinner. A few hours after dinner they were embroiled in a drunken game of trivial pursuit and Jane was stuck on a particularly poignant question.

"Which English club won the European cup in 1977."

"If you get this wrong, I'm pouring this beer over your head," Shipsey threatened.

"If you pour that beer over my head, I'll pour this wine over yours," Jane retorted.

Sure enough, she answered incorrectly and the drink throwing ensued, followed by quite a bit of abusive taunting.

"How can you not get that right, you thick cow?"

"At least I'm not coming last you big Spa."

Ten minutes after the row broke out Matt, and a shell-shocked Samantha, had left for home. Five minutes after that Shipsey and Jane got down to some serious sex.

Matt's post school career decisions were quite a bit more calculated than his best friend's. After finishing a four year commerce degree, he interviewed with quite a few financial institutions, before taking a job with a small stockbroking firm. Here, he learned the ropes, in what at first was a largely administrative role. After a while, he passed the relevant exams and the partners started allowing him talk to some of their smaller clients. After three years, he landed a plum job within the equity trading arm of a large Irish Bank. Here, he was given a lot more responsibility and paid a lot more money. Using his charm and sense of humour, he built up good loyalty in his customer base, many of whom had followed him over from his previous firm. But never did he put his charm, sense of humour and handsome looks to such good use, as the night he met Samantha Kearns.

She was the most beautiful girl he had ever seen and he felt his heart trying to beat its way out of his chest as he approached to ask her to dance. Being tall, tanned and handsome, with dark hair and deep blue eyes, Matt had always been able to attract the prettiest of girls, but shuffling slowly around the dancefloor holding the stunning Samantha Kearns in his arms, he felt like Quasimodo. It came as little surprise to him, when she told him that she was a fashion model. And she seemed quite impressed when he stretched the truth a little, telling her that he was a stockbroker. It was a balmy August evening, when they left the nightclub hand in hand. They walked and talked, sat and talked, kissed and talked for two hours before he hailed her a cab and they arranged to meet in the same place the following night. When Matt eventually got home, he took his calendar down from the wall and wrote under the 6th of August, "The night my life changed." Three and a half years later, he was still in love with Sam and she still had the ability to take his breath away with a smile, but in many ways their relationship had become a lot more complicated. His main worry was that, although they were the same age, she was a couple of years ahead of him in terms of wanting to settle down. Their relationship wasn't nearly as fiery as Shipsey and Jane's, but they did have their disagreements, most of which involved issues like, joint bank accounts, moving in together, and the amount of time Matt spent drinking with the lads.

On the same page of his calendar, was a date that despite having no entry beside it, left Matt with a cold hollow feeling. On the 22nd of August 1998 his mum died. It was a beautiful sunny Saturday morning and he and Shipsey had decided to hack a few golf balls around Stepaside golf course. His mum had been suffering from, what doctors called "a peculiar strand of meningitis" for six weeks. There had been a few brief periods in between those when she felt fine, that she became very weak, but everyone seemed certain that she was going to shake it off. The doctors were still doing tests on her and the medication she was on seemed to be helping. But just as he was about to tee off at the short eighth hole, Matt's mobile phone rang. As soon as he heard his sister's voice on the other end, his blood went cold. The next few hours, days and weeks of his life were a hellish blur. After mourning deeply for a while, he started drinking heavily to numb the pain. He came very close to quitting University, but it was his mum who had been the proudest when he'd qualified to take his degree. She'd spent a lot of time boasting to friends and neighbours, about how bright her Matt was. Four and a half years later he still felt a huge emptiness when he thought about her, but his biggest regret was not going to the hospital that morning. It had been agreed the previous day, that his two sisters would go in the morning and he and his brother in the afternoon. Although he had been brought up a Catholic, Matt was not a religious guy and he no qualms about calling God a "fucking bastard," for not giving him a chance to say goodbye.

*****

"Can you try not to make too big a deal tonight, about us moving

47

in together?"

"What? It *is* a big deal"

"Yeah, I know it is. It's just, well… Dave's gonna be there."

"So? He's a big boy."

"I know, but I've been living with him for over six years, so it's like the end of an era."

"Surely that's a good thing? The two of you are starting to remind me of Bert and Ernie."

"Yeah, it *is* a good thing and I'm looking forward to it. It's just…well…Dave's not going out with anyone and he doesn't have very many other friends in Dublin, so I don't know what he's gonna do."

Matt and Sam had been getting ready to go out and celebrate Jane's birthday for the last hour. Well, in truth Matt had been ready for the last half hour and was drinking a beer on the sofa, watching TV. Sam was in his room trying on her fifth outfit. In the three and half years they had been going out, and she had "occasionally" been staying over at his flat, Sam had slowly invaded Matt's wardrobe space, until now all he had left hanging up were his two suits and seven work shirts. Being in the middle of her pre night-out routine, Sam had spent the last hour, showering, washing and drying her hair, and doing her make-up. The next forty-five minutes would be spent trying on every single outfit she has at least once, until the bed is littered with clothes, shoes and bags. Through a process of elimination, which Matt would be forced to participate in, she would finally choose one and after re-touching her hair and make-up another three times each, she would be ready. On average the whole process took two hours, but on a really big night out, Matt could be half-pissed by the time she's ready. When he first witnessed this routine, it staggered Matt and almost brought him to breaking point, but he learned quickly and painfully not to interfere with it and just lie to her about what time the table was booked for. What was ironic to Matt, was that Sam could wake up, forget about her hair and make-up, throw on an old tracksuit and still be the most beautiful woman wherever she went. He even tried to use that line once, but it didn't wash.

This night however, he was happy to have a couple of beers before they went out, just to settle his nerves. Not only was he not looking forward to the whole "moving in together" discussion and what might go with it, he was particularly worried that somebody might get drunk and let it slip to Sam that he had recently blown a portion of their down payment on a racehorse. Dave, who had to go into work for a couple of hours, had come up with the idea that they use a code, so that if anyone had anything to ask Macker about the horse, they would phrase it as if they were asking about something else that was going on in his life. The best they could come up with was to pretend that Macker was training for a triathlon. Matt slowly shook his head as he cracked open his fourth can. *Fuck me! This is gonna go tits up.*

"Lads...I'm in love...plain and simple," said Macker, taking his seat at the dinner table.

"What?!," exclaimed Matt, relieved that the conversation was starting on a subject other than marriage or horses.

"Yeah, I went to get my hair cut in the usual spot around the corner from work yesterday, and there was a new bird workin' there. She's an absolute babe. She gave me a proper head massage when she was washing it and then we had a nice friendly chat while she was cutting it. But to top it all off, she didn't compliment my hair once."

"What do you mean?" asked Dave, struggling to grasp this concept.

"Not once in the whole twenty minutes did she say anything nice about my hair."

"And that's a good thing?"

"In all the years women have been cutting my hair, I can't remember *one* that didn't give it some sort of compliment."

"So, did you ask her out?"

"Nah, I bottled it, but I'm going back again next week."

"You're gonna get her to cut your hair again next week?"

"Yep."

"And what if she compliments it?"

Macker pursed his lips and squinted his eyes. "Right, I'll tell ye what...If she compliments it, I won't ask her out, if she doesn't, I will."

It was just as the main courses were arriving that they started trying to use the code, to find out how their horse was doing. Thankfully, from Matt's point of view, Sam and Jane were engrossed in a conversation about *ikea* beds.

"So, how's the trainin' goin' Macker?" Shipsey asked.

Macker, who had been to visit their horse and its trainer during the week, was keen to fill them in as much as possible.

"Well, as you're well aware, I'm in pretty good shape anyway and have been doing lots of light training for the last six months. My intention is to crank it up during the next couple of months."

"And when will you go in your first serious race?"

"Barring injury, April or May."

49

"And what are your chances of winning?"

"Well, baring in mind, I'll be up against other inexperienced athletes, I would certainly want to finish in the top half of the field and hopefully even get a place." Macker took a sip of wine, then smiled proudly "You never know, a man of my pedigree, I might bloody well win it."

Shipsey leaned in to the table, lowering his voice slightly. "So, you know the way lots of triathletes put a nickname on the frame of their bike? What will you be calling yours?" Shipsey was quite proud with how he was sticking to the code.

Macker raised his eyebrows. He'd forgotten to tell them about the cool name he'd come up with, but he was equally determined to keep up the code speak, and had to think fast.

"No, I wasn't aware of that, big man," he grinned."But if I decide to put a name on it, I would probably use a cross between the nicknames of my two favourite BMX bikes I had when I was a kid. They were "Devil's Valley" and "The Cat's Whiskers," so I was thinking possibly *"Satan's Whiskers."* It's also the name of a cocktail I used to make in the states."

"Sounds good," said Matt.

"Yeah, pretty cool," Dave nodded. "I like it."

"You used to have nicknames for your bikes?" Shipsey chuckled.

Samantha suddenly stopped talking to Jane and looked at the lads. "What on earth are you guys talking about?"

Matt's heart stopped. The four lads looked at each other for what felt like a lifetime, before Dave finally spoke.

"Ah, just the fact that McCann used to have nicknames for his BMX bikes."

"Whatever you're into Macker," said Sam, before downing the last mouthful of her Chicken Parmagiana. Matt's heart started beating again.

A couple of hours later, they were drinking toward closing time in a pub across the road from the restaurant, when they bumped into a face that was familiar to Matt, Shipsey and Macker.

"Howye Stinger!" said Shipsey, spotting him first.

"Ah, howye big man! All right Matt. Howye Macker ye skinny bollix."

Andy Belton, also known as Stinger, had been known to Matt and Shipsey since their school days. In fact, it was Matt who had given Stinger his nickname. Stinger knew Macker through football and for a few years had played on the same team.

"Jaysis lads, it's gas I bumped into yiz. Do you know what's on tomorrow?"

"What?"

"The 5-A-Side comp down in Loughlinstown. Remember we won it about five years ago." It was actually seven years since they won it and they were all a lot fitter at the time, but nonetheless, by last calls Stinger had convinced them to roll back the years and enter a team.

"Why's he called Stinger?" asked Dave on the way home in the taxi-van.

"Well his name is Andrew Belton, so his initials are A.B," said Matt.

"Oh God," Dave cringed. "Who came up with that?"

"Who do you think?" said Shipsey, pointing at Matt.

"Well, it's also because, when he was learning to play the piano, he only got to learn how to play the theme tune to "The Sting," before he gave up"

"I thought it was cos he's good at poker," added Macker.

"That's another good reason." Shipsey nodded. "He's the jammiest bastard I've ever seen!"

"How does that go again?" asked Dave.

"How does what go?"

"The theme music to "The Sting?"

At this point Macker starts whistling the start of *"When I'm 64,"* by *The Beatles.* Half way through the second line he stops abruptly, frowning and shaking his head.

"That's the fucking Beatles!" laughed Shipsey.

"Yeah." Dave started singing the start of the song to confirm Macker's error. *"When I grow older, losing my hair, many years from now...*

"Oh yeah," said Macker, who was still racking his brain for the tune.

...will you still be sending me Valentines, birthday greetings, bottle of wine."

"OK OK, I'm with ye! How does it go then?"

"I can't remember," said Dave, shaking his head. "It's the same as the old intro tune for the snooker back in the eighties."

At this point Matt remembered the tune and whistled the first line. By the end of the second line all four lads were whistling in sync.

Whu whu whu whu-whe whu-whe whu-whe whe
Whe whe whe whe-whu whe-whe whe-whe whu

Whu whu whu whu-whe whu-whe whu-whe whe
Whu whu whu whu-whu whu whu whu-whe

Tucked away in the two front seats of the van were Sam and Jane. As is often the case, they'd spent most of the evening talking to each other, as the four lads amused themselves. Jane had found her 26th birthday particularly hard work, as Sam has been relentless in wanting to talk about her big move. Every time Jane managed to steer the conversation on to something less serious, Sam would soon find a way back to topics like DIY or mortgages. The lads, who were now in singing mood, were trying to come up with a birthday song for Jane. To do this, they had slightly modified another Beatles number and as the van pulled up to let her and Shipsey out they were roaring to the tune of *"Penny Lane"*

"Peggy Jane is in my ears and in my eyes.
There beneath the blue suburban skies."

Matt, who had spent the first couple of hours of the evening uptight was now fully relaxed and leading the singing. It was his way of paying a tribute to Jane for keeping quiet about the horse purchase *and* spending most of the night talking to Sam about *IKEA* and freeholds and down payments. Jane was putting on a brave face, smiling and saying her goodnights. Just before she turned to walk up the drive, she made eye contact with Matt. Through the van window she could see him wink and mouth the words "Thank you."

Chapter 7

"For fuck sake lads!" Matt roared. "We're running around like headless chickens. Let's keep the shape!"

Three minutes into their first match they were already losing two-nil. The shape they had agreed was Shipsey in goal, Stinger and his friend Cob at the back, Matt in midfield and Macker up front. Unlike most of the other teams, they had no substitutes on the sideline, only Dave, cheering them on. Shipsey had been at fault for the first goal, which was a speculative 25-yard drive he'd let slip through his fingers at the near post. For the second Cob had brought the ball up field and couldn't manage to get back when he lost it. Just before half time, Matt and Macker pulled off a lovely one-two, which sent Macker clean through on the keeper. He calmly drilled the ball into the corner, 2-1. Macker, whose confidence was now on the up, made it 2-2 shortly after the restart. The opposition were now rattled and chose to defend in greater numbers. The lads struggled to convert their territorial advantage into a victory until the final minute when Matt struck a pile driver from thirty yards that took three deflections, before nestling in the back of the net. Their second game proved to be quite a bit easier and they cruised through it 4-0.

Their final group game was crucial and would decide who would progress to the semi finals. They were up against a team called "Brack," which was full of ex-Ballybrack players. They had also won their other two group games, but had a superior goal difference, courtesy of 4-1 and 6-0 victories. This meant that the lads had to win the game to advance to the semi-final. From the off, the pace of the match and the harshness of the tackles were heightened. One of those tackles was on Macker and resulted in a penalty, which he duly converted. In the second half he made it 2-0 with a brilliant piece of individual flare. After beating one of their defenders by rebounding the ball off the sidewall he beat their big centre half by nut-megging the ball through his legs. This was a move he'd practiced hard when he has sixteen and any time he managed to pull it off he'd call out the word "nuts" as he did it. Needless to say, this infuriated the foolish looking defender, but there was little he could do as he turned around to see Macker tucking the ball into the far corner of the net.

Macker was to spend the remainder of the match jumping out of the way of tackles, while his teammates desperately tried to defend the lead. With two minutes to go "Brack" got a goal back and then things started to get out of hand. They were so desperate to get the equaliser that they started to hack players down to regain possession of the ball. Macker was coming in for some particularly rough treatment and the referee wasn't keeping the game under control. In the last half minute Shipsey made a great save from a powerful shot, but didn't manage to hold on to the ball. Just as their centre forward was about to smash home the rebound Stinger managed to stretch out his leg and poke it sideways to Matt. In doing so he received the full force of the centre forwards boot on the side of his ankle. Matt now had two of their players bearing down on him, but managed to keep his cool and find Macker with a pass off the wall. Macker again beat one of their defenders with a rebound off the wall, but instead of heading goal-ward he dribbled the ball into the corner to waste time. Bad idea. The big centre half, who by now had had enough, came charging in from behind and smashed in to the back of Macker's legs, leaving him moaning in a crumpled heap on the floor. Although they were a good forty yards away, it didn't take long for Matt and Cob to arrive on the scene. Matt was there first and went straight for the big guy slamming him into the boards behind the goal. Within a second of that Matt received a hefty punch to the side of the head from the other defender. In no time a free-for-all punch-up had commenced. Cob was not coming off well against their big defender and blood was flowing from his nose. Macker, had got back to his feet and was trying to help Cob, but was being pushed away by one of their other players. Matt was now well on top of his battle with the other defender, but the referee made the mistake of grabbing him around the chest from behind. Before he realised who it was, Matt had knocked the referee to the ground with a thumping elbow to the mouth. There were a small handful of non-participants at this point. Two of "Brack's" better players were standing in the semi-circle calling their own team mates "wankers." Stinger and Shipsey were also struggling to join the melee. Stinger wanted to get involved, but was struggling to make it to his feet in the far goalmouth. Shipsey, who had started his run, when he saw Matt getting hit from behind, was now approaching the action at top speed. As he homed in on his victim, he lowered his shoulder. When contact was made, it was Shipsey's shoulder being driven hard into the chest of the big defender. The impact drove the big guy back with such force that when he hit the waist high backboard the momentum caused his whole body to flip over the top and make a hard landing on the far side.

*****

"I can't believe I missed all that," complained Stinger, adjusting the ice-pack on his ankle and taking a gulp from his pint. "I haven't had a scrap since fifth year. Probably just as well though, one of them was my cousin"

Shipsey nearly choked on his pint. "Wha? Which one?"

"The one that Cullen beat the crap out of."

"Jaysis Stinger!" said Matt. "I didn't know. Sorry about that."

"Don't worry about it," laughed Stinger, "I never liked the prick!"

Moments after Shipsey exploded onto the scene, the fight was over and both teams were ejected from the competition. The lads spent the first hour in the pub reminding each other of how brilliantly they had performed, firstly on the playing side, but more importantly on the fighting side. Each one of them had their own heroic tale to tell and there was a battle to get centre stage.

"Did ye see the way I nutmegged that defender?"

"Did ye see the way I blocked that shot?"

"Did ye see the way I burst the referee's lip?"

"Did ye see me knock that ape clean out of the stadium?"

Spirits were high and the drink was going down quick and easy. None of them wanted to finish up when it was approaching closing time, so they decided to get a few more beers to takeaway and head back to Matt and Dave's flat to play some cards.

There were some quite different thoughts going through those six minds on the way back to the flat. Matt was feeling a bit sorry for himself about how he was going to miss this sort of night when he moved in with Samantha. Cob was also feeling sorry for himself, because the pain in his nose was still pretty sore. Dave was disappointed that they were going to have to wait until at least April for "*Satan's Whiskers*" first race as that meant he probably wouldn't see Kate again until then. Stinger who was starving was just hoping there was a pizza delivery place near the guys flat. Macker was making plans for how he would go in for the kill with his dream hairdresser. Shipsey, for good reason, was the only man with his mind on the task ahead. The last time he'd played cards with Stinger had been a very expensive night for him. Even though it was over three years ago, he could still remember some of the big hands he lost and it seemed to be Stinger that stung him every time. He was reminding himself that with six players it didn't make sense to get involved every time he had half a hand and to save his big bets for when he was pretty sure he had the winning hand.

As was usual in their games, it was Macker who set the pace. It had always been his style to bet hard and fast almost disregarding the quality of his cards. Not unlike his formula for success at the horse auction, he hoped that doing this would scare the other players away. Matt and Shipsey who knew this better than the others always tried to avoid sitting next to him. They found it impossible to tell when he was bluffing and only knew that he couldn't have a good hand every time. Most of the time they were playing seven-card stud with a three euro ante for the dealer and a limit on the maximum bet of half the pot. With six players, this should have worked out at an average pot of about twenty euro, but with Macker around it was more like twice that. It got to the stage where both Stinger and Cob were so fed up with Macker raising every bet they made, that they left the betting up to him even when they had really good cards. This was the obvious flaw in Macker's tactics. The only people who were calling his raises were the people with good cards and with six players there was almost always at least one of them who fancied taking him on. His system continued to fail and after nearly three hours he was down 220 euro. His two biggest losses had been to Matt and Stinger who had both pipped him with higher flushes.

"So Macker, are we going to go and see the horse some time over the next few months?" asked Dave.

This was the only obvious way he could think of that he could bump into Kate between now and the first race.

"Yeah, well I'll definitely be heading out once or twice. So if you wanna come along, then cool."

"Yeah, that would be good craic. We should all go."

Matt knew exactly what Dave's angle was and winked across at his flatmate. "Sounds like a good idea to me." He'd agreed with Dave that he wouldn't say anything to Macker about Dave's interest in Kate.

Shipsey stood up so he could reach the money in his back pocket. He only had a hundred Euro left, but he was confident. He tossed it nonchalantly into the pot and smiled across at Stinger.

"I'll see your forty and raise you sixty."

Stinger couldn't believe his luck. On his last card he managed to fill a full house and was sure he had the best hand. He saw the bet of sixty and raised it a further onehundred and fifty Euro. The smile fell away from Shipsey's face as he plonked down into his chair with a thud. He hadn't seen that one coming.

Stinger was now positively beaming on the other side of the table. It was not the face of a man that was bluffing. Shopsey let out a deep sigh. He looked like he was about to be stung by his old poker nemesis again. Or was he?

He took another peek at his own cards. A full house of threes was a pretty good hand. Of Stinger's seven cards he had a pair of Jacks, a two and an eight showing. All he needed was another Jack and an eight in his other three cards and he would win. Or a pair of eights… or a pair of Jacks… or a Jack and a two… or a Jack and any pair… or three eights… or three twos. Basically there were lots of cards he could have to beat a house of threes.

Shipsey placed his hands over his eyes and let out a loud groan. He knew he should probably fold, but he didn't want to. This was the best hand he'd had all night. He removed his hands from his eyes to see that Stinger was still smiling contently.

"Are you bluffing?" Shipsey asked.

Stinger's smile broadened further. "You'll have to pay and see."

Shipsey studied the clock on the wall. "Ah fuck it. It's gettin' late anyway. Matt, can you lend me one fifty to see what this wanker has?"

Matt counted out the cash and handed it to his friend. Shipsey rested it gently on top of the massive pot.

"The only thing I don't wanna hear is 'Full House', ok what ya got?"

Stinger turned over his three blind cards to reveal a pair of twos and a six.

"Full House…"

"Wha?"

"A house of twos."

"A house of twos?"

"Yeah, a house of twos! What the fuck have you got?"

"Oh…only a house of THREES! Get in! You little fuckin daisy!" Shipsey couldn't hide his relief and excitement and started singing and dancing the 'Macarena' all around the table. He'd learned the words on a holiday to Marbella two summers previously.

Dale a tu cuerpo alegria Macarena
Que tu cuerpo es pa' darle alegria y cosa Buena
Dale a tu cuerpo alegria Macarena
Heyyyy Macarena!

Within half an hour the rest of the lads had left and Matt and Dave were clearing up the debris.

"I'm gonna miss nights like these," said Matt.

"What dya mean?"

"Well just look at today. I left the flat at 4pm to play in a 5-A-Side competition that we heard out about in the boozer last night. We get kicked out of the competition for fighting, so we go to the nearest drinking hole and get completely wankered. But we haven't had enough, so we get more beers and come back here to play a civilised game of poker. That ends up with my six foot four, seventeen stone friend, breaking one of our chairs from dancing on it, cos he's just lifted about 500 euro out of the pot."

Dave was shoving the remnants of their kitchen chair into a black bin liner.

"You're gonna miss times like these?"

"Yeah. I'm hardly gonna be able to do this when I move in with Sam"

"Come on Matt, you're pissed and maybe a part of you wants to be a student forever, but you're gonna move in and start settling down with one of the best looking girls in the world and you're madly in love with each other."

"Yeah…Ok, but does it have to be so final. Couldn't I live with her Monday to Thursday and come back here for the weekends?"

"No. So you'll just have to get all this drunken debauchery out of your system over the next few months. Come on, let's leave the rest of this shit till the morning."

As the two of them waddled out of the kitchen with their arms around each other's shoulders, Matt was having difficulty with the words of *The Doors* song *The End*.

> *"This is the end…beautiful friend, the end*
> *Of our elaborate plans…the end.*
> *I'll never look into your…glands again."*

Chapter 8

"Can you do a blade two on the sides and back please and just trim a bit off the top."

It was exactly eight days and one hour since Macker sat in the same chair receiving the same haircut from the same beautiful hairdresser. He'd let two other people skip ahead of him in the queue waiting for his girl to be free. He spent almost an hour sitting on the waiting bench, pretending to read "Hello" magazine, but really checking out her sexy legs. By the time it was his turn he had become quite nervous. He always performed better when he didn't have too much time to think about what he was going to say. While he had been waiting he started mentally rehearsing some lines, but they all sounded incredibly cheesy

The sexy hairdresser was standing behind him, frowning at his reflection in the mirror. "Weren't you here last week?"

Uh oh, thought Macker… *rumbled!*

After a while he regained his composure and in the short time it took her to retouch his haircut, they had quite a nice chat. He learned that her name was Rachel, she was from Sutton and as the conversation wore on, Macker was getting more and more confident that she might be single. When the time came to pay and say goodbye, he took a deep breath and asked her out.

*****

Matt slid a pint across the table to where Macker was taking his seat.

"So how did it go Romeo?"

Macker looked up and smiled. "I'll tell you in a minute. First, it's konch time."

"We want the story of the non-complimentary hairdresser first," said Dave.

"Don't worry its all related. Basically she said I could take her out Saturday week, if I brought along another couple. So the loser of the spin has to come with me."

"Bollix. Ye must be jokin" laughed Shipsey.

"Yeah, fuck right off!" agreed Dave.

59

Macker looked at Matt with pleading eyes. "Matty baby! Wadye say? I'll be your best friend."

"I think you're stretching the use of the konch a bit. Why won't she go with you on your own? You're hardly the scariest fucker in the world."

"I don't know. She says she had a bad experience before or something."

"Ok, well how about this? We do the spin and whoever it lands on goes on the date with you, but straight away you owe that person one konch sacrifice in return, no spin. Deal?"

"I'm ok with that."

"Ok, fuck it. I'll do it," Shipsey agreed.

"What if it lands on me?" asked Dave "Who the hell am I supposed to bring?"

Matt winked across at him. "You'll think of someone."

Macker was happy to get away with paying a small price for their agreement. He knew the lads would make a big deal out of what he was asking them to do. As he was preparing to spin he was hopeful, he could land it on Matt. Although he was a bit too good-looking for Macker's liking, the other alternatives were a bit frightening. Shipsey would probably be his second choice, but Macker wasn't sure how well Rachel would get on with his biggest and loudest friend. Shipsey was a difficult man to tone down and there was always a chance he would have one of his blazing rows with Jane. He was still a comfortable second ahead of Dave. To the best of Macker's knowledge, the only woman Dave had ever spoken to in his entire life was his mother. Even *finding* a date for Dave with only ten days notice, would be a miracle. On top of that Dave had shown talent for dreaming up particularly nasty konch-tasks. Macker's spinning skills let him down and moments later he was contemplating going on a double date with a guy who hadn't been out with a girl in over three years.

"So, who the hell are you gonna bring?" asked Macker.

"Oh, I've got a couple of ideas," said Dave as coolly as possible.

He had literally that, two ideas. The first was obvious. He would ask Macker's cousin Kate who had been dominating his thoughts since their first meeting. Asking someone out on a double date is a lot easier than a normal date, especially if you can convince the datee that they would be helping out their own cousin. If Kate said no, he would ask Helen, his University girlfriend. Although that would be a call that he would make in trepidation, she might just say yes out of sympathy.

Although she dropped him like a bad habit back in College, Dave still felt that Helen had a soft spot for him and he knew he had a soft spot for her.

"A couple of ideas? You haven't been out with a bird for years! You're not gonna pay for an escort are you? 'cos I think that would be a bit obvious."

"Only if my couple of ideas fall through," Dave retorted.

Macker got to his feet, shaking his head. "I don't know. I just don't know," he said, breathing out heavily. He turned and headed towards the gents muttering something about his lousy konch spin.

When Macker was out of earshot, Matt whispered towards Dave. "So, are you gonna ask his cousin?"

"I guess so."

"Nice one, she's lovely," Matt encouraged.

"And what's plan B?" asked Shipsey, less confident of his friends chances.

"Helen."

"What? The bird from college who gave the great blow jobs? The one who dumped you years ago? How the fuck are you gonna swing that one?"

"Thanks for your confidence, Shipsey. We've bumped into each other a couple of times since then and we've got on all right."

Matt nodded his head slowly. "You're going for the sympathy vote."

"Yep."

"You know you're gonna have to tell Macker you're asking his cousin. You can't just turn up with her on the night."

"I don't have to tell him unless she says yes. Anyway here he comes, so shush."

As Macker was sitting back down, three broad grins were looking up at him.

"What the fuck are you guys smiling at?"

"I've been thinking about what sacrifice I might make you do," said Dave.

"Oh fuck! Now take it easy on me Dave. None of that crazy coin-tossing shit."

"Don't worry it won't be as easy as that. Dave's grin was now broadening. I was wondering if you got the compliment you were looking for from your hairdresser?"

"Her name's Rachael and no, the only thing she said was "your hair is very fine.""

"That's not bad, is it?"

Macker shook his head. "Your hair is very fine is not a compliment. Your hair makes my knickers wet, that's a compliment."

Dave chuckled and then began to explain the complicated task he had dreamt up for Macker. "OK, here's what you have to do. During the course of the meal, you have to illicit three compliments from Rachael. If you get three or more, you have completed your task and you gain control of the konch. However for each of the three you don't get, you must buy one course of the meal for the whole table."

Macker slumped back in his chair. "What?"

So if you only get one compliment you don't have to pay for our starters. If you get two all you have to pay for is dessert. Got it?"

"You're some evil bastard Massey! Yeah, I get it. But what if people don't want dessert?"

"Good question," said Dave folding his arms and trying to come up with another twist. "If Rachael doesn't order dessert and you get less than two compliments, you have to pay for the drink."

"The drink! Fuck off!"

"That's only if she doesn't order dessert. If she does, that might be the only one you have to pay for."

"Don't worry, she will." Macker slowly folded his arms. "If I have to force feed it to her, she will."

That Sunday Dave finally got up the courage to ring Kate and ask her on the double date. To his great joy and relief, she said yes. Half an hour later he was still on a high, looking forward to the date, when his mobile phone rang. It was Macker.

Shit, how did he find out so fast?

"Good afternoon Mr. McCann."

"Good afternoon Mr. Massey. Just ringing to see how the hunt for the Loch Ness monster is going."

"If you mean, have I got a date? The answer is yes."

"Oh yeah? How much did you have to pay her?"

"Not as much as two haircuts."

"No seriously…what's she like…is she the right species?"

"Whaddya mean?"

"Is she a female human being?"

"Oh yes…a very pretty one actually. You may even recognise her."

"Yeah? Who is it?"

"Your cousin Kate."

"What?"

Dave was glad this conversation was taking place on the phone.

"Is that a problem?"

Macker had to think long and hard about this. Did he mind that his cousin was going out with a short, fat, bald, blind, smoker? *Yes.* Did he like the fact that it meant that he could go on the date with his tall, slim, beautiful hairdresser? *Fuck yes!* And at the end of the day, Dave's a good bloke and he was quite proud of Kate for seeing the potentially nice interior under the sloppy packaging, even if she could do a lot better.

"No, I suppose that's all right," Macker agreed. "Are you sure she's not going out with anyone?"

"Not entirely sure...why? Do you think she is?"

"I don't know."

"It doesn't really matter," said Dave. "She's just helping *me* help you."

"Ok, fair enough. Should be an interesting night."

*****

When the day of the double date came around, Dave was really nervous. At midday he found himself wondering what he was going to wear. That was definitely a first. Normally he would take the first pair of jeans and the first ironed shirt he found in his wardrobe and put them on without a thought for whether they looked good together. Often when he couldn't find an ironed shirt, he'd just put a fleece on over a creased one. But tonight he decided he was going to make the effort and off he went to the Blackrock shopping centre. Dave hated shopping, particularly for himself. Trousers were always a problem. With a thirty-eight inch waist and a twenty-nine inch leg, he wasn't well catered for in the trendier shops. After a sweat-inducing four hours he managed to find a pair of black casual trousers and a charcoal shirt that he thought were acceptable.

He'd arranged to meet Kate a half an hour before the table was booked in a bar across the road from the restaurant. He got there twenty minutes early and proceeded to calm his nerves with a couple of swift pints. Five minutes after Kate was supposed to arrive his phone rang.

Oh shit! She's not coming! he thought. But when he lifted the phone he could see Matt's name flashing in the screen.

"Howye."

"Has she arrived?"

"Not yet."

"Ok, I'll call again in ten minutes."

"What for?"

"So it'll look as if you're a really popular bloke."

"Ah no, you're all right."

"You sure?"

"Yeah, it's fine. Thanks anyway."

"Well how about I ring just to make sure she shows up?"

"If you ring again and she's here, I'll switch the phone off to let you know, ok?"

"Ok, seeye good luck."

Kate rushed through the door ten minutes late. Dave felt an electric charge going through his stomach when he saw her. She looked like she'd been running and when she saw him she waved enthusiastically. As she walked swiftly towards him Dave was taken aback by how well she looked. He thought she was quite good looking when they met at the horse auction, but now she looked fantastic. Her long hair was down and had obviously taken an age to do. It was longer than Dave had thought. She was only wearing a small bit of make-up, but it made her pretty face look even more beautiful. Her big blue eyes that had looked friendly before, now looked downright sexy. Dave's mouth was still slightly ajar when she got to where he was sitting.

Kate leaned in and pecked him on the cheek. "Hi"

"Hi."

Kate started to take off her coat. "I'm so sorry I'm late. I always get lost out this way. I asked the bus driver to let me know when we got here, but he forgot."

"No worries…Sit down." Dave got to his feet. "What are ye havin' "

"No, you stay sitting. I'll get them." She put her coat on the back of the chair and made her way up to the bar. She was wearing dark blue wide ankle jeans over a pair of black boots and a simple almost T-shirt-like white top. She looked sexy as hell.

"Guinness I presume?" she asked resting the two drinks on the table and sliding her stool closer.

"Yes. Thanks"

"I really hate being late. I don't believe in that 'fashionably late' crap."

"Don't worry about it. It's only ten minutes. I would have waited a lot longer. You look great." He was sure she'd lost weight, since they last met, but how do you say that to a girl without suggesting that she was a bit overweight in the first place.

"Thanks," said Kate. "So do you. I like your shirt."

What Dave didn't realise is that Kate could tell from the faint horizontal and vertical creases on his shirt, that he'd just bought it. She liked the fact that he'd made the extra effort. When his phone rang he switched it straight off.

"Sorry about that I meant to switch it off when you got here."

"That reminds me. How did you get my number? Does Michael have it?"

"Yeah, I nicked it from his phone last weekend. Is that all right?"

"I suppose so. It shows initiative anyway. And what does he think of you bringing his cousin on a double date?"

"I don't know. You'll have to ask him. He seemed ok with it. I think he's just happy that the whole thing is going ahead."

"And why didn't he pick Matt or Shipsey for the task?"

"Eh…well…y'see…it's eh…Ok…here's the truth."

Dave knew this was probably one of those times when a little white lie should be used to good effect, but he proceeded to tell her about the konch.

When he'd finished Kate glared at him with an indignant expression. "So, I'm like some sort of prop in this laddish game of yours?"

"No, it's not like that" Dave swallowed hard. "I…eh…wanted to ask you out anyway."

Kate's glare melted and she started giggling.

"Dave, relax, I'm just kidding with you."

Half an hour later, Dave, Kate and Macker were sitting at the restaurant table when Rachael arrived fashionably late and fairly unapologetic.

"I hope you didn't wait for me to order?" she asked.

Kate smiled at Dave. "I knew we shouldn't have," she whispered.

After they'd all settled down and ordered, Macker decided to go to work on his konch task.

"Why don't we play the "what I like" game?"

"The what?" asked Dave.

"Y'know, the game where you say what you like about your date or partner."

"That's a game?"

"Yeah, I'll start," said Macker determined to get the ball rolling. "Ok, well I was going to say her luscious lips, but what I like most about Rachael, are her long sexy legs."

Macker was hoping that by mentioning two compliments for her, Rachael might give him two compliments in return.

"Cringe," said Kate who was looking at Macker and poking two fingers towards the back of her throat.

Macker ignored his cousin "Ok, who's next? Let's go around in a circle…Davey boy?"

Dave could think of a thousand compliments to lay on Kate, but her reaction to Macker's one told him that he might want to tone it down a bit.

"What I like about Kate, is that she buys me Guinness without asking what I want."

Kate smiled. She was glad that Dave hadn't gone over the top. "Oh that's so sweet. You really mean that?…Well, what I like about Dave is he's charming, he's honest and he bought a new shirt for our first date."

Dave felt proud, but slightly embarrassed at the same time. Receiving three compliments was cool, but getting caught out by the creases of a packaged shirt was not so cool. All eyes were now on Rachael who'd been pretty quiet since her late arrival.

"Rachael?" Kate prompted.

"What I like about Michael is ehhh….

Dave was just about to swallow a mouthful of wine

…he smells nice."

Dave's wine stopped halfway down his throat and reversed sharply. What didn't come out his nose came out his mouth onto his prawn cocktail starter.

He grabbed his napkin and held it over his mouth and nose. "Sorry."

Kate was also trying to hold in the laughter, but was a bit disappointed that her cousin wasn't getting credit for more than just smelling nice. "Is that it?" she asked. "Not his twinkling blue eyes or his soft blonde hair?"

"No, I'm not mad about his hair…it's a little bit…girlie."

By now Dave was almost choking and had to leave the table.

The evening went downhill from there for Macker. Forget compliments, he had trouble getting Rachel to say anything pleasant at all. Dave on the other hand was having a great night. Not only was he spending it in the company of a beautiful woman with a deadly sense of humour, but his friend who was squirming beside him was going to have to pay for it. When it came to ordering desserts both Dave and Kate passed and ordered Irish Coffees instead. That put Macker under added pressure. It was going to be a very expensive meal if he couldn't get Rachel to eat a dessert. Unfortunately he must have tried to coax her a bit too much, because he almost started a row.

"Some of us have to work harder than others, to maintain our figures!," she growled. With that, Macker had made up his mind. Not only would he not be calling Rachel, he would never step foot inside her hairdressers again. When she got up to go to the ladies, he leaned across the table and whispered to Dave and Kate.

"Come on, let's ditch this bitch."

"What? Now?" Dave gasped.

"No, we pay the bill, then I say I've got an early start and am getting a cab home. The three of us are heading south, she's heading north… job done."

In the taxi on the way back to *The Banner Man*, Dave and Kate had a good laugh at Macker's expense. You couldn't keep Macker down for long though. Within minutes of arriving back on home turf and spotting Michelle, his favourite lounge girl, he was back to his old self.

"Howye Michelle! Are you still going out with what's 'is name?"

"Hi! yeah, 'fraid so."

"Ok, well I'll let my friend know. Don't forget to tell me if it ends."

"I won't." Michelle smiled and turned away. She'd gotten used to Macker and his cheeky routine and found it quite charming.

At the end of the night Kate walked home with Macker. She was staying with her relatives. Dave made his way home on his own, going over and over in his mind the previous five hours he'd spent with Kate. He'd enjoyed every moment of it and couldn't see how it could have gone any better. He even avoided making any clumsy overtures towards her at the end of the night…just a simple kiss on the cheek. He was definitely up for more, but didn't want to take any chances. They had arranged to meet the following Saturday when the lads would visit "*Satan's Whiskers*" at his stables. As the taxi pulled into his estate, Dave realised that he still hadn't answered either of the two main enquiries he had about Kate. He still didn't know if she was going out with anyone or whether she'd be interested in taking things further than just a double date to help out her cousin. He would call on Matt's help to find out some answers.

Chapter 9

Shipsey poked an elbow into Dave's ribs. "Well at least if you get that far, you know she's a great ride," he whispered.

After a little bit of coaxing the trainer, Paddy Mulryan, had agreed to let Kate take *Satan's Whiskers* out for a run. He didn't usually let part owners ride their own horses, but he knew Kate was experienced and in the short time he'd had *Satan's Whiskers*, the horse had shown himself to be well behaved.

"Don't do anthin' shtewpid now Kate," he advised in his thick Kildare accent. "He's already had a run today so don't go beyond a canter."

The four lads watched in awe as Kate handled their horse beautifully, at what appeared to be a couple of gears above a canter. Kate couldn't take the grin off her face, as she held tight to the reigns of this magnificent galloping animal. He was easily the best horse she had ever ridden. In all her years at riding school, she had gradually fallen in love with every horse she had spent time riding and was always broken hearted when one died or she had to move onto a new horse because she was getting too big. But this was different. This was love at first sight. The power, the speed even the *smell* of this horse was superior. It was as if she'd traded in her smelly old Skoda with the broken taillight and dodgy clutch for a spanking new BMW with tinted windows and leather seats.

So this is the difference between a racehorse and a work horse, she thought, as she slowed to canter back to the lads.

As she approached them, they were all clapping and cheering.

"That was great, Kate."

"How was he Kate?"

"Kate for the National!"

"My turn," said Shipsey, pretending to climb over the fence.

This was the first time they had seen *Satan's Whiskers* up close and they were all very impressed. He was a tall lean beast with a dark brown coat that was gleaming in the sunlight. With his bright eyes and rippling muscles he was the picture of health and he was hardly even puffing after what seemed like a pretty decent workout. There were only three white patches breaking his beautiful dark brown colouring, one on each of his hind feet and a small diamond shape in the middle of his forehead.

Dave was mesmerised by the whole scene. He found few things more stimulating than the sight of a beautiful fit woman in jodhpurs. Ok, Kate was wearing jeans and not jodhpurs, but it wasn't taking away from the fantasy going on in his mind. He could feel the beginnings of an erection stirring in his pants as Kate bounced down from the horse and bent over to adjust the saddle.

This will not do! Dave started to panic. *Getting a stiffy in broad daylight is a bad idea, especially when you're wearing chinos!*

Stop staring at her ass! his brain said to his eyes. *Think of econometrics.*

But his eyes were under the control of another part of his anatomy. He was relieved when Paddy offered to take them for a tour of the yard. Sometimes the only way to deal with a misbehaving middle wicket is to walk it off.

Until the age of forty, Paddy Mulryan had been a cattle farmer. On his fortieth birthday he decided to buy and train a couple of racehorses for personal interest. After a few years, word got out that he knew what he was doing and other owners started to ask him to train their horses. Every five years since then he added a new block of stables to his land that had long since said farewell to the cattle. What had begun as a hobby had transformed over twenty-two years into a very enjoyable, if at times stressful vocation. The yard and stables were a hive of activity on this sunny February afternoon. He employed three full time and three part time staff to help him cope with the forty-five horses he was responsible for. Stables were sprawled out in three different directions from his farmhouse, which faced onto the rolling gallops. As he was showing the new owners around the facilities, Matt started to chat to Kate. As promised, he was going to try to help Dave find out what his chances were. The problem would be doing so without making it obvious.

"So what do you think Kate? Is he gonna make us lots of money?"

"He's absolutely amazing. I've never ridden a horse as fast and powerful as that. It was such a buzz and you can tell he wants to race. I had to hold tight to keep him from taking off!"

"Really? That good?"

"Well, to keep it in perspective, that's the first time I've been on a proper racehorse, so I don't know if they're all like that. But he looks *extremely* fit and healthy."

"You're not lookin' too bad yourself. You look like you've lost a bit of weight?" As soon as the words came out, Matt bit his lip.

"What? You mean I looked like a big fat trollop before?"

"No no! I was just eh thinkin'-

"Relax Matt. I'm just kidding with you."

Kate was actually pretty pleased that Matt had noticed she'd lost weight. After breaking up with her last boyfriend back in November, she'd let herself go a little bit, but since the auction she'd lost five pounds on a new low-carb diet.

"God you had me goin' there for a sec," said a relieved Matt. "But seriously, you looked great up there. It can't be easy to manage a horse like that for the first time. How'd you become such a great...em...*rider*, for want of a better word?"

Kate frowned at first and then started giggling. "*Rider*? Are you flirting with me?" She was enjoying having a man as handsome as Matt on the back foot and could see his cheeks were starting to redden.

Matt grimaced and shook his head. "Sorry, *rider* was the best of the three words that came to mind at the time."

"Oh? Were the other two really that bad?"

"Well, *jockey* was the first one. But I'd associate that more with short, forty-year-old men with leather skin. And then there was...eh...*horseman*, which just sounds crap."

"You're right, it *was* the best of the three."

"Thanks, I try hard," said Matt, regaining his composure. By now he and Kate had drifted away from the back of the group, so he felt safe to start asking her some more pertinent questions. *Softly softly,* he said to himself.

"So, did you have a good night last weekend?"

"Oh I see," smiled Kate. "You're Dave's best mate and he's asked you to find out if I'm interested in him."

Oh shit, rumbled already, thought Matt. "You're a bit of a "Quicker Wit" aren't you?"

"Don't tell me you've heard of the *Quicker Wits*!" said Kate, taken aback.

"Yeah, I used to read all about them with my mum when I was a kid."

"Me too! That's amazing. You can't get them now, you know. I went to a couple of libraries and bookstores to try and find them for my little cousin, but people were looking at me as if I'd asked them for one of their kidneys."

Matt *was* truly amazed. It was about twenty years ago that his mum had borrowed a series of tattered booklets from the local library called "The Quicker Wits." While the other kids in his class were being bored to death with stories about Peter and Jane he and his mum read about a clever tribe of indiginous people who came up with cunning solutions to solve the problems they encountered in their primitive lifestyles. He could clearly remember lying in bed turning those tattered pages, his young mother beside him. It was a long time since he'd cried for her loss, but this memory was evoking real emotions.

"That *is* amazing." Matt swallowed back a tear. "I'd say I've been using that phrase for years, but I can't ever remember anyone who knew what the hell I was talking about. I'd nearly forgotten myself."

"Well, now we can be "Quicker Wit" buddies," said Kate, linking her arm around his.

"Well, if we're "Quicker Wit" buddies, you're gonna have to give me something I can go back to Dave with."

"Like what?"

"Like, are you going out with anyone?"

"What do you think?"

"I don't know."

"Would I have gone on a date with him, if I was going out with anyone?"

"Jesus Kate, you're one tough cookie to crack. Do you always answer a question with another question?"

"Ok, sorry, I'm just not used to this...Right, ask me another one and I'll try to be more helpful."

"Ok...eh...right, what happened with the last guy you went out with?"

"I broke up with him three months ago after going out with him for four months. He turned out to be another in a long line of losers."

"What do you mean by *losers*?"

"Guys who think they're either more intelligent or better looking than they actually are."

"Ah, well Dave couldn't be accused of that."

"No."

"*So*?"

"So *what*?"

"So, do you fancy him?"

"I had a great time with him and we got on really well, but I wouldn't say he's my type exactly."

"Ok, so what *is* your type?"

"Oh I don't know," Kate paused momentarily and looked up at Matt. "About six foot tall, tanned skin, dark hair, nice blue eyes."

"Now, you're flirting with me!"

71

"Only cos I know you're safe. You're practically married."

"And I'm six foot one," Matt added.

"Well then you're definitely safe."

Matt was starting to see exactly what Dave had been going on about for the last few weeks. Kate really was a bit special. There was a lot more to her than a kind face and ample breasts. She was friendly and warm with a great sense of humour and not afraid to be a bit forward.

"So, if he asks you out again, what are you gonna say?"

"He already has. We're going to some *big* football match next Saturday."

"You're joking! He's bringing you to our cup final?"

"Yeah, we're going for a bit of a drive first and then he said if I fancied it, we could catch some of your match."

"And you said *yes* to that?"

"Yeah, I love soccer. Ok, its not as good as hurling or Gaelic football, but soccer players have the best legs."

"I'm not so sure you'll think that next Saturday."

"Ah, I bet you have a fine pair."

Matt noticed that the rest of the crowd were quite a bit ahead. "Come on, we better catch up to the others."

"So, what will you say to Dave about our chat?"

"I'm gonna tell him you're a psycho and he should stay away from you. That way I can have you all to myself."

"No, *seriously*?"

"Ok, I'm gonna tell him the truth and add on some of my own advice."

"What's that?"

"Well, I'm gonna tell him that you had a great time on the date and you really enjoyed his company, but that you may not be as physically attracted to him as some of your previous boyfriends, none of whom treated you right."

"Ok…and your advice?"

"That would be telling."

"Come on."

"I don't know, I guess I'm gonna tell him to hang on in there. I'll say that, I think you've got your work cut out pal, but she's definitely worth chasing."

"Good advice."

"Thanks."

"Are you going to tell him that I sussed you out straight away?"

"What do you think? Should I?"

"Nah, probably not."

*****

At twenty-five Kate McCann was the eldest of three kids born to Liam and Eileen McCann. She was a bright girl with plenty of spirit and a heart of gold. Parents aren't supposed to have their favourites and Eileen was always diplomatic, but Liam often whispered to Kate over the years that *she* was *his* little favourite. After doing a three-year language degree in Waterford RTC, she moved to Dublin and got a job teaching English to Foreign students. While she enjoyed living in Dublin and made many new friends, she still travelled home most Friday evenings to spend the weekend with her family and friends in and around Naas. In October 2001 Kate's world came crashing down when her mum's health started to fade. Her younger brother and sister were both in Universities on the west coast of Ireland, so there was just her dad at home to take care of her mum. Within a week, Kate had quit her job and moved home to help out. Shortly before Christmas that year, her mum was diagnosed with systemic lupus. Lupus is a disease, which causes the immune system to become hyperactive and attack normal tissue. Symptoms can include arthritis, muscle pain, weakness, fatigue, sun-sensitivity, hair-loss, anaemia, fever and headaches. Systemic lupus is the worst strand of the disease as it can lead to attacks on the major organs and nervous system.

At first, dealing with her mum's illness took a great toll on Kate and her dad, but after a few months when they had learned more about the disease and the helpful medications, they began to formulate a routine and cope much better. Kate tried to earn what money she could, working from home. Some of the jobs she did included, proof-reading for a local firm of solicitors and typing dissertations for the students in UL and UCG that were known to her brother and sister. The most difficult thing was seeing her mother so tired and weak all the time. This really upset Kate and at times she just had to get out of the house and let her father take over nurse duties. Her involvement in the horseracing syndicate, although not planned, was a welcome distraction. Here she was, spending the day with her mad cousin and his three best friends, riding a magnificent horse and flirting with a very handsome man. This was the first full hour she'd spent that week not concerned with the health of her mother. Even when she took a break from looking after her mum to go for a stroll around Naas town, she invariably bumped into people who would be asking after Eileen. Kate was disappointed in herself that this bugged her, but the truth is that there is

73

no cure for lupus. Her mum would always be tired and weak. If she wasn't tired and weak, she would be tired and weak *with* a fever or a headache or worse. There was no light at the end of this tunnel.

In a way, it was more refreshing for Kate to spend her spare time with new people who didn't know of her mum's plight. But there would always come a time when she would have to open up. This made relationships quite difficult. Her last boyfriend whined non-stop that she didn't spend enough time with him, until she explained very clearly to him exactly where he figured in the order of merit for her time and affection. He coped very well with the setback and the whining dissipated rapidly. *That's very mature of him,* thought Kate, until she guessed correctly that he had started to see another local girl to fill in the rest of his time. Little did he realise that Kate had a built-in lie detector when it came to men and he was not the first one to send the needle rocketing.

Her one and only love, Paul Hennessey was another to be betrayed by the same lie-detecting needle. She'd gone out with him for two fun-packed years when they were in college together and declared their undying love and fidelity to each other as he was boarding the plane for Australia. A month later during a telephone conversation Kate's lie detector developed mild epilepsy when Paul gave a simple one-syllable answer to a softly loaded question.

"So are there lots of good-lookin' girls down there?"

"No."

Inside a week, Kate had followed up her suspicions and had Paul tailed by a friend of hers also staying in Sydney. Not only was Paul spotted shoving his tongue down a busty brunette's throat he was also spotted shoving a suspicious white substance up his own nostrils.

Maybe I was a bit harsh on him, thought Kate after dumping Paul over a twenty-second reverse charge conversation, but she found it hard to ignore her infallible lie detector. Honesty was her biggest attraction to Dave. In the short time she'd known him, he'd shown himself to be intelligent, considerate, funny, caring, but above all honest. Not once in his company had Kate's lie detecting needle so much as sneezed. So what, if Dave didn't get her juices flowing the same way Paul Hennessey did. Maybe it was time to give up on racehorses and enjoy the benefits of a good reliable workhorse.

*****

74

At a quarter to one the following Saturday afternoon Kate pulled in to the estate of her favourite workhorse. When she arrived at the entrance to Dave's block it was open, so she made her way upstairs to flat 8, which was denoted *Cullen and Massey*.

How sweet, thought Kate as she neared the door. There was a lot of noise and shouting emanating from inside. She could clearly make out the words "where the fuck are my shinpads?" Followed shortly after she knocked on the door by "who the fuck is that?"

Kate recognised Matt's voice. Dave's voice sounded further away, but she thought she heard the words "stop" "shouting" "shit" "Kate" and "early" followed by "you" "get" and "door."

Dave was busy in his room making some last minute alterations to his CD changer. He'd removed *The Jam, Led Zepplin* and *The Clash* and replaced them with the more easy-listening tunes of *Stereophonics, Radiohead* and a new CD he bought that morning called *20 Driving Classics.* He'd left in *U2, The Doors* and *Pink Floyd.* Kate could now hear footsteps approaching the other side of the door.

"Kate, is that you?" asked Matt softly.

"Yeah."

"I hope you don't mind a little bit of nudity?"

"The more the merrier," she answered, looking forward to this unexpected treat.

When Matt opened the door, she wasn't disappointed. The only thing he was wearing above his tracksuit bottoms was a smile. Kate did her best to maintain eye contact, but couldn't resist taking a peek at the goods. She would have guessed he'd have a nice body, but it was even more toned and tanned than she'd expected.

"Sorry about the shouting, he whispered. I presumed it was one of our pain-in-the-ass neighbours…How did you get in?"

"The door downstairs was wide open."

As Matt bent down to adjust the mat inside the door Kate took a good long look at his muscular chest and shoulders. "So…are you nervous?" she asked.

Matt stood back up and frowned. "Nervous? Why do you ask? Are my nipples sticking out or something?"

Kate snorted back a laugh. "No, I meant about the big match."

Matt smiled. "A little bit I suppose…I mean, it's not exactly Liverpool I play for, but it's a big game. This team beat us in the semi-final last year so we'll be up for it today."

Matt backed away from the door gesturing for Kate to come inside. "Right, well I better get ready. I'll go get his majesty."

Dave took Kate on a nice long drive to Glendalough. The weather was perfect and the conversation was flowing. Kate was pretty impressed with his CD selection and especially enjoyed *Pink Floyd*, a CD she had herself, but hadn't listened to for a while.

"Oh, I love this song!" she cried as *Comfortably Numb* came on. "Can I turn it up?"

Beautiful girl, beautiful scenery, beautiful music, thought Dave as he pumped the volume up a notch or three. When they got to Glendalough, they went for a short walk, followed by lunch in a country pub that seemed to be full of Americans.

"So, how's your mum?" asked Dave.

Kate thought about giving Dave her usual answer, but changed her mind. "Can I be blunt with you Dave?" she asked.

"Of course," he answered, worried that he'd asked the wrong question.

"I hope you don't think I'm horrible," Kate continued. "But, y'see, I spend most of my week looking after my mum and her condition hardly ever changes, at least not for the better. I hate seeing her that way, but I also hate the fact that any time I get to take a break from it all, I have to answer people's questions telling them how tired and weak and feverish she is. I'm sorry Dave, I know it sounds cruel and selfish, but sometimes talking about her illness can get me down as much as having to help her up so she can go to the toilet."

Dave could see a tear gathering in the corner of Kate's eye. "I'm sorry Kate, I understand," was all he could think of saying.

"If you understand so much, then why aren't you giving me a hug," said Kate trying to break a smile through her tears. Dave reached over to hold her, softly patting her back and hair. "I'm sorry," he whispered into her ear.

"Oh shut up, you big softie!" she said, sitting back into her seat and wiping her eyes.

Dave felt an actual physical pain in his heart. It may have been from eating his carvery lunch too fast, but his guess was that he was falling in love with this beautiful woman and it ached him to see her so hurt.

"Wanna go see some football?" he asked, trying to lift the air.

"Let me see," she mused. "The smell of men's sweat, the crunching tackles, twenty-two pairs of muscly legs. That might just take my mind off things."

They arrived at the match at a good time. Just as she and Dave were joining Shipsey on the sideline, Macker poked home the first goal of the game following in on a parried free kick.

"Wahayyyy, good man, Michael!" Kate cheered.

The first seventy minutes of the game had been relatively uneventful, with both teams defending well. But now the players were getting tired and mistakes were starting to seep in. With ten minutes to go the opposition equalised after their centre forward intercepted a back-pass to the keeper that fell short. With two minutes left it looked like they were going to lose the game when the same centre forward rounded the keeper and rolled the ball goal-wards. From out of nowhere Matt found the energy and speed to make it back in time to scoop the ball off the goal-line.

"Well done Matt!" Screamed Kate.

Fuck! That hurt thought Matt, looking down at his bloodied knee which had been sliced up on the hard turf.

Three quarters of an hour later Matt had to block out the pain in his knee as he walked from the centre circle to the penalty spot to take a vital part in the penalty shoot-out. He had been asked to go fourth and Macker, the regular penalty taker was to go last. But as it panned out, with the opposition already missing two of their kicks, if Matt scored, his would be the winning penalty.

"I can't watch," said Kate, covering her eyes.

"Don't worry," said Shipsey confidently. "He won't miss."

To their communal relief Matt smashed the ball into the roof of the net.

*****

Matt was the man of the moment when the team arrived back at *The Banner Man* to celebrate.

"Here's to Matt Cullen, man of the match," said Gary the big centre half, raising his pint. "Good man yourself Cullen."

"Yeah, well done Matt," agreed the others.

"I was hopin' you were gonna miss," laughed Macker.

"You probably *were*, ye little bollix!"

Despite having a great time, Kate grabbed Dave's hand after a couple of drinks and told him she had to leave. Dave pleaded with her to stay a bit longer, but she was adamant. "No, I have to drive."

"You can stay at our place," Dave offered.

"Nice try studley," she smiled, "but I have to get home."

"Ok, I'll give you a lift to your car."

Ten minutes later he and Kate were engaged in a very passionate kiss leaning against her Yellow *Renault Clio*. They had been casually saying their goodbyes, when Kate reached out with one hand grabbing him by the shirt and pulling him close. The kiss started soft and gentle, but gradually became firmer and wetter, with Kate leading the pace. She was leaning back against the car door and holding him tight against her warm body. Dave was in such shock that he didn't know what to do. That is…ninety-nine percent of his body didn't know what to do. He could hear a little voice coming from his trouser region and *he* seemed to know what *he* wanted to do.

Come on buddy! Rip open her blouse and let's get in there! Come on! It's hammer time! What the fuck are you waitin' for? Just pick her up, carry her up that stairs, fling her onto the bed and I'll take care of the rest!

Despite this very persuasive argument, Dave decided to ignore the advice of his miniature friend. When Kate finally broke from their kiss, he was almost out of breath. "Are you sure, you don't want to come inside for a while?"

"Nah, I better not ," said Kate, opening the car door. "I have to get back to my mum." As Dave was waving goodbye through the back windscreen of her car, he heard the little voice again.

You fucking moron! You just never listen do you? That was our chance! Are you turning gay or something? Is that what it is? Has it been so long since you've seen a woman's soft bits that you've turned into a big pufter?

Dave was doing his best to ignore the little voice.

Helloooo bender…can you hear me? Take that cock out of your mouth and say something.

"Shut up!"

Oh, you are still alive! Come on, let's go inside and watch that video with the lesbians again.

C h a p t e r   1 0

Over the next few months, Dave and Kate's relationship developed a bit like a test cricket match. At least, that's the analogy he used when talking to the lads in *The Banner Man*. Between February and April they saw each other only six times. Just like in cricket when it seemed like the action was starting to get exciting, a tea break was called and he wouldn't see her again for another fortnight. When they did meet they spent the first half hour practically reintroducing themselves. The long distance between their homes wasn't helping and most of their dates took place in the city. This journey was awkward for Kate and often she would have to leave just as they were starting to have a good time. Dave offered plenty of times to travel out to Naas, but Kate always seemed reluctant. The one time he did make the journey, she met him in one of the pubs in the town. As usual they enjoyed each others company, but when it came to the end of the night Dave had to practically beg her to get into his car to drive her home. They parked outside her house and kissed for a while, but she didn't invite him in for coffee, or anything else for that matter. Dave's guess was that Kate didn't want to bring him in to her house because of her mother's condition.

Their last date was the worst. Kate had travelled all the way out to *The Banner Man*. As usual she had spoken to Macker's parents beforehand and they were delighted for her to stay in their spare room.

"This is your chance lad," said Dave to his reflection in the mirror. He was psyching himself up to make a move. "At the end of the night you turn on that old Massey charm and take her back here."

Charm, my Bollox! said a little voice from just below his waist.

Just ply her with alcohol, drag her back here by the scruff of the neck and give her a damn good shafting. That'll put all three of us out of our misery... you, me and your right hand.

During the night Dave felt quite nervous and awkward. This was the first time he'd really been out with Kate as her boyfriend in the company of the rest of his friends. He spent most of the night wondering where to sit and what to do with his hands and getting a little bit too drunk in the process. Shipsey and Matt were both showing him up. They had brought out Jane and Sam and Dave watched as they effortlessly ensured that their parners were sitting in good seats and never left out of the conversation. Occasionally he would see Shipsey reaching for Jane's hand and giving it a rub or Matt making eye contact with Sam and winking as if to say, "*whoops, I seem to have got slightly separated from you during that last game of musical chairs when three people left the table at the same time to either go to the toilet or to get cigarettes, but y'know, even if I don't spend the whole night sitting beside you, I'm still here making sure you're having a good time and we both know we'll be spending the night together.*"

Dave was in awe. *How the fuck can he wink at her from across the table and say all that!* But when he saw Sam smiling back, he knew the message had been received loud and clear. *Jesus, how will I ever get to be that in tune with Kate*, he wondered. *Not by seeing her once a fortnight.*

Kate had also been a bit nervous coming out to see all of Dave's friends as his official girlfriend. This was also the first time she got to meet Samantha and Jane. Not long after sitting down though, she began to feel comfortable in their company and got on particularly well with Jane. It turned out that Jane's office was just around the corner from Kate's old school. They both used to frequent the same sandwich bars and pubs so it's likely they had crossed paths some time before. Jane was able to let Kate know that there was still a flock of foreign students who congregated on the green across from her school any time the sun was kind enough to drop by. Kate thought it funny, that nobody asked the usual questions about why she had left or what she's doing now, but figured that Dave must have prepped them and asked them not to touch on the subject of her sick mother. If this was the case she was impressed and thankful. She would take him to one side later on in the night to show him her appreciation.

When it came time to go home Dave was nicely drunk. Or at least that's what he thought. To everyone else he looked a bit of a mess. As the others walked on ahead down the side of the pub, Kate kept Dave behind outside the front door to find out if it had been down to him that nobody had asked any questions about her mum.

"Yeah, sorry, is that ok?" asked Dave stumbling slightly forward.

"Yes, it's ok. In fact it's very sweet," said Kate leaning forward to kiss him on the cheek. Dave put his arms around Kate and turned his head to get his mouth on hers. He started kissing her hard and passionately. She was returning his kiss for a while, but when he started to hold her too tight and grab her ass, she broke free.

"Dave! Take it easy!"

Kate was holding her hand to her mouth where she was sure he had drawn blood with one of his teeth.

"What's the problem?"

Dave hadn't seen Kate look at him with this expression before. She looked angry, but also as if she was on the verge of crying.

"You were squeezing too tight and hurting me *and* I think you cut my lip."

"I'm sorry if I was a bit forceful," slurred Dave, "but we're a couple aren't we?"

"Yeah, but your friends are just down there."

"So what?"

"So, we're not *sixteen*."

A part of Dave knew he should have shut up and taken Kate softly by the hand and walked her back to the rest of the group. But unfortunately that part of Dave wasn't functioning very well and his drunken evil twin had taken over the controls.

"Come on Kate. Come on back to my place."

"I don't think so."

"Why not."

"Not tonight. You're too drunk."

"Ah, I'll be fine. I promise."

"No, I'm staying at my uncle and aunt's tonight."

"Ok, when then?"

At this point Kate decided to ignore him and marched off to catch up with the rest of the group. Dave spent the next ten minutes trying to catch a hold of her to apologise, until Matt finally stepped in to take him home.

The following day Dave spent forty minutes on the phone to Kate apologising and he was sure towards the end he had redeemed himself somewhat.

"Ok, stop saying sorry," said Kate. "Let's just forget about it you big oaf."

She had been with men before who wouldn't call at all after such an incident, so Dave's over-the-top contrition was welcome. When the phone call had finished, they both spent the next half hour thinking about the future of their relationship. Kate knew that she was making it tough on Dave by not being available to see him more often. She really loved that Dave was honest and smart and witty and until last night, a complete gentleman, but she still wasn't bowled over by his looks.

Ok, he's not ugly, she reasoned, *but he's no Brad Pitt either. Maybe if I was more attracted to him, I would have gone back to his* *place. If he **was** Brad Pitt, I'd still be there now!*

Dave was still thinking in terms of cricket when he examined their relationship.

There are way too many breaks, the action doesn't get very exciting and I haven't a fuckin' clue what the result is gonna be! ...Still, even if all the highlights would only take up five minutes and it looks as if we're heading for a long unspectacular draw, I'll settle for that ahead of a loss any day.

While Dave and Kate were struggling through their marathon cricket session, Shipsey and Jane were trying to get the best out of their roller-coaster ride of a relationship. Since it began, their partnership was one of many ups and downs and very few plateaus. Both had become familiar with this pattern and would be bracing themselves for a sharp decent if they'd just gone through a good period together. Paradoxically, when they were getting on really well together and it didn't seem as if they could have another fight that was usually when their sexual activity was at a low. When they felt happy and content in each other's company, they tended to kiss and cuddle a lot, rather than wear out the bedsprings. They were both aware of this so perhaps that's why they rarely went through a full week without having a blazing row. They fought over the simplest things, from hair in the plughole, to clothes left in the washing machine. But when Shipsey and Jane went to war they did it in style. If war was a mixed-doubles Olympic sport they would proudly represent Ireland. Mostly they resorted to verbal warfare only. Between Shipsey and the rest of the lads this was known as DEFCON 1 and would usually result in hurt feelings, a short period of silence and then great sex.

DEFCON 2 included verbal warfare, but also involved the destruction of property. Over their years of living together, DEFCON 2 had been reached a dozen times and the financial damage was mounting. Jane had a habit of throwing cups and other items of cutelry, but luckily for the big man her aim was pretty woeful and she rarely hit his large frame. As a joke, Matt made a point of bringing them back a souvenir cup every time he went on holidays. DEFCON 2 usually resulted in the occasional bruise, approximately twenty-euro worth of damage, a shorter moment of silence, followed by even better sex.

The lowest slope of their roller-coaster ride was reached two years previously when for the one and only time they reached DEFCON 3, or all out nuclear warfare. It had followed a two-week high period when they had been kissing and cuddling each other to sleep every night, so

Shipsey should have known to expect trouble when he arrived home one night very late, very drunk and very horny. He had clearly forgotten the rules of engagement when he jumped into bed beside his sick, slumbering girlfriend. When he started to snuggle up to Jane to show her just how happy he was to see her he was met with a shrug of the shoulders and a very loud "Fuck off!"

Undeterred, he swung his leg over and straddled the hostile enemy who was still lying in the foetal position.

"Come on Janie babe, it's been a while."

Jane's next move was to elbow him in the ribs, *hard*. Shipsey had three good-sized brothers and none of them had ever delivered a blow as painful as that. He was left holding his side, lying on his back on the far side of the bed.

"Ahhh you fuckin' cow! That hurt!"

A short while later the pain died down and he started to move slowly back towards Jane. Foolishly, he had not given up on the idea of sex and delivered a stinging smack to her bare ass. "I was only lookin' for a bit of action!"

Little did he know, he was about to enter DEFCON 2. Maybe if he knew Jane had been struggling to get to sleep for the last four hours due to agonising period pains, he would have thought twice before slapping her bum, but it was too late.

"You want action! I'll give you fucking action!" she roared. Jane jumped out of bed, made her way to the dressing table and picked up the first weighty object she could find, which turned out to be Shipsey's electric razor. Maybe it was because Liverpool had just qualified for the second round of the Champions League, or maybe because he'd spent three hours staring at other women in a local nightclub or perhaps it was just down to the poor lighting in their bedroom, but for once Jane's crazed throw hit the spot. Shipsey was now standing at the other side of the bed with his right hand holding his ribs and his left hand covering the word *Phillips* which was clearly imprinted backwards just above his eye. Now that her arm was in, Jane hadn't finished throwing. The next item was a bottle of CK1, but she was back to her old form and it went crashing into the wall behind Shipsey. He looked down at the unbroken bottle thinking, *Wow! You really do spend most of your money on the packaging!* This thought was quickly followed by *Fuck me! How am I gonna get out of here alive?* He decided he needed to get closer to Jane before she picked up the sharp metal-framed photo of them at some New Years party. He rushed across the room and grabbed her by the shoulders forcing her into the corner away from all throwable objects.

That is, of course, unless you consider feet and fists throwable objects.

Welcome to DEFCON 3 Mr Boate. Strap yourself in. Jane started swinging all four limbs in his direction like some demented epileptic octopus. The first blow to make any damaging contact was a left foot to the groin.

"Oh Jesus fucking Christ!" roared Shipsey, doubling over with pain. Just as he was stumbling around in agony, holding his bruised testicles and thinking, *Oh sweet Jesus, there's nothing quite as painful as a kick in the bollix!* Jane introduced him to something that was. As he was coming up for air she caught him with a right hook to the throat that nearly sent his Adam's apple out the back of his neck. Shipsey collapsed on to the bed and rolled up in a ball. He was gasping for air and didn't have enough hands to sooth all his injured areas. Although his eyes were closed he could feel Jane moving in for the kill. With all his strength he managed to gather enough air into his lungs and through his throbbing throat, he croaked out five words that possibly saved his life. "Jane stop! I love you."

With that, Jane collapsed in an exhausted heap in the corner. Just above his own moans, Shipsey could hear her crying.

*****

"DEFCON 3 ain't much fun," he told the lads in *The Banner Man* a few nights later. "Not only is it the most painful, but it is also the only one that isn't necessarily followed by great sex."

Shipsey was genuinely frightened by Jane's behaviour that night and after spending the night on the couch ice-packing his wounds, he stayed with Matt and Dave for a few days to let the dust settle.

Shipsey and Jane spent most of the time on this roller-coaster ride of "friendly, but no sex" followed by "angry and fighting" and finally "getting over fight and good sex." Their relationship clearly wasn't perfect, and both of them were feeling worn out emotionally. They never really discussed how they might improve things, which is just as well, because they both had very different ideas. Shipsey thought at one point of suggesting to Jane that she might go an anger management course, but he backed away from this idea in case it pissed her off. His other solutions revolved around getting married and having babies. He felt that this may provide the greater stability they required. When they had discussed these topics in the past they had both agreed that marriage and kids might be something they'd be interested in when they got close to thirty. But now Shipsey was thinking in terms of, *well if we want to start having kids when we're say... 29, then we'll have to get married at 28 and it takes so long to organise a bleedin' wedding these days, we'd have to get engaged when we're 27 or even sooner! Holy shit!*

Both he and Jane were 26. Shipsey wasn't sure if he was ready for all that business, but that spring, he found himself doing double takes when he was walking past jeweller's shop windows.

Jane was a bit more analytical in her examination of their relationship. Her first conclusion was that they weren't spending enough quality time together. They both worked hard and if they went out after work, it was usually in separate groups. The last proper night out they'd had just by themselves, was three months ago when she'd insisted they go to a local restaurant that had just opened up. The time they spent at home together was usually in front of the TV. Even if they were eating at the same time, which wasn't often, they always brought their plates into the living room and switched on the box. But the biggest problem as far as Jane could see was the sex or lack of it. Over the years their sexual attraction towards each other had diminished and laziness had settled in. Jane was sure that this lack of sex was leading to their constant fighting. They seemed to have to resort to foolish bickering to heighten the sexual tension in the house. Another problem was that neither of them were natural leaders when it came to lovemaking. When they were getting on well together, it was as if they were both too shy and polite to make the first move.

If only he'd just grab me and fling me on the bed the odd time, she thought. Jane was sure that if they spent more energy having sex that they wouldn't have enough left for the fighting. *What we really need is a bit of spicing up and maybe it's gonna be up to me to make the first move.*

*****

Matt and Samantha had no such problems. Their attraction for each other was as strong as when they first met. On Valentines Day, Matt took Sam out to an extremely posh restaurant. The restaurant was known to be very exclusive and difficult to get into so he'd made the booking two months in advance. Neither of them had been there before and he knew Sam would love it, as he had overheard her talking to Jane about it on the phone. They spent the perfect night together, smiling and holding hands across the table, enjoying delicious food and wine and spotting some celebs sitting around them.

85

"There's yer man from the news."

"That looks like the fiddle player from *The Corrs*.

In the taxi on the way home Matt had the idea of visit the nightclub where they first met. They spent only an hour inside, but that was enough time to enjoy two drinks, a couple of slow dances and a snogging session that a couple of sixteen-year-olds would have been proud of.

If Shipsey and Jane were great fighters in the mould of Tyson and Holyfield, then Matt and Sam were great rowers in the mould of Redgrave and Pinsent. Like the Olympians, they looked like an unbeatable outfit, using perfect Synchronisation to push towards a common goal. And they appeared to be able to achieve the impossible almost effortlessly, or at least that's how it looked from the shoreline. But when the TV cameras got a close up, you realised all was not so rosy in the garden of Messrs Redgrave and Pinsent. Ocassionally they *would* go out of sync for a brief moment or sometimes it would look like Redgrave was trying harder than his partner. Even the great men themselves had their own doubts. *What if an oar breaks? What if the current catches us? What if he finds another partner, who's fitter and stronger than me?* Thus it was with Matt and Sam. What appeared to be a well-oiled machine occasionally became slightly unhinged and required some work to get it back on track. Sometimes Sam would have a go at Matt for drinking too much or Matt would complain that Sam never took an interest in his football, but these were small glitches in their stroke pattern that could quickly be forgotten. Their doubts did not involve oars or currents, but usually centred around the pace at which they were going. While Sam thought they could push a little faster, Matt was straining to keep up. He'd bought himself some time by lying to her about when his lease was up, but now Summer was looming on the horizon and it would be time for a new regime of cohabitation. Matt's main worry was that he wasn't ready for this step-up in pace and he would have to go into altitude training to keep up with his partner. Slovenliness and drunkenness were a huge part of the curriculum when living with Dave. Over the six years they lived together, they had not fought once. Their only unwritten rule was, "thou shalt not tell the other one what to do." Under this law, they lived in perfect harmony and over the years they became so attune with one another that they developed their own new form of communication. This would be a typical conversation that might occur when Dave arrived home from work to find Matt drinking a beer on the couch.

"Alrigh?" "Good evening Dave. How was your day?"

"Ye, nudder one? "Not bad at all. Would you like another beverage, as I'm getting myself one?

"Yup." "Oh, yes please. That would be very kind."

"Ahhh" "Oh, this *is* tasty and refreshing, just like they say on the ad."

"Ahhh burrrp" "Yes, very tasty and a great way to unwind after a days work."

"Hm" "I know exactly what you mean."

"'Son" "What have we got in store for this evening's entertainment?"

"Match" "There's a premiership football match on."

"Ah" "Great. I love watching football."

"Score?" "What's the scoreline at the moment?"

"Zip" "Nil-Nil"

"Who" "And which two teams might be playing?"

"Arse and Shite." "Arsenal and Manchester United."

Matt was quite sure that things would be very different when he started living with Sam. Not only would he have to become a lot more domesticated and drink considerably less, he would also have to relearn the whole English language.

Chapter 11

While Dave and Kate were in the middle of a test cricket series, Shipsey and Jane were on their roller-coaster ride and Matt and Sam were trying to row their boat in sync, Macker was playing the dating game. Macker viewed dating as being similar to buying scratch cards. When you buy a scratch card, you effectively take a very small risk that has huge payout potential. Until you start scratching away at the surface of the card, that potential is fully intact. An unscratched lottery card is in itself perfection, but it's not until you start to remove that surface that you find out what that card really has to offer. This is normally when the potential of perfect happiness gives way to the reality of flaw and disappointment. Over the spring Macker scratched the surface of a number of different lottery cards, but not the same way the rest of the world does. Macker uses a technique all of his own. While most people remove the entire magnesium surface and see if they've won a prize, Macker has a unique way of doing it. He would slowly scratch the surface revealing symbols one by one until he was halfway through. Then he would estimate his chances of winning the top prize and if they didn't look promising enough he would throw away the half-scratched card. Macker wasn't happy to settle for the lesser consolation prizes, so if he *wasn't* going to win the yacht or the 50,000 euro, he'd simply dump the card and move on to the next one.

The closest he'd come to the top prize that spring was with a girl called Sarah Lynch. He'd bumped into her one evening after work in a busy pub just off St. Stephen's Green. He had been drinking with his fellow I.T. colleagues until he saw a beautiful blonde walk down the steps and start looking for her friends. She had a gorgeous shapely body and sexy blue eyes and when Macker offered to help her find who she was looking for, she revealed a beautiful set of gleaming white teeth. He was relieved when she found her two friends that neither of them turned out to be blokes. Macker decided to stick around and see if his luck was in. It turned out to be Sarah's first week working for a firm of solicitors and she was full of talk. Macker did the right thing, avoiding chat up lines and just asking her questions about her new job. As she was telling him about her exciting week, Macker was running through the checklist in his mind.

Hair: check, long, blonde and smells like a spring meadow.

Face: check, pretty as can be, eyes are a particularly sexy feature.

Smile: check, ten out of ten.

Breasts: check, two of them, symmetrical in shape, cleavage reading meets the minimum requirement.

Legs: check, two of equally sufficient length, surface appears to be wax treated.

Bum: yet to view the subject from correct angle.

Fingers: seven, eight, nine, ten, check, all there and looking good. Houston I'm preparing for lift off.

Toes: negative Houston, I can't get a look at her toes. The crowd is too big and I'm standing too close to her. If I look down, not only will I not be able to see them, I will be staring straight at her tits.

Toes!: negative Houston, I'm too close to tell, unless I take off my shoes and start counting them with my own toes...Houston, I suggest we go out on a limb here and assume she has ten of them...I'm about ready for lift-off.

Bum?: Oh shit Houston. Sorry, I forgot about the bum.

By the end of the night, not only was Macker able to confirm that Sarah had ten dainty toes and a very nice rear end, but that she was single and would be happy to go out on a date with him.

They saw each other four times over the next few weeks and things were going really well. Not only was Sarah a bit of a babe, she also had a good sense of fun about her. On one of their dates she insisted on taking Macker to her local go-kart track followed by a round of crazy golf. Macker was starting to think that this particular scratch card was going to reveal three yachts when all of a sudden on their fourth date a plum symbol was revealed. They met in a pizzeria in town for a bite to eat, which they planned to follow up with a night on the tiles. When Sarah was turning to the waiter to order her hawaain pizza Macker noticed something that he'd somehow managed to miss before.

Eh Houston, we got a problem here.

What is it Commander McCann?

It's the ears

Too many?

Negative

Not enough?

Negative

Unsymmetrical?

Negative

Not positioned correctly on the head?

Negative

Wrong size?

Correctomundo Houston! They are most definitely the wrong size! And the wrong shape!

Describe please?

They're fucking huge Houston! Absolutely fucking enormous with great big fucking points on them!

Is this an exaggeration Commander McCann?

Negative Houston! This is a fucking abomination! These things belong to Mr Spock!

Macker was now trying to work out how these ears had previously passed the checklist and he suspected foul play. On the three previous occasions he'd met Sarah, she had worn her hair down, now it was tied back and her massive goblin ears were on full display. Macker was well pissed off. He felt like he'd been conned. Sarah was recounting a story about something that had happened to her while shopping that day, but Macker wasn't listening. He wasn't even making eye contact with her. All he could look at and think about were her horrific novelty ears.

How the fuck did she hide them till now? I can't believe I missed them! They must stick out through her hair when she has it down. And why the fuck has she got them on display now? I bet she thinks, cos this is our fourth date that I'll overlook this little blemish. Fuck that! She is a sly bitch, reeling me in with her fantastic smile and great personality. I should have known there was a shock like this just waiting for me...And what's with that laugh?I thought it was kind of cute at first but, actually it sounds like a chipmonk been strangled!

Macker was becoming over critical with the rest of Sarah's attributes and if there was one thing he was good at, it was finding imperfections.

I'm not sure I like her hands either. They're a bit bony and let's face it her tits could definitely be bigger.

By the end of the night he had reduced Sarah to a spotty, sly witch with a scary laugh and joke ears. Even her smile, which he had previously given ten out of ten, he was now describing as "a bit toothy."

While his interest in Sarah and the other girls he dated that spring didn't last the test of the test of time, he had one interest that more than made up for it. When the football season came to a close he started visiting "*Satan's Whiskers*" on a much more regular basis, usually driving down on Saturday mornings to have a look at him work out. On one of those trips Shipsey came along for the ride. On the way there, he asked Macker how things were going with Sarah. The revealing of the ears had been the previous Saturday night and Macker hadn't called Sarah that week.

"Oh, I had to dump her."

"Wha?"

"Yeah."

"Why? I thought you liked her."

"Well, I did until I saw her ears."

"Her ears?"

"Yeah, fucking massive," said Macker, shaking his head.

"What?"

"Her ears were fucking massive!"

"You broke up with her 'cos her ears were too big?"

"Not just too big. These things were like fucking satellite dishes!"

"Jesus," said Shipsey shaking his head. "Y'know Macker, some day you're gonna have to settle for a bird who isn't perfect in every way!"

"Why?"

"Because, none of them are!"

"Yeah, but Shipsey, you didn't see these things!"

"Ok, maybe they were huge, but in a way it's the imperfections that make a relationship great."

"What?"

"Yeah, over time you'll find that what you first saw as a flaw, will become an endearing attribute of someone you care about."

"Get the fuck out of here!"

"I'm serious! Take Jane for example. Sometimes when she chews her food, her jaw starts clicking. Now when I first heard this, I found it so annoying I was gonna get my coat, but now I find it quite cute and when I hear it, all I want to do is love her even more."

"Shut up, you soppy tart."

Shipsey starting doing an impression of Mr. Miyagi from "The Karate Kid."

"You have much to learn Danielson. You must learn to embrace the ears Danielson."

As they pulled in to the stable yard, they could see four horses out on the gallop and Paddy Mulryan leaning over the fence watching them closely. As they were walking down to join Paddy, Macker recognised *Satan's Whiskers*.

"There's our one! You see him? Second from the back."

Shipsey spotted their horse and noticed that he looked even bigger

91

and stronger than he had on their first visit. They joined Paddy and asked him how *Satan's Whiskers* was getting on.

"Ye just watch boys," said Paddy, chewing on a piece of hay. "That's all four three-year-olds I have out there. They have about three and a half furlongs left of a mile and a half."

At this point *Satan's Whiskers* started to tackle the horse for second place. "Come on Satan!" roared Shipsey. Within a few strides, he had drawn level with the second place horse. At this point Paddy let out a huge roar. "Go!"

It was so loud and unexpected, both Shipsey and Macker jumped. This was the signal to the jockeys to run them flat out for the last couple of furlongs. You could visibly see all four jockeys, getting down to business, working their shoulders and arms hard, but one horse responded better than the others.

"Come on Satan, yeboyo!"

Satan's Whiskers glided into second place and started to eat into the leaders advantage. The horses were now getting closer to where the lads were watching from.

"Come on *Satan's Whiskers*!"

By the time the horses passed them and started to ease up, not only had he taken the lead, but he had left all the others for dead. You wouldn't know it was only a training session from the way Macker and Shipsey were cheering and jumping up and down.

The lads were very excited when they settled down in Paddy Mulryan's kitchen for a cup of tea and a chat.

Macker could barely sit still. "He looks great, doesn't he?"

"The only way I could be any happier with this horse, is if I owned him myself," Said Paddy.

Macker and Shipsey smiled and winked at each other.

"He's easily the best of my three-year-olds and barring injury I'm sure he's gonna win some races."

"So, when does he start racing?" asked Macker.

"Possibly very soon. He's still only getting used to hurdles, so it might be best to keep him out of hurdle races for another month or so, but there's a flat bumper race on here in Naas in a fortnight that I've spoken to your uncle about putting him into."

"Really? That soon."

"Why not? You can see yourself he's as fit as a fiddle. He's definitely one of the fastest three-year-old I've ever had. It's just down to whether he can do it in the right company and on the right day. The race is one mile six and by the time he gets there he should be able to stay that long."

"So, do you think he'll win?" asked Shipsey.

"He's definitely got a chance, but it'll be tough. I ran a horse in this race last year...actually, I think it was his half-brother and he came sixth of twenty-two." Paddy smiled and pointed at the two of them. "But your one's better."

"Excellent, so every chance of getting a place?"

"Yeah, but don't get too carried away. It's a feckin' big field so there's lots that can go wrong. And they'll all be inexperienced horses, so it could be run at a silly pace and that might not suit him. But I'll ask young Daly if he'll ride him. He'll keep him out of trouble."

"Kevin Daly?" asked Macker.

"That's the one."

Macker knew all about Kevin Daly. He had only been on the scene for a few years, but had rapidly become one of the top Irish jockeys and had ridden a whole host of famous horses.

"Do you think he'll do it?"

"I'm sure he will if he's available. Sure, he rides for me all the time."

"And you think he'll come to Naas and ride our horse?"

"He won't have far to come. He only lives down the road."

This was the icing on the cake for Macker. Not only would their horse be realistically contesting a race very soon, but he would be doing so with one of the most successful jockeys of the last five years on his back. Macker was almost as excited about getting to meet Kevin Daly as he was about getting to see *Satan's Whisker* line up in a real race.

"What sort of odds do you think he might be?" asked Shipsey

"That's always difficult to say," Paddy mused, "but I suppose you might get him at about fourteens or sixteens on the morning, it depends on how many runners there are and how many of them have run before."

"Sixteen to one?"

"Yeah, you might get that, if you go to a betting shop in the morning. God only knows what you'll get at the track."

Shipsey was busily trying to work out what return he would get if he backed it 100 euro each way.

"So, you could win two grand if he you put 100 euro each way on him and he wins!"

"And if he only gets placed, you'd still win 300 euro," added Macker. The lads were getting quite excited at the prospect of winning large sums of money on the success of *Satan's Whiskers*. Shipsey had even figured out where he would go that Saturday morning to place his bet.

One of his local bookmakers was owned and run by an old schoolmate of his called *Slim Shady*...or at least that's what Shipsey knew his as. Barry Quinn had followed his father into the bookie trade as soon as he left school and by twenty was running his own betting shop in Sallynoggin. He was apparently doing quite well, because a few days after his twenty-first birthday he walked into Shipsey's car showroom and handed over 42,000 Irish Punts for a brand new BMW. It was around this time that Shipsey gave him his nickname. The *Slim* part was as much to do with the odds that Barry offered, as it was to do with his skinny waistline. And Shipsey was sure there was something *Shady* about a bloke walking around with that much cash in a plastic bag. While Shipsey was happy to earn the commission on the sale of a new BMW, he found it a little disconcerting that the purchaser was two months younger than himself. Even more disconcerting was the fact that Shipsey had contributed in no small way to this extravagance. Over the years he had entered *Slim Shady's* establishment around thirty times, but never managed to emerge with more money than he went in with. A lot of that money was lost backing Liverpool to win the premiership. This wouldn't have been so annoying if "Slim Shady" wasn't a Man United fan. Every year they would go through the same pre-season ritual. It would usually begin with Shipsey complaining about Slim Shady's stingy odds.

"For fuck sake Barry! Ladbrokes are making them 5 to 1, what's this 9 to 2 bullshit?"

"Ok big man, just for you, I'll match the 5 to 1."

"Right, I'll have my usual ton on it."

By now, Slim Shady would be shaking his head. "Jaysis Shipsey. Don't you ever learn? They're just not good enough."

"Fuck off and print the ticket! I have a good feeling about this season."

"You said that last year and United pissed all over them!"

Shipsey tended to lose his mastery of the English language when it came to Liverpool versus Manchester United arguments.

"Fuck United! That shower of scummy wankers! Don't even talk to me about that slimey bunch of fucking tosspots or I'll puke all over your fucking counter!"

Macker and Shipsey were in high spirits as they were driving home. They'd phoned ahead to Matt and Dave to let them know of the high hopes that Paddy had and what great shape "*Satan's Whiskers*" was in.

"Here listen to this," said Macker who had been working on a limerick.

> *There once was a champion called Satan*
> *Who gave the other horses a batin'*
> *The lads won a load of cash*
> *And bought a shitload of hash*
> *And flogged it to a bunch of Jamaicans!*

"I like it!" laughed Shipsey, who quickly turned his attention to his own limerick.

After two minutes he was finished. "Here! Try this one on for size!"

> *Five years now I've been waitin'*
> *For a horse to come along like Satan*
> *Slim Shady's been getting' rich*
> *But I'm gonna treat him like my bitch*
> *When The Whiskers comes home with the bacon!"*

Chapter 12

On the Saturday morning of *Satan's Whiskers* first race, Barry Quinn opened his betting shop at 10am as usual. Shipsey, who had been waiting outside for ten minutes was his first customer.

"Good morning Mr Quinn."

"Ah, good morning Mr Boate! What has you up so early?"

"Ah, I'm heading down to Naas for the racing later on and was wondering if you have any early prices."

"Really? Well to be honest, I haven't had a chance to look yet, but I'm sure I can come up with something for a valued customer such as your good self. Any particular horse you're looking at?"

Shipsey didn't want to give up this information, so he asked for the full run down on the last race.

"Jaysis Shipsey!" said Barry, who was now examining the Naas racecard. "That's a flat bumper race for maidens with 24 runners declared!"

"That's the one." Shipsey had a copy of *The Irish Racer* under his arm. Number twenty of those twenty-four horses was *Satan's Whiskers* and it was in his paper at forecast odds of sixteen to one.

"And you want prices on all of them?"

"Ok, I'll tell you what," reasoned Shipsey, "just give me the odds on the last eight."

"All right," said Barry taking out his mobile phone, "but it'll take a minute."

He phoned his father, who ran two of the largest betting shops in the city, to see if he had seen any action on this race. When he was happy that there didn't appear to be anything funny going on, he agreed to show Shipsey the prices that were quoted in *The Irish Racer*.

"All right then," said Shipsey, emptying 1,200 euro onto the counter. He was placing the bet for all the lads. "I'll have 600 euro each way on number 20 *Satan's Whiskers*. He's sixteen to one."

"Holy shit big man! That's not your average bet! What's goin' on?"

"Nothing. I just like the name."

"Bullshit! There's obviously something going on if you're heading down to Naas to watch some Mickey Mouse race."

"That's very good Slim," laughed Shipsey, "that rhymes."

"Well I can't let you put the full amount on at sixteens. I'll have to make it fourteens."

After a couple of minutes of haggling, during which Shipsey repeatedly reminded Barry of his dismal gambling record, he persuaded the nervous bookmaker to show him odds of fifteen to one. He had guaranteed the rest of the lads that he would secure them odds of at least fourteen to one so he was happy with his work. Barry was still trying to garner more information as he was registering the betting slip.

"So, come on Ship, tell us, what's the story?"

"No seriously, I just like the name. It's the name of a cocktail I used to drink a lot."

"Yeah, right. What goes in it then?"

Shipsey had guessed he might be asked this question and had done his homework.

"Gin, sweet and dry vermouth, grand marnier, orange juice and a dash of orange bitters."

"Sounds fucking disgusting!" Barry protested.

"No, its yummy." Shipsey rubbed his belly. "If you don't like the sound of the grand marnier, you can replace it with orange curacao, but that gives you curled whiskers. I prefer mine straight, even if it is a bit more expensive."

As he was reeling off the ingredients, Shipsey decided that he would have to try one of these *Satan's Whiskers* one day.

"Right, I'm off," he said, taking his betting docket. "Are you open tomorrow?"

"Yeah."

"Ok, I'll be back then to collect my winnings." Shipsey was doing his best to keep a straight face, but couldn't hold back his grin. He had thoroughly enjoyed putting Slim Shady under a bit of pressure. Even if the horse didn't win, he'd had a bit of fun.

The lads agreed that they'd alternate driving to each of *Satan's Whiskers* races and Dave offered to do the honours first. He was a bit nervous about the trip, as he hadn't seen Kate since he'd made a fool of himself outside *The Banner Man*. Add this to the fact that he was going to meet Kate's dad for the first time and he concluded that it was a good idea for him not to drink. On the way down, Macker surprised them all by producing the konch from his pocket. He hadn't forgotten the nasty task that Dave designed for him and he was hoping to repay the favour.

"Ok, I'll explain what the task is after the spin," he said placing the konch on the back of his "Racing Post." To his disappointment, the spin landed on Shipsey who was sitting beside him on the back seat.

"Right, here you go," said Macker, handing Shipsey a piece of paper. "For every non-runner there is in a race, you have to use one of those words in a sentence talking to my uncle, before that race begins."

Shipsey was frowning and scanning down the list of ten words. "Royal, cricket, Maggie Thatcher, Commonwealth, Londonderry! Jesus Macker! I take it your uncle isn't exactly a lover of all things British! Rugby, Tory, BBC, Soccer and Copulate! Oh for fuck sake! I have to use all these words in sentences talking to your uncle?"

"Yep...well for each non-runner there is in a race you have to use one of those words. So if there are two non-runners in the first race you have to use two of those words in sentences, before the first race is off."

"Am I allowed to repeat them?"

"No, your mission is to get through the whole list."

"Ah fuck off. *Londonderry*, for Christ sakes! I've never called it that in my life! Even *I'd* go ape shit if someone started talking about *Londonderry* to me! And what's the story with *copulate*? How the hell am I supposed to use that in a sentence talking to a sixty-year-old man? You'll have to give me some sort of prize if I get through the whole list."

"Yeah, that sounds fair," said Dave, who knew that this list had been designed with him in mind.

"Ok, I tell you what. If you use all ten and then our horse wins, I'll give you a tenner."

"Fuck your tenner! If our horse wins, I won't need a measly tenner!"

"All right...what then?"

"Ok, hows about this?" said Shipsey thinking hard. "If I use all ten words and then our horse wins you have to get each of Dave's cigarettes lit up by a different girl for the rest of the day."

"What?"

"Every time Dave wants a cigarette, you have to go and get it lit by a different girl."

That didn't sound like a terrible prospect to Macker. In fact, he might well enjoy it.

"All right then, you're on."

The lads arrived at Naas racetrack half an hour before the first race. The crowd was quite small and it didn't take them long to find Kate and her dad Liam. Macker introduced the lads to his uncle. Liam smiled as he shook all their hands.

"You boys must have been busy this morning."

"How do you mean?"

"Well you can't get any better than twelve to one now on *Satan's Whiskers*. He was sixteen to one first thing this morning. I assume you had something to do with that?"

"Well yeah, we put a few bob on it between us," answered Macker, "but nothing massive."

He genuinely didn't consider their bet *that* big, certainly not compared to some of the large wagers he knew his uncle had made in the past.

"I'd say you put a few sheckles on it yourself?"

"Oh, I just about managed to get a few quid down, before the sixteen to one was gone."

As they chatted about their horse's prospects, Shipsey examined the large board, which was displaying the runners and riders, but most importantly the non-runners for the first race.

Oh shit, three non-runners in the first race! Better get to work, he thought, shifting closer in proximity to Liam and quickly glancing down at his list of ten words.

"So Liam, do you fancy anything in this first race?" he asked, interrupting the previous conversation.

"I hadn't really looked yet," said Liam, flicking through the pages of his race programme.

Shipsey had already checked out the names of the horses. "I was thinking of backing that "Ballykelly Boy," what do you think of him?"

Liam moved his head slowly from side to side. "Eh, I don't really know anything about him. He doesn't seem to have any sort of form."

"Ah yeah, but it's a great name though. Ballykelly's up in Derry isn't is?"

"I believe so."

"Jaysis, did ye see that programme on the BBC the other night about Bloody Sunday? They kept callin' it Londonderry! I mean whose idea was that? Sounds like Maggie bleedin' Thatcher!"

Shipsey smiled broadly at Macker who was genuinely impressed. In a couple of sentences he's already gotten three of the more difficult words out of the way. Liam, whose head was spinning, was just trying to figure out how they had moved from talking about *Satan's Whiskers* form, to discussing Bloody Sunday so quickly.

"I'm not really a fan of the BBC," he said finally.

"Oh I know what you mean," said Shipsey, perking up and glancing quickly at his task-list of words.

"Too much Rugby and Soccer and documentaries about the Royal family." Shipsey took another look at the list while Kate's dad frowned at him. "…and the Commonwealth games! I mean, *come on!*"

Shipsey was practically getting giddy from how well he was doing.

Seven before the first race! Who's the man? He was now standing so close to Liam that his clenched fist of victory was outside the peripheral vision of Macker's uncle. Matt and Dave were doing their best to keep their laughter in. Kate could see that something was going on, but couldn't figure out what. Macker was staring at Shipsey and shaking his head slowly in amazement. Liam was just praying to god that the big loudmouth standing next to him wasn't the one who was dating his beloved daughter. He made an excuse about wanting to check the odds on the first race, so he could get away from Shipsey's insane ranting. When he was out of earshot, the lads finally burst into laughter.

"So how many is that so far?" asked Shipsey "I reckon it was seven."

"Yeah seven," confirmed Matt, patting his friend on the back. After they explained to Kate what they were up to, she chastised them for using her father as a guinea pig in one of their juvenile experiments, but eventually admitted that it was funny.

"So what words are left?"

"Cricket, Tory and Copulate. Cricket and Tory should be a doddle, but copulate is a tough one," Shipsey scratched his chin. "Might need a few beers to mull that one over."

After a couple of races and quite a few beers Shipsey decided to pounce on Macker's uncle again. This time he approached him from behind announcing, "hold still Liam!" Then he brushed his hand down the back of one of Liam's shoulders before claiming, "got it! Looked like a cricket or something. Jaysis I was up on Tory Island last year and I saw millions of the things!"

"Millions of what things?" asked Liam, wondering why this big man kept harassing him.

"Crickets."

"Crickets?"

"Yeah crickets…or maybe they were grasshoppers. Come to think of it, I don't know what the difference is myself. I think crickets are bigger and that one on your shoulder was enormous, but then again, it might have been just a really big grasshopper. Anyway, never mind that. What do you fancy in the next race?"

Not for the first time that day, Liam McCann was left staring at Shipsey with a confused look. Dave was enjoying watching his friend behaving like a maniac around Kate's father.

I must look like a mature, sober, well-adjusted saint next to that mouthy monster, he thought.

He wasn't wrong. Liam rarely prayed for anything other than the health of his wife, but that afternoon he found himself standing in the betting ring of Naas race course praying that the guy his daughter was dating wasn't the six foot four mad man with the propensity to discuss all things obscure. However, he was resigned to the fact that it was Shipsey who was his potential son-in-law. Why else would he be behaving so strangely? He didn't want to say anything to Kate, as she had seemed quite happy the last couple of months.

At five fifteen that afternoon the build up to the last race commenced when the runners and riders took to the parade ring. Macker was the first to spot *Satan's Whiskers*. "There he is lads, number twenty, second from the back!"

Satan's Whiskers entered the ring majestically and proceeded to follow the other horses around in a circle. His six owners were leaning over the perimeter fence of the parade ring staring at their magnificent racehorse.

"Jaysis, he looks great," whispered Shipsey.

"Yeah, he looks even stronger than before," whispered Dave.

"Why are we all whispering?" whispered Matt.

"No idea," whispered Shipsey.

Liam was pleased that the horse seemed to be handling the occasion well. "He doesn't seem too bothered by the whole thing. I've seen some first-timers that go mad when they get into the parade ring."

"Jesus lads, I've got serious butterflies in my stomach," said Matt.

"I've got butterflies, humming birds, a rattle snake and Rolf Harris playing the fucking kazoo in mine," laughed Macker.

This is the moment he had waited for. He had dreamed for years about owning his own racehorse and now here he was at the parade ring of a real racecourse watching excitedly as his horse walked by. OK, maybe it wasn't all his horse, but a reasonable portion of it was and *Kevin Daly* was in the saddle. *"Satan's Whiskers"* was getting close to them now and he could clearly see Kevin Daly's face. He looked relaxed, professional and very smart in his navy and sky blue epaulettes.

"Wahay, he's carrying the Dublin colours!" cheered Matt. The colours were actually those registered by Liam McCann when he became an owner for the first time five years earlier.

"So Liam, you know the way he's been gelded," whispered Shipsey.

Liam slowly turned to Shipsey fearful of what the harebrained fool might say next.

"Does that mean he's not able to…y'know… copulate?"

Dave, who was on the other side of Shipsey, was nearly choking trying to hold back the laughter. Liam, who had been closely studying *Satan's Whiskers* as he walked past, was now standing upright and staring quizzingly at Shipsey. "Copulate?"

"Yeah, y'know" said Shipsey, jerking his fists towards his waist "*copulate*."

"Are you for real son?" asked Liam, his eyebrows disappearing into what was left of his hairline.

"Well, yeah, I was just wondering if you knew."

"Well I'm no expert," said Liam, shaking his head, "but I'd imagine he's not able to do it properly anyway."

At the end of his sentence, he turned his back to Shipsey and whispered softly to Kate, who was giggling on the other side of him. "Tell me that's not the one you're datin' Katie."

Within a few minutes all the horses were at the starting line and the owners of *Satan's Whiskers* were gathered together on the stand. Liam was extremely relieved when Kate informed him that it was *Dave* and not Shipsey that she was going out with. "Oh thank God Kate! That's excellent!"

"So, you like him then?" asked Kate.

"Oh yes, I like him a lot, mainly because he's not *him*," he said pointing his thumb firmly at Shipsey, who he was doing his best not to stand beside.

"The white flag is raised."

"Holy shit! I think I'm gonna have a heart attack!" announced Macker, clutching his chest.

"And they're off!"

"Come on *Satan's Whiskers*!"

There were twenty-two horses in the field, so the lads spent most of the first half of the race simply trying to see their horse.

"Is that him there towards the back?"

"Where?"

"No, I think he's in that bunch in the middle."

"Really?"

"Yeah, I think that's him on the far side of that big bunch."

"Matt, do you see him?"

"Nope, I haven't a fuckin' clue where he is. Shoulda brought some binoculars."

With that, the lads turned their attention to Liam who was standing on the step in front of them peering through a huge pair of binoculars. "Liam, can you see him?"

"Yeah he's on the outside, back in about ninth or tenth, but he's lookin' pretty handy. Kevin's keepin' him outa trouble. He'd probably want to have him in about sixth when they get to the turn and then get to work on him from about three furlongs out."

As they approached the corner, the field was becoming more spread out and they could all see "*Satan's Whiskers*." He was about to challenge the sixth place horse. Ahead of him then was a gap of about two lengths to the five front-runners who were tightly grouped. When they were halfway around the turn, the lads heard their horse mentioned by the racecourse commentator for the first time.

"As they approach the four furlong pole it's *Yours Sincerely*, vying for the lead with *Earl Street*, behind these two we have *Thou Shalt Not* on the inside of *Rebel yell* and *Mighty Mouse*, then a gap to *Satan's Whiskers* who's getting the better of *Three's a crowd*."

"Come on *Satan*! Get up there my son! Come on you good thing!"

"As they pass the three furlong marker, it's *Yours Sincerely* by half a length from the favourite *Thou Shalt Not*. *Earl Street* is going backwards and is about to be passed by *Rebel Yell* and *Satan's Whiskers* is taking the long way round *Mighty Mouse*. The rest look beaten."

"Jesus lads! He's lookin' good for a place!"

"Fuck the place! He's gonna win it!"

"As they enter the last two furlongs *Thou Shalt Not* has a length advantage over *Rebel Yell*. *Satan's Whiskers* is being steered into third past *Yours Sincerely* who looks spent. Kevin Daly makes a move on *Satan's Whiskers* who's now looming up on the outside of *Rebel Yell*. He looks the stronger of the two, but can he do anything about the lead of *Thou Shalt Not*?"

"Yes he fucking can!" roared Shipsey. "Come on yeboyo!"

"It's down to who has the stronger finish now as *Satan's Whiskers* tries to get on terms with *Thou Shalt Not*. *Satan's Whiskers* on the outside of *Thou Shalt Not*, this is gonna be a close one."

"Come On *Satan*!"

"And as they approach the line, it looks like *Satan's Whiskers* might nick it. He seems to have *Thou Shalt Not* tapped for toe. Yes *Satan's Whiskers* wins by a neck from *Thou Shalt Not*. A blistering finish by Kevin Daly's mount!"

"Waaaaaahayyyyyyyyy!!!!"

Chapter   13

"Hi, can I have seven *Satan's Whiskers* please?"

"Sorry?"

"Seven *Satan's Whiskers* please."

"You wha?"

"*Satan's Whiskers.*"

"Satan's Whispers?"

"*Whiskers.*"

"Ahh, whiskers!   *Satan's Whiskers.*"

"Yep."

"Sorry son, but I haven't got a clue what yer on about."

Macker realised that ordering seven exotic cocktails from the proprietor of *The Haystack House* in downtown Naas, might be a tall order in more ways than one. The closest the owner, Danny Donoghue, had come to making a cocktail that week was when an English tourist asked him for a lager top. Macker could see all the required ingredients for his *Satan's Whiskers* on the dusty shelf behind the barman, so he offered his help. Five minutes later he and Danny were loading seven orange coloured concoctions onto a tray.

"I don't even know what to charge you for these," said Danny.

Macker, who had explained the reason for the peculiar order, handed him a 50 euro- note saying, "here, keep the change. We've had a good day."

A "good day" was something of an understatement when you added up the profits of the seven people who were now sipping their brightly coloured drinks. Between them they had won over 30,000 euro. Both Liam McCann and the trainer Paddy Mulryan had placed bets of 500 euro each way at sixteen to one, making them ten grand each. Between them, the lads would be collecting 11,250 euro from Slim Shady. Even Kate got in on the act with a last minute bet of 10 euro to win at twelve to one. It was the first bet she'd had since the 1997 Grand National and even the harsh taste of her *Satan's Whiskers*, couldn't take the smile off her face.

"I think I'll call Slim Shady," announced Shipsey, "just to make sure he doesn't flee the country or anything." The lads enjoyed listening to one half of the conversation between Shipsey and the bookmaker they had taken to the cleaners. Shipsey could never be accused of being magnanimous in victory.

"Howye Slim? I was wondering if you like apples?"

"Well, you owe me 11,250 euro. How do you like them apples?"

"Nah, no rush. I'll be around first thing in the morning for it."

"What if he doesn't cough up?" asked Dave after Shipsey had finished taunting the bookie.

"I'll drag him over the counter by his scrawny little neck and treat him to the most severe beating of his life. Then I'll go to my car showroom where I have a copy of the key to his Beamer. I'll walk casually up to it and drive it away from the front of his betting shop, whilst waving out the window and beeping the horn."

While the other horse owners were busy discussing the future of *Satan's Whiskers* with Paddy Mulryan, Dave and Kate were trying to figure out what their future held in store. "I wasn't sure if you'd be here today," said Dave.

"What? Oh yeah, my sister is home from university. She's looking after my mum."

"Oh right. Back for the weekend is she?"

"Well actually she's been around for a while."

This admission didn't go down well with Dave. *How long had her sister been around for? Why hadn't he been seeing more of Kate if there was someone else there to take care of her mum?*

Almost every time he had suggested to Kate that they meet up, she had used her mum's illness as the reason she couldn't get out. Now he hadn't seen her for a fortnight and he finds out that her sister was there all that time!

I don't like the sound of that, thought Dave, reaching for his cigarettes.

"Eh, excuse me Dave. What do you think you're doing?" Shipsey interrupted.

"What?"

"What's that?"

"This is a *cig-a-rette*," said Dave, as if he was talking to a three year old.

"And what are you doing with it?"

"Well, I was planning to *smoke* it, until you interrupted me."

"Now David, you know you're not supposed to be lighting your own cigarettes this evening. I'm sure Michael can help you with that."

By now Dave had remembered the terms of Macker's task and

reluctantly offered up his cigarette. Macker stood up, took the cigarette and casually walked over to a small group of thirty-year-old women. The rest of the lads watched from a distance as he effortlessly chatted up the best looking of them and got her to light his cigarette. Two minutes later he left the women, who had been reduced to giggling teenagers, returning with a lit cigarette in his hand and a smile on his face. This whole scene annoyed Dave massively. Firstly because his conversation with Kate had been interrupted at a crucial point, secondly because he was now smoking a cigarette that already had Macker's germs on it, but most of all, because in a brief encounter, Macker seemed to have built up more of a rapport with a total stranger than Dave had with Kate. He decided it was time to confront Kate. He'd had enough of seeing her only once or twice a month and not knowing where the relationship was going. Luckily enough Kate had a ready-made solution for his inquiry.

"Maybe we should just call it a day then," she said staring down at the bottom of her empty cocktail glass.

"What?" Dave started to panic. This wasn't quite the solution he had been hoping for.

"Yeah, I'm sorry. I realise now that I haven't been fair on you," said Kate, looking up from her glass. "It's probably best if we just call it a day and stay friends. Otherwise, you'll just get more and more annoyed with me."

Dave was seriously regretting putting Kate on the spot. Yes, he was finding it very frustrating seeing so little of her, but he would rather be frustrated and going out with her than frustrated and *not* going out with her. He wasn't brave or cruel enough to say it, but the solution he had in mind involved her moving back to Dublin and leaving the nursing of her mum up to someone else. He knew this was a non-starter, but part of him believed that if Kate really wanted their relationship to work that she could compromise a little by sharing the time spent caring for her mum a bit more equally with the rest of her family.

Kate felt awful. She knew she could make herself available more often to see Dave if that's what she really wanted. The problem was she hadn't made up her mind if that *was* what she wanted. She had hoped that over time that she would become more attracted to him and eventually they could take their relationship on to the next level, but she was starting to understand that she couldn't force herself to fancy a man just because she really cared for him. So, while she knew she didn't want to lose Dave as a friend she didn't think she wanted to take him as a lover. She recognised the fact that she was hiding behind her mother's illness and that sooner or later Dave would see through this. So she figured it would be better for her to finish the relationship, before she ended up hurting him. In many ways Kate's bond with Dave was different from her previous relationships. Normally, when she started to date a guy, she would be physically attracted to him and would end up sleeping with him sometime in the first month. After that it was customary for her to find out that he was a complete jerk. Then they would break up and she would be left hurt. She was tired of being hurt. With Dave she didn't feel as if she could be hurt. She found herself thinking of a *W.B. Yeats* poem she learned in secondary school, called *Never Give All The Heart*. It was another poem that Yeats wrote lamenting the unrequited love of Maud Gonne:

> *Never give all the heart, for love*
> *Will hardly seem worth thinking of*
> *To passionate women, if it seem*
> *Certain, and they never dream*
> *That it fades out from kiss to kiss;*
> *For everything that's lovely is*
> *But a brief dreamy kind delight.*
> *Oh never give the heart outright*
> *For they, for all smooth lips can say*
> *Have given their hearts up to the play.*
> *And who could play it well enough*
> *If deaf and dumb and blind with love?*
> *He that made this knows all the cost*
> *For he gave all his heart and lost.*

Kate realised that she was protecting herself from being badly hurt again by going out with a guy who she really liked, but could never really fall in love with. She had taken Yeats' advice and got herself into a comfortable relationship, which she was in control of and didn't threaten to break her heart.

So, if I don't feel like I can be hurt, where's the harm? She asked herself.

Her answer was in Dave's eyes. He was desperately trying to talk her around, by explaining that he would rather see her once in a blue moon than not at all. He acknowledged that the momentum of their relationship was not being helped by such infrequent encounters, but insisted that it was not a good enough reason to throw in the towel. Kate could see the hurt in his eyes and she hated herself for it. After a while of grovelling on his behalf she agreed that there was no need for them to break up and promised to try and see him more often.

When Dave left *The Haystack House* to drive the lads back to "The Banner Man" he was riddled with doubts about his future with Kate. While he was glad he managed to keep their bond in tact and definitely felt that Kate was worth fighting for, a part of him worried that there would be more difficulties to overcome. In the back of his mind was the niggling doubt that it may be more than just her mum's illness causing Kate's lack of enthusiasm. Thankfully the other three occupants of the car were quite drunk and were helping him take his mind off things. He was looking forward to ditching the car outside *The Banner Man* and joining in on their antics. While he had been having his sobering conversation with Kate, the other lads had been getting merrily pissed chatting to Macker's uncle and Paddy Mulryan about the future of *Satan's Whiskers*.

"So lads, Cheltenham here we come!"

"Yeah imagine that, us four over at Cheltenham! How many of us would make it back alive d'you reckon?"

"Well count me out for certain," said Macker, "If the drinkin' and gamblin' doesn't do me in, the women are sure to."

"So Matt, are you gonna tell Sam about the horse now?"

"Reckon so, I'm feelin' pretty brave and now I've won back all the money I spent on it, there's not too much she can get pissed off about. We're goin' to the cinema tomorrow afternoon so I'll wait until the middle of the film and casually lean over and whisper it in her ear. She's less likely to blow a gasket in the middle of a movie."

"Eh Macker, we've got a problem," declared Dave.

"What's that?"

"It'll be half an hour before we get back to *The Banner Man* and I fancy a cigarette now."

"Ok, well you'll have to stop at the next town or petrol station or something."

Macker was quite enjoying the task that had been set for him. Getting a cigarette lit was such a good excuse for chatting up strange women he was even considering taking up smoking himself.

"You're gonna struggle to get a light in a petrol station," said Dave.

"He might not have to worry about that," said Matt, peering through the windscreen. "Look what I see ahead."

"Wha?"

"Well unless I'm sadly mistaken, it appears as if two female hitchhikers have been sent down from heaven to help us in our plight."

Shipsey was now leaning through the two front seats to get a look at the backpackers.

"Well dip me in shit and roll me in sugar! Dave, you have to pull over!"

"Fuckin' right I'm pullin' over!"

Macker was worried. This would be a real challenge. "What the hell am I gonna say to them?"

"Don't know, but you better think fast," said Dave slowing down and pulling in twenty yards ahead of the backpackers.

When Macker rolled down the rear window and stuck his head out he realized that Matt had, in fact, been sadly mistaken. He was not looking at two female hitchhikers, but one blonde female and one long-haired bearded bloke. From the expensive and loud-coloured clothing they were wearing it was obvious they weren't Irish.

"Hi, Sorry we don't have enough room to give you a lift, but I was wandering if you might have a light?"

Macker had the unlit cigarette in his mouth. He was doing his best to aim the inquiry at the girl, but she was practically hiding behind her hairy friend.

"Exscouzen me pleece?" said the foreigner.

Macker held his right fist up to the cigarette and started wiggling his thumb up and down. "Have you got a light for my cigarette?"

"Ahh!" Said the man, raising his index finger and his eyebrows to the sky. He then proceeded to turn his female companion around and start to open her rucksack.

"Jost one momenten boye. Aye haf da fiar."

The other lads in the car were starting to chuckle. "Did he just call you boy?"

"Yeah, this guys a fucking nutcase," whispered Macker.

"He must have spent the last week down in Cork."

"Where d'ye reckon he's from?"

"Dunno, he sounds a bit like Arnie Shwarzenegger."

"Vee go too Doblin," said the man, who had fished an enormous box of matches from the girl's rucksack and was handing them to Macker.

"I see, very nice, thank you," said Macker taking the matches and pulling his head back inside the car. "Right, what the fuck do I do now?"

"You have to get the bird to light it," Shipsey reminded him.

"Ok, ok," said Macker slowly removing one of the long matches from the oversized box, while trying to figure out how he was going to get the timid female hiker to do the honours. He smiled out the window at the two tourists before slowly but deliberately snapping the match against the side of the box.

"Oh woops, sorry. It's a long time since I've used matches, at least ones this size. Do you think you could help?" he asked, trying to hand the box to the girl.

"Diss iss not prowblemen boye," said the man stepping forward to take the matchbox.

Macker removed the matches from his grasp and nodded towards the man's female companion. "I was hoping your girlfriend could do it."

The man turned to his fiancée and then back to Macker, who was doing his best impression of an innocent ten-year-old altar boy.

"No, diss iss ok. I do it," the man nodded.

"I'd really prefer if she did it," insisted Macker. "I don't want your beard to catch fire."

"Excouzen me pleece?"

"Your beeeard," said Macker, scratching his own chin, "it might go on fire."

"Ha no! You believen me, diss iss ok." The man was smiling manically while at the same time trying to free the box of matches from Macker's grasp. Then Macker noticed the engagement ring on the finger of the young lady and came up with a new line of attack.

"You're getting married, yes?" He was nodding in the direction of the girl's bejewelled finger.

"Ahh yesss!" roared the man, who had taken the matches from Macker and was opening the box.

"Well you see it's an Irish custom to get your cigarette lit by a bride to be. It's for good luck."

The chuckles coming from inside the car were beginning to get louder. The man was staring at Macker as if he had asked him to perform oral sex on the car's exhaust pipe. He could tell the man either hadn't understood him or didn't believe what he was saying. He decided to repeat himself slowly. "It's a trad-i-tion in Ireland for a woman who is getting married to light your cigarette. It brings you good luck."

"A tradischun? I haf not hert off diss beforr boye?"

"Ahh well y'see it's more of a *Dublin* tradition. They don't do it down in Cork."

"Ah! You orr from Doblin?"

"Yes."

"Ah very goot! My name iss Schtefan." Stefan was now guiding his fiancée closer to the car and handing her the matches. "Diss iss my feyonsay Cattareen. Ve orr frrom Dortmoonde."

Macker was craning his neck out the window and sucking with all his might to make sure the cigarette caught light from the match that Katarine had just struck. When he was sure it was lit, he dropped back into the car. "Dave, I've got it, now put the foot down!"

As Dave was putting the car into first gear, Macker turned back to the German tourists. "Thank you very much Heidi, thank you Fritz. Viva Borussia Dortmund! Auf weidersein pet!"

An hour later the lads had settled down at their usual table in *The Banner Man*. Dave was drinking and smoking fast, firstly to try and catch up with the others, but also to try to wash away his worries about Kate.

"Jaysis! That one was all over me!" exclaimed Macker. He had just arrived back to the table, having gotten another of Dave's cigarettes lit.

"The one at the bar?"

"Yeah, she introduced herself and everything! I think she thought I was trying to chat her up! She kept grabbin' my hand!"

"Jesus Macker!" said Shipsey looking over at the woman. "She must be about fifty!"

"I know! I only asked her for a light, but I got the impression she would have been happy to give me more than that."

"Maybe you should get back over there. You might learn a few things, y'know, mature woman and all that."

"Don't think so, she must be twice my age."

"Don't knock it till you've tried it," laughed Shipsey. "Matt was with a forty-seven-year-old when we were in Greece and we were only nineteen at the time!"

Dave and Macker had now turned their attention to Matt. "Were ye?"

"Well yeah, but I didn't shag her or anything."

"*And* she was a lesbian," Shipsey added.

"Really?" Asked Macker. "How d'you know that?"

"Well, she was with three other women and they had just arrived from the island Lesbos."

"Cool."

By the end of the night the lads were quite drunk and the conversation had reached a suitably low ebb. In between visiting almost

111

every female smoker in the lounge to have Dave's cigarettes lit, Macker was playing devil's advocate in the ongoing debates.

"Do you thinks it's a coincidence," asked Shipsey, "that our hands conveniently hang down to our waists? That's God's way of telling us that it's ok to play with yourself."

"I don't think so," argued Macker. "It's unruly, it's unhealthy and eventually you will go blind."

"Who says it's unhealthy? I read an article recently that said the more you wank the less likely you are to get prostrate cancer."

"Oh yeah? And what wholesome magazine did you read that in? If it's so good for you why don't people do it in public?"

It had been a long day. Shipsey was very tired and getting a bit sick of Macker arguing for the sake of it. "Ok, shut up for a second you skinny little git! Firstofall, there are lots of healthy things people do that they wouldn't do in public and secondly, apart from possibly Dave, you're the biggest wanker sitting at this table!"

"Cheers," said Dave. He hadn't been participating much in the debate. Sadly, masturbation was a subject he was all too familiar with and judging from his earlier conversation with Kate the situation wasn't going to change in a hurry.

"Name one," said Macker.

"Name one what?"

"One healthy thing people do, that they wouldn't feel right doing in public."

"Take a shit."

"That's just a normal bodily function."

"So is wanking."

"Yeah but *not* shitting is unhealthy, *not* wanking is *not* unhealthy."

Macker was very drunk and not entirely sure what he was saying made sense, but he was determined not to be defeated in the argument even if he didn't thoroughly believe in his own side of it.

"So Macker," Shipsey leaned forward. "Are you saying you don't wank?"

"Of course I wank, but that's not what we're arguing about."

"So you *do* wank?"

"Yeah, but that doesn't mean I think it's a clean, healthy and natural thing."

"So you're a tosser then?"

Macker shook his head. "Look, we all do it, but the point is that…"

Shipsey interrupted before Macker could get to his point. He

112

wanted to go home to bed and knew that Macker would be happy to argue all night.

"You know what McCann?" Shipsey leaned over and put his arm around Macker's shoulder. "I love you...but you're a complete wanker and I think we've talked enough shite for one night. Come on, let's get out of here."

As they were making their way out of the pub, Macker was taken to one side by the bar manager Niall Harrison.

"Macker, what the fuck were you up to tonight?"

"Oh just the usual Harry, getting pissed...talkin' shite."

"Well, I received a complaint about you from one of the female customers."

"What?"

"Yeah, she said you came up to her and asked her for a light and while she was lighting your cigarette, you were staring down her top."

"So?"

"She then said that you proceeded to the same thing with every other woman in the pub!"

"That's bollix! There's a few of them I didn't get around to."

"So you're admitting it then?"

"It's a long story Harry."

"Enlighten me."

"Look Harry...if women go around wearing tight tops and showing loads of cleavage, do they really have the right to complain if us men take a look at the goods?"

"Listen Macker," Harry, lowered his voice. "I know what you're sayin', but do you really have to go up to every single one of them and have a good old gawk? Can you not just take a sly peek from a distance, like the rest of us?"

Macker smiled and stumbled towards the door. Harry had no intention of barring one of his most valued customers, but still wanted to get the message across that he was in charge. "I don't wanna hear any more complaints Macker! You don't even smoke for fuck sake!"

Macker didn't bother turning around. "I know," he laughed, "but I'm thinkin' about takin' it up."

Chapter 14

Shipsey woke up the next day with a horrendous hangover. He had planned to visit Slim Shady as soon as his betting office opened, but it was already half past eleven.

Jane was reading a book in the bed beside him.

"Good morning!" She said chirpily.

"Owwwww! I've got a wicked headache."

"Yeah it sounded like you had a good day. I'll go get you some *Neurofen*."

Shipsey instantly became very suspicious. He couldn't remember speaking to Jane, but he had obviously phoned her from *The Banner Man* to tell her of his win. The main reason for his suspicion, however, was that in all the years they had been living together, he couldn't recall one occasion when Jane had fetched him Neurofen before. He was much more used to her picking on him when he was ill and he found this new approach unsettling. They had been getting on really well for last ten days, which meant two things. They hadn't had sex in that time and the next fight was imminent. Shipsey was praying he could avoid combat that morning, but feared the worst when Jane arrived back with two pills and a glass of water in her hands and a scary smile on her face.

"Do you fancy watching a video?" she asked, getting back into bed.

"Not really. I was planning on just crashing out until this headache goes," he said, knocking back the tablets.

"Do you mind if I watch it in here?"

"Of course not babes. Just not too loud please." Shipsey plonked his head back down on the pillow and pulled the duvet up over his ears. He could just about hear Jane loading up the video and switching on the TV as he started to doze off.

Shipsey spent the next fifteen minutes falling in and out of consciousness. His banging headache and the noise from the video were preventing him falling back to sleep properly. Even though Jane had the volume turned down, the main character of whatever movie she was watching, had such a monotonous voice, it was antagonising his migraine. He couldn't make out what the guy was saying, but his dull speech seemed to drone on forever.

"Sorry Janie, would you mind turning it down just a smidge more?" he asked, pulling the duvet tighter around his head.

But the man's voice seemed to get louder. Shipsey held his breath to try and confirm this. *Yes she definitely has turned the volume up! This can only mean one thing...ladies and gentleman. That's right! It's showtime! The main event of the evening is a battle for the heavyweight championship of the world. In the blue corner is the challenger, weighing in at seventeen stone. His record reads 33 professional fights 33 defeats all by way of knockout. Let's hear your groans of sympathy please for Alan "The Big Ship" Boate. And in the red corner is your champion, weighing in at nine stone three pounds of steeled fury. Her record is 33 wins in 33 fights, all by knockout. Ladies and gentlemen, bow before the might of Jane "The Guvnor" McGovern!* Shipsey was in no way ready to rumble, so he stayed still under the duvet cover and tried to block out the noise from the TV. "Monotoman's" voice was coming through more clearly now.

"It's important to spend time exploring your parner's body."
What?

"Some people are shy and prefer to do this with the lights off."
What the fuck?

"Candles often create the best atmosphere for lovemaking."
Oh my God!

Shipsey finally popped his head above the covers. "What the fuck are you watching?" On the TV he could see a naked man kissing a very good-looking naked woman on the hipbone.

"It's *The Good Lover's Guide,"* answered Jane, without removing her gaze from the screen.

"Where'd ye get that?"

"I bought it yesterday."

"I seeeeee," said Shipsey very slowly. "Why?"

"I thought it might spice things up a bit for us."

"Oh"

"What d'you think?" she asked, turning to face him.

"Of what? The idea or the video?"

"Both"

"I suppose it's not a bad idea," he hesitated, "but that bloke's voice is giving me prick ache and not in a good way."

"Yeah, I know what you mean," chuckled Jane. "He sounds like a complete arsehole!"

Shipsey began to relax. "He's ruining a perfectly good video." He was glad that the atmosphere had lightened and he may not have to go ten rounds with Jane, at least not in the fighting sense.

"Do you wanna have a look at the other one I got?"

"What's that, *The Good Lover's Guide 2*?"

"No," said Jane, reaching down into a bag at the side of the bed. "It's called *'Sorority Chicks 3'*."

Shipsey couldn't hide the look of astonishment from his face, as he studied the cover of *Sorority Chicks 3*. It wasn't the naked flesh on the cover that had him in a state of shock, it was the fact that Jane had gone out and bought it. In all the years of going out together, he had never got the impression that she might be into watching dirty videos. After a moment his shock started to give way to another emotion that left him with a lump in his throat. He realised that the problems they had been having hadn't *just* been affecting *him*. Jane was also hurt and emotionally worn out by their roller-coaster love life. There were times when he thought that she really loved to fight, but he knew now that that wasn't true. While he had been foolishly thinking that getting married and having kids was the solution to helping them lead a more even-keeled coexistence, Jane had been dreaming up solutions of her own. Her going out and buying this video said a lot more to him than "*I want some good sex now!*"

It *said "I love you and I'm tired of fighting. Maybe this will help us get things back on track."* Without speaking, Shipsey slid across the bed and gave Jane a firm hug while kissing her on the side of the head. Jane wasn't quite sure what this meant, but she thought she could see a tear gathering in his left eye.

"So do you wanna watch it or not?" she asked finally.

"Fuckin' right I do." Ten minutes later Shipsey was placing soft kisses in the vicinity of Jane's hipbone. Miraculously, his headache had completely cleared up. This could have been thanks to the *Neurofen*, but more likely it was down to *Sorority Chicks 3*.

*****

"Don't you ever listen to your messages?"

"Did you leave me a message?" asked Matt, looking at his mobile phone.

"No, not on that! On *that* thing!" said Sam, pointing at the answering machine in his hallway.

"*You* left me a message on *that*?

"No *I* didn't, but somebody obviously did, look!"

Matt looked at the machine and could see the number 3 flashing in the display. He hadn't noticed it before, but then again he didn't tend to pay much attention to the answering machine. Dave had received it as a

Christmas present from his mum three years earlier and before long it was given the nickname "Jack" as it spent all its time it the box it arrived in. Jack remained in that box for a full ten months before Dave finally connected him up to the phone. He was interviewing with recruitment agencies at the time and didn't want to miss any calls. This was the most exciting time of Jack's life and he really hoped he could help Dave get the extra five grand he was hoping for. He finally felt like he was part of the family. For three weeks he diligently took messages and churned them out as clearly and accurately as he could. Unfortunately their quest failed. Dave couldn't find a better paying job and over time the phone rang less and less. Both Matt and Dave had mobile phones that made Jack sick with envy. Not only were these little phones prettier and more sophisticated than him, they also seemed to get all the good calls. The only calls that came through to Jack were from salespeople or work colleagues that weren't popular. There was one other call that came through at the same time every Wednesday night without fail. Jack dreaded this call for two reasons. Firstly, because it was from Dave's mum and boy could she go on! Several times he had run out of memory because she just had too much to say about uncle Dermot's kidneys or cousin Sheena's dancing. But the main reason Jack hated taking her call was because it reminded him of the first time his new owners mistreated him. It was a cold Wednesday evening in February, when bang on eight o'clock the phone rang. Jack knew that both of his owner's were watching football in the next room so he ignored the ringing phone and waited for one of them to take the call. Then he heard the immortal words that broke his heart.

"Oh bollix! That's my mum…Fuck it! I'll let the machine get it."

Jack let the phone ring a few more times in the vain hope that Dave would change his mind. Then he gave up and realized that he would have to go against his programming.

"Matt and Dave aren't here at the moment. Please leave a message."

While he loved taking messages, he hated being party to such deceit and from that day forward Jack whinced when he heard the words "let the machine get it."

"So, are you gonna listen to them?" asked Sam.

Matt had retreated to his bedroom to try and locate his wallet. "What?"

"Are you going to listen to your messages?"

"Nah…Where the fuck did I leave that bloody thing?"

"Why not?"

"Wha? Ah, I don't have time and nobody ever leaves messages on that yolk anyway."

This hurt Jack's feelings, but only because it was true. He found few things more upsetting than callers who didn't leave messages and some callers were downright ignorant. He'd lost count of the number of times he'd heard the words "fucking machine" followed by a hanging up sound. Matt was passing through the hallway on his way to the kitchen to continue his search for the lost wallet. He was still pretty hung-over from the night before and had only fallen out of bed forty minutes earlier. In that time he had managed to shave, shower and give Dave a lift to the pub to collect his car. He had only just arrived back before Sam rang his buzzer. Their plan was to grab some lunch before going to the cinema. For the second time he opened the fridge to check for his wallet. Sam realized she may have to wait a little while longer and plonked herself down in the chair beside the phone. Matt never seemed to lose anything, but he often forgot where he put things, especially when he'd been out drinking. She often joked with him that he was showing early signs of senility. He'd once driven home from football training with his gear bag on the roof of his car. It was almost annoying to see how absent-minded he could be and yet never lose anything. Sam found herself looking at the flashing 3 on the answering machine. Here was something else that annoyed her about Matt. He couldn't care less what was on his own answering machine! Sam got depressed if she wasn't first to know who was snogging whom at work or which two celebrities had been photographed together in St. Tropez. While this little answer machine couldn't volunteer such juicy information, she still found herself magnetically drawn to the blinking red light.

"Do you mind if I check these out?" she asked finally.

"What?"

"Do you mind if I listen to your messages?"

"If it makes you happy."

Jack had been keeping these messages for a few days and was glad to get them off his chest.

"You have three new messages. Message one left at 1.26pm on Wednesday the 10th. Click. Beeeeeeeep...Message two left at 4.40pm on Friday the 12th. "Good afternoon, my name is Ray. I'm calling from Wilson's Windows and I have a question for the homeowner. How much do you think it would cost to double glaze...beeeeeeeeep, message deleted."

Even Sam wasn't interested in *that* information.

"Message three left at 7.56pm on Saturday the 13th. "Howye Matt, it's Paul from work. Just givin' you a quick call to thank you for the tip. Stuck a score each way on it myself, so headin' out now to celebrate. Saw the race in the bookies. That's a helluva horse you've got. Let me know when he runs next. Anyway, thanks again. I'll seeya on Monday. Bye."

The ensuing fight did not go well from Matt's point of view. In fact it's a bit of an injustice to even call it a fight. There was little he could do to appease Sam's rage and he realized that all he could aim to achieve was damage limitation. Everything he tried, however, just seemed to infuriate her even more.

"I was going to tell you today, I swear."

"Oh how fucking convenient! I suppose you were gonna whisper it in my ear half-way through the movie?"

Matt decided it would be best if he didn't answer that. He had never seen her so angry. Getting angry was not really Sam's style. Normally when they argued she would resort to using tears or the silent treatment to sway things in her favour. Sam detested foul language, so to hear her using the F-word scared Matt into silence. It was almost a year since he'd last heard her use the word "fuck" and that was when she'd spilt some nail varnish on an expensive dress.

"When did you buy this fucking horse?"

Two fucks inside a minute. She really is pissed off! Thought Matt.

He briefly contemplated lying to her, but decided against it. "January."

"January! You bought it in fucking January! And you were going to tell me today! Three months later! How much money did it cost?"

When Matt explained the intricacies of the syndicate and that he'd parted with 2,500 euro she started heading for her car.

"So you're all in on it! Who else knew? Did Jane know? How could you waste all that money on a horse! What about our deposit for the house?"

"Don't worry, I won it all back yesterday!"

As soon as the words were out of his mouth, Matt knew it was a mistake to mention that he'd gambled a further 200 euro on the horse. Sam was now sitting inside her car and starting up the engine. Matt was holding open the car door and pleading with her to calm down.

"I'm sorry Sam. I meant to tell you sooner. I just couldn't find the right moment. I knew I'd have the money for our deposit anyway when I get my work bonus. The other lads were gonna do it with or without me and I didn't want to be left out. I'm sorry."

"That's the problem isn't though Matt? You always put the lads first!"

Sam grabbed the car door and pulled it shut, only narrowly missing Matt's fingers in the process.

"Wait Sam! Hold on a minute!"

But it was too late. She had already put the car into reverse and was rolling the front wheel over the bridge of his foot.

"Ahhhhhhhhhhhhhhhh! Sam! STOP!"

As the car made it's way over Matt's aching foot they made eye contact for a split second.

"Ahhhhhhhhhhhhhh! Sam!"

He could see the hurt and hate on her contorted face. "Fuck off you lying prick!"

Wow she really has got the hang of the cursing. He watched her car spin out of the estate while trying to ease his throbbing foot from his shoe.

It took Matt quite a while to hobble back upstairs to the flat. He was feeling pretty sorry for himself and not just because his foot was in agony. It had frightened him to see Sam that furious and he hoped he hadn't messed things up for good. He couldn't help flashing back to the ugly expression on her face as she pulled away in the car. It was far detached from the elegant features he had fallen in love with four years earlier. He was at fault for this horrific transformation and he would have to work hard to get his beautiful Sam back. When he arrived at the door of the flat, Dave was waiting for him.

"All right?"

"Been better," said Matt, collapsing into the hallway chair.

"So I see…Come on." Dave was handing Matt his jacket.

"Where we goin'?"

"The boozer."

"Ok, hold on *one* minute." Matt grabbed a hold of Jack, reefed the plug from the wall and wrapped the wire tightly around his neck. He limped as far as the kitchen, before forcefully slotting the answering machine deep into the large swing-top bin.

Chapter 15

Matt looked down at what was left of his fifth pint of Guinness. "Y'know what my favourite quote is from the sitcom *Cheers*?"

"No."

"It's when Norm's wife Vera rings him at the pub to nag down the phone at him. After Norm hangs up he turns to Sam and says, "Women! Can't live with them...pass me the beer nuts."

This had Dave chuckling. "Well, at least I'll know what to bring you as a moving in present. A year's supply of beer nuts. Hey! I just thought of something you could get Sam as a peace offering, y'know, to make things up to her."

"What?"

"A framed photograph of *Satan's Whiskers*."

Matt felt a lot better for this early afternoon visit to *The Banner Man*. Not only had the fresh alcohol cured his hangover and eased the pain in his foot, it had also made him more confident that he and Sam could overcome this hurdle in their relationship.

A bit of time and a lot of grovelling, that's all it takes, he thought.

"Anyway enough of my strife," said Matt, looking up at Dave. "What's the story with you and Kate? I saw the two of you having a bit of a tete a tete yesterday."

Dave told Matt about how he had talked Kate out of breaking up with him.

"Why did she wanna break up?"

"Well, as you know, we haven't exactly been seeing much of each other because she spends a lot of time looking after her mum. So she basically said that she'd rather keep me as a friend, than lose me as a frustrated boyfriend."

"And *are* you frustrated?"

"Well, yeah, a bit...ok a lot. We've been going out for three months and I think she's absolutely perfect, so of course I wanna see a lot more of her."

"A lot *lot* more of her, I'd say?"

Dave understood that Matt was asking if he'd slept with Kate yet. Matt was probably the only person he was willing to share that sort of information with.

"Ok a lot *lot* more," Dave admitted.

"Right, I see," mused Matt. "Well, this is all pretty fucked up really. You're madly in love with Kate and you would do anything to stay with her, but you really need to bone her soon or you're going to do yourself an injury. And she's too busy taking care of her sick mother to realise the urgency of the situation." Matt scratched his chin thoughtfully. "*Opportunity* seems to be the big problem here."

"Whaddya mean?"

"Well, you live in Dublin and she lives in Kildare with her folks. You're not exactly gonna be able to shag her in the room next to her ailing mother and any time she spends the night in Dublin she stays in Macker's house."

"Right...so?"

"So, as I see it, there are two potential solutions."

"Really? What?"

"Well, you could invite her away for a weekend."

"I tried that actually, but she used the old mother excuse again. What's the other idea?"

"You need to get her up to Dublin on a night when Macker isn't out and you need to get her drunk...very drunk."

"Why very drunk?"

"So drunk that she wouldn't consider driving back to Kildare and drunk enough to consent to getting naked in a bed next to you." Matt pinched dave's love handles. "So I reckon *very* drunk."

"Fuck off!" Dave pushed Matt away. "Although in principal it sounds like a good idea...Hey! Maybe you and Sam could do a double date with us? That way it would feel quite natural for us all to go back to the flat."

"You're forgetting that three hours ago Sam ran over my foot in her Peugot 205, I don't think she'll be up for a double date for at least a couple of weeks."

"That's all right. I usually have to give Kate about two weeks notice anyway."

Matt and Dave were cheered up even more when Shipsey and Macker arrived to the pub. Shipsey was in particularly high spirits as he sat down at the table. Not only had he enjoyed the best sex of his life that day, he had also just collected their winnings from Slim Shady. He casually dropped the large brown envelope on to the table.

"Pick the bollix out of that one lads! 11,250 euro. Not bad for a weekend's work."

"Nice one! Any problems collecting it from Slim Shady?"

"Unfortunately not. The fucker had it waiting in an envelope in his safe. He even managed to smile the whole way through the transaction. He almost ruined the whole thing for me. I was really hoping to see him cry. What a fucking wanker!"

"Yeah, what a bastard!" nodded Macker, opening up the envelope. He fished inside and grabbed one of the large wads, which was bound with an elastic band. As he was removing it, he noticed Michelle, the beautiful lounge girl, walking towards their table.

"Well, I know what I'm gonna spend mine on," he said, gazing at Michelle.

"What?"

"I'm gonna offer it all to Michelle for one night of passion."

The lads had to stop their chuckling short as Michelle stopped to see if they needed anything.

"Howye Michelle! I was just thinking about you," announced Macker.

"Really?" She smiled down at him.

As usual she looked fantastic in her short black skirt and white T-shirt.

"Yeah, I was wondering if you're still going out with what's 'is name?"

"Yep, 'fraid so." She had lost track of how many times Macker had asked her this question and wondered what his follow up would be if she didn't always give the same answer.

"Did ye hear that Matt? She's still going out with him."

By now, Matt was pretty sick of this routine, but as usual he humoured Macker.

"Ok, thanks Mack."

Macker winked up at Michelle. "You'll let us know if anything changes, yeah?"

"You'll be the first to know." Michelle was about to turn away when she stopped. "But actually I'm only working here for one more week."

"Oh no! Why's that?" Macker's heart sank. He really did like Michelle. Apart from her sexy looks she had a very sweet personality. Although she was probably about four years younger than him and clearly involved in a happy relationship, Macker had always fancied his chances of dating her some day.

"I'm heading to Australia for a year."

Macker shook his head. "That's a bad idea Michelle. Australia's full of dangerous snakes and insects and...eh...koala bears. They're everywhere!"

Michelle laughed sexily.

"I'm serious, I don't think you should go there. They treat women like second class citizens!"

"Who? Koala bears?"

"Ha ha very good, but it's no place for a young elegant lady like yourself."

"Well thanks for your concern, but I've already spent two grand on flights and accommodation."

"Are you going with what's 'is name?" asked Shipsey.

"Yes, I'm going with what's 'is name."

"What *is* his name anyway?"

"Jason."

"Jason! Ugh! Jason! I think I prefer what's 'is name! So when's your last night here?"

"Friday…I fly out on Sunday."

"Ok, well we'll make sure we're here on Friday to give you a good send off."

The lads were a bit down after this bad news. They all had a soft spot for Michelle, especially Macker. To lift the mood they spent an hour talking about *Satan's Whiskers* and how great the previous day had been. Macker, who had spoken to his uncle earlier, was able to tell them that the horse was fit and well and the trainer would be looking to run him in a hurdle race in three to four weeks time. By eight o'clock Matt and Dave were well into double figures for the number of pints they had drank and the topic of conversation had come down to a more suitable level.

"So what *is* the difference between 32EE and 32F?"

"Let me tell you somethin'. If you're goin' out with a bird who's stuck somewhere between 32EE and 32F, you're gonna be so happy that you won't give a shit what the difference is."

"Yeah, that's true I suppose," said Matt struggling to his feet and hobbling snail-like towards the gents.

"What's wrong with him?" asked Shipsey.

"I think he's – hic - had too much to drink," slurred Dave.

"No, I mean why is he walkin' like that?"

"Oh, he had a bit of an automobile acshident earlier."

When Matt finally made it back to the table Shipsey decided to pursue the subject further. "What the fuck happened to you?"

"Whaddya mean?"

"Well, on the way back from the jacks Old Quirkey passed you out!"

"Oh that, well y'see, Sam kinda ran over my foot in her car, by acshident, I think."

"What do you mean, "you think"? You think Sam ran over your foot? Or you think it was an accident?"

"I think…well I hope it was an acshident."

"Why would she want to do it on purpose?"

Matt proceeded to explain to Shipsey how Sam had found out about the *Satan's Whiskers*. In the meantime Dave was trying to delicately garner some information about Kate from Macker.

"So y'know I really like your cushin Macker?"

"Yeah."

"J'reckon she really likes me too?"

"Well, I suppose she must. She's been going out with you for a couple of months now."

"Thatsh good, cos I really really like her."

"Right, so you said."

"I wuz wondrin if you knew…like…how any of her udder rela'ships worked out?"

"I haven't a clue. I think she's been out with a few dickheads. Whaddya mean?"

"Well I wuz hopin' you knew…like…how long like it takes b'fore she…y'know…gets…eh…fizzicle with a guy?"

"Wha?"

"Y'know, how long she –hic- goes out with a bloke b'fore she…y'know…"

"Ok, I understand what yer askin' me! But what the fuck makes you think I'd know that?"

"Shorry, no afence like or anthin'. I jusht…y'know…thawt you might have an idea like wedder she's more of a…Mudder Terrayza or a Madonna?"

"Do you like actually y'know like *WANT* me to punch you in the face?"

"No datsh ok. Shorry Macker, I'm a bit pished. I'd like to…y'know…retract the queschun if thatsh ok."

Half an hour later Matt and Dave were making their way home. With the aid of lampposts, walls and each other they advanced with the pace and grace of two blind geriatrics.

"What time izzet?" asked Dave, unable to read his own watch.

"Way too early to be thish pished."

"Are you pished? I'm not that bad. Bit merry mebby."

"Yeah me too ashally. I wuz thinkin' of ringin' Sam, but Shipshey said I wuz too pished…but I r'ckon om alrigh'."

"Ahsher yer grand."

"Righ' den here goesh," said Matt, taking his phone from his pocket and dropping it on the ground. On the fourth attempt he dialled the right number. For no apparent reason, when he heard Sam's voice he started whispering.

"Hi Sam…itch me…Matt. How are you?"

"What? No…well yeah, but just two or chree."

Ten seconds later it was apparent to Dave that the conversation was over when Matt said "OK" and started trying to locate the hang up button through one squinted eye. "What d'she say?"

"Eh letshee, she called me a "lying turd" and den I tink shhee told me to "wank off!"

"Wank off? What dozzat mean?"

"I dunno…I s'pose it cud be conshtrued in a number of ways. It cud mean tha I won't be gettin' anny punani furra while, but I think she jusht needs to brush up on her cursin'."

Chapter 16

Shipsey couldn't make up his mind between *Busty Babes*, *Hot Flesh* and *Amazon Women 2*. When he first walked into the adult section he was a bit nervous and started behaving like a spy, but it's difficult to make yourself inconspicuous when you're six foot four, weigh seventeen stone and are trying to conceal a semi-erection behind a video called *The Slut Cruise*. After a while though, he relaxed and began to examine the video covers in earnest. He definitely liked the look of "Busty Babes" which lived up to its title and the cover of *Hot Flesh* boasted some pretty interesting scenes. *Amazon Women 2* was also very tempting, because it starred Tiffany Tongue, who was his favourite girl from *Sorority Chicks 3*.

Not only does Tiffany have an amazing body and a mind-blowingly long tongue, but she's also somewhat of a sequel expert, thought Shipsey, checking to see if anyone had noticed how long he'd been studying these three video covers. In the end the decision was too difficult so he stuffed all three videos under his arm and made his way to the checkout queues. There were four separate queues being manned by four young people and to Shipsey's relief one of them was a bloke. He happily joined the back of that queue despite it being the longest. After a short while he realised that not only was it the longest, but it was also by far the slowest. The guy at the cash register must have been new to the job, but Shipsey was happy to stick it out with him to avoid the embarrassment of going to one of the girls. Some of the other customers weren't happy to stick it out, however, and not long after he'd joined the queue, the woman in front of him was tutting and excusing herself whilst making her way to the back of a shorter queue. Shipsey froze with fear when he realized that this person squeezing past him was familiar.

Oh fuck, oh fuck. Don't look up. Don't look up!

It was his older brother's fiancée Fiona O'Sullivan. Shipsey was now standing with his back to her, pretending to be looking at the blank tapes, which were on special offer. Fiona and he had always got on really well together, but now was not the time for a chat. As casually as possible he withdrew from the queue and hid in the easy listening section. The armpit under which he was concealing his pornographic material was perspiring heavily.

I wander if Jane went through this much hassle. He stood still, admiring the cover of "Tubular Bells" until Fiona had paid for her goods and headed downstairs on the escalator. Ten minutes later he was making his way downstairs with his purchased goods when he saw Fiona looking at some calendars at the bottom of the escalator.

Oh shit, oh shit! Shipsey briefly toyed with the idea of turning and running back up the escalator, but he had visions of that ending in disaster.

Don't panic, stay calm. As he neared the bottom of the escalator Fiona looked up to see him. A split second before she covered her face with a friendly smile, Shipsey was sure he had seen embarrassment in her eyes. When he made it to the bottom of the escalator, he realised why.

"Howye Fi, Big Justin fan are ye?" he asked, nodding at the semi nude picture of Justin Timberlake on the front of his calendar.

"No, eh, I was thinking of getting it for my niece. She's...eh...six."

"I seeeee, whatever you say," laughed Shipsey, delighted that he wasn't the one on the back foot.

"What are you doin' here?" asked Fiona, keen to change the subject.

"I just picked up a couple of...videos."

"Oh, whadya get?"

Shipsey started to panic. *Did she see me in the adult section? Did she notice me ducking out of the queue? Jesus! This is more hassle than it's worth! If I get out of here alive, I'm never buying porn again..*

"I got...eh... *"Leathal Weapon."*"

"Oh, is that it?"

"Yeah...*Leathal Weapon...1,2* and *3."*

"I seeee, you must be a big fan," she smiled.

Shipsey could feel his face taking on a deep shade of red. *She knows you muppet, she knows! Let's get out of here!*

"Listen, I've gotta split. You need a lift?"

"No thanks, I'm driving as well."

Thank god for that, thought Shipsey, saying his goodbyes and making a hasty exit. He walked at top speed to his car avoiding eye contact with passers by for fear he'd bump into someone else he knew. The cool April air didn't stop him from breaking sweat and by the time he got into the driver's seat he was panting heavily and mopping his brow with his sleeve. He looked down into the plastic bag on the passenger seat and sighed heavily.

"Hot Flesh, Amazon Women, Busty Babes, you guys better be worth it."

128

*****

"Well, I see you're walkin' ok," said Dave.

"Huh?"

"You're walkin all right. That means she didn't chop your nuts off or run over your other foot."

"Oh…yeah," said Matt making his way to the kitchen and grabbing himself a beer. He'd spent most of the week trying to weasel his way back into Sam's good books. After several grovelling phone calls, an apology card, a bunch of flowers and an invitation to a very posh restaurant she finally succumbed to meeting him. He was still reviewing how the night had gone when he plonked himself down in the armchair beside Dave and cracked open his beer. Dave could see that his friend was in dreamland.

"Are you ok?"

"Huh, oh yeah."

"So, how was it?"

"Very expensive."

"Well you brought her to *The Mint Leaf.* Of course it was expensive. How much was it?"

"Well including taxis, almost 300 euro."

"Holy shit! Was it worth it?"

"Dunno." Matt was happy to be back on talking terms with Sam, but things were still quite awkward between them. When he picked her up in the cab, she looked absolutely stunning, but Matt could tell by her eyes that she was still very angry with him. He spent most of the first part of the night continuing to apologise for his dishonesty and begging her to forgive him. Later on in the night, he managed to steer the conversation away from the past and toward the future. They talked about where they might buy a property together and he agreed when Sam suggested they should start looking soon. She was keen to find somewhere near her parents in Killiney. He tried to point out that they wouldn't be able to afford anything nice in the Killiney area, but didn't put up too much of an argument, as he was more eager to keep things amicable. A number of times during the night Sam reminded him of how disappointed she was and how things needed to change when they started living together. Most of these changes revolved around Matt spending less time in the pub with the lads and more time with her visiting restaurants, museums and theatres. Matt went along with everything she suggested. He was so keen to win back her love and avoid further conflict, he would pretty much agree to anything.

Colonic irrigation? No problem my dear.
Genital cuffing? It would be a pleasure.

"Helloooooo." Dave was calling to Matt from the adjoining sofa.

Matt shook himself out of his trance. "Sorry lad. What were you sayin?"

"What do you mean, you don't know?" asked Dave. "You must be back on talking terms?"

"Well yeah, but there seemed to be a lot more *negotiating* than talking going on. I spent most of the night conceding ground on things like where I'm gonna live, how much money I'm gonna spend and what I'm gonna do in my spare time."

"What does that mean?"

"Well, as she pointed out, not only do I go drinking with the lads three or four times a week and play football every Saturday, but now I've got a racehorse to follow. So she's saying that if things are to work out when we move in together I'll have to spend more time with her and less time with the boys."

"Well, that seems fair," said Dave. "In fact you're bloody well lucky! Your girlfriend wants to spend more time with you. Meanwhile I can hardly get any face time with mine!"

"You wanna swap?" joked Matt.

"Yeah, ok then," countered Dave, "but just for one night."

"Ha ha Massey! Forget about it. You wouldn't even last one night. She'd chew ye up and spit ye out."

"What's yer problem?" Asked Dave rubbing his inflated gut. "Are you afraid once she'd driven the Rolls Royce that she'd forget about her Mini Cooper."

"Ha! Rolls Royce? Bleedin' moon buggy more like it!"

"Anyway did ye say anything to her about the night out with myself and Kate?"

"Yeah, we can do it Saturday fortnight."

"Great, I'll call Kate and try to get her on board."

"On board what? The moon buggy?"

"Fuck off!"

"Sorry lad. So, are you still having trouble meeting up with her?"

"Yeah, it's a real pain in the arse! And I'm not one hundred percent sure about her excuse either."

"Whaddya mean?"

"Well she says she's spending all the time looking after her mum, but I know for a fact that her sister is at home at the moment as well."

"I seeeeeee...so what does that mean?"

"Well, it means her sister could look after her mum and she could spend some time with me."

"I figured that much out Einstein. I'm askin' you why that ain't happening?"

"I wish I knew," said Dave, shaking his head. "I can sense that she's holding back on me, but I can't figure out why."

"Well, maybe it's time to bring things to a head."

"Whaddya mean?"

"You know, put her on the spot. Ask her some tough questions."

"Yeah, maybe you're right."

Dave's mind started to drift. Bringing things to a head hadn't worked before and deep down, he knew if he put Kate on the spot, there'd be a good chance he'd lose her, but maybe Matt was right. Maybe it was time he found out whether they had the possibility of a real future together. Cricket as a sport, was designed to be a draw, but Dave was starting to see that a draw wasn't good enough. He would have to risk defeat in going for the victory.

*****

The following night all the lads were in *The Banner Man* to say goodbye to Michelle. At the end of the night Macker took her to one side and gave her a large rectangular amber ring.

"Wow! I love it," said Michelle sliding the ring onto her finger. "You shouldn't have."

"Ah, we had to get you something. You know, we've been coming to this pub for seven years and you're by far our favourite lounge girl."

"Well, thanks a million. Did you pick it out?"

"Yeah, I noticed you liked to wear oversized rings and I've seen you wear a really nice amber necklace once or twice, so I thought this might suit your taste."

"It does! It's perfect." Michelle was truly impressed with the gesture and particularly the thought that Macker had put into it. She leaned forward on her tippy-toes hugging him and kissing him on the cheek. For a split second Macker felt like he could fly. Her lips were silky soft and she smelt divine.

Damn! I'm gonna miss this girl! He thought.

"You take care down there Michelle," he said backing towards the door. "Remember what I said about the koala bears."

As Macker took in Michelle's beautiful young smile for the last time, it frightened him how much he cared for her. Even though she'd

131

only been working in *The Banner Man* for a few months, Macker felt like he knew her better than most of the girls he'd gone out with. It worried him that he was approaching his twenty-fifth birthday and he'd yet to be involved in anything approaching a serious relationship. He imagined himself lying on a psychiatrist's couch trying to explain away why most of his relationships didn't go the distance.

"What makes you think you may have problems with commitment Mr. McCann?"

"Well Doc, as soon as I start going out with a girl, I think I'm too busy looking for her faults to even notice her redeeming features."

"And why do you think that is?"

"I don't know. I think I'm just a bit of a perfectionist."

"A perfectionist tends to seek perfection in themselves, not in others."

"Ok smart arse! Why do you think I do it?"

"Maybe what we need to do is look at some examples of these so-called imperfections. Can you give me a recent case study?"

"Ok. I went out with this girl from work a couple of weeks ago. She was pretty cute, but she used to say the word "like" all the time. It drove me mad, so I dumped her halfway through our second date!"

"Does that not seem harsh to you?"

"Well, like, why don't you like, try to have a conversation like, with someone who keeps like, sticking in the word like, like all the time. Before long like, you start like, counting the number of times like, she says the word like, until like, you don't even like, hear the words in between like, all the likes."

"Ok, I see like, how that could be pretty like, annoying."

"And it got even worse when she started completing sentences with the word "like" followed by a strange sound."

"Like how?"

"She was saying things like, "when I saw them like, kissing in the corner, I was like euuughhh. And he like, followed me like, outside, giving it all like, blaa blaa blaa blaa blaaaaghhh. So I was like, duhhhhh whatever."

"And you lasted a whole date and a half with this woman?"

"Yep."

"Well that's not bad."

"Thanks Doc."

"No worries…Are there any girls who you feel you treated particularly harshly?"

"Well, maybe Sarah Lynch."

"And what was wrong with her?"

"Her ears were big and pointy."

"And apart from that?"

"Apart from that, she was fine. I really liked her."

"That's it? You dumped her, because her ears were too big?"

"Not just too big! They were fucking humungous, with big pointy tips!"

"Couldn't you overlook them?"

"Only if I had a step ladder."

"Ha ha, but you said yourself that maybe you were a bit harsh."

"Yeah, I could've given her a chance to do something about them. Y'know, plastic surgery maybe."

"Oh, I see. But the solution couldn't have involved you focussing more on her attractive features and less on her oversized ears?"

"Doc, you didn't see these things. They were the size of Peter Schmichael's hands!"

"Oh well, if they were too big, they were too big, I suppose."

"Thanks Doc. I knew you'd understand. This has been a very helpful session."

"Don't thank me. Thank yourself."

Chapter 17

Matt and Dave had planned every last detail of their double date with military precision. Matt's relationship with Sam was still reeling from it's recent troubles so he was keen for everything to go smoothly, but the meticulous preparation that they put into the date was really for Dave and Kate's benefit. Dave hadn't seen Kate in the three weeks since *Satan's Whiskers* first race. He was determined to make up for lost time and with that in mind, Matt helped him devise and formulate "Operation Bed Kate."

"Operation Bed Kate" was an elaborate campaign consisting of five strategic manoeuvres. Each manoeuvre had its own code name. In turn they would be known as "Appetize 'er," "Moisturize 'er," "Liquidize 'er," "Tenderize 'er" and "Gehinside 'er." Matt had wanted to code name the fifth manoeuvre "Sodomize 'er," but Dave overruled that on the basis of bad taste. They spent over an hour in their kitchen that Saturday afternoon redefining and perfecting the strategy. Unlike most military commanders they used beer cans and stale pieces of pizza crust to map out their manoeuvres. The greatest obstacle they had to overcome was Kate's sobriety. It was of paramount importance that they render Kate at least semi-drunk. If Kate didn't have too much to drink, there was a chance she would drive back to Kildare and the plan would be dead in the water. Dave had requested that Kate arrive to their flat at nineteen hundred hours as they had a restaurant booking at nineteen thirty. This early start would give them more than adequate drinking time. The restaurant was only a five-minute walk away, so if Kate arrived on time they would even have twenty-five minutes for a glass or two of wine, before departure. Dave had commandeered and stocked the fridge with six bottles of wine. Three white and three rose, all brands amenable to Kate's taste. They had chosen to eat in *The Vinegar Yard*. Matt and Dave were not particularly fond of this restaurant, but they both agreed it would help them with their line of attack. *The Vinegar Yard* was notorious for slow service and they reasoned that the slower the food was, the more they would drink. It was also a very dimly lit restaurant, which made it easier to covertly top-up wine glasses. Using the beer cans, stale pizza and a bottle of ketchup, Matt demonstrated the best way to top-up a persons wine glass without being detected. He pointed out that when you are sitting at a square table, such as they have in *The Vinegar Yard*, it is preferable if your target is seated in one of the two right hand seats. Someone sitting in a right hand seat is likely to spend more of their time looking left, away from their right-handed wine glass. The sniper then takes up his position opposite the target making sure to pour the wine with his left hand. This gives him the best chance of not being discovered. Another tactic is to move his own glass to the left side of the table to act as a decoy. It was decided that Dave would order the wine, ensuring that any wine bucket would be placed to his left. According to their calculations the estimated time of meal completion would be between twenty-one hundred and twenty-one thirty. Regardless of whether or not the target was sufficiently inebriated by this time, Matt and Dave agreed that Kate *herself* would deem any time before twenty-two hundred hours, too early to depart.

There were two pubs in the near vicinity of *The Vinegar Yard*. *Quaids* which closes at twenty-four hundred hours and tends to attract an older, quieter crowd or *The Cauldron* which stays open till 0 two hundred and is usually packed with young, heavy drinkers. The boys had done their reconnaissance and on the basis of comfort and easier access to the bar they had chosen Quaids as the venue to continue their offensive. It did not matter that Quaids closed early, as the next manoeuvre would be to get the girls back to their flat and open up a bottle or two of wine. There were two two-seater sofas in the lad's flat. That afternoon they studied the layout and moved them both into new strategic positions. They decided that for "Operation Bed Kate" to have the best chance of succeeding, Dave and Kate should share the first one, with Dave sitting to the right of Kate. That would leave Matt and Sam to share the second one. Matt would position himself on Sam's left. This would make him the closest person to the light switch, the kitchen and the coffee table. It now became Matt's responsibility to make sure the room was dimly lit and the wine glasses were full. He would also be in the ideal position to receive any hand signals that Dave sent to him from behind Kate's back. They agreed on four basic signals. The "thumb down" signal was to alert Matt that more wine was required. The "screwdriver" signal of twisting hand and wrist was to call for the lights to be dimmed further. The "OK" signal of thumb and index finger creating a circle denoted that everything was fine. And the "thumb up" signal indicated that it was time for Matt and Sam to go to bed and leave Dave to execute the final phase of the operation.

Dave's bedroom, which was to be the scene for the final push of "Operation Bed Kate," was an utter mess. That afternoon they gave it a complete makeover. All the clothes that were on the ground were thrown into the washing machine. His CDs, which were scattered all over the place, were put back in the rack. The bed linen was changed, the carpet was vacuumed and the windows and mirrors were polished. "There's still a problem," said Matt surveying Dave's newly tidied room.

"What's that?"

"The smell."

"What smell?"

"You can't smell that?"

Dave walked slowly around his room, sniffing high and low. "What does it smell like?"

"I dunno…it's a stale sort of B.O. kinda smokey stench. I can't believe you don't smell it!"

Dave was leaning over his bed, inhaling deeply. "I can't get it! Where's it coming from?"

"The whole room! You need to get your fucking nose checked lad! It smells like a big gang of sweaty tramps spent the night in here, farting and passing the duchie!"

"Really? Fuck! How am I gonna get rid of it?"

"Wait there." Matt went to find the scented plugs that Sam had bought for their flat. When he retuned Dave was frowning and still trying to locate the smell.

"Here," said Matt, throwing him a small package. "Plug in one of those…actually, fuck it, plug them all in. That should sort it out."

"Is it really that bad?" Dave was worried that he had lost his sense of smell.

"Put it this way. It smells pretty rank to *me* and women are *known* to have a far more acute sense of smell. While we're on the subject of odour, maybe you should lay off the smokes for the night as well."

"Are you serious?"

"Of course I'm serious. Do you think Kate enjoys the taste of Marlborough lights when you stick yer tongue down –"

"No, I mean about women having a better sense of smell?"

"Yeah. Did you not know that? It's a scientific fact. Sam can *actually* smell my farts before they've left my ass!"

Dave was down on his knees, inserting the second of these apparently odourless plugs into the wall socket. The thought of Sam chastising Matt for the mere contemplation of farting brought a smile to his face.

136

"And you think I should quit the ciggies?"

"A clean smelling room and a fresh breath would definitely increase the chances of success for our operation."

"Cool, now all I have to do is put on about six inches in height, lose about three stone in weight and grow a full head of hair in the next three hours."

"You said it. We'll start with five laps of the block."

"No I'm serious," said Dave, collapsing on to his bed. "What if this is all a waste of time? What if she just doesn't fancy me?"

Matt didn't know how to answer that question and wasn't particularly keen to try.

"What do you mean?"

"You know what I mean Matt. I've never had sex with anyone who even came close to being as good-looking as Kate."

Matt was stumped. He couldn't deny that he saw something of a gulf in the league of looks between Kate and Dave. While Kate was comfortably in the Premiership, challenging for a Champions League place, Dave was lurking the depths of the Vauxhall Conference. But now was *not* the time to be pointing *that* out to his friend. He briefly toyed with the idea of consoling Dave with the fact that lots of very beautiful women date rich ugly men, but then he remembered that Dave wasn't rich. In the end he came up with the sort of support and encouragement he thought Dave needed.

"Don't worry lad. Tonight's the night that changes. Tonight is, 'Revenge of the Fatties'."

"Well, maybe there's something else we could include in our plot that might help."

"What's that? Chloroform?"

"Very funny. No, I was thinkin' that whenever you get the chance, maybe you could try to make the conversation a bit more...y'know...racy."

"Racy? Whaddya mean?"

"Y'know...risqué...sexy."

"You want me to talk sexy?"

"Yeah...Not like phone sex or anything. Just try and steer the conversation towards y'know sexy sort of things."

"Oh, right...like what?"

"I don't know. I can't give you any specifics. But if at any time you think you could leave the impression that it's perfectly normal for a couple in their mid-twenties who have been going out with each other for three months, to be having sex, that would help."

"Ok, gotcha."

*****

"So, you guys must be looking forward to moving in together," said Kate.

Well, I'm looking forward to the increase in the amount of sex we'll have, thought Matt.

And the more he thought about it *that* was probably just the sort of thing that Dave wanted him to say. But unfortunately, he was chewing a large piece of steak and Sam got her response in ahead of him.

"Yeah, we are, but we've just started looking at places and everything seems ridiculously expensive."

Matt was tempted to point out that if they looked further a field than Killiney and Dalkey, they might find something larger than a garden shed that they could afford, but he let it go.

"What about you?" asked Sam. "Have you any plans to move back up to Dublin? Maybe you could move in with Dave?"

Dave's ears pricked up on hearing this. By innocently asking a question that he didn't have the balls to ask, Sam had suddenly become an unexpected ally. Unfortunately, the response was predictably disappointing.

"No, I'm gonna be staying in Kildare with my folks. My mum is still quite sick."

"Oh sorry...of course...no improvement then?"

Like most military campaigns "Operation Bed Kate" did not go entirely to plan. The "Appetize 'er" phase went quite smoothly, with Kate arriving on time and knocking back two glasses of wine. It was when they arrived at the restaurant for the "Moisturize 'er" manoeuvre, that they encountered their first hitch. As planned Dave and Matt unceremoniously sat down first, ensuring that they were seated in the two left-sided seats. Unfortunately, their partners decided to sit beside them and not opposite them as predicted. This meant that Matt was opposite Kate and in the best position to stealthily top-up her wine glass. He quickly adopted this role and ordered the wine, making sure that the waiter placed the wine bucket to his left. The next hitch came in the topic of conversation they had landed on. Instead of talking about sexy underwear and dirty weekends, they were listening to Kate tell them about her mother's debilitating illness. Dave was glad when the waiter interrupted to see if they would like dessert. The lads both ordered Irish Coffees and were encouraged when Kate followed suit. It was clear that Matt had done a pretty good job topping up her wine, as

Kate was definitely edging past the stage where she could drive. Half an hour later, they were standing by the bar in Quaids and the "Liquidize 'er" phase had commenced.

"Did you know myself and Dave are telepathic?" announced Matt proudly.

"What?"

"Yeah, look…I'll hold one, two, three or four fingers up behind my back and Dave will read my mind and tell you how many."

Matt put his hand behind his back and held up two fingers. Kate and Sam craned their necks around him to see his V-sign. Meanwhile Dave had his eyes closed tightly and was rubbing his temples. He finally opened his eyes, smiled at Matt and said "two."

"How'd ye do that?" asked Kate, suspecting foul play.

"We told ye…telepathy."

"Ok, do it again and this time I'll keep an eye on Matt."

"All right," said Matt, "but let's make it a bit more interesting." He bought two shots of Aftershock and the girls agreed that if Dave got it right again and they didn't spot any foul play that they would down the shots.

"Ok, ready," said Matt holding up four fingers. Sam was standing behind him, making sure that his fingers stayed out of Dave's view. Kate was keeping a watchful eye on his face to check for any telltale signals.

"No blinking or moving your eyes," she said harshly.

"What am I supposed to do with them?"

"Either close them or keep them on me."

"Ok then," smiled Matt, looking into Kate's eyes. Dave was a bit concerned to see this semi-flirting going on between his girlfriend and his best friend, but at least it meant that Kate's attention was distracted from where Matt was sending him the signal. Matt was holding his pint down by his side and Dave could clearly see that three of his fingers were wrapped around the front of the glass, while his thumb and little finger were hiding down around the bottom of it. He continued to rub his temples for effect.

"I'm starting to hear you now brother. Speak to me. Tell me how many fingers are you holding up behind your back? Ah, thank you. Dave opened his eyes and smiled. "Three".

"Three is right!" announced Sam.

"Wow! That's pretty impressive," said Kate knocking back her shot. "Do it again and I bet ye we'll suss it."

Six Aftershocks later both girls were drunk and they still hadn't figured out the telepathy trick. Sam was starting to feel sick and refused to drink any more shots. "Come on! Just tell us how you do it," she pleaded.

"I'm tellin' ye. There's no trickery to it," said Dave. "We've just known each other a very long time and we've developed mental telepathy."

"Poppycock!" said Kate in disgust. "It's definitely a trick."

"*Poppycock*?" laughed Matt. "You don't get much *poppycock* these days!"

"Not nearly enough," giggled Kate, stumbling slightly backwards.

Matt and Dave looked at each other and nodded. "Operation Bed Kate" appeared to be alive and well. Time to move back to their flat and proceed with the "Tenderize 'er" phase.

"Ok," said Matt, searching through the movie channels, '*Goodfellas*' or '*Steel Magnolias*'?"

"*Steel Magnolias,*" said Sam and Kate together. Twenty minutes later, both girls were asleep and the lads were watching *Joe Pesci* and *Robert DeNiro* kick the crap out of some guy who had been foolish enough to question whether or not they had the balls to kick the crap out of him. The lads hadn't allowed for the eventuality of Kate falling asleep on the sofa and there was confusion as to what was best thing to do. After several minutes of hand gestures and whispers they gave each other the thumbs up. As Matt was picking Sam up to carry her to his room, Kate stirred. She looked up at Dave, whose shoulder she had been using as a pillow. Dave smiled down on her beautiful face. He had been stroking and smelling her hair as she dozed and had felt a powerful combination of love and lust rising within.

"Sorry babes," said Kate, rubbing Dave's shoulder. "Those *Aftershocks* knocked me out."

"You're not the only one," whispered Matt, pushing past their sofa with Sam in his arms. "Good night."

Dave and Kate were now alone and they turned their attention back to the movie. *DeNiro, Pesci* and *Ray Liotta* were having a good laugh digging a grave for the guy they had just murdered.

"Do you wanna watch a bit of this or go to bed?" asked Dave.

"Eh…let's watch a bit of this," said Kate putting her head back on his shoulder.

By the time the next set of adverts came on she was asleep again.

Dave kept his eyes on the telly, while his brain wandered elsewhere. On the TV a very handsome clean-shaven man was water-skiing on a crisp clear lake. He seemed to be having the time of his life zig-zagging skilfully across the fresh wet surface and having a shave at the same time. Kate was sleeping softly with her head on Dave's belly and her hand on his thigh. Dave was still stroking her hair, slowly tracing his fingers around the back of her ear. Her hair was soft and silky, her neck smooth and warm. Her peaceful beauty contrasted sharply with the violent scenes that had returned to the telly, so he turned the volume off. He couldn't decide whether he wanted to carry her to bed and fall asleep with her in his arms or rip off her clothes and give the wall a good pounding with the headboard. Either way it was time to take his lovely girlfriend to bed. It felt like a crime even considering waking her from her peaceful cocoon. What would he say? He rehearsed the words in his head.

Kate, it's time for bed.

Wake up Kate. It's bedtime.

Kate, sweetheart, let's go to bed. Or maybe I should use Kitty? She likes when I call her that.

Kitty, sweetheart, let's go to bed. That sounds good. It's soft and gentle yet with an air of authority. Important to use the word "let's," rather than saying "it's time for bed," thus implying that it's a two-person activity. Ok ready, here goes. Wait, knock back that wine first, just to calm the nerves.

Dave pretended to be setting his alarm clock, as he watched Kate undress on the far side of the bed. She had her back turned to him and was quickly down to socks, bra and what appeared to be some sort of black lacy hot pants.

Holy shit! thought Dave.

Holy shit! Came a little voice from his boxer shorts. *What are you waitin' for dickhead? Get over there! She's gaggin' for it!*

Hey! You're the dickhead. You shut up and leave this to me!

Leave it to you? Oh great. What are we gonna do? Spend the night knitting cardigans?

Kate turned around. She looked absolutely spectacular. "Have you got a T-shirt or something I can wear?"

Fuck me dude! Check out the body on that! Booyaka Booyaka! Yeeeeeeeeehaaaaar! Azza gawna git me sarm lurvin tanide!

Dave was doing his best to ignore the little voice coming from below, but he was truly in awe of this sexy stunner in his bedroom. He could feel his hands starting to shake and his throat going dry. Looking at Kate's shapely figure had given him a screaming erection, so he didn't feel able to go and get her a T-shirt.

"Ahem...eh...try the second drawer behind you there," he croaked.

Dude! What are you doing giving her a T-shirt? Please don't fuck this up for us. If we don't get action tonight, I'm never speaking to you again!

"Second from the top or bottom?"

Top? Bottom? Honey, I don't care. Hows about a bit of both?

As Kate was putting on his black Guinness T-shirt, Dave decided to make his move. By the time her head popped out of the neck of the T-shirt, he was upon her. He planted his lips on hers and pulled her close by the waist. She was shocked at first, but then started kissing him back and put her arms his neck. Dave was pleased he'd managed to stay off the smokes for the night.

That's more like it Dude! Now don't give her a chance to change her mind. Grab that ass and squeeze it tight! Pull her right in and I'll show her what's on offer!

Dave did as he was told. He took a firm hold on Kate's ass and held her body tight against his erection.

Ok that's good! You're learning choirboy. Now, rip that T-shirt off her, throw her on the bed and bury your face in her panties!

That's my good Guinness T-shirt!

Just do it! I'll buy you a fucking new one!

Dave's hesitation was fatal. Kate was pulling out of the kiss, trying to loosen his vice-like grip.

"Sorry Dave," she whispered, withdrawing her head far enough to look into his eyes. "I'm really tired."

"NOOOOOOOOOOOOOOOOOOOOOOOOO!! You've got to be fucking kidding me! You must be the biggest loser in the world! That's it! I've had enough! You are such a fucking tosser! I want a new owner! I'm putting an ad in the paper. Wanted: New owner for underused and over-abused cock. Only applicants with balls need apply. You are a fucking disgrace to the whole of mankind! I must have done something really bad in a previous life to be sentenced to being attached to your disgusting body!

Dave lay awake for an hour staring at the back of Kate's head and trying to ignore the muffled voice that was still ranting from beneath the duvet.

Ok buddy. I'll give you one more chance. All might not be lost. Just move in a bit closer and I'll give her a bit of a nudge.

But Dave feared that all was, in fact, lost. His mind wandered back to the handsome young water skier who had been advertising shaving gel on the TV. He realised that he and the water skier, whose name was probably *Chad*, had a lot more in common than he'd first thought. Fair enough, with his amazingly square jaw and smooth skin and perfect hair and bronze tan and rock-hard pecks, Chad probably just about has the measure of him for looks. And given that Dave's only attempt at water skiing resulted in a minor hernia, Chad probably had the upper hand there too. What they did have in common was a lack of control over their own destiny. Yes, at first glance, Chad did appear to be in effortless control of his skilful movements, but the truth was that he was at the mercy of the person driving the boat. Without warning the driver of the boat had it in their power to make life very difficult for poor Chad. At the drop of a hat they could take Chad out to sea. If the mood caught them they could speed up, slow down or even stop. They could go in search of choppier water or stronger currents or if they got a bit bored of Chad's company they could just cut the rope. At the end of the day they could do what they dam well pleased and Chad would just have to live with the consequences. The driver of the boat calls all the shots and while giving somebody a tow with a rope and two planks of wood is an enjoyable novelty, it's a novelty that soon wears off. Chad was in no more control of his water skiing than Dave was in his relationship with Kate.

On the edge of the bed Kate lay awake with her eyes closed. Her mind was racing. She knew she couldn't have driven home, but it was a bad idea to be spending the night in Dave's bed. At least it forced her to come to terms with one clear fact. She didn't love Dave and probably never could. By getting involved in the relationship in the first place, she'd let her head overrule her heart. Going out with Dave was the comfortable and painless thing to do. She'd felt enough hurt from her previous relationships to make that combination quite enticing. She'd got herself into a situation where her downside was limited, but so too was her upside. She knew she could never feel the same sort of love for Dave that she had felt for her college sweetheart, Paul Hennessy. Kate realised that in matters of love the heart would always have the last word and while she was busy protecting her own, she had forgotten to consider Dave's. Now she recognised that she would be administering the same sort of pain to him that she had received in the past and she hated herself for it. She didn't sleep a wink that night. When Dave awoke, she kissed him softly on the cheek and proceeded to gently break up with him. This time she didn't spare him from the truth. Honesty was the least he deserved. Dave thought of the helpless water skier. He realised his own ski rope was been cut through and there was

143

nothing he could do about it. When Kate left he was holding an unattached rope, bobbing up and down, at sea...alone.

Chapter 18

Matt had a great night with Sam and felt they were finally putting the whole *Satan's Whiskers* trouble behind them, but the next morning he couldn't wait for her to leave, so he could find out how things had gone between Dave and Kate. He'd heard Kate leave at about seven that morning and couldn't wait to get the juicy details. After kissing Sam and closing the door behind her, he charged back up the stairs to the flat, taking them three at a time. Dave was sitting up in bed, staring at the wall and listening to his *Coldplay* CD. One look at his face told Matt that "Operation Bed Kate" hadn't been a success. He'd never seen his friend look so miserable.

"What happened bud?"

Dave kept his eyes on the wall. He took in a deep breath and let it out with a sigh. "She dumped me."

"Shit, I'm sorry lad. What went wrong? Things were looking promising when I went to bed?"

Dave was taking a long time to answer. He was going over and over the ten-minute chat he'd had with Kate that morning. On the stereo the lead singer was whining in a high pitch. *"Nobody said it was easy, oh it's such a shame for us to part. Nobody said it was easy, no one ever said it would be this hard."*

Dave exhaled and shrugged his shoulders. "At the end of the day...she didn't fancy me as much as I fancy her."

"Oh...right...is that what she said?"

"Pretty much," said Dave trying to manage a smile. "Well at least she stopped using her mum's illness as the excuse."

"Are you pissed off with her?"

Dave shook his head. "Nah, she was crying and kept saying sorry and that she didn't wanna hurt me, cos she'd been hurt before herself. In fact, if anything I think I love her even more now."

"What?"

"Yeah, I shoulda seen this coming really...actually...when I think about it, I probably did."

"So, is that it? It's over?"

Dave swallowed and nodded.

"You wanna go for a few beers?"

Dave smiled and looked at his bedside clock. "It's half eight in the morning."

"Yeah I know, but whatever you wanna do today to take your mind off it, just gimme a shout."

"I'll be all right."

"You sure?"

"Well, actually no. I'm gonna be pretty fuckin' miserable for a while, but eventually I'll be ok."

Matt started heading for the door, but stopped when he realised he hadn't fully satisfied his curiosity about the success of "Operation Bed Kate."

"So, should I take it that you didn't get the leg over then?"

"Unfortunately not."

"But she spent the night didn't she? Did she sleep in here?"

"Yep."

"Did you try anything?"

"Of course I did!   Jesus! You wanna see her in her bra and panties! She looked absolutely amazing. I swear…you wouldn't believe how sexy her body is!"

"So, you got a bit of action, but you didn't bone her."

"Pretty much," nodded Dave. "And it's a crying shame, cos I had a stiffy the size of a baseball bat the whole night."

*****

"Coming up to the fifth hurdle, and it's *Pink Powder* on the inside of *Hellovagame* followed closely by *Satan's Whiskers* then a gap back to *Badger Bill* and *The Hot Stepper*. *Pink Powder* and *Hellovagame* land together over that one. *Satan's Whiskers* catches the top of it and loses about a length on the leaders."

"Shit! He didn't get over that one very well."

"No, he's struggling a bit with his jumping."

"As they approach the next, it's *Pink Powder* and *Hellovagame* being rejoined by *Satan's Whiskers* with a slight gap to *The Hot Stepper*. They all get over that one safely and have opened up about a four or five length lead over the rest of the field.

"He's in there with a good chance again! Come on Satan!"

"Come on yeboyo!"

"Three fences left to jump now, and it's *Pink Powder* and *Hellovagame* being challenged by *Satan's Whiskers*. And here comes *The Hot Stepper* on the outside putting them all under pressure. *Pink Powder* and *Hellovagame* get over that one smoothly. Oh and there's a faller! *Satan's Whiskers* is down! *Satan's Whiskers* has taken a tumble and there are only three left in with a shout."

"FUCK! BOLLOCKS! SHITE!"

"Is he all right?"

Matt was peering through his binoculars. "Well Kevin looks all right…hold on…yeah…he's getting up…yeah he's up…he looks all right…he's shaking his head a bit."

"Not Kevin!" roared Macker. "The fuckin' horse!"

"I'm talkin' about the fuckin' horse! He's up, but I think he's hobbling…fuck…yeah…he definitely seems to be lame."

"SHITE! BOLLOCKS! FUCK!" Macker started to panic. He'd seen lame racehorses being put down before. A broken leg is all it could take. He could see that the jockey, Kevin Daly had now got a hold of "*Satan's Whiskers*" reigns, but the horse wasn't budging. Macker swallowed hard. "Please don't bring out the covers."

Shipsey frowned at Macker. "The covers? What are the covers?"

"Shut up Macker!" Matt shouted. "He's gonna be all right!"

"How do you know? That was a heavy fall. He coulda broken his leg."

Shipsey was starting to get annoyed that his question hadn't been answered.

"Will someone please tell me what the fucking covers are?"

"If they're putting a racehorse down, they erect a big partition around it, so the crowd won't see."

Matt could see the vets ambulance whizzing around the outside of the racecourse. He started to worry that Macker might be right. Maybe *Satan's Whiskers had* injured himself badly. He focussed the binoculars in as close as possible. The horse was standing up, but not moving. Kevin appeared to be examining the lower part of the horse's front left leg. The ambulance had stopped and two white-coated men were slowly approaching. When they arrived beside *Satan's Whiskers* Kevin took a few steps forward and pulled at the reigns. He was trying to see if the leg could take any weight. Surely this was a good sign. He wouldn't be doing that if he believed the leg was broken. But the horse wasn't budging. Kevin had his neck at full stretch, but *Satan's Whiskers* refused to move forward. Matt could see his front left leg was cocked and slightly off the ground.

"Oh bollocks. He's not walking. His front left leg is fucked."

The two white coats were now approaching the problem area to take a closer look. As they bent down, Kevin took a sharp pull on the reigns. *Satan's Whiskers* hobbled forward on to his left foot. He took two full strides and ended up in the same position, with his injured leg

147

cocked.

"Come on, let's get down there!"

On the way down to the track Kate took Matt to one side to find out why Dave hadn't come to the race that day. When they were breaking up, she had made Dave promise to stay friends and part of their agreement was that they would meet the following week at *Satan's Whiskers* second race. If Kate had known Dave wasn't going to show up, she wouldn't have come herself. She'd left her mum at home with her auntie Maeve who was visiting, but she knew her mum didn't like to be left alone with her dad's sister. Auntie Maeve was an ex-nun and had a habit of using quotes from the bible in every second sentence. To those who didn't know her, she was creepy and depressing. To those that were lucky enough to know her, she was just depressing. Matt told Kate that Dave was still very down in the dumps.

"He just wasn't up to it Kate. He said he needed to catch up on some work stuff, but he's been pretty miserable all week."

The thought of Dave moping around the flat with a broken heart made Kate feel terrible. "Does he hate me?"

"No, of course not. He's still crazy about you. It would probably be easier for him if he *did* hate you."

"Is he really that down?"

"Yeah, he's pretty bad. I've been trying to lift him, but with no success. He's even refusing alcohol."

"Do you think I should call him?"

"I don't know." Matt had to think about this one. Hearing Kate's voice on the other end of a phone might just lift Dave's spirits. Maybe it would help him realise that while Kate was no longer his girlfriend, she could still be a good friend. Or then again, it might just depress the hell out of him.

"Why don't you give me your number and when I get home I'll see how his mood is and I'll send you a text."

"Ok, thanks Matt. You're a good friend. Can I ask you another favour?"

"Sure."

"I asked Michael already, but he said you were driving. I was hoping you could drop me home after the last race? My dad drove us here and he always likes to go for a drink with Paddy, but I'm not really in the mood."

"No probs...We can go sooner if you want. I'm not really in the mood myself after seeing that fall."

"Yeah, I know. I hope he's ok."

By the time they reached the edge of the race track "*Satan's Whiskers*" was being gingerly loaded into the back of a horsebox. Paddy Mulryan was on the scene to fill them in on the details. The lower part of the horses leg was badly swollen, so it was difficult to tell exactly what was wrong.

"I don't think it's broken anyway," said Paddy rubbing the top of his forehead. "He's definitely done some damage to his coronet, but hopefully the rest is just bruising. They've injected him with a pain killer and are taking him for x-rays."

Kate closed the passenger door and put on her seatbelt, while Matt fiddled with the CD changer. There were still three races left so he had plenty of time to do the twenty-minute return trip to her house before picking up the other lads.

"So, am I the only one who doesn't know what a coronet is?" he asked, starting the car up.

"Oh good choice!" smiled Kate, recognising the guitar intro to *The Counting Crows* song *Round Here*. "Eh...the coronet is like a band of tough skin that joins the hoof to the foot, a bit like the quick on your finger."

"The quick?"

"Yeah,"said Kate, holding up her hand and pointing to her finger nail. "That little bit of skin that joins the nail to the finger."

"Oh right. I didn't know that had a name."

"Well you learn something new every day."

"Yeah, thanks to you I know all about the quick and the coronet."

"Actually, you haven't learned everything about the coronet."

"Oh? There's more?"

"Yeah, don't laugh, but I was watching this nature programme recently all...

"I love nature programmes," Matt interrupted.

"Me too. Well this one was all about sea horses."

"Ah, the famous sea horse. The only species of animal where the daddy has the babies."

"Exactly! Well in this programme, some old scientist guy had been studying sea horses for like a million years and he was particularly interested in the coronet. I bet ye don't know where the coronet is on a sea horse."

"Eh...his head?"

"That's right! Was that a guess?"

"Total fluke," laughed Matt.

149

"It's a small growth coming out of the top of his head," said Kate, gesturing with her hands.

"Don't tell me it's his todger!"

"No," Kate snorted, "that's the thing, you see! They didn't know what it was there for. But the study showed that down through the years it was getting bigger. So the scientist guy decided to study them in captivity to find out its purpose."

"Don't tell me, don't tell me. All the little daddy seahorses had given themselves big headaches from complaining about being pregnant all the time!"

"Ha ha, very funny."

"That *would* be funny. Imagine two seahorse blokes clinging onto a twig with their little tails, complaining about being up the duff! ...

"All right there Jeff?"

"Oh I tell ye Bill! Never again! As soon as I get this lot out of me, that's it. I've had enough! The missus is gonna have to get her tubes tied!"

"I hear ye Jeff! Look how badly swollen I am! I can't remember the last time I could see my tail! And her indoors couldn't care less. She's off galavantin' with yer man who lives two branches down!"

"Actually," laughed Kate, "I quite like that explanation! It's much better than the real one!"

"So, what is it?"

"It's a bit boring after all that, but it's to make them look bigger. The study showed that the males with the biggest coronets were chosen as sexual partners ahead of the others."

"Oh...right...I see."

"Yeah, they reckon that it fooled the females into believing that a bigger coronet meant a bigger pregnancy pouch and therefore a greater number of eggs could be deposited."

"Wow, that's amazing."

"Yeah it's pretty cool...Anyway," said Kate, pointing out the windscreen. "It's just another two minutes down here on the right. I'll tell ye when we get close."

"Ok...eh....listen Kate...I know you don't like talking about it. So, if you want me to shut up, just say so, but I thought it would be rude to drive you all the way back here and not ask about your mum."

"Oh, she's ok...actually, recently she's been pretty good, but still quite tired and weak."

"It must be tough. I was reading a bit about it on the internet...y'know...lupus."

"Yeah, it's tough for all of us really." Kate was impressed that

Matt had taken the time to find out about her mum's illness.

"So, what did the internet have to say about it?"

"Well…em…the main symptoms seem to be achy joints, high temperature and fatigue, but there can be lots more depending on which type you have. And…eh…there's medication you can take, but no cure yet."

"Ok, slow down a bit, it's just here on the right."

Matt pulled into the yard of an old grey country house.

Kate thanked him and started to get out of the car when she stopped and turned around. "Do you wanna come in for a cup of tea?"

"Nah, that's all right. I don't really drink tea."

"Okaaay," Kate said slowly, "Do you wanna meet my mum then?"

"Oh…sorry…yeah, all right. Are you sure it's ok?"

"Yeah, she likes meeting strangers, as long as it's one at a time."

As Kate was turning her key in the door, she turned to Matt and whispered, "don't get too freaked out by my auntie Maeve."

"Ok," whispered Matt, starting to get freaked out.

He was surprised to see that Kate's mum was not in bed, but sitting on the sofa watching TV.

"Hello Mrs McCann. Very nice to meet you," he said, gently shaking her hand. He had expected her to look older, but this woman was in pretty good shape and was no more than early to mid fifties. Probably about the same age his own mum would have been if she were still alive.

Kate's mum smiled up at him. She had the same kind blue eyes as Kate.

"Call me Eileen," she said. "The only one around here who calls me Mrs McCann is that Dr. Shields and he's a miserable beggar."

"Eileen, that's *my* mum's name too."

"Well, there you go. You shouldn't have any trouble remembering it."

"Matt, this is my Auntie Maeve."

Matt held out his hand to the old woman. "Hello." She was older than Kate's mum by a good ten years. She wore incredibly thick glasses, which gave her wide staring eyes.

She took Matt's hand limply. "God bless you."

"Thank you."

"God blesses those whose hearts are pure."

"Oh…I see…well hopefully that includes me."

"The lord is close to all who call on him sincerely."

"Right." Matt didn't like the way auntie Maeve was peering at him through her thick glasses. Her eyes started to squint and her eyebrows met in an angry V. Could she tell he hadn't been to mass in over ten years? Was she able to see that he didn't have a whole lot of time for God, after his mother was taken from him. He looked nervously at Kate, not knowing how to stop this onslaught of religious verbatim.

"Now Auntie Maeve," said Kate, trying to lend him a helping hand. "What does God tell us about strangers?"

"The Lord says, don't forget to be kind to strangers. For some who have done this have entertained angels without realizing it."

"There ye see," said Kate, chuckling and patting Matt on the arm. "This man could be an angel and we might not even know it!"

Kate's mum smiled and gestured for Matt to sit down. "Well you'd be the first angel this house has ever seen. So, how did my favourite horse get on? You know I won sixty euro on it the last time?"

"Well I hope you didn't have anything on him this time. He fell I'm afraid."

"Oh no! Is he all right?"

"We think he'll be ok, but he's gone for x-rays on his leg."

"Well, we'll say our prayers for him won't we Kate."

Kate's mum loved hearing about the horses her husband owned, but had a particular fondness for "*Satan's Whiskers*," because Kate was involved. She was delighted that Kate had something to interest her and get her out of the house every now and then. Since her illness she had grown closer than ever to Kate and would choose her company over anyone else's. She loved the chats they had and how Kate always managed to lift her spirits when she was having a bad day. But a lot of the time she felt guilty about taking up so much of her eldest daughter's time. When she felt up to being on her own, she always tried to encourage Kate to do her own thing.

"So, how have you been mum?" asked Kate, returning from the kitchen with a tray of teas and coffees and a glass of milk for Matt.

"Oh, I've been havin' a barrel of laughs, listening to Maeve's jokes and watching the goggle box...This programme's really good. Wait till ye see what this little fish does."

On the TV a very small fish was hovering just under the surface of a clear stretch of water. Six inches above the water was a tiny fly resting on a green twig. Suddenly and with deadly accuracy the little fish spat a big mouthful of water at the fly, knocking it clean off its perch. The poor fly spun in the air and dropped onto the water just above the fishe's head. Before the fly knew what was going on, the little fish had gulped him down for tea.

"Wow, that's amazing," said Matt.

"Yeah, cool," Kate agreed.

"Isn't it?" smiled Kate's mum. "Mind you, spitting wasn't really the done thing in my day. That fish would just have had to get that fly down some other way."

Ten minutes later Matt was at the front door saying goodbye to Kate.

"Your mum's lovely Kate."

"Yeah, I know…thanks."

"You're a lot like her."

"You think so."

"Yeah, definitely. Very friendly and a great sense of humour…and you've got her eyes. And then there's the whole nature programme thing."

Kate was always very proud to be compared to her mum who she saw as a beautiful, gentle, loving person. Recently, however, it had started to worry her a bit, because she'd found out how genetics can play a large part in the contraction of lupus. Dr Shields often seemed as concerned about Kate's health as her mum's. When Kate returned to the living room her mum had a very broad grin on her face.

"So who's he Kitty? Not the one you broke up with."

"No mum, that's one of his friends. He was just giving me a lift home."

"Just a friend then?" asked her mum, a little bit disappointed. She loved hearing updates on Kate's love life and hoped that at least one of her children would be kind enough to marry before God blew the whistle on her.

"Yes mum, just a friend…He has a girlfriend."

"I'm not surprised," Eileen smiled "he's a bit of a…what would you call him these days…a hunk!"

*****

"I'm tellin' ye the only way for him to get over her is to go out and pull someone else," said Macker.

"I don't have much experience in this particular field," admitted Shipsey. "but I reckon you're right."

On the way back to Dublin that evening Matt, Shipsey and Macker chatted about how they might lift Dave from his post-Kate depression. They were in agreement, that the best way for Dave to get over her was to get it on with someone else.

"But you know what he's like lads," said Matt. "He's never been

153

on the pull in his life! How he started going out with Kate in the first place is a mystery."

"If I remember correctly," said Macker, "I forced him into it by using the konch. Remember? We went on that double date."

"Oh yeah, maybe we could do something like that again."

By the time they'd got back to Dublin they'd come up with a plan. They coaxed Dave down to *The Banner Man* by refusing to tell him how *Satan's Whiskers* had got on unless he came for a pint. Matt sent Kate a text, suggesting that she leave it for a week or so before ringing Dave. When Dave arrived down the pub that night he walked straight into a trap.

"Lads I was lookin' for the konch earlier on," said Macker, shrugging his shoulders "but I couldn't find it anywhere."

"Are you sure you had it last?"

"Yeah, remember the day I had to light up all Dave's smokes."

"Ah well, if you've lost it, that's tough shit," said Shipsey.

"I have it somewhere. I just couldn't find it tonight. I'll just have to chose my victim some other way."

"Why don't we just play the numbers game for it?" offered Matt. "Last one out loses."

"All right then."

"What's the task?" Dave asked.

"I have a different one for each of ye. So I'll tell ye after we've done the numbers."

After a well-rehearsed game, Macker was dictating his task to a suspicious Dave.

"All right Davey son, next Saturday you and me are going on the pull in town. You're task is to either A Score or B Chat up a minimum of five birds."

Dave couldn't help but feel as if he'd been set up. He'd never been so clinically defeated in a game of numbers before.

"Why do I feel like I've been done up like a kipper?" frowned Dave. "What tasks did you have waiting for the other two?"

Macker had to think quickly. He hadn't bothered to prepare tasks for Matt and Shipsey, as the numbers game had been fixed so precisely.

"Eh…no I don't think I'll tell ye that. I'm saving them for a later date."

Dave was now convinced he'd been set up, but decided not to argue. He knew the lads had done it with his interests at heart. What good was he doing moping around the flat in his dressing gown? Maybe the only way for him to get over Kate was to get back in the game.

Chapter 19

"This is the bathroom." The estate agent stayed outside, as Matt and Samantha filed in for a closer inspection.

"Bloody hell!" whispered Matt. "That's pretty risky use of the word *room*." He turned around on the spot, admiring how the plumber had actually managed to install a bath, a sink and a toilet into such a small space.

"Forget swinging a cat, you'd have trouble swinging a tadpole in here!"

In 1976 Matt's parents bought a large four-bedroom house in Cabinteely for £15,000. When his mum died in 1998 the house was valued at £320,000. By 2003 it was worth close to 600,000 euro. Essentially anyone who had bought property in Ireland in the twentieth century, had either a little or a lot of equity, come 2003. Matt was worried about where things might go next. What happens when interest rates start rising from their all-time lows? What happens when new developments aren't sold out before completion? What happens when buy-to-letters start to panic because their rental incomes take a dive? What if a huge number of people no longer need to live close to Dublin City, because they can do their work from home? Between his and Sam's savings and the bonus he was due to get, they would have enough for the deposit on a property worth roughly 300,000 euro. Five or six years ago that sort of money could have got them quite a nice home anywhere in Dublin. But in 2003 on the south-side of Dublin, it didn't go very far. In the Killiney/Dalkey area it didn't go anywhere at all. It ran out of breath at a tiny one bedroom flat, with hollow walls and low ceilings. Still, the view wasn't bad if you're hobby was spotting JCB diggers and cement mixers. Matt and Sam were now inside the kitchen. The estate agent waited at the door, so as not to crowd the "room." Matt was becoming familiar with this trick. He hadn't had many dealings with estate agents, but he was beginning to find them a pretty detestable breed. This slick operator was no more than twenty-three years old and yet leaning against the doorframe, with his black folder under his arm he was attempting to give off the aura of a man who knew everything. Matt was really starting to dislike him.

"As you can see the kitchen is south-facing so it catches a lot of sun. The drawers and units are shaker and it's a granite style work top."

Matt eyed up the pimple-faced poser. He felt the overwhelming urge to slam one of the shaker drawers shut on the guy's hand and bang his head repeatedly off the granite style work top.

What the fuck is shaker you smug twat? Doesn't that just mean the knobs on the drawers are fucking metal and not wood! And granite style work top! Ask my bollocks! It's a piece of fucking chipboard with a speckled grey plastic coating, you greasy fuckwit! But thank you so much for pointing out that it's south facing! Is that supposed to make up for the fact that the fucking living room is facing north onto the main road! In a square flat there's a good chance that one of the poxy rooms will be south-facing! So brilliant! In this little cesspit it's the fucking kitchen! Now all we have to do is close the door, turn on the oven and make it into a fucking sauna!   Or, at least, that's what he wanted to say.

Instead he whispered to Sam. "At least my kitchen has enough room for a table and chairs!"

It was becoming apparent to Matt that, they would have to look further a field than Killiney and Dalkey if they wanted to buy anything half decent. He just hoped he could convince Sam to move that extra few miles away from her parents.

By six o'clock that Saturday Matt and Sam had seen nine flats and were completely exhausted. In the car, on the way back to Matt's flat, they were both glad they weren't going out that night.

"I think the second flat was about the best," said Sam, going through the property profiles on her lap. Matt was trying to cast his mind back to the second flat they had visited. He recognised it when Sam held up the profile with the photo on the front. Sam was right. That was probably the best flat they'd seen, but Matt didn't really want to encourage her as he still thought it was a long way away from being worth the 315,000 euro asking price.

"Yeah, but it was a good bit away from the DART Station. About a twenty minute walk."

"Yeah, that's true, I suppose," agreed Sam.

She wasn't fond of walking. Matt could see that she was pretty disappointed with the standard of property they could afford in the area around where her parents lived, but now was not the time to be sympathetic. Now was the time to drive the point home and make her agree that they should look at properties in less expensive areas.

"And the toilet was tiny, remember?"

"Yeah."

"I mean, if we invited Shipsey over, he'd have to take a crap outside on the street, 'cos he wouldn't fit into that jacks."

"Ok, I take your point. You don't have to be quite so graphic."

"Listen babes, how about I get some estate agents further south to send us details of what they have and we just compare them. I really think we're gonna have to look outside Killiney and Dalkey to find anything decent in our price range."

"Ok," sighed Sam, "but where are you talking about?"

"Well, we'll stick to what's on the DART line, so let's say, Shankill, Bray and Greystones."

*****

Dave's heart skipped a beat when he looked at the face of his ringing phone and saw Kate's name flashing on the screen. "Hello."

"Hi, it's Kate."

"Hi...how are you?"

"I'm fine. And you?"

"All right I suppose."

When they had been going out together it was usually Dave who called Kate, so he was quite surprised to be receiving a call from her two weeks after they'd broken up. Hearing her voice again brought back all sorts of emotions. A small part of him wanted to be angry with her for breaking his heart. But, in the main, he just felt love. He'd spent the last two weeks trying and failing to think of anything other than Kate. He'd ignored the advice of his friends who all said the key to getting over her lay somewhere between the bottom of a bottle and the arms of another woman. He'd made himself so miserable that he was actually looking forward to the ordeal of going for a night on the pull with Macker. He'd spent too much time lying on his bed, staring at the wall, listening to a string of lead singers telling him how badly love can hurt.

"I was a bit disappointed you didn't come to the race last weekend," said Kate.

Dave didn't know how to respond. Kate had made him promise to go to the race and he'd let her down, but he didn't feel up to seeing her so soon after the break up.

"You promised we'd stay friends," Kate pushed.

"Yeah, I know Kate. I'm sorry. Next race, I promise."

Dave had heard from Macker that due to his injury and the end of the season, *Satan's Whiskers* next race wouldn't be until at least September. This would give Dave a good three months to move on with his life or, at least, get Kate out of his head for more than ten minutes at a time.

"That's ok," said Kate, not wanting to push it too far. "Just don't do it again or I'll come round there and beat you up!"

"Ok boss," said Dave, relieved that the tone of the conversation had been lifted.

When Matt and Sam arrived back, Dave was still on the phone to Kate. Matt was knackered after all the property viewings and looking forward to a quiet night in with Sam. It suited him that Dave was heading into town with Macker. On the way home, they'd bought some chips and dips and rented two videos. He went to his room to get into his comfy shorts and T-shirt. He could hear Dave saying goodbye on the phone and a moment later knocking on his door.

"Come in lad…what's up?"

"That was Kate on the phone."

"Oh, right. How is she?"

"Fine," said Dave. A frown was starting to take over his face. "I hear you met her mother."

"Oh yeah, just for a few minutes…she's really sweet."

Dave was a bit annoyed. He'd gone out with Kate for three months without meeting her mother. Why did she invite Matt in to meet her? He didn't know what to say to Matt, so he just came out with it.

"I went out with Kate for three months and never met her mother."

Matt turned to Dave and nodded slowly. "Okay." He waited for the rest of Dave's point, but it didn't come. "Is that a problem?"

"It just doesn't seem fair. How come you got to meet her?"

"I dunno…Kate *did* say that she was feeling pretty well that day."

Dave didn't say anything. He couldn't quite pinpoint why he was pissed off, but he was. Matt stopped hanging up his clothes and looked at Dave who he could see wasn't happy. "Look Dave…did you ever give Kate a lift home?"

"Yeah…once."

"Well I presume *that* day, Kate didn't feel her mother was up to seeing a visitor,"

Dave remembered the night he drove Kate home. It was actually quite late when he dropped her off, so he couldn't really have any complaints for not being invited in.

"So what's her mum like?"

"Really nice. Great sense of humour and she's younger than I thought she'd be. No more than fifty-five I'd say. A bit frail maybe, but generally in pretty good nick."

"So she didn't seem particularly sick?"

"Not really, but I was only there for five minutes and as I said, Kate told me that she was going through one of her better spells."

"I see." Dave tapped Matt's door twice and left to get ready for his night on the town. He knew his reasons for being annoyed were pretty flimsy, but he was still annoyed. As he dressed in front of his mirror he was more determined than before to get Kate McCann out of his system.

*****

The atmosphere in the *The Endzone* nightclub was drenched with the smell of alcohol, sweat, and testosterone. Dave held firm to the bar to avoid being lifted away by the wave of passers by. Saturday was always its busiest night, but this particular Saturday in late June, when the students had finished their exams and the summer mood was kicking in, it was simply too crowded. From a hundred feet above, the packed nightclub must have look liked one giant moving organism. Dave's whole body was covered in a blanket of perspiration. He was sweating from areas he didn't think he could sweat from. His chin, his elbows, the back of his knees were drenched! *Well, at least I might lose some weight*, he thought, trying to cheer himself up. After pub crawling around the Temple Bar area for four hours, Macker came up with the idea of going to *The Endzone*. Situated below the *Touchdown* sports bar, *The Endzone* was well known as a no nonsense pulling joint. It was full of young single people, or at least people who were pretending to be single for the night. Speckled around the throbbing crowd were newly formed couples that didn't even know each other's names, but were more than happy to swap bodily fluids for the night. Suddenly, someone crashed into Dave's elbow. He managed to hold on to his pint glass, but most of the contents went up into the air and landed on the back of the girl in front of him.

"Oh for fuck sake!" It had taken him twenty minutes to order that drink! There weren't many things that angered him more than the sight of spilt alcohol. He turned to see what idiot had caused the commotion.

"Sorry chief," came a deep voice from about fifteen inches above the top of Dave's head.

Oh great, thought Dave, tilting his head upwards, *it's Arnold Schwarzenegger's big brother!* He briefly shook his head at the monstrous mutant, but quickly turned back towards the bar to avoid any real confrontation. The girl who his beer had landed on was now facing Dave and giving him filthy looks. She was shouting something at him, but was being drowned out by the echoing boom of *The Prodigy's* hit *Firestarter*. Dave tried to read her lips. He couldn't make out whether she was saying, "I'm the firestarter, twisted firestarter!" or "You're after soakin' me fuckin' back, you fat prick!" Dave was not enjoying his first visit to *The Endzone*. Here he was stuck between Yeti and the *Twisted Firestarter*, saturated in sweat, with only a dribble of beer left in his pint and all he could think of was Kate. As soon as Macker returned from the toilet, he was going to suggest they call it a night. As he tried to focus on his watch, a bead of sweat dived off the end of his nose and landed on its face. Macker had been gone for over half an hour.

Finally, Dave saw Macker's blonde hair making its way through the crowd.

Dave wanted nothing other than to go home and was happy to accept defeat in his konch task. Earlier on in the night he'd tried to chat up an American tourist while Macker chatted up her friend, but Dave never got far when chatting up girls. He felt he needed to know a girl before he made any attempt at pulling them. All five of his previous girlfriends he had met through work, college or other friends. The whole concept of going up to a strange girl with a view to sticking his tongue down her throat didn't rest easy with Dave.

"Grab your pint and follow me," Macker shouted into Dave's ear.

"Where the fuck have you been?"

"Just follow me."

"Come on, let's just head home. It's too fuckin' packed in here. I'm sweatin' like a jack rabbit at a bunny pageant."

"Don't worry. I've found somewhere nice and airy with seats and an endless supply of women."

"I told ye, I'm not goin' to *The Fly Trap*!"

The Fly Trap was the nearby lap-dancing club. The lads had passed in on their way to *The Endzone*. "It's too expensive Macker!"

"It's not *The Fly Trap*, Macker shouted. He scythed his way through the crowd until two minutes later they arrived outside the door to the ladies toilets. Macker stopped and smiled proudly at Dave.

Dave looked up at the Ladies sign. "You're fuckin' jokin! You've been in there for the last half hour?"

"Yup."

"You're fuckin' mad. I'm not goin' in there!"

"Come on. It's perfect. You wanna see the size of it! It's at least three times the size of the Gents! It's lovely and cool and there's even seats!"

"I can't believe you've already been in there!"

"Yeah, it was a genuine mistake actually," laughed Macker. "I just walked in behind some girl with a shaved head. I thought she was a bloke!"

"And did the girls not go ape shit?"

"One or two gave me funny looks, but most of them were quite nice. I've been chattin' to some honey from Donegal for the last half hour."

"It *would* be nice to get a bit of air, I suppose," Dave sighed.

Macker pushed through the door before he had a chance to change his mind.

As they were entering, a good-looking blonde was on her way out.

"Sorry guys," she said, putting on a fake smile and giving them an entirely unimpressed look, "this is the ladies."

Macker smiled back and winked, slowly looking the blonde up and down. "So I see," he exclaimed. "And what a beautiful young lady you are."

Dave watched in awe as the ice around the blonde's smile started to melt. He couldn't believe she was falling for such an obvious line.

There's hope yet, he thought, as he moved towards the chairs on the far side of the room. It was nice to be able to breathe and move freely again. The nightclub owners had obviously gone out of their way to keep the girls happy when they designed these plush toilets. Or maybe it was just that accessories like red carpet, pot pourri, chairs, hand creams, perfumes and space were wasted on men.

Why the hell would you need a chair in a toilet? Dave wondered.

"Oh, that's good," he sighed, nestling his backside into the red velvet upholstery.

"Comfortable?" asked a tall, thin girl who was drying her hands nearby.

"Yes, thanks," said Dave straightening up and trying not to sound too smart.

She smiled, threw her paper towels into the bin beside him and made her way towards the door, where Macker was still chatting to the good-looking blonde. Dave was starting to think that Macker was right. Maybe this wasn't such a mad idea. They had comfort and space and a conveyer belt of girls passing through. If ever he was going to have a chance to complete his konch task it was in here. Just then a chubby girl with short dark hair entered and started bounding straight towards him. She was wearing a very revealing belly top and a tight skirt that went well above the knee. Parts of her were threatening to escape the skimpy

161

outfit as she bounced across the red carpet. She was not Dave's type, but he decided to have a go at chatting her up anyway. As she got closer he realised that she wasn't walking straight for him, but for the two vending machines on the wall beside him. Dave looked at the contents of the machines to see if he could find inspiration for an opening line.

Let's see, condoms, chewing gum, mints, tampax, tights, and perfume. No nothing there.

The girl stopped in front of the vending machines and started rooting in her tiny purse for the correct change. She paused and frowned down at Dave, who was smiling up at her from his chair.

"Whad a you lookin' at?" she asked, in a gruff voice.

"Eh? I was just admiring your entrance."

The girl looked down at her white spandex skirt. "You were admirin me wha'?"

"No...I mean."

"Are you some sorta weirdo?"

"No...sorry...I was-"

"What the fuck are you doin' in here anyway?"

Think brain! Think fast!

"Eh...I'm just...eh...making sure the machines are fully stocked," Dave, tapped the side of one of the vending machines.

"Oh yeah? Well why are you sittin' on your fat arse then?"

Dave wasn't happy with the fat arse jibe. It was a bit below the belt coming from such a chubby antagonist, but he decided to let it slide.

"Just waitin' for my colleague with the key," he said, gesturing towards the door.

The girl turned around, only to see Macker snogging the face off the good-looking blonde.

"Has he dropped the key down her throat or somethin'?" The chubby girl shook her head and inserted some coins into the vending machine. Dave was sure she would be buying tampax.

"You and your buddy better get outa here or I'm tellin' the bouncers," she threatened. She collected her condoms from the bottom tray, smiled meanly at Dave and started bouncing back towards the exit. On her way out she bumped into a friend of hers. "Howye Trace?"

"All righ' Shaz?"

"Listen, watch out for the pervert over by the Johnnie machine."

"All righ', tanks."

Shaz was now looking over Trace's shoulder straight at Dave. For some reason Shaz looked a bit familiar.

"I'm just headin' out to the car park with...yer man...Shane!

162

Jaysis, I nearly forgot his name!"

Trace was giggling and showing Shaz her newly purchased packet of condoms.

"All righ'. Will you be long?"

"Hopefully about ten inches!"

The two girls started cackling loudly. Just then, Dave realised where he knew Shaz from. She was *The Twisted Firestarter* he had spilt his drink over! He sprang from his chair and started to panic. Without thinking, he darted into the nearest empty cubicle.

Dave didn't emerge from the cubicle for a good twenty minutes. This was long enough to convince himself that Shaz was gone and that Trace hadn't bothered to alert the bouncers to the male invasion of their toilet. His plan was to walk calmly, but swiftly from the ladies, keeping his head down to avoid eye contact. He would say goodnight to Macker on his way past and go straight outside and hopefully get the nightlink home. Unfortunately, he only made it halfway to the ladies exit, before he was stopped.

"Well, if it isn't David Massey!"

Dave knew who it was before he looked up. It was his old college girlfriend Helen Campbell.

"Howye Hells Bells!"

"What the hell are you doin' here?" frowned Helen.

"What…in the ladies toilets or in *The Endzone*?"

"Both."

"Well basically I'm in *The Endzone* cos I'm supposed to be on the pull and I'm in here cos it's too bloody packed outside!"

"Yeah, it's unbearable isn't it?"

"I was sweatin' like a hooded rapist!"

"You always did have a lovely turn of phrase," laughed Helen. "So, since when does Dave Massey go on the pull?"

"Since tonight."

"Oh? What's the occasion?"

Dave explained how he'd recently broken up with Kate and that his friends deemed it the best way for him to get over her. He even explained the intricacies of his konch task and how he was attempting to chat up a certain quota of women.

"So, how's it going so far?"

"Not great. The last one I tried to chat up thought I was some sort of weird pervert." Helen laughed. "You never were any good with the chat up lines."

"Thanks. That'll do wonders for the confidence."

Helen spotted Macker and the blonde girl canoodling in the corner. "I take it that's one of your pals."

"Yep."

"And you're supposed to be doing what he's doing?"

"Pretty much, but it's just not happening. I was about to head home actually."

Helen felt sorry for Dave. She had always had a soft spot for him and didn't like to see him so low. She decided to stick around and try to help him.

"Listen Dave, I personally think you're too decent and honest for the pulling game, but if you want, maybe I can help?"

"Oh yeah?," Dave smiled cheekily. "What have you got in mind?"

Helen smiled back. "Well, I'd say the key to chattin' a girl up is confidence and eye contact. Guys always worry too much about what to actually say and when it finally comes out it sounds totally corny. As long as you give her a few compliments and ask her some questions, what you say is pretty irrelevant."

"I see," Dave said, making sure to maintain eye contact. "I like your hair that way."

"Not bad," said Helen, pretending to bat her eyelids.

Dave nodded down at her feet. "Nice shoes as well."

"You like them? Are they not a bit tarty?"

Dave looked down at the shoes again. They were bright pink with high heels and straps going up her ankles. Yes they were pretty tarty and not the sort of thing she used to wear in university, but he still liked them. He smiled and shook his head, happy that he'd bumped into Helen again. They were friends before they started going out together and although they didn't see much of each other, they were still friends now.

"Now, the biggest thing you have to overcome is lack of confidence. If you go around chatting girls up and you don't have confidence, it makes you look desperate. And girls will run a mile from any guy who looks desperate."

"Ok…confidence…gotcha. How do I get that?"

"Well, that's where you might struggle a bit, unfortunately. Y'see some people have natural confidence, but you *don't*, which means any confidence you get will only come as a result of success. But the success will be difficult without some sort of confidence."

"So you're saying, I can't score without confidence and I can't get confidence unless I score?"

"Pretty much…I'm saying you shouldn't be in a place like *The*

Endzone. You're also way too honest to be in here."

"I thought honesty was a good thing?"

"Of course it is in a relationship. But if you're out on the pull it just gets in the way."

"Really?"

"Yeah...look...what does your friend do?"

Dave looked over at Macker who had the blonde pinned up against the wall. "He's in IT support."

"Right, now do ye reckon he told Claudia Schiffer over there that he's some sort of computer geek?"

"Probably not."

"Face it Dave. You're just too nice to be in this meat market. And you can take that as a compliment."

"What are you doing here then? You going out with anyone these days?"

"Good question. Officially, the answer is yes, but in my mind I've already broken up with the two-timing reject."

"I see. What happened?"

Helen explained how one of her friends had spotted her boyfriend in *The Endzone* with another girl the week before.

"So I figured what's good for the gander is good for the goose."

"So, you're here on the pull too?"

"I guess so."

"Any joy so far?"

"Nope."

"Maybe I can help," winked Dave. "Did I mention how sexy you look in that tight top?"

"That's pretty good Mr Massey!" Helen grinned and paused for a minute, while Dave did his best to keep eye contact. He couldn't quite read the expression on her face. She looked as if she was trying to decide whether to have a starter or skip straight to the main course.

"Ok, listen," she said finally, taking him by the hand. "This is not Helen and Dave getting back together. This is just a one night thing."

"Ok...great," nodded Dave. "What's the plan?"

Helen led him by the hand to the nearest empty cubicle. She pulled him inside, locked the door, sat down on the toilet seat and started to undo his belt. In seconds she had his trousers around his ankles and her hand around his stiffening cock. She slowly massaged his shaft in one hand and started to squeeze his balls with the other. Dave had almost forgotten just how good Helen's blow jobs were. She locked her wet lips around his member and started to slowly move her head up and down. Dave could feel her hot breath and her tongue swirling around the head of his cock. Helen loved the feeling of control she got when giving head. Her special gift was recognising when the man was on the brink and prolonging the ecstasy by adjusting her pace. With Dave she could always tell when he was about to come, because his breathing became very loud and his calf muscles started to spasm. She knew the excitement of getting a blowjob in a public toilet would probably be too much for him, so she kept a slow steady pace. Every now and then she withdrew him from her mouth and looked up at his face, while slowly tracing her tongue along his firm length. Dave had his eyes shut tight and was trying to control his breathing. Suddenly Helen tightened her grip around the base of his shaft and started to quicken the pace, taking him deeper and deeper into her mouth.

Macker was about to leave the ladies with the good-looking blonde when he realised Dave had gone missing. There was a strange noise coming from one of the cubicles. It sounded like a deep-sea diver had just come up for air to be greeted by the Boston strangler. Macker's curiosity got the better of him and he bent down to take a peek under the cubicle door. He saw a pair of black slacks resting on the back of two hairy calves. Suddenly the muscles in the calves started to twitch and the noises reached a crescendo. The owner of the calves was now on his tippy toes and between his feet Macker could see a strappy pair of high-heeled pink shoes. *Nice one my son!*

Chapter 20

Matt looked at Dave as if he'd asked him to spend the day hot air ballooning over O'Connell Street. "You what?"

"You heard me," said Dave, not looking up from his bowl of cereal.

"Are you serious?"

"Yep."

"What brought this on?"

"I just think it's time."

Matt had noticed that there was something different about Dave that morning. He couldn't quite put his finger on what had changed, but the post-Kate depression certainly seemed to have eased.

"Are you still pissed or something?"

"No. Why?"

"There's something strange going on with you."

"Whaddya mean?"

"I don't know. There's something very un-Dave-like about you this morning. What happened last night?"

"Ahh, not much really."

"I think I'm gonna have to play my bullshit card on that. Something definitely happened. Did ye get yer leg over?"

"Not exactly...I bumped into Helen."

"Helen Campbell?"

"Yeah."

"I knew it! I knew there was something going on!So did she give you a Helen special?"

"What's a Helen special?" asked Dave, pretending not to comprehend.

"Eh...hellooooo?" Matt picked up a bottle of Heinz ketchup and started to deep throat it. "Does this ring any bells?"

Dave couldn't hold back a smile, but at the same time was a bit disappointed that all Helen ever got credit for was giving great blowjobs. Of course, this was mainly *his* fault. He was the one that used to describe them to Matt in graphic detail when he and Helen were dating. But last night was different. After the incident in the cubicle, he walked Helen home. They walked and talked fondly to each other for forty-five minutes. Then he went into her flat and they sat and talked for

167

another hour and a half. It was as if they were rediscovering each other. Helen had a way of making him feel good about himself and it wasn't just the oral sex. Dave looked up at Matt going to work on the ketchup bottle.

"All right, all right! I got a Helen special! But there's a lot more to it than that!"

"Really?"

"Yeah…I mean we had a really great night together. We got on better than when we were going out. I'm telling' ye, she knows me better than I know myself. She really made me see that I need to take control of my life a bit more."

"Take control of your life?"

Matt was delighted that his friend had found the perfect antidote to lift him from his depression, but a bit worried that Dave was going overboard.

" And t*his* is your idea of taking control of your life?"

"Yeah. It's one of a few changes I plan to make. I'm also gonna try to give up the smokes and go on a diet. I may even try to cut back on the beer."

"Holy shit! When Helen sucks dick, she sucks dick good! So are you two going out with each other again?"

"Nah, we're just friends, but we'll probably stay in touch with each other a bit more." Dave neglected to tell Matt that he asked Helen out three times the previous night, but she turned him down. He failed to realise that the chances of her saying yes were greatly reduced by the fact that he'd spent most of the night banging on about Kate.

"So, are you gonna do it or not?" asked Dave, looking up from his bowl of cereal.

"Why do *I* have to do it? Can you not just do it yourself?"

"Nah, I'd probably only make a balls of it."

"What if *I* make a balls of it? Then it's *my* fault!"

"Don't worry about it. You won't fuck it up. And if you do, I won't blame you."

"You promise?"

"Yep."

Matt hesitated. "Are you sure you're not still pissed?"

"Positive."

"Ok, fuck it, I'll do it. But I want a written guarantee that you won't blame me if it goes wrong."

He went and got a pen and piece of paper and placed them in front of Dave.

"What do you want me to write?"

"I, Dave Massey do solemnly swear that I will not hold Matt Cullen in any way responsible for any mishaps that may occur during the shaving of my head."

Dave scribbled it down fast. "Ok…there you go."

"Have you signed it?"

"Yep."

"Right, I'll go get the clippers."

Halfway through his haircut, Dave's mobile phone rang. It was Macker.

"All right stud?"

"Howye lad."

"Good night last night then?"

"Yeah, I suppose it was in the end."

"*You suppose it was!*," mocked Macker. "The last I saw of you, you were getting' yer fuckin' langer chewed off in one of the cubicles! I thought you were gonna have a bleedin' heart attack with the noise comin' out of ye!"

When Matt realised it was Macker on the phone he snatched it off Dave.

"Howye Mack! Listen, what the hell did ye do to my boy last night? He's woken up a different man this morning!"

"In what way?"

"Well, at the moment, I'm shaving his head and then he's talking about going on a diet, quittin' smoking and doin' exercise!"

"Seriously?"

"Yeah, it's like someone replaced him with a U.S. Marine!"

"Well, I'd love to take the credit for it, but I think it's probably down to that bird that sucked him off in the ladies toilets."

Matt looked at Dave in amazement. He'd assumed the action had taken place in Helen's flat. "The ladies toilets!"

Dave took the phone back off Matt. "Macker, how'd ye get on with that blonde?"

"Not bad. Guess where she was from?"

"Where?"

"Blackpool. She was over with her mates for the weekend."

"So did she take you back to her hotel?"

"Yep."

"Nice one!"

"I told ye going into the ladies was a good idea. Anyway, listen, I have to run. I was just ringin' to make sure you hadn't been strangled.

I'll seeya later."

"Right then, seeya. Oh hold on! Quick question for ye."

"What?"

"What did ye tell her ye do?"

"What?"

"The blonde. Did ye tell her you work in IT?"

"Not quite."

"What then?"

"I told her I was a Formula 3 racing driver."

Macker was starving. He jogged downstairs to knock himself up a good hearty fry-up. Just as his sausages were starting to sizzle, his sister Sinead and her boyfriend Frank walked in. They'd returned form their walk to the local newsagents with a litre of milk and the Sunday newspaper. Chit-chat was kept to a minimum.

"Good night last night?"

"Yeah...you?"

"Yeah...not bad."

Macker watched as they divided up the newspaper. Main section and business for Frank. Reviews, fashion and gossip for Sinead. Thankfully Macker was able to settle down for his breakfast with the sports section. But he wasn't really reading it. He spent more of his time watching his sister and her boyfriend of six years. Frank was standing by the toaster, while Sinead was getting their mugs ready for the boiling kettle. She took down the largest mug for Frank and poured a drop of milk into it. The toaster popped up and Frank took two of the four lightly toasted pieces of bread from it, before pressing the toaster back down. Sinead poured the boiling water into her own slim mug, which contained a tea bag. After vigorous stirring, she removed the tea bag and deposited it into Frank's mug. She then filled it to about three quarters of the way before adding another drop of milk. Frank popped the toaster and removed two dark pieces of toast. He placed them on the breadboard beside his own jam laden toast and lightly covered them in Slimline Flora. Not a word was spoken throughout this whole process. But through occasional eye contact and gentle touching an air of comfort and satisfaction permeated. It was as if they'd taken a vow of silence just to prove how stable their relationship was.

Macker started to wonder if he'd ever get to that stage in a relationship. Would he ever reach the point where he knew exactly how his girlfriend took her tea or her toast? He'd always looked at Sinead and Franks's relationship as boring and lifeless, but he was starting to see that there were certain comforts to be had from knowing your partner so well. It must be nice to feel as relaxed in someone else's company as your own. Comfortable enough to just shut up and not worry about what to say next or what the other person might be thinking. Macker's relationships were always dead and buried long before this stage was reached. He was happy to stick around while the excitement lasted, but as soon as it ran out, he was on his bike. The moment it looked like a bit of effort might be required, Macker would give up and go in search of that initial buzz again. Last night was the perfect example. Sure, the Blackpool girl was good looking, but what he found most appealing about her was the fact that she was only in Dublin for the weekend. There would be no opportunity for anything between them to become, messy or boring. In any of his relationships that did last longer, he was an expert at coming up with excuses to head for the door as soon as the initial spark started to fade.

She lives too far away or she's a little older than me or her ears are too big.

As he munched through the last mouthful of his fry, he made a pact with himself that the next time he was in a relationship that began to require a bit of effort on his behalf, he would roll his sleeves up and get stuck in.

Chapter 21

Dave's hairline wasn't the only move that took place that summer. His waistline moved down from a stretched 38 to a comfortable 36. In late august Matt moved out of the flat and in with Sam. The following week Macker moved out of his parent's house and in with Dave. *Satan's Whiskers* moved off the injured list back towards full health and was only a month away from his next race. And in the meantime Shipsey moved from being a casual user of pornography to being a serial user.

"Does anyone want to buy any pornos?" asked Shipsey, taking his seat in *The Banner Man*.

"You what?"

"Pornos…y'know…mucky movies…filthy flicks…"

"Is that what's in the bag?" asked Matt, pointing at a large sports bag beside Shipsey's chair.

"Yep."

"Holy shit! How many do you have?"

"Thirty two."

"Where the fuck did ye get them?"

"Ah y'know…few here…few there."

"So they're all yours!"

"Yeah, but I'm lookin' to shift some of them."

"I didn't know you'd branched out from the car selling trade to the pedalling moody videos trade," laughed Matt. "All along we thought you were Boycie, now we realise you're Del Boy!"

Macker had his head down the side of the table and was peering into Shipsey's goody bag. "For fuck sake bigfella! What are you doing with so many of them?"

"Ah…y'know…the collection just builds up over the years. And then this guy from work gave me a whole load when he was moving to the States."

This was a lie, but Shipsey wasn't about to tell them that he had built up a collection of forty-two dodgy videos on his own over the last three months. After his stressful shopping visit to HMV, he'd found an easier way to satisfy his dependency. On an almost weekly basis he started sending away for videos advertised at the back of dirty magazines. It wasn't until the end of august that Jane realised just how many he had. This left her in a bit of a dilemma. On the one hand she was happy that they're sex life had improved immensely and they weren't fighting nearly as much, but on the other hand there was the worry that her boyfriend was turning into a pervert. She decided to set down three basic ground rules. Firstly, he had to keep his collection to under ten videos. Secondly, every other time they had sex had to be without the aid of video. And lastly, if there was a video on while they were having sex, he wasn't allowed look at the screen when he was climaxing.

Shipsey picked up the bag and plonked it on the table. "So, who wants some?"

"I'll take a few off your hands," Macker offered.

"Good man. How many do you want?"

"I dunno…five?"

"Right, I tell ye what. I'll give you five for a score or you can have ten for thirty euro." Shipsey had to get rid of all thirty-two to bring his private collection back within the regulatory ten, but he wanted to make some money at the same time.

Macker looked at Dave. "Whaddya reckon my follically challenged flatmate? You wanna go halves on ten for thirty euro?"

It had taken the lads the whole summer to get used to Dave's shaved scalp and more slimline look. He had lost a stone and a half over the previous two months, by eating healthier and cycling to work three times a week. He'd also invested in a few loose weights and was starting to beef up a bit. He'd cut right back on the cigarettes too and generally only smoked after a few drinks. All in all he was a much healthier, happier and more confident man than when Kate had broken up with him, but he still thought about her all the time. Perhaps an overdose of pornography might take his mind off her for a while, but he fancied haggling Shipsey down a bit. He pursed his lips and started to move his head from side to side.

"I dunno, thirty sounds a bit steep to me. I reckon ten for a score sounds a bit more like it."

"I tell ye what," said Shipsey. "I'll give you twenty for thirty euro! Now, it doesn't get much better than that!"

"What are we supposed to do with twenty of them?" argued Dave "Open up a fuckin' library?"

"You'd be amazed how quickly you go through them," smiled Shipsey. "What about you Cullen? How many will I put you down for?"

"Eh…let's see," Matt mused. "How about zero."

"Come on! It would be a great house-warming gift for the new gaff."

"Nah, I think I'll pass. Sam would have my balls in a sling if I arrived home with a bunch of pornos."

"Actually," Shipsey chuckled, "there's a guy in one of them who does have his balls in a sling. It doesn't look all that bad really."

As it happens, Matt's sex life was in no need of spicing up. He and Sam had just moved in together and they were thoroughly enjoying their newfound freedom. By the end of the first week they had christened every room in their new house apart from the bathroom. It took two months of searching before they agreed on a property to buy. Sam had not wanted to move far from Killiney, where she grew up, but Matt wasn't happy with the size of flat they could afford in that area and was keen to look elsewhere. In the end, a small townhouse came on to the market in Killiney that helped them meet somewhere in the middle. It was in the right locality for Sam and it was big enough to satisfy Matt. The drawback was that the house was in pretty poor condition and would require plenty of work. Matt's father offered to help with the painting and decorating, while Sam's father lent them some money to repair the roof, before they moved in.

"So how's the gaff?" Dave asked Matt. "Has the roof fallen in yet?"

"No, we've got the roof sorted. Still a load of painting and shit to do and eventually we'll probably have to get a new kitchen...and bathroom maybe."

"And how's cohabiting working out?" asked Shipsey. "You had a shag in every room yet?"

"Yep...well actually...we haven't done it in the bathroom yet, cos there's a weird smell in there, so we did it twice in the kitchen to make up for that."

"Ah...sex in the kitchen," sighed Shipsey. "I remember it well. Mysef and Janie even had sex in the back garden when we moved in together."

"Really?" Matt was trying to figure out if he could match that feat, without being seen by the neighbours.

"Yeah, it's like marking your own territory I suppose...but the novelty soon wears off. Give me a comfy bed any day."

"A comfy bed and a dirty video y'mean," said Macker, getting up to go to the toilet.

When Macker was out of sight Matt leaned closer in to the table.

"So tell us Dave," he whispered. "What's it like livin' with

Macker?"

"Ah, it's all right I suppose…I mean…nah…yeah…it's fine."

"What?" asked Matt, sensing that Dave was about to say more.

"Nah…it's nothing."

Shipsey was also getting the notion that Dave was holding back and leaned closer in to the table. "Come on Davey lad, tell us."

"Ah, it's nothing really." Dave was trying to soften the blow of betrayel he was landing on his new flatmate. "It's just that his bird is a bit…loud…y'know… in bed."

"Who? Laura? I didn't even know he was still going out with her," said Matt.

Shipsey wasn't interested in her name. He wanted to find out the finer details before Macker arrived back from the toilet.

"Hold on…what do you mean by loud? Is that…like…moaning or screaming?"

"More screaming really…and a bit of shouting."

"Shouting?"

"Yeah…a bit."

"Shouting what?"

"I dunno…different things."

"Come on tell us…is it like…encouragement or instructions?"

"Whaddya mean?" Dave was stalling for time in the hope that Macker would return.

"Well is she saying "Yes, yes oh God yes!" or "Come on! Harder! Faster!"

"You've definitely been watching too many of those dodgy videos," said Dave, relieved to see Macker returning from the gents.

There was a moment's silence when Macker arrived back to the table during which the other three lads exchanged grins. As usual it was Shipsey who broke the hush.

"So Macker…How's "Loud Laura"?"

Macker looked accusingly at Dave who was admiring the paintwork on the ceiling. He decided to ignore the "loud" comment. "She's fine…not a bother."

"I hear the sex is pretty good."

"Yep, not bad at all." Macker was refusing to take the bait.

"I heard that from my uncle in Donegal!" said Shipsey, unable to hold in the laughter.

"Ha ha." Macker had promised himself to start taking his relationships more seriously and work harder at them and therefore wasn't about to join in the joke. In any case, he found Laura's vocal approach to sex, quite a turn on. It was just a shame there was somebody in the next room.

Laura Dillon worked on the fourth floor of Macker's building and he had fancied her for ages. She was a very pretty, outgoing twenty-two year old who had worked in the telesales department for three years. Macker knew her quite well and immediately became excited when he heard that she split up with her boyfriend. Within a couple of weeks, they had started dating and everything was going really well. There was just one slight predicament. Three weeks before Laura and her boyfriend broke up they paid their final deposit on a holiday to Portugal. Neither of them could get their money back and Laura was very restricted as to when she could take her two weeks. She decided she was going on the trip and spent most of July and August trying to convince her ex to pull out. When it got to two weeks from the holiday and her ex was standing firm, she decided she'd have to tell Macker.

Macker was gutted and didn't know what to do. He knew he was unlikely to get any sympathetic advice from the lads, but then again it couldn't do any harm. In any case, it might just distract their attention away from the noisy sex issue.

"Actually lads," Macker cleared his throat, hoping he could induce a more solemn atmosphere. "There is one slight problem...y'know...between Laura and me."

The clearing of the throat had worked. There was about two seconds of grave silence before Matt spoke. "Don't tell me you got her up the duff?"

"No." Macker waited for any remaining guesses.

"She's wondering why you're not driving Formula 1 cars every weekend?" Dave offered.

"No, but not bad."

"You can't afford to soundproof your room?" Shipsey asked.

"Ok, very good. Are we all done?" Macker asked in a serious tone. The lads hadn't seen this staid version of Macker before and took it as their queue to shut up and listen. When he'd finished explaining his quandary to them, Matt was the first to speak. "Can you not just take yer man's place?"

"No the ticket is non transferable and I don't think I could get the time off work anyway."

"When is the holiday and how many are going?"

"It's next Saturday. There's six of them. Two couples and Laura and her ex. The two couples have agreed that each of them will spend a

176

week in different rooms."

"What does that mean?" asked Matt.

"What do you think it means?"

"I don't know! It could mean there's a fuckin' orgy going on!"

"It means," Macker asserted. "For the first go, one of her girlfriends sleeps with Laura while *her* boyfriend sleeps with Laura's ex. On the second week the first couple switches with the second."

Matt frowned at Dave and Shipsey who also looked confused. "Well, I'm glad that's cleared up!"

Macker could tell he hadn't done a good job explaining the bedroom arrangements. "Look!" he said, shaking his head and reaching for some beermats to use as visual aids. "There's three rooms right?"

"Right."

"Laura stays in this one for the whole two weeks. For the first week she shares it with female friend number one, let's call her *Heineken*. Which means *Heineken's* boyfriend will be staying with Laura's ex." Macker reached for Dave's cigarettes. "We'll call him *John Player* which is handy cos his name *is* John."

"Hold on," Shipsey interrupted. *John Player* is *Heineken's* boyfriend or Laura's ex?"

Macker wasn't sure if Shipsey was really struggling to follow or was taking the piss, but he was starting to lose his Patience. *John Player* is Laura's ex!"

"And," said Shipsey, pausing and raising his index finger. "Laura's ex's name is *actually* John."

"YES! And I'm conveniently representing him in my fucking diagram with a box of John fucking Player!"

"Ok." Shipsey decided to swallow the obvious next jibe.

"Right," said Macker regaining his composure and placing his finger on top of the box of *John Player*. "He stays put in room number two for the whole two weeks. Now in the second week *Heineken* and her boyfriend switch with the couple who had been sleeping in room three." Macker picked up a *Bulmers* beermat. "Ok, so the third girl *Bulmers* switches with *Heineken* and stays with Laura, while *Bulmer's* boyfriend keeps "John Player" company. Now *Heineken* is reunited with her boyfriend in room three." Macker nodded his head contentedly and sat back in his chair. "Any questions?"

Shipsey raised his hand. "What if John the Player fancies a *Snake bite*?"

Macker ignored Shipsey. "Any *serious* questions?"

Matt raised his hand. "Are they double rooms or twin rooms?"

"I'm pretty sure they're twin rooms."

"Pretty sure?"

"Yeah, pretty sure, but as I've explained, it doesn't really make a difference."

"Well it makes a difference to "John the Player." He could be sharing a bed with two of his best mates!"

Macker was getting fed up. "Look! Your concern should not be for John the fucking Player! It should be for "Macker the fucking chump who drinks with you muppets! So if you haven't got any sensible questions or advice, then let's just drop it!"

"All right lad, calm down," said Matt. "How long did Laura go out with this guy for?"

"They broke up in June after going out for two years."

"Ok, and who broke up with who and why?"

"She said she broke up with *him* cos he was too immature."

"So hold on a second," Shipsey interrupted. "She chose *you* as the mature one?"

"Yeah, I know…funny isn't it. I think she just assumed cos I'm older that I'm automatically more mature."

"Right...ok." Matt was getting back to his line of questioning. "Now, is "John the Player" involved in a new relationship?"

"How the fuck would I know!"

"Ok…let's assume he isn't," Matt continued. He looked into mid air before asking his next question. "Have you ever met John the Player?"

"No."

"Ever seen any photos of him?"

Macker exhaled deeply. "Noooo."

"Are you sure?"

"Yes I'm fucking sure! She's hardly going to carry his photo around is she?"

"No, but you may have seen one at her place. They *did* go out with each other for two years."

"No, I haven't seen one! I haven't even been to her place! I don't know what he looks like and I couldn't give a shit! What difference does it make anyway?"

"It's all relevant," said Matt, logging the information in his memory bank. "Now this is important."

Macker folded his arms and slumped back in his chair with the realisation that Matt's inquiry was going to be thorough.

"Is Laura still in touch with John the Player?"

"As far as I know she's only been in touch with him over the phone trying to get him to pull out of the holiday."

"Ok...and have you been in her vicinity when she's been making these calls?"

"No."

"Right...interesting," Matt murmured..."How close is *John Player* to *Heineken* and *Bulmers*?"

Macker scrunched up his face and looked in bewilderment at the box of cigarettes and the beermats "What?"

"I'm trying to find out is John the Player closer to *Heineken* and *Bulmers* than Laura is...or is he just mates with the lads?" Matt made a little chopping movement with his right hand. "Y'know...what's the group dynamic?"

"Oh for fuck sake Matt! Where are you going with all this shit?"

"I'm just trying to gather as much info as possible before I come to a conclusion."

"Ok, well as far as I know Heineken's boyfriend is John's best mate and Bulmers is Laura's best mate."

"Is that Bulmers as in the girl........or *Bulmers'* as in the boyfriend belonging to Bulmers?"

"Right...fuck it...that's it!!" Macker threw the "Bulmers" beermat up into the air. "Forget about it! Let's talk about something else!"

"Relax Macker," said Matt, showing him his two palms. "I'm nearly finished."

"No...fuck it! I don't care! No more questions. Either skip straight to the advice or I'm goin' home."

"*Advice?* You wanted *advice*? I thought you just wanted odds on the likelihood of Laura shagging John the Player.

Matt could see that Macker was ready to follow though on his threat to go home. "Nah relax, I'm just kidding...I've taken everything into account and I honestly think there's absolutely fuck all you can do."

Macker folded his arms in disgust and moved his head from side to side.

"Oh! Well, that's just fuckin' brilliant! We go through all that shit and you tell me there's nothing I can do!"

"Well, what were you thinking of doing?" Matt countered. "Bribing the guy not to go on the holiday?"

"Yeah...why not?"

Matt shook his head slowly. "Don't even think about it Macker. That's the worst idea you've had since wearing your hair in a ponytail."

"Why?"

"Because ponytails are for girls," Shipsey muttered.

"*Because*," said Matt "if the guy accepts the bribe, Laura will find out and you'll look pathetic and untrusting. And if he doesn't accept the bribe, he'll tell her that you tried to bribe him and not only will you look pathetic and untrusting, but "John the Player" will be boning *your* Laura for the whole two weeks!"

Macker raised his eyebrows and then nodded slowly. "Ok, fair enough. I see your point."

There was a moment of silence during which Macker looked from friend to friend hoping they would come up with an inspirational solution to his problem. It was Shipsey who finally broke the hush.

"Soooooo…" during this pause, he shifted his stare from the table to Matt. "What are the odds anyway?"

Macker looked up from his pint in disgust. Matt pretended not to know what Shipsey was talking about. "Sorry?"

"The odds…y'know…on Macker's bird shaggin' John the Player."

Matt stalled and looked at Macker, waiting for some form of protest, but Macker just picked up his pint and shrugged his shoulders.

"Well…it's tricky," said Matt, "but I reckon it's around even money."

Macker planted his pint firmly back down on the table. "Even money! Even fuckin' money! You reckon it's a straight fifty fifty call on whether Laura does the dirt on me or not!"

"Under these circumstances…yeah," Matt nodded. "But the odds are slightly longer on *you* actually finding out."

"*What?*" gasped Macker in annoyance.

"Well, the chances of it happening are fifty fifty," Matt explained. "But the odds of you finding out are slightly longer…y'know…maybe two to one or something."

"Well that's just fuckin' charming! How'd ye work all that shit out?"

Matt could sense the anger rising in Macker. So he explained how he arrived to his conclusion with complete composure.

"Well, as I see it," he said, raising his right thumb, "there's absolutely no doubt that "John the Player" will try to make a move at some point in the two weeks. I reckon inside the first three days. He's got the motive, the means and he'll have plenty of opportunity. He may even have an accomplice in "Heineken" or her boyfriend. So the only question is…will Laura put out?"

Macker started shifting awkwardly in his chair as Matt continued. "They're gonna be in a beautiful foreign country with the sun shining and the alcohol flowing. They've only just broken up with each other after a two-year relationship. The pressure will be on Laura, not just from "John the Player," but possibly from other people who want the group to behave like three couples. And then there'll be a late drunken night when "The Player" will fancy his chances of getting back in the game. Laura will be sloshed. Her defences will be down and before she knows what's goin' on   Ol' John Boy will be slippin' her the tongue. At this point she might get a bit angry or maybe even feel a bit guilty, but at the end of the day…from what we've heard…she does enjoy a bit of sex."

The lads sat in silence for a moment, taking in Matt's prediction. Shipsey couldn't help but nod his head. Dave just looked at Macker waiting for a response. Macker's stare was alternating between Matt and mid air. He felt his temper rising, but at the same time had difficulty arguing with any of what Matt had said. In the end he opted for a different line of attack.

"Ok then…how much do you want on it?"

"What?" Matt frowned.

"How much do you want to bet?"

"I don't wanna bet. I was just saying what might happen."

"Come on! Put yer money where yer mouth is!"

"You want me to bet that your girlfriend sleeps with her ex?"

"Yep."

"Nah, I don't think so."

"Come on!"

"Nah, you're all right."

Shipsey held up his hand. "I'll do it."

Macker stopped staring Matt down to turn his attention to Shipsey. "All right then bigfella," smiled Macker. "How much?"

"What are the odds?"

"Evens."

"Nah, it should be two to one."

"Ok, I'll give you six to four."

"Fair enough," smiled Shipsey. "I'll have a score on it, if that's all right?"

"Ok, that's done," said Macker, before turning back to Matt. "Cullen, are you sure you don't want a piece of the action?"

"Ok…fuck it," said Matt…"I'll do the same."

As Matt offered his hand out for Macker to shake, Dave leaned forward and took it. "I'll take that bet if it's all right with you Mack."

It had been the first contribution Dave had made to the conversation in a while and one of the reasons he did it was just to feel

181

involved. But also he felt a duty to back up his new flatmate and even out the numbers. And besides, he was the one being kept awake at night by the loud sex sessions of Macker and Laura.

In the middle of all the handshaking banter, Shipsey's phone rang.

"Hello, is that Mr. Boate?"

Shipsey hated being called Mr. Boate. Especially over the phone as it was a sure sign that someone was selling something. Shipsey had alarmingly little time for his fellow salespeople. He'd once responded to a guy who asked him,

"Would you mind if we came around to measure your windows for a quotation?"

"Yes...please *do* come round and bring your fucking measuring tape...it'll come in handy for measuring up your coffin!"

Shipsey quickly realised however that this caller wasn't trying to sell him anything.

"Hello Mr. Boate, this is Gavin from *The Video Palace*, Cabinteely. We have a slight problem with the video you dropped back earlier this evening."

"Oh yeah, what's that?" asked Shipsey, getting ready to be chastised for not rewinding the tape.

"Well...," Gavin hesitated "it's the tape...y'see." Shipsey was preparing to give Gavin a very hard time, but allowed him to continue meekly. "It's not...eh... *Lord Of The Rings*...it's something called...em...*Big and Bouncy.*"

Shipsey glanced up at the rest of the lads. Thankfully they weren't paying much attention to him, but nonetheless he turned slightly away to continue the conversation.

"Oh...I see...yes...eh...that's my...eh...Australian wildlife documentary...it's about giant kangaroos."

"Right." Gavin didn't sound convinced.

When Shipsey had finished his call he knocked back his drink and got to his feet. "Right, I'm off. Early start tomorrow."

He stepped away from the table and slung his bag over his shoulder.

"Aren't you forgetting something?" said Macker, pointing at the sports bag. "What about our videos?"

"Oh yeah," Shipsey frowned. "What did we agree again?"

"Thirty for twenty euro," Dave lied.

"Fuck off ye chancer! It was *twenty* for *thirty* euro!"

"Thirty for twenty seems to ring a bell with me," said Macker, smiling up at Shipsey.

"All right, I tell ye what," said Shipsey, scratching his earlobe. "I'll give ye the whole lot for twenty euro, if ye drop *Lord of the Rings* back to *The Video Palace* for me."

The Video Palace? Macker frowned. "That's on your way home!"

"Yeah, I know, but I don't really want to go in. I owe them a bit of money."

Macker and Dave looked at each other, nodded and started reaching into their pockets for the money. "Right then. You're on."

Shipsey plonked the goods down in the middle of the table and took the twenty euro. "I want that bag back...right?"

"Yeah sure," nodded Macker "Thanks Ship...that's a pretty good deal."

"Ah, no probs. I had to get rid of them anyway."

"So, where's *Lord of the Rings*?" asked Dave.

"It's in the bag...inside the case of "Big and Bouncy.""

Macker started rummaging through the bag. "What the fuck's it doin' in there?"

"Slight mix up," Shipsey coughed and started to turn for the door. "Just ask for Gavin when you get to the video store. He'll have *Big and Bouncy* for you."

Chapter 22

"Macker you're gonna have to pull over in the next town," said Shipsey, squirming in his seat. "I'm dyin' to go to the jacks."[*]

"Ah...no way Shipsey! I've stopped three times already and it took me ages to get past that last patch of traffic! If we don't get there soon, the hotel will give away our rooms!"

"Yeah, well if you don't get me to a *toilet soon*, I'm gonna make a real mess of your car!"

"Look," said Macker, checking his rearview mirror. "We're on a quiet road, there's no-one around. Just kneel on the seat and go out the window."

Shipsey looked at Macker with raised eyebrows. "You want me to kneel on the seat and take a crap out the window? What am I? Some sort of contortionist?"

It was a Friday night in late September and the lads were on the road to Listowel, County Kerry. *Satan's Whiskers* was running in his third race the following day. The horse had healed well during the summer and had been training hard over hurdles for the previous six weeks. Paddy Mulryan was more than pleased with his progress and had entered him in a tough two-mile hurdle at the Listowel Festival. The lads couldn't wait to see him run again and because they had so far to travel, they had decided to go down on the Friday night after work. That way they could spend the following day drinking and gambling instead of enduring the five-hour journey. Yet speeding down the country roads on the outskirts of Newcastle West, not one of their minds was on drinking, gambling or horse racing.

Macker was thinking about his latest in a long line of short-lived relationships. As Matt had predicted, Laura called him from Portugal during the second week of her holiday to tell him that she had gotten back with John. Apparently, the warm Iberian sun had helped her ex-boyfriend develop into a more mature and considerate twenty-two year-

---

[*] Jacks is slang for toilet. Jackeen is slang for Dubliner. To create confusion Jackeen is sometimes pluralised as Jacks.

old. It was the first time in years that Macker had been hurt by a girl. His reward for having his heart trod on was to hand over thirty euro to Shipsey. He was starting to query the wisdom of moving away from his tactic of keeping his relationships brief and uncomplicated. Maybe he just wasn't cut out for the long-term thing. Perhaps it was time for a return to the good old days of hit and run.

In the back seat Matt was gazing out the window. For the previous three hours he'd been enjoying the beautiful scenery of a cross-country drive in Ireland, but in the last half hour it had gone dark. In his mind he was reliving the fight he'd had with Sam the previous evening. It wasn't a bad fight (He described it to Shipsey as a three-rounder), but it was their first in their new home. He'd had a late meeting on Thursday with his boss and some clients, which had adjourned to the pub. The drinking went on a little later than he'd anticipated, but he was still home by ten o'clock, albeit slightly the worse for wear.

Not too bad he'd thought, looking at his watch and turning the key in the front door. Sam disagreed. The row started pretty slowly, but took some rapid twists and turns along the way. In the end Matt wasn't sure what Sam was annoyed about. It seemed less to do with the fact that he'd been working late and hadn't called her and more to do with the fact that they weren't spending enough time together. Matt had a lot of difficulty grasping this concept. *What the hell does she mean, we're not spending enough time together? We live together for Christ sake! I mean...I fully intend to be with her for the rest of my life! So what's the problem with the odd weekend away with the boys?*

Sitting beside Matt, Dave was rubbing his fingers against the grain of the bristles on his shaved head, a habit he still hadn't shaken. After Matt moved out he had to buy his own set of hair clippers. The previous evening Macker had given him a blade one and Dave loved the soothing feeling he got from stroking the prickly surface. At first he had his doubts, but now that he was used to it, he was well pleased that Helen had talked him into going for the shaved look. She was right. It did make him look a bit more "street." But what made him happiest and most confident about himself was losing almost two stone over the summer. He'd been to visit his parents the previous weekend for the first time in months. At first he nearly scared his mother to death, but when she was convinced he was her son and he wasn't taking drugs, she was overwhelmed with how well he looked. It was time for the new improved Dave to reintroduce himself to another important person he hadn't seen for over three months. Kate would be driving down to

Listowel in the morning, leaving her father behind to look after her mum. The thought of seeing her again gave Dave butterflies in his stomach. He'd spoken to her on the phone a few times over the summer, but had purposely neglected to tell her about the steps he had taken to transform himself. He wasn't about to share his ambitions with the lads, but he had high hopes of winning her back.

Shipsey, who was still squirming in the front seat, had two things on his mind. In his lap was a very old and furry baseball cap. It was circa 1977 with a thick dark blue centre stripe with light blue on either side. On the bridge of the peak it said "Dublin" and on the back it had the phrase "The Jacks Are 'ack." It was supposed to say "The Jacks Are Back," but the "B" had fallen off. As loser of the latest konch spin, it was Shipsey's task to wear the cap for the entire time they were in County Kerry. It was an evil task designed by Dave and Shipsey wasn't looking forward to the verbal if not physical abuse that was likely to be dished out by the passionate Kerry people. Shipsey was doing his best to think up a few excuses for wearing the cap that might keep him out of trouble, but what he was really concentrating on, was not soiling his good work trousers. He'd been holding back nature for far too long and if they didn't get to the next town soon he was afraid he might do himself or Macker's car some permanent damage. All of a sudden he saw a sign at the side of the road that almost made him relax his anal muscles a little bit too much.

"Well praise the fucking lord!" he yelled. "Welcome to Newcastle West. Home of *Ballygowan Water*. Jaysis, I thought I wasn't gonna make it!

Newcastle West...I...love...you."

Five minutes later Shipsey emerged from the doors of *The Heather Tavern* with a grin from ear to ear.

"Oh lads," he groaned, getting back into the car. "You don't know how good that was. That was actually *soooo good* it was almost worth the pain I went through tryin' to hold it in. I think I *now know* what Freddy Mercury was goin' on about. *Pain is so close to pleasure*."

"Y'know," said Dave, clearing his throat. "Some scientists believe there is no such thing as pleasure, only the release of pain."

"What?" gasped Matt. He could only just make Dave's face out across the back seat.

"Yeah, they believe the feeling we associate with being pleasurable is in fact just a release of pain."

"Makes a lot of sense to me," Shipsey sighed.

"Sounds like bollocks to me," said Macker.

"Yeah Dave," Matt agreed. "There's lots of things that give you pleasure with no pain."

"Name some."

"Well, *orgasms* for starters."

"Well if you really think about it," said Dave thoughtfully. "When you're about to come you're not exactly singing and smiling are you? No, you're making an ugly face and going oh ah ah ah oh ah oh oh ohh ohhh! ahhhhhh! ...yeah! ohh yeah God yeah."

"That was pretty good," Matt complimented him. "But you're still talkin' shite."

"Yeah," Macker agreed. "What about the pleasure you get from eating something really nice, like a chocolate cake."

"That's the same thing really," said Dave. "You're satisfying your hunger pains or maybe a sugar deficiency."

"All right then," said Matt. "What about the pleasure you get from going on a roller-coaster ride?"

"That's just adrenalin."

"What about watching your team score a goal?" Macker tried.

"That's also adrenalin," said Dave, happy that he was still on top of the argument.

"Yeah, but it's a pleasurable feeling and it doesn't involve the release of pain."

"Well, actually, adrenalin is a hormone secreted in response to stress," said Dave quite pompously.

"What about that nice feeling you get when you wake up late in the morning and then suddenly realise its Saturday and you don't have to go to work?" asked Matt.

"Ah, well y'see," said Dave. "For a split second you're panicking cos you think you're late for work. After that it's just a feeling of relief really."

"Ok then," said Shipsey, finally joining in the debate. "What about the enormous feeling of pleasure I'll get when you lot shut the fuck up and stop talking bollox!"

Dave stuck his head between the two front seats to look at Shipsey. "Shouldn't you be wearing your cap?"

"We haven't crossed the border yet."

With that, they crossed the border. Macker was the first to spot the roadside sign.

"Welcome to County Kerry!" he cheered "All Ireland football champions a record 32. Jaysis and they're not afraid to harp on about it."

The way the sign was erected with a removable panel for the "32" told you two things. Firstly that Kerry didn't fancy the chances of any county trying to steal their record, but more importantly that they fully intended to win plenty more. A big cheer went up when Shipsey donned the silly looking Dublin cap and broke into a verse of *The Auld Triangle*.

> *"A hungry feeling*
> *Came o'er me stealing*
> *And the mice were squeeling*
> *In my prison cell"*

As the car sped towards Listowel the rest of the lads joined in the chorus. They were roaring loud enough to rouse the spirit of *Brendan Behan*.

> *"And that auld triangle, went jingle jangle*
> *All along the banks of the Royal Canal"*

They followed up *The Auld Triangle* with *Molly Malone, The Rare Auld Times* and *The Rocky Road to Dublin*. By the time they hit Listowel, they were ready to do battle with the locals. With the provocatively coloured cap on his head, Shipsey feared he may have to.

A pretty young girl called Marie greeted them at the hotel reception. After she'd handed them their keys Shipsey leaned over the desk to ask her the question that was on everyone's lips.

"What time does the residents bar close?"

Marie smiled up at him, trying not to stare at his silly cap. "Oh, well…PJ is doin' the bar tonight, so as long as you buy him the odd pint, he'll keep it open as late as you want."

"Thank you very much Marie," Shipsey grinned. "After the journey we've had, that sort of thing would bring a tear to a glass eye." Shipsey bent down to pick up his bag.

"No problem," said Marie. "Nice cap, by the way."

Shipsey popped his head back above the desk. "Really? Do you like it?"

"No, not really." Marie curtly shook her head, but then managed one last smile. "Welcome to Kerry."

After a lengthy pub-crawl around the town, the lads settled down in the resident's bar to put Marie's theory to the test.

"Jaysis, I'm glad we're back here," sighed Shipsey. "Did ye see the way those lads were lookin' at me outside the chipper! I feel like I'm walkin' down the Falls road in a fuckin' Rangers jersey!"

"Relax," said Dave, looking up at the offensive cap. "You'll be fine. Just think of it as a conversation starter."

In truth Dave was feeling a bit guilty about the task he'd set and was glad he wasn't the one in the Dublin colours.

"A conversation starter?" laughed Shipsey. "The only thing this yolk is gonna start is a civil fuckin' war!"

"Relax Shipsey! Who the fuck's gonna start on you?"

"Well, I'm not too keen on the look of that PJ fella," said Shipsey, nodding his head towards the bar. The lads turned to have a look at PJ. They saw a tall, muscular, tattooed skinhead roughly their own age. He had a ring going through the corner of his left eyebrow and a large scar taking up most of his right cheek.

"Fuck me!" said Macker. "He does look like a bit of a head case!"

"Look at that fuckin' scar!" Shipsey gasped. "He didn't get that from poppin' zits!"

"Whose round is it anyway?" asked Macker, glad that he'd got the last one in before they'd arrived back to the hotel. "Shipsey?"

"Ah, bollocks lads!" Shipsey groaned. "You can't make me go up there, wearing this fuckin' thing on my head!" He took a twenty-euro note out of his pocket and placed it on the table. "Someone else can do the honours." He looked from face to face, praying for some help.

Eventually Matt stood up. "Right, fuck it…I'll go."

By 2am, the bar was almost empty and the lads decided it was time to start a sing-song. During the previous few hours they'd built up a bit of rapport with PJ by buying him a couple of pints. They still didn't feel totally comfortable in his company, but he gave them a smile and the thumbs up when Matt burst into the first verse of "Nancy Spain." The only other group left in the bar were three couples from London. By the end of the third song, they'd moved to the table beside the lads to join in the action. PJ, who was sitting on the bar just across from them, was also giving a helping hand through the odd chorus. After a while, the English crowd started to sing a few of their own songs and it turned into a Eurovision song contest of sorts. PJ was happy to act as compere and award the teams points. Macker was standing up with his eyes shut tight. If he could nail the last two verses of *Dirty Old Town,* he'd put Ireland into a commanding lead.

> *"Clouds are drift-ing across the moon*
> *Cats are prowl-ing on the beat*
> *Springs a girl in the street at night*
> *Dirty old town, dirty old town*
>
> *I'm gonna make me a big sharp axe*
> *Shining steel, tempered in the fire*
> *I'll chop you down, like an old oak tree*
> *Dirty old town, dirty old town."*

"Irlande, dix points!" roared PJ, in his best French accent. He wanted to give Macker twelve points, but didn't wish to appear biased towards his fellow Irishmen. The English crowd were whispering amongst themselves for a while before the three lads stood up to give a rousing rendition of *Swing Low, Sweet Chariot*. When they'd finished PJ clapped his hands high above his head. "Not my favourite song," he smiled, "but I'm gonna give you dix points aswell. I thought the hand gestures were pretty good."

"All right lads," said Shipsey, clearing his throat. "It's time to put this lot to bed."

He started off in a low gravelly voice...

> *"Well, how do you do young Willie McBride*
> *Do you mind if I sit here down by your graveside*
> *And rest for a while 'neath the warm summer sun*
> *I've been walkin' all day and I'm nearly done*
> *Well, I see by your gravestone, you were only 19*
> *When you joined the great fallin' in 1916*
> *I hope you died well and I hope you died clean*
> *Or young Willie McBride, was it slow and obscene*

The rest of the lads and PJ joined in the chorus while the English crowd made plans for bed.

> *"Did they beat the drums slowly, did they play the Fife lowly*
> *Did they sound the death march as they lowered you down*
> *Did the band play the Last Post and Chorus*
> *Did the pipes play the Flowers of the Forest?"*

Four verses later, the couples from London said their goodnights.

As a reward for the home victory, PJ pulled the lads four creamy pints on the house.

"Irlande, douze points!"

Chapter 23

After gulping down breakfast the following morning, the lads went in search of a base in the heart of Listowel. The headquarters they were looking for had to meet three criteria. It had to serve alcohol, be close to a betting shop and have a table big enough to accommodate four pints, a racing post and a sporting life. Before long they settled down in "The Whiskey Stream," a dark wooden pub, next door to Hannigan's bookmakers. Shipsey went to get the papers while Dave ordered the drinks. As Shipsey was returning to the pub he heard a loud voice behind him.

"I hope yer wearin' that fuckin' cap as part of a bet!"

Shipsey turned around slowly and was relieved to see a friendly, if slightly scary face.

"Ah, PJ...how's it goin'?"

"All right ye big fuckin' Jackeen. How are you?"

"Not bad ye Kerry muck savage."

PJ's face turned to indignant anger. "I might be a muck savage, but I'm not from Kerry!"

"Where are ye from?"

"Just the other side of the Limerick border...Newcastle West."

Shipsey thought back to his pleasurable visit to the toilets of The Heather Tavern.

"Great spot that Newcastle West."

PJ frowned. "You takin' the piss?"

"No it was a shit actually...in the Heather Tavern. You ever drink in there?"

"The odd time."

"Well the next time yer in there and yer goin' to the jacks, don't go in trap one."

"Ok, fair enough," said PJ convinced that Shipsey was still drunk from the night before. "Whaddya up to anyway?"

"Ah, y'know," said Shipsey breathing in a large pocket of Listowel air. "An Irishman's favourite pastimes. Drinkin' and gamblin'."

"Ye left one out."

"What's that...Ridin'?"

"No...singin'." They both laughed and as Shipsey was pushing open the door to "The Whiskey Stream," he turned back to PJ. "Do you wanna join us?"

"Asher, why not?"

PJ had enjoyed the previous night immensely and was happy to spend more time with the lads. His average Saturday afternoon was spent crumpling up losing betting slips with the sixty-year-old locals in the smoke-filled Hannigan's bookmakers. It would make a nice change to spend a few hours downing pints with kindred spirits of his own age, even if they were from Dublin. He may even manage to scab a few free pints off them. If they were staying in Listowel again that night he could pay them back at the expense of the hotel bar.

"So, are yiz stayin' in the hotel again tonight?" he asked, as Dave went up to the bar to get him a pint. The lads explained that they were going to the races to watch their own horse and would be hitting the road back to Dublin at six o'clock.

"Ye have your own racehorse?"

"Yeah...well, we own half of him between us."

"Jaysis...that's deadly! What's he called?"

Macker rotated "The Racing Post" on the table so it was facing PJ. *Satan's Whiskers*. He's running in the second last race."

PJ shoved his face to within an inch of the page. *"Satan's Whikers"*. he murmured. "Cool name. Did you guys come up with it?"

"Yeah, I did," said Macker proudly. "It's the name of a cocktail."

"So, is he any good? Should I be backin' him?"

"He *is* good, but it's his first race back after injury. So we're not too sure. It's the toughest race he's been in so far, but the trainer reckons he's got a good chance of a place, if he stays on his feet."

"What odds is he gonna be?"

"Probably around twelve to one."

"Jaysis, that's not bad. I'll have to put a few quid on him each way."

"Yeah," Macker nodded. "That's what I'm gonna do...Are you goin' to the races?"

PJ shook his head. "Nah, I don't think so. I'll probably just watch it on the box."

He was disappointed the lads weren't staying down an extra night. He really fancied another sing-song.

"Why aren't yiz stayin' down here tonight? You'll be in no mood to drive back to Dublin after the racing."

Macker looked at Matt. They had discussed this option earlier in the week, but Matt had voted against it, because he knew Sam wouldn't like the idea.

"Well...y'see," said Matt hesitantly, "we couldn't really afford it."

"Right, well let's see if we can do somethin' about that," said PJ, picking up *The Sporting Life* and giving it a purposeful shake.

Within an hour a number of new agreements had been made between PJ and the Dublin lads. They'd decided to pool some of their funds and do a huge cumulative bet on nine of the soccer fixtures taking place that afternoon. The lads agreed that if "Satan' Whiskers" won his race or if they collected enough money on their football bet that they'd stay in Listowel the extra night. PJ agreed that he'd join them in their trip to the races and if they ended up staying the night he'd keep the bar open until first mass on Sunday morning.

*****

Kate had wandered around the crowded betting ring for five minutes before she finally spotted Matt. Her view was obscured, but she was sure it was him standing between two skinheads, looking up at the odds on the first race. She decided to approach him from behind and started meandering her way through the mob. When she arrived behind him, she threw her hands over his eyes.

"Hello handsome! Guess who?"

"That would be the bauld Kitty McCann," said Matt, smiling and turning around. They embraced each other warmly.

"Long time, no see. How have you been?"

It wasn't until she released from their hug that Kate realised that the two skinheads on either side of Matt had turned around also. She glanced at the one on the right first. He had a face that looked like it had been in a few battles and a ring through his eyebrow, but quite a nice smile all the same. When she glanced at the one on the left, her eyes nearly popped out of her head. She took a half step backwards, partly to steady herself, but really to assure herself that it was in fact Dave. Despite the newly grown goatee, the completely shaved head and the fact that he'd lost about two stone, he still had the same warm eyes.

"Jesus Dave!" said Kate, finally managing to speak. "I didn't recognise you."

She started to feel a bit guilty about hugging Matt first *and* calling him handsome. She held her arms out to Dave, to even things up. "You're looking well. Come here."

And then they hugged. As Dave held her tight, he whispered in her ear. "I've missed ya."

After introducing her to PJ, the lads sent Kate off to the bar where Macker and Shipsey were holding fort. PJ turned to Matt and Dave when she was out of sight.

"So, who's the babe?"

"That's Macker's cousin," said Matt. "She has a small part in the horse too."

"Well," PJ grinned. "I wouldn't mind havin' a small part in her!"

Matt let out a short snort of laughter and then coughed. "She's also Dave's ex."

"Oh sorry about that Dave." PJ punched him lightly on the shoulder. "How long ago did ye break up?"

"Three months ago."

PJ frowned. Something about all this didn't quite add up. He wanted to ask more questions, but decided against it, in case he pushed the wrong buttons.

Kate spotted Shipsey in his blue fur-covered cap as soon as she entered the bar. "What's with the Dublin cap?" she asked, as she was hugging her hellos.

"Trying to take the attention away from Dave's head," Shipsey answered. "Have you seen him?"

"Yeah!" Kate gasped. "I nearly didn't recognise him!"

"So, whadya think?"

"I think he looks good. I'm not sure about the goatee, but I think the shaved head suits him. How much weight has he lost?"

"Dunno," Shipsey shrugged, "but the local pizza company has gone out of business."

Kate turned to Macker who was glued to the halftime scores on the big screen.

"How are *you* cuz?" she asked, ruffling his blonde hair.

"Not bad. I'd be even better if Charlton would score another goal."

Kate shook her head and smiled at the same time. "Only you lot could travel three hundred miles to a racing festival and then gamble on the football."

As they made their way back to the bar Dave asked Matt for a favour.

"Listen, if we end up going back to the hotel again tonight, do you think you could ask Kate to join us? Y'know…ask her back for a few drinks."

"Yeah, I suppose so, but why don't you just ask her yourself? You *are* just friends now aren't you?"

"Yeah, but y'know…it's still a bit awkward…she might get the idea that I have an ulterior motive."

"Which, of course, would be wrong," said Matt.

"Of course," Dave smiled.

He wouldn't usually try to mislead Matt like this, but he was afraid that if he told him that he was planning to ask Kate out again that Matt might try to talk him out of it.

By the time they made it back to the bar, Macker was getting pretty excited about their football bet. He'd written down all the relevant half time scores and it looked like they had a good chance of making some money.

"Lads, check it out! In our nines matches, six of our teams are winning and two are level. The Crystal Palace match kicks off at six o'clock. It's on Sky Sports."

"Nice one," said PJ. "We can watch it back in the hotel bar."

Matt hadn't really contemplated the possibility of their football bet being successful. It was an outcome that gave him mixed feelings. Sure, he wanted to win pots of cash, but the fact that it meant he could be staying an extra night in Listowel worried him. The way he'd left things with Sam, he knew it wouldn't go down well if he didn't make it back to Dublin that night.

A short while later the lads were taking up a good position in the stands directly opposite the finishing line. "*Satan's Whiskers*" was about to start his third race and Matt, Shipsey and Macker, who had all brought binoculars, were ready to deliver commentary. It became clear at an early point in the race, however, that their commentary skills weren't up to scratch.

"Oh bollix!" shouted Shipsey, halfway through the first furlong. "He's last! He's fucked!"

"Are you sure that's him?" asked Macker.

"Yeah, he's the one in the blue, going backwards!"

"Well, I count one, two, three, four horses wearing blue…well not the horses…obviously…the jockeys."

"What about that one in the middle?" asked Matt. "Behind the one in yellow."

"The yellow jersey or the yellow cap?"

"The one in the blue jersey behind the one in the fuckin' yellow jersey! Right in the middle of the field!"

"That's not him!" Macker shouted.

"How do you know?"

"Because that horse is fucking grey! Our horse is dark brown...remember."

"Oh yeah. What about the one that's two ahead of the one in yellow?"

"Two ahead of the one in yellow," Macker repeated, while adjusting his focus. "Right, I see the one yer talkin' about. It could be him. It's either him, the one in last or...there's another one in blue...in about fourth place."

"I don't think he's the one coming last," said Matt.

"Why not?"

"Cos, I can see the number on that one. It looks like eighteen."

"It couldn't be eighteen! There's only sixteen horses in the fucking race!"

"Does that mean they have to be numbered one to sixteen? Maybe they have squad numbers?"

"They don't have fucking squad numbers!"

"Ok, well then he's number sixteen!"

"And what number is *Satan's Whiskers*?"

"I don't know, but he's not sixteen...or eighteen."

"Wait a minute," said Shipsey. "He's fifteen!"

"Oh, well then we're fucked!" roared Macker. "That's him coming last! I can see the number fifteen on him!"

"How do you know he's number fifteen?" asked Shipsey.

Macker took the binoculars down from his eyes and started waving them around. "Cos I can see him using these fucking things!"

"No, I mean, how do you know *Satan's Whiskers* is number fifteen you fuckin' spanner?"

"What? You just told me he's number fifteen, ye big gobshite!"

"No I didn't! I said the one comin' last is number fifteen!"

"What?"

"I never said *Satan's Whiskers* is number fifteen!" yelled Shipsey. "You two morons were arguing about the number of the one coming last and I just told you that it was fifteen!"

"So, what number is our horse then?"

"I haven't got a clue!"

Dave, who'd been rifling through the pages of his racing programme, finally found "*Satan's Whiskers*." "He's number eight! Now do ye think ye can find him before the fuckin' race is over?"

"Ok," said Matt... "we know through a process of elimination that he's either the one in fourth place or the one in six, seven, eighth place…woah…ninth place…wait a sec…tenth place…shit…eleventh place! What the fucks goin' on with this horse? He looks like he's been shot!"

"He's gone lame," said Macker. "Yeah, he's definitely limping…..the jockey is pulling him up."

"Shit…fuck! bollix!"

"Wait a minute!" shouted Macker. "He's number twelve!"

"Oh nice one! You beauty! Come on Satan!"

And then they heard the racetrack commentator mention their horse's name for the first time. "Five furlongs left to race and its *Secret Mission* and *Yellow Brick Road* followed by the favourite *Goody Gumdrop* who's been tracked by *Satan's Whiskers*.

"Come on Satan, ye good thing!"

"Four more hurdles to jump and its *Yellow Brick Road* now, getting the better of *Secret Mission* who's starting to look tired and is being caught by *Goody Gumdrop*…a length further back in fourth is *Satan's Whiskers*.

"He's lookin' good lads," howled Macker. "Travelling really well."

"*Yellow Brick Road* has opened up a length advantage over *Secret Mission* who's been challenged on the outside by *Goody Gumdrop*. *Satan's Whiskers* is tracking the favourite and is still travelling well."

"I told ye he was travelling well!" Macker roared. "Come on Satan, ye fuckin' good thing!" His heart was starting to do an impersonation of Michael Flately on speed.

"As they jump the second last it's "Goody Gumdrop" looming up on the outside of "Yellow Brick Road." They both get over that one cleanly. "*Satan's Whiskers*" jumps it like a stag and is hot on their tails."

"COME ON SATAN, YEBOYO!!"

"One fence left to jump and it's "Goody Gumdrop" looking strong as he takes a half length lead over the weakening "Yellow Brick Road." The challenge may well come from "*Satan's Whiskers*" who's cruising in third."

"COME OOOOOOOOOOON!!"

""Goody Gumdrop" gets over the last safely. Ooooooooooh! "*Satan's Whiskers*" hits the hurdle hard and is almost brought to a halt!"

"FUUUUUUUCK!!"

"Kevin Daly has done well to stay on board, but it looks like this one's over…or is it? "Goody Gumdrop" is tiring and *Satan's Whiskers* is starting to pick up steam again! The gap is four lengths, but with half a furlong left, it's closing fast!"

"COME ON SATAN!!"

"Only two lengths between them now and "*Satan's Whiskers*" is closing with every stride! But can he get there before they cross the line. Only a length between them now and "*Satan's Whiskers*" is finishing much the stronger.

"COME ON SATAN, YE FUCKIN' BEAUTY!!"

"As they cross the line it's *Goody Gumdrop* who just holds on by a head to beat the fast finishing *Satan's Whiskers*. *Yellow Brick Road* follows them home a distant third."

"Fuck!"

They adjourned to the racetrack bar to hold a quick and conclusive post mortem. Matt summed up how they all felt.

"He would have won that by about five lengths if he hadn't crashed into the last hurdle."

"Yeah," Macker agreed. "He just looked like he was going so fast that he couldn't find his stride."

"Cheer up lads...and lassie," PJ smiled at Kate. "He's a bloody good horse and he's bound to win his next race."

But it wasn't until *Satan's Whiskers* trainer joined them for a pint that they heard news that really cheered them up.

"Cheltenham!" gasped Macker. "Jesus Paddy, are ye serious?"

"Yep, sure he's easily the best horse I've had in the last ten years. He would have won that race handily if he'd jumped the last and the time was very fast...not far off the track record. I've just spoken to the trainer of *Goody Gumdrop* who told me that *he'll* be going to Cheltenham."

Macker couldn't believe his ears. The thought of their horse running at Cheltenham got his heart doing the Riverdance again.

"Have you thought about what race you might run him in?"

"Well possibly the Triumph Hurdle, but that sort of decision is up to you guys and your uncle."

"The Triumph Hurdle! You think he's good enough to run in the Triumph Hurdle?" Shipsey and Dave weren't familiar with the Triumph Hurdle, but were getting the impression that it was one of the bigger races at the Cheltenhem festival.

Macker was grinning from ear to ear. "Jaysis lads! The fuckin' Triumph Hurdle!"

"First things first," said Paddy. "Over the next few days we see how the horse is and then try to make up our minds if Cheltenham is the way to go."

Paddy explained to them the many implications of bringing a

horse to Cheltenham. He pointed out that to give a horse a good chance at Cheltenham you might only run him twice between now and then. Otherwise you could run him four or five times before March. He gave them a rough idea of what it might cost to fly him over and enter him in a big race. He tried to make them see that it was as much a financial decision as a horseracing decision, but his words were falling on deaf ears. The disappointment of losing a close race had been forgotten and the owners of "*Satan's Whiskers*" were now daydreaming about Cheltenham. The lads were smiling and winking at each other all the way through Paddy's advice. They just about managed to keep their composure, but after Paddy had left, the glass-clinking, back-slapping and Cheltenham banter took over. For five of the six owners of "*Satan's Whiskers*," the Cheltenham decision had been made.

Matt knew from the excitement buzzing around the table and the fact that Macker was ordering six *Satan's Whiskers* up at the bar that there was little chance of him returning to Dublin that night. Sooner or later, he'd have to make an awkward phonecall to Sam. When Macker arrived back to the table with a tray full of orange-coloured cocktails, Matt asked him how the football bet was going.

"Jaysis!" Macker gasped. "I forgot all about that! I'll have to check them on text." While Macker went to get the remote control Matt convinced Kate to join them back at the hotel bat for a while. Dave sat still and pretended not to notice.

"We're laughin' lads!" Macker announced. "Seven of our nine teams have won and we still have Crystal Palace to play! If they win, we'll be up a good bit of money!"

"Nice one!" howled PJ. "How much?"

"Well that's the difficult part," said Macker. "We'll have landed one eight-way accumulator and I think about eight seven-way accumulators. So as it stands we're roughly all square, but if Palace win we could make over a grand. I'll need a calculator to figure it out."

Five minutes later they were all speeding back to the hotel to watch Crystal Palace V Sheffield Wednesday. Kate had offered to take a couple of them in her yellow Renault Clio to even out the load between the two cars. Dave was the first to jump forward and was gutted when PJ followed suit. This should have been the perfect opportunity for Dave to get chatting to Kate and find out if she might be interested in going out with him again, now that he was a new man. But, with PJ sitting in the back seat he was limited to small talk. Still, at least he'd beaten PJ in the race to get the front passenger seat. PJ was slouched in the middle of the back seat. He was beginning to take a shine to the good-looking lass from Kildare and was pissed off when Dave had barged past him to claim the front seat. Then he noticed that in the rearview mirror he had the perfect angle for observing Kate's beautiful face. He spent the rest of the journey admiring her lovely soft features. Most of the time when she looked into the mirror he looked away shyly, but occasionally he would maintain eye contact for a second and smile. PJ had noticed how Dave had jumped at the opportunity to travel in Kate's car and had practically shoved him out of the way to sit beside her. Something told him that Dave wasn't quite over his ex-girlfriend and he decided to have a bit of fun with it.

"So, you guys used to go out with each other?" PJ blurted it out loud enough to drown out both the car stereo and the small talk.

There was a moment's hesitation during which Dave's muscles tensed.

"Yeah," they both answered together.

"But you're just friends now?" PJ continued.

"Yeah," Kate answered first. "Yeah," Dave followed. He turned slightly around in his seat. Not far enough to make eye contact, but he hoped it would be far enough to convey some sort of message to PJ. The message wasn't received and PJ continued.

"Tell me this then," he said, looking at Kate in the rearview mirror. "Why didn't you recognise him earlier on in the betting ring?" PJ knew it was a rude question to ask, but he was genuinely curious and thought, *what the hell! I'll probably never see these two people again after tonight.*

Dave didn't budge as they both waited for Kate to answer.

"Well," said Kate, slowly. "He used to have his hair longer…and he didn't have a goatee…and I'd say he's lost a bit of weight too."

*A **bit** of weight!* thought Dave angrily, but he didn't say a word.

"Oh I see," said PJ. "Is it a long time since you broke up?"

Dave knew for sure now that PJ was fucking about. He'd asked that question earlier! But he remained motionless in his seat and waited for Kate to answer.

"Not that long really" Kate answered warily. "Three or four months."

"Oh…right," PJ nodded. "So he's changed quite a bit in that short space of time?"

"Yeah," said Kate.

Dave managed to gather enough energy to turn and shoot PJ a quick look. But all he got in exchange was a menacing grin. PJ looked back up into the rearview mirror and caught Kate's eye.

"For the better?" he asked.

"Sorry?"

Dave wanted to tell PJ to shut up, but he also wanted to hear Kate's answer. He shrugged his shoulders and exhaled sharply as if to say "who is this lunatic?," but then he turned his attention to the passing scenery and prayed for the right answer.

PJ sat forward brashly. "Would you say he's changed for the better?"

"Yeah," Kate nodded and giggled at the same time. "I think he looks great."

In the car in front Matt was trying in vain to get the score of the Crystal Palace match from the car radio.

"I can't believe we have a grand riding on a match between Crystal Palace and Sheffield Wednesday," Shipsey Laughed. "Who picked Palace anyway?"

"I did," said Matt.

Shipsey shot forward in his seat. "Are you serious?"

"Yeah...why?"

"Well, if you picked them they're a certainty."

"I hope so," said Matt. "It would be nice to win a little bit of cash to go along with the black eye I'm going to get for staying down the extra night."

Macker looked in his rearview mirror to check that Kate was still behind him. She was there and so was Shipsey's big head still wearing the Dublin cap.

"So, Shipsey...you must be getting' used to the cap by now."

"Yeah, I suppose so. To be honest I thought the reaction would be a lot worse. Apart from those young lads outside the chipper last night people have been pretty decent about it. I even got a few smiles and handshakes at the races. Although they were probably Dubs on tour."

Macker slowed down when the light went amber. Normally he'd put the foot down, but he decided to wait for his cousin. As they pulled up in the outside lane of the Dual carriageway a large saloon car pulled up inside them. In the front two seats Mr. And Mrs. O'Shea were discussing which secondary school to send their eleven-year-old daughter to the following year. Mrs. O'Shea would be happy for her to go to the local co-ed community school, which she had attended herself almost thirty years earlier. Mr. O'Shea wasn't too keen on the idea of his only daughter going to a school with boys. Jacquiline O'Shea, or Jack, as she insisted on being called, was sitting by the window in the back seat, quietly playing on her video game. She was oblivious to the potentially life-altering debate going on in the front of the car. Suddenly she felt as if she was being watched. She looked out of the window into the car beside. Sure enough there was a big brute of a man staring straight at her from the back seat of the car in the outside lane. As he smiled at her she noticed he was wearing a dark blue and light blue cap. The big man smiled and waved at her and she waved back. An innocent smile spread across her angelic face. When the traffic lights turned green, the smile turned to a frown and the hand that had been waving, rotated and turned into a fist with an impressively extended middle finger. She may have only been eleven years old. Not even half as old as the cap on Shipsey's head, but Jack O'Shea knew how she felt about Dubs.

The half time score was Crystal Palace 0, Sheffield Wednesday 1. Matt got up and went to the lobby to phone Sam. He was looking forward to another night in Listowel and decided to get the call out of the way. He would simply explain to her that he was being held hostage by the rest of the lads and there was no way for him to get back to Dublin. A minute later Kate got up to go to the ladies. Dave looked at her almost empty glass on the table. When he'd bought it for her she'd told him it would be her last before she hit the road for Kildare. As he watched her traverse the hotel lobby to the toilets he made up his mind to intercept her on the way back and ask her out. He could feel his pulse quickening as he rehearsed what to say in his head. After what seemed like an hour she emerged from the ladies and started making her way back. Dave sprang to his feet and started to move. He'd timed it so that he'd bump into her just as she got to the bar entrance. In his determination not to miss the appointment, he almost stood on a toddler's head. He ignored the protests of the onlooking parents. Suddenly he was very aware of the size of his tongue. Had it always been way too big for his mouth? The confidence he'd gained from hearing Kate say that he looked great was leaking out of every pour of his body. He slapped the back of his right hand into the palm of his left.

Come on, he said to himself. *Dithering Dave is long gone. Dynamic Dave is here to stay*. He almost smiled when he realised how corny that sounded, even in the privacy of his own head.

Suddenly Kate stopped walking. Half way across the lobby she just stopped and turned and smiled. Then Matt came into view. He'd finished his call to Sam and was now chatting to Kate in the middle of the lobby. Dave stood for a second at the bar entrance watching them chat.

FUCK!!

Realising he was caught in No Mans land he elected to continue his pretend visit to the gents with as much composure as he could muster. Neither Kate nor Matt noticed him pass.

BOLLOCKS!!

Twenty minutes later Kate was gone and Dave was gulping his way to the bottom of another pint. *Crystal Palace* had equalized and the other lads were roaring at the TV screen. But Dave wasn't joining in. Even when Palace scored the winner with two minutes to go he could only manage a half-hearted "yay!"

According to Macker's calculations they'd won just under thirteen hundred euro between them and a huge cheer went up when the referee blew the final whistle. There was a real buzz going around the table as they tucked into their celebratory round of drinks. It had all the credentials of being a great night. Spirits were high on the back of their big win. They were three hundred miles from Dublin in a lively little town with a bountiful supply of creamy Guinness. Their new best friend was a mad barman from Newcastle West who'd promised to serve them till the sun came up. And to top it all off they'd just found out that their racehorse was potentially good enough to run in the *Cheltenham Festival*. It looked like one hell of a night lay ahead, yet one of them would rather have been sitting on the passenger seat of a yellow *Renault Clio* on its way back to Kildare.

At eight o'clock PJ had to get behind the hotel bar. He'd already had quite a few pints and wasn't looking forward to the challenge of balancing the till. The lads decided to go on another pub-crawl around the town. With each watering hole they visited the crowd got bigger and louder. *Even The Whiskey Stream*, which had been empty that afternoon, was straining to contain the throng. Shipsey could almost taste the sweat in the air as he forced his way up to the bar. After seven long minutes of pushing, squeezing and holding his breath he could finally rest his elbows on the beer-soaked counter. As he was trying to get the barman's attention a good-looking brunette squeezed in beside him. He checked out her reflection in the mirror behind the bar. *Wow, pretty cute!* he thought. *But there's no fucking way she's getting served before me!*

Chivalry is about as popular as leprecy when it comes to ordering alcohol in a packed Irish pub. Just as the barman spotted him, Shipsey felt a sweaty hand grab a hold of his shoulder.

"Where the fuck dya tink yer goin' in that cap boy?"

The crowd was packed so tightly that Shipsey could barely manage to turn around. When he did he was face to face with a big rusty-haired local. Shipsey deemed from the angry expression on his freckle-faced adversary that he meant business. In an attempt to buy some time and come up with the right response Shipsey cupped his hand behind his ear and tilted his head slightly forward.

"I said, where the fuck dya tink yer goin' in that cap? Is it supposed to say, The Jacks are Cack?"

As he wiped the spit off his face, Shipsey considered a variety of responses.

"Get out of my fuckin' face you sweaty mullah!" Was the first one that came to mind.

Possibly a bit too confrontational, he thought.

"Je ne parle pas Anglais." That might work, unless of course this sweaty Kerryman is able to translate his abuse into French.

Shipsey looked past the drunken antagonist to see where the other lads were. They were about twenty yards away on the far side of the bar. Between him and them were another two hundred rusty-haired freckle-faced locals. Shipsey decided to try and ignore the abuse and turned back to the bar. The pretty brunette was collecting her change and two bottles of alcopop. Another two blokes had come to his area of the bar to compete for service. One of them had positioned his elbow between two of Shipsey's ribs. From behind, the rusty-haired yob was squeezing tightly on his shoulder again. A bead of sweat rolled down the side of Shipsey's protruding temple vein. His ears felt like they were about to catch fire.

"Did ye hear me ye fuckin' Jackeen? Where dya tink yer goin' in that cap?"

Ah, what the heck, thought Shipsey. He turned around to face his challenger while trying to make himself look as big as possible.

"I'm goin' outside ye fuckin' bollix! You wanna come?"

As Shipsey was attempting to push his way past, the guy grabbed his arm. Shipsey tensed his bicep and prepared himself for the worst.

"Relax bud, I was only messin' with ye. I'm from Stoney Batter." His accent had indeed made a rapid journey from the banks of the river Feale to the banks of the Liffey. Shipsey frowned at the guy for about five seconds, before giving him the benefit of the doubt and shaking his hand.

"Howaye, I'm Ray."

"All righ', I'm Shipsey."

"That's two things you have to explain then," said Ray.

"How dya mean?"

"Where d'ye get a name like Shipsey and what the fuck yer doin' wearin' a Dublin cap in the Kingdom of Kerry."

*****

Ray and his friend Conor, a real Kerryman, came in very handy when the pressure was on to remember the second verse of *The Fields of Athenry*

> *"By a lonely prison wall*
> *I heard a young man calling*
> *"Nothing matters Mary, when you're free*
> *Against the famine and the crown*
> *I rebelled, they cut me down*
> *Now, you must raise our child with dignity"*
> *Low lie the fields of Athenry*
> *Where once we watched the small freebirds fly*
> *Our love was on the wing*
> *We had dreams and songs to sing*
> *It's so lonely round the fields of Athenry"*

It was approaching five thirty in the morning and the sing-song had been in full flow for over four hours. Of all the sessions PJ had witnessed in the hotel bar this was by far the best. Ray's talents were not limited to impersonating the Kerry accent. He was a very good singer and had an enormous array of ballads at his disposal. PJ was absolutely exhausted and to conserve energy was allowing the lads to go behind the bar and pull their own pints.

"Come on PJ!" roared Shipsey. He'd spotted that PJ was getting more and more horizontal on top of the bar. "Give us a good Limerick song!"

PJ shook his head. He preferred to join in rather than lead songs.

Ray looked at PJ in confusion. "You're from Limerick?"

"Yeah."

"Well, I suppose that would explain the big scar on your face then," Ray chuckled.

"Ha ha very funny, ye big Jackeen bollocks! I got that from hurling actually."

"Well if you're from Limerick," said Matt, "ye must know *Sean South from Garryowen*."

"Of course I know *Sean South*!" said PJ, sitting up straight. "I practically wrote the fuckin' thing!"

"Well, ye'll have to sing that then."

PJ knew all the words and had joined in singing "Sean South From Garryowen" a hundred times, but he was genuinely reluctant to sing any song on his own, particularly such an esteemed Limerick ballad. Only once before had he sang the martyr's song solo and that was after drinking way too much the night of his grandfather's funeral. He had no real recollection of the event, but people told him that his grandad would have loved it.

PJ shook his head. "Nah, I don't think so. I can't sing solo till I've had at least fourteen pints. This is only number thirteen."

"Come on lad! We've done about a hundred songs and yer the only one who hasn't sang solo."

"I don't remember Dave singing solo," said PJ.

The lads looked at Dave. He was clearly having trouble keeping his eyes open and PJ was right. He hadn't played the role of lead singer at any point. In fact, at times he looked like his mind was elsewhere. Matt came up with a plan to draw these two shy voices out of their shells. He staggered in behind the bar and started emptying some tequila into a tall slim glass.

"Right...here's the deal!" he said. "PJ and Dave have to sing a song each or else they have to drink this...PJ have you got any tobasco behind here?"

PJ and Dave tried to voice their complaints, but were shouted down by the rest of the group who, seeing the triple shot of tequila with the tobasco head, thought it was a great idea.

"I reckon the one who sings the worst song, should have to drink it anyway!" Macker shouted.

Dave looked at the concoction that Matt was placing on the table. "What the fuck is that?"

"That's a prairie fire. Tequila with a tobasco head."

"That's all tequila! Fuck me! How many shots did you put in there?"

"I don't know, three...maybe four."

"Ah, for fuck sake Matt! You know I can't drink tequila without puking!"

"Yeah, but I also know that you can sing."

"When did ye ever hear me sing?"

"I remember you singin' yer head off one night in the university bar."

"Really? What did I sing?"

Matt couldn't remember clearly, so he decided to bluff Dave. "You sang "The Wild Rover" and then you did a great version of "Spancil Hill.""

"Spancil Hill"! I don't know the words to "Spancil Hill"!"
"Well, sing *'The Wild Rover'* then."
Dave looked at the glass of tequila and decided to give it a go...

> *"I've been a wild rover for many a year*
> *And I've spent all my money on whiskey and beer*
> *And now I'm returnin' with gold in great store*
> *And I never will play the wild rover no more"*

The rest of the lads roared the chorus while Dave tried to recall the second verse.

> *"And it's no, nay, never*
> *No nay never no more*
> *Will I play the wild rover*
> *No never, no more"*

Dave couldn't remember any more verses, but luckily Ray was able to reel them off. When the song was finished a big cheer went up and Macker awarded Dave a generous eight of ten. Dave looked at PJ who was getting to his feet on top of the bar and then to the glass of tequila. He crossed his fingers and said a quick prayer that PJ would fall on his face.

> *"It was on a dreary new years eve*
> *As the shades of night came down*
> *A lorry load of volunteers*
> *Approached a border town"*

By this point Dave knew he'd have to drink the prairie fire. Not only did PJ have the perfect voice for this song. He was standing proudly on top of the bar marching like a soldier on the spot. There was real emotion in how he was delivering the ballad and never a question that he'd forget the words. Towards the end of the first verse Dave and the other lads found themselves belting out the last two lines.

> *"There were men from Dublin and from Cork*
> *Fermanagh and Tyrone*
> *But the leader was a Limerick man*
> *Sean South from Garryowen*

And as they marched along the street
Up to the barracks door
They scorned the dangers they would face
Their fate that lay in store
They were fighting for old Ireland's cause
To claim their very own
And the foremost of that gallant band
Was South from Garryowen

But the sergeant foiled their daring plan
He spied them through the door
Then the sten guns and the rifles
A hail of death did pour
And when that awful night was past
Two men lay cold as stone
There was one from near the border
And one from Garryowen

No more he will hear the seagulls cry
Or the murmuring Shannon tide
For he feel beneath a northern sky
Brave O'Hanlon by his side
They have gone to join that gallant band
Of Plunkett, Pearse and Tone
Another martyr for old Ireland
Sean South from Garryowen"

Everyone cheered and clapped loudly, apart from Dave that is. Nobody fancied following PJ's superb performance, so there was only one act left to watch. The rest of the lads closed in around Dave as he began to consume the toxic-scented potion. As soon as he'd knocked back the "Prairie Fire" Dave knew he'd have to get sick. He looked to the hotel toilets on the far side of the lobby and shook his head.

I'll never make it! He'd have to settle for a good spot in the near vicinity. Shipsey was standing beside him, his Dublin cap clinging on at an angle to his head.

"Shipsey," Dave groaned. "Give us yer cap."

"What?"

Dave started to gag. "Give us yer fucking cap!" he shouted.

He had one hand on his stomach and the other covering his mouth.

"What for?" Shipsey wasn't in any hurry to give up the cap-wearing task at this late stage in the weekend. Only a few more hours and he'd be back across the Kerry border. Dave was in convulsions trying to keep himself from wrethcing.

"Hurry up! I'm gonna puke!"

PJ who had been watching from the sidelines didn't fancy having to clean up any tequila-scented vomit. He reached up, took the cap from Shipsey's head and tossed it to Dave. Before Shipsey had a chance to argue, Dave had filled the cap. There was a small ripple of applause from the non-Dublin contingent. Dave left the cap resting on the table and collapsed back into his chair, groaning and clutching his stomach. Shipsey leaned over and examined the contents of the cap.

"Don't even *think* of asking me to put that thing back on my head."

"Don't worry," said Macker, sliding around the table and delicately picking up the cap. "I know just the place for it." He gingerly made his way towards the toilets holding the cap in both hands.

Late the following morning four hungover bodies were making their way back to Dublin. As they crossed the Kerry border, Macker pulled over. He went to the boot and retrieved the Dublin cap. Although he'd washed it out it still carried a strong aroma of vomit. He stood in front of the roadside sign. "Welcome to County Kerry. All Ireland football champions a record 32 times." Using all his height and a bit of a jump he just about managed to balance the cap on top of the supporting pole. It was facing perfectly forward with the "Dublin" in clear view. A chorus of whistles and cheers welcomed him back to the car.

Chapter 24

Harry, the bar manager of *The Banner Man*, had always been a bit of a scrooge when it came to Christmas. This year he'd left it till the last minute before getting his staff to put up the pub decorations. They were the same crummy decorations he'd bought on the cheap in a January sale seven years earlier. As usual the artificial Christmas tree was being suspended from the ceiling so as not to take up valuable floor space. The young lounge staff were running in all directions with cellotape hanging from their lips shouting, "a bit to the left, now just a smidge higher, yep there!"

Matt was doing his best to ignore the chaos going on around him and reply to Shipsey's question. It shouldn't have been a difficult one, but he had to strain his eyes to the northeast corner of their sockets to try and tease the answer out of his memory bank. Then it suddenly came to him. "Soap."

"Soap!" Shipsey coughed and placed his pint back on the table. "How the fuck did you have an argument about soap? Wait a minute...don't tell me...You left scrape marks in it from cleaning your finger nails?"

"No."

You left behind a piece that was too small to use, instead of throwing it in the bin?"

"No."

"When you finished, there were a few pubic hairs still attached to it?"

"Euuugh...no."

"Ok...I give in. What did you do?"

"I didn't return it to the soap dish," said Matt, nodding his head guiltily.

"You didn't return it to the soap dish? You fucking rebel!"

"I know...I'm one *bad motherfucker*. I looked straight at that soap dish and thought...*No...fuck you...this baby's goin' on the side of the bath along with the shower gel and hair products*."

Shipsey couldn't help laughing. He knew only too well that when you're living with your partner, your arguments tend to begin over the silliest of things.

"Soap, that's a good one! But I betcha the argument wasn't really about soap, was it?"

"Honestly…I haven't got a fuckin' clue what it was about!"

Shipsey chuckled some more. "Ah…I love it! This is classic stuff."

"What's so fuckin' funny?"

"You fought with Sam for half an hour, followed by what? *four hours* of silent treatment and you haven't got the foggiest idea what it was all about! *That's* funny!"

"*That's* fucked up!"

"Ok, it's a bit fucked up, but it's funny too. You just won't see the funny side for another few days."

"There's nothing funny about getting my ass whooped in an argument over a bar of soap."

Shipsey shook his head. "But the argument wasn't about a bar of soap, was it?"

"I don't know!...That's how it started! Whatever the fuck it was about… well I just had no way of defending myself, cos she just kept switching from one subject to another! She was coming at me from different directions with all kinds of shit!"

"Wait a minute," said Shipsey, holding up his index finger. "You *tried* to *defend* yourself?

"Of course I did!"

Shipsey shook his head and started tutting. "Schoolboy error."

"What?"

"You've just made one of the most basic errors a cohabiting man can make."

"What?" Matt gasped angrily. "You think I shouda just sat there and taken a whole loada crap over a fucking bar of soap."

"Look," said Shipsey, raising his hand. "Just calm down and listen." He was secretly enjoying having a vastly superior knowledge to Matt on this particular subject. "Firstofall, this argument was not about a bar of soap. In fact it wasn't even an argument and the sooner you stop thinking of it as an argument the better."

"What *was* it then?"

"Try to think of it as a dressing down…y'know…that little chat the referee gives to you before he shows you the yellow card."

"What are you on about? It went on and on for over half an hour!"

"That's only cos you answered back. If you'd said nothing it would have been over in a minute or two."

"So, you're telling me I should have stood there like a naughty little toddler and said "sorry mammy, next time I'll be sure to put the soap back in the soapdish.""

Shipsey was starting to get impatient with his pupil. "For fuck sake Matt, forget about the fucking soap! This is not about a poxy bar of soap! This is about avoiding *The Store of Gore*!"

"The *store of gore*? What the fuck's that?"

"The *store of gore* is the can of worms a woman will open up if you engage her in a domestic argument. It's all the shit you did in the past that pissed her off. It's everything she said to you yesterday after she was finished giving out about the soap."

Matt fell silent. He knew Shipsey was right.

"So tell us," Shipsey smiled. "What else did she give you grief over?"

"Well, after the soap it was the cap on the toothpaste, then it was last weekend when I played football twice…on Saturday for my own team and again on Sunday when Stinger rang me up. Then she brought up the trip to Listowel when we ended up staying that extra night. And I think last on the list was work, cos I've been out with clients a fair bit lately."

Shipsey nodded. "That's not the worst *store of gore* I've ever heard."

"It's a load of crap if you ask me! I mean…it's Christmas for fuck sake! Everyone goes out more at Christmas! And the Listowel trip? That was three months ago and I copped a load of stick for that at the time!"

Shipsey laughed. "Janie still gives me shit over stuff I did three *years* ago."

"And the football thing!" Matt gasped. "She said nothing to me about that last weekend!"

"That's something else they do," Shipsey chuckled. "Some stuff they just put straight into the store without even mentioning it at the time."

"Well that's not exactly fair is it?"

"Fair? What's fair got to do with anything? Women don't play by the rules when it comes to fighting. Trust me…I've got the scars to prove it."

While Matt and Shipsey were bitching about the irrational behaviour of the women in their lives, Macker and Dave, who were on their way to the pub, were complaining about the lack of women in *their* lives. Since going out with Laura, Macker had been going through a very lean spell. In the last three months he'd managed a total of one nightclub snog. Every girl he chatted up seemed to be morose, moronic or married, or a combination of the three. He was beginning to get sick of the chasing game and just wanted to find the right girl and settle down, at least for a couple of months. He was still doing a damn sight better than Dave. Since the night in the cubicle with Helen, Dave hadn't even chatted up another girl. The reason for this was simple, but he wasn't about to tell Macker or the other lads that he was still in love with Kate. He just couldn't get her out of his system, not that he was trying very hard. He was regularly calling her on the phone under the guise that they were still friends, but he was desperate to find out if they could be more than friends again. By the time they'd made it to *The Banner Man*, Macker and Dave had convinced each other that being single sucked and that the grass was definitely greener on the side of the man in a relationship.

"Seriously lads," said Matt, "it's not as great as you think. I mean...you totally give up your freedom. All of a sudden you've got somebody else you have to answer to."

"Yeah," Shipsey agreed. "And if you wanna keep her sweet, you've gotta start doing all sorts of stuff you wouldn't normally do."

"Like...*sex*...y'mean?" asked Macker.

"Like going to museums and art galleries."

"I wouldn't mind that," said Dave. "Beats going to the pub all the time."

The other three lads paused and looked at Dave as if he'd let a very loud, smelly fart. Dave held his hands up in apology. "Sorry....I didn't mean it...I love pubs...must be the cold weather messing with my head."

"I just think it would be nice," said Macker "to...instead of being stuck out in the cold waiting for a taxi...to be at home in front of a warm fire, curled up on the couch with a cute chick, watching a video."

"Like *Big and Bouncy*", Shipsey chuckled.

"No, seriously lads," Macker continued. "I definitely think you have the better of it, being involved in good relationships. It's just a hassle trying to meet girls all the time."

Dave nodded. He hadn't been trying to meet any girls or gotten stuck out in the cold waiting for a taxi, but the idea of being curled up on a couch with Kate definitely appealed to him.

"Ok, maybe we have slightly the better of it," said Matt, "but it's not all strawberries and cream y'know...especially when you're livin' with your bird. Enjoy your freedom while you have it."

"Yeah," Shipsey agreed.

"Ok, I'm sure you have your tough times" Macker nodded, "but it's better than being on your own."

"I don't know though," said Matt. "there are times when I think I wouldn't mind being single again...Y'know...just for a few weeks. It would be fun to go out on the pull again."

"That's not a bad idea!" said Shipsey, leaning forward and pointing at Macker and Dave. "Next Saturday, you two guys stay in with Janie and Sam and myself and Matt will go out on the pull."

Macker was about to say, "only if I can have Sam," but decided against it. Instead he reminded them that *Satan's Whiskers* next race was that day and that he would happily miss out on a threesome with Pamela Anderson and Jennifer Lopez to see it.

Satan's Whiskers had picked up some bruises on his shins when he hit the last hurdle at Listowel, but after a months rest he was back in training. Following Paddy Mulryan's advice, the owners agreed to put him in the top hurdle race at the Christmas festival at Leopardstown. If he could finish in the top three of that race they would send him to Cheltenham in March. The fact that their horse was running at the Christmas Festival at Leopardstown was almost as exciting for the lads as the idea of it running at Cheltenham. Leopardstown was not exactly exotic to them, being only two miles down the road, but the Christmas festival was the best attended race meeting in Ireland and one they had been to many a time before. Macker was a big fan of the festival and had been to it every year for the last twelve years. He even made the journey four years ago when he was suffering with a temperature of a hundred and two. He finished the day with a temperature of a hundred and three, but with an extra fifty quid in his back pocket, so he was happy.

They discussed how they would travel to and from Leopardstown and Matt came up with the best idea.

"Right, so...Shipsey takes Jane, Sam and Myself. Macker takes Dave. We all go on the piss, get taxis home whenever we want and on Sunday morning I'll pick up Shipsey and Macker and drop them back up to their cars."

"Sounds good," Shipsey nodded and then looked at Macker. "Are Liam and Kate both coming this time?"

"Not sure," Macker shrugged. "I'm sure Liam will be there this time, but..."

"Yeah, they'll both be there," Dave interrupted.

Macker looked at Dave. "How dya know that?"

"I was talkin' to Kate about a week ago."

"I didn't know you bumped into Kate."

"No…on the phone. I still talk to her on the phone every now and then."

They were all surprised to hear this. It wasn't strange or sinful that Dave might still be in touch with Kate as a friend. The suspicious thing was that he hadn't mentioned it to any of them over the last six months. Matt was particularly surprised that Dave hadn't told *him*, because Dave had confided in him all the time when he was going out with Kate. And why didn't Macker know about it? He was Dave's flatmate, not to mention Kate's cousin. Maybe this wasn't a big deal, but Matt looked Dave up and down with one eyebrow slightly raised and had a feeling that it was. He was about to put Dave on the spot and ask him what the story was when three young ladies entering the pub caught his eye.

"Jaysis lads!" Matt whispered loudly and started gesturing towards the door. "Is that who I think it is?"

Macker, Dave and Shipsey strained their necks to get a look. They didn't recognise two of the girls, but the third one definitely rang a bell.

"It is!" Shipsey gasped.

"Yeah, I reckon so," nodded Dave. "Jaysis, she's lookin' well… Nice tan!"

"She must have just come back," said Matt. "It's summer down there."

"I thought she was supposed to have gone for a year," Shipsey muttered. "She must have just come home for Christmas"

"If you're in Australia for a year," said Matt. "You don't fly home and back for Christmas. Not unless you're fuckin' loaded."

"S'pose not," Shipsey agreed. "Somethin' must have gone wrong then. Maybe she broke up with what's 'is name."

They all looked at Macker who was still staring speechlessly across to where the girls were taking their seats. His pulse was racing, his eyes were glazed over and his head was cloudy, but he finally managed to speak.

"Meeechelle…my belle."

After three more swift pints Macker finally got up the courage to go and talk to Michelle. His heart was pounding as he made his way across the lounge. He'd never been so nervous in all his life. Since his first kiss at the age of eleven he must have chatted up ten thousand girls, but suddenly it felt like he was doing it for the first time. It was as if all prior encounters had been dummy runs leading up to this moment. And now rehearsals were over, the theatre was packed, and for the first time ever, it actually mattered. He felt really awkward and had to concentrate hard on not dropping his pint or tripping over his own legs. Finally when he got to within five feet of her, Michelle looked up, raised her eyebrows and smiled warmly. She still had the same beautiful smile and Macker responded with a smile of his own...Not so much a smile...as a manic grin. The kind of smile a demonic executioner might show to his next lucky customer.

"Hi!" Michelle said cheerily. "How are you?"

"Hi, how are you?" Macker repeated. "I mean...I'm fine....how are you? Happy Christmas!"

"Happy Christmas to you too!" Michelle giggled.

Macker continued to grin...manically.

Michelle introduced him to her two friends as Michael. He'd almost forgotten that was his name. Even at work the people who didn't call him Macker called him Mick, which until this moment he preferred to Michael. But coming from Michelle's lips Michael sounded smooth, confident and sexy. As she invited him to sit down, he felt anything but smooth, confident and sexy. He started talking to himself to try and calm down. It was a conversation between the part of his brain that usually drove the bus of social interaction and the lunatic who'd just hijacked it.

Stop smiling so much would you!

Was I smiling? Sorry, I wasn't.

You're still doing it!

Am I? Oh well...nothing wrong with smiling.

There is when it's a big goofy stupid smile like the one you've got on!

It's just my normal smile.

No it's not! You look like someone has taken out all your teeth and replaced them with scrabble tiles!

Really?

Yes! And they're spelling out the word "dick"!

I'm just trying to be friendly.

You look like a fucking axe murderer! Try and tone it down a bit.

She looks great, doesn't she?

Yes, but stop staring at her! Ask her how she got on in Australia.

With the noisy debate still raging on in his head Macker didn't catch much of what Michelle had to say about Australia.

Dude! You're still staring at her!

Am I?

Yes! Now look away! Just glance down at your pint or around the

217

bar for a sec.

OK, in a minute.

No! Now!

What's your problem? I'm just trying to maintain eye contact.

You're gonna scare the shit out of her! You've been staring deep into her eyes for the last five minutes!

Couldn't be that long.

It is! You haven't even taken a peep at her tits for Christ's sake! You need to look away right now! Imagine there's a sexy woman walking through the pub. Just take a casual look around.

I can't!

Of course you can! Imagine its Melinda Messenger she's standing in the middle of the lounge totally naked!

So

She's just been joined by Penelope Cruz and an Irish wolfhound and they're having three way sex!

Take a photo for me.

Suddenly Michelle stopped talking and looked at Macker as if she was expecting a response to a question.

Oh you're fucked now! You haven't been listening have you?

Shit! That's your fault! You distracted me!

Hey, don't look at me buddy. You're the one driving the bus tonight.

What the fuck am I gonna say?

Dunno, but you better say it soon!

For the first time in five minutes Macker blinked. As, he cleared his throat, the corners of his mouth edged even closer to his ears.

"It's great to see you. You look …great!"

Oh, that's just brilliant! Nice use of the word "great" Einstein. Fuck off.

"Thanks" Michelle smiled. "You look pretty good yourself."

She lifted a few fringe hairs away from her pretty face and blushed slightly. That's when Macker noticed the ring on her finger. It was an amber ring. It was a big amber ring. It was a big rectangular amber ring on a silver band. It was the big rectangular amber ring on the silver band that he had given to her when she left for Australia. In that fleeting moment, the old composed and confident Macker returned and there was only one question left to ask.

"So, are you still goin' out with what's 'is name?"

Macker walked Michelle home that night, smiling all the way. He'd managed to tone his smile down from psychotic to ecstatic, but that was as far as it would go for the moment. They stood outside her parent's house until three in the morning, chatting, cuddling and snogging. Macker could feel a warm buzz in his stomach the whole time. When they kissed the buzz was more like an electric shock. After they'd said their final goodnight he turned to face the long walk home. It was a crisp, wintry night and the wind had plenty of bite in it, but Macker was too warm inside to feel the cold. As he slushed through the leaves on Shrewsbury bridge he stopped to look at the river. One of the owner's of the houses backing on to the river had made a special effort with their Christmas decorations. All the trees in the garden were lit up like stars and in the middle of them was an artificial snowman. The garden was facing onto the river about fifty metres away, but the snowman was facing the bridge where Macker was standing. The lights that made up his right arm were flashing in a way that gave the impression that he was waving. As he smiled and waved back, Macker wondered if the snowman knew that he was waving to the happiest man in the world.

Chapter 25

The morning of *Satan's Whiskers* fourth race, Macker woke up and let out a long satisfied sigh. He could feel the warmth of Michelle's body next to him and could tell from her breathing that she was still asleep. He smiled to himself as he went over in his mind what had been the perfect evening. He'd taken her to an expensive restaurant in Blackrock, where they'd washed down some delicious food with some very tasty wine. After dinner they'd decided to walk back to his place via the video store. It was a clear crisp evening and the stars were out in numbers. Back at his flat he learned how Michelle liked her coffee and committed it to memory. Strong, no sugar, tiny drop of milk. They curled up on the couch together and not long into the video she dozed off. After watching a bit of the video on his own, Macker finally decided to wake her up with a few soft kisses on the lips. It had the desired effect, because ten minutes later they were on his bed, making love for the first time.

It had been the perfect night...or had it?

He remembered the bill from the restaurant. Way too expensive for the minuscule food portions they'd received. And the waiter was a French snob who spent half his time trying to look down his nose at Macker and the other half trying to look down Michelle's top. The wine hadn't been perfect either. Macker preferred white, but Michelle was a red drinker so he had to compromise on that. It wasn't the only time he let Michelle get her own way. In the video shop, he'd wanted to rent Samuel L Jackson's latest thriller, but they ended up getting a romantic comedy starring Hugh Grant. The cuddle on the couch wasn't without its drawbacks either. After a while Macker started to feel unbearably hot and uncomfortable. Then there was the awkward moment in the bedroom when he had to go fidgeting for a condom in his bedside locker. The sex itself had been pretty good, although Michelle didn't quite match "Loud Laura" for flexibility and sheer enthusiasm. And somewhere in the middle of it she'd managed to cut his shin with one of her toenails. Macker smiled to himself as he looked at the beautiful girl lying next to him. Her mouth was open and she was snoring softly. He recalled a conversation he'd had with Shipsey many months earlier and started chuckling to himself. Shipsey had been right. The perfect woman doesn't exist. The perfect night doesn't even exist. Macker leaned over and kissed Michelle on the forehead. But perfect love does.

*****

The last day of the Christmas festival was the busiest. The weather had improved a bit and the previous three days of racing had obviously not deterred the enthusiastic Dublin crowd. The lads had never seen the racecourse so packed and were continually bumping into people they knew. They couldn't help mentioning that there was a very special horse named "*Satan's Whiskers*" running in the second last race. Just in case everyone they met also backed their horse, they decided to get their money down early. Between them they put just over a thousand euro on him each way. Macker had wanted to back him to win, because the odds were only six-to-one, but the other lads had overruled him. They had agreed that any winnings would go into a fund for Cheltenham, so they needed to collect some sort of return if the horse was only placed. After the first couple of races they adjourned to one of the busy bars to warm up. They were clearly not the only ones feeling the cold, because the crowd was full of punters ordering hot whiskies and ports. The bar manager, who was worried they were going to run out of cloves had instructed his staff to reduce the number they put in each drink. The owners of *Satan's Whiskers* and their partners were spread out in small groups at the busiest end of the pub. The area they were in was so heavily crowded that it was impossible to have a conversation with more than two other people at the same time. Macker was holding Michelle's hand and talking to Stinger. He'd bumped into his old football buddy down in the betting ring and was now telling him all about the adventure they'd been having with "*Satan's Whiskers*." Not far away Shipsey was chatting to Kate's dad about Cheltenham. Shipsey hadn't been before, but Liam's stories of heavy drinking seesions, games of poker till the small hours and the rivalry between the Irish and the English were getting him in the mood. Another few yards away were Dave, Jane and Samantha. Sam was talking excitedly about her newborn niece. Her sister gave birth to a baby girl on Christmas day, which she had very imaginatively named Noelle. Although if you asked Dave what her name was he might have guessed Rudolf, because he wasn't really paying attention. Two yards over Sam's shoulder he could see the back of Kate's head. They'd been at the races for an hour and a half and he still hadn't had a chance to speak to her. With the crowd being so huge he was worried he'd never get the opportunity to talk to her alone and ask her out. He was beginning to regret not being up front with Matt about his feelings for Kate. He could have used the help and Matt would have come up with a way to get him that valuable face time.

Matt, who had just bought a round of hot drinks, was chatting to Kate. She was explaining to him that she had been in two minds about coming to the races that day on account of her mum being ill with the flu.

"So, who's looking after her?"

"My brother and sister are home from university," said Kate. "My mum practically shoved me out of the door when I told her I wanted to stay home from the races to make sure she was all right."

"Well, I think your mum's right," Matt nodded. "You're the one looking after her all the time. It's only right that you take a break when you can."

"Yeah, I know," said Kate. "I just feel bad leaving her when she's stuck in bed."

"It's only the flu. She'll be fine," said Matt. "Don't worry."

But Kate was worried. The doctor had given her mum some antibiotics for the flu, which simply added to the glut of drugs that she was already taking. Kate knew that while her mother had the flu, her strength for fighting the lupus would be diminished. She thought of her frail mum lying in bed next to a locker full of medication and felt her eyes starting to water. Matt could see the tears forming in Kate's eyes. At the same time he noticed Dave looking nervously over at Kate and quickly tried to lighten the subject.

"So, whadya think of the new Dave Massey?"

Kate could just about see Dave's shaved head when she looked over her shoulder. He was only a couple of yards away, but there was about five tonnes of crowd between them. "I think he looks pretty good." Kate smiled and dried a tear. "Much healthier anyway. The hair definitely looks better shaved. I'm getting used to it now. And I see he got rid of the goatee. Yeah, he looks quite well."

"Well enough to go back out with him?" asked Matt.

"What?" gasped Kate. "Did he send you over here to find that out?"

"No," Matt smiled. "I swear he didn't. I don't even know if he wants to get back with you…I mean…he's said nothing to me."

"So, why are you asking me that then?" Kate frowned.

"Well, it's like this," Matt smiled. "I reckon he still fancies the ass off you and I was wondering if your feelings had changed for him now that he's a new sleeker version of the old Dave."

"What makes you think he fancies me?" asked Kate.

"Just call it male intuition." Matt didn't want to give too much away. He had a couple of reasons for thinking it, not least of which was the way Dave kept glancing awkwardly over at her.

"I see," Kate mused.

"I know it's a bit of a blunt question," Matt whispered. "But I decided against the coy approach. I tried that with you in the past and you spotted it straight away."

"Well I am a fellow "Quicker Wit," said Kate, raising an eyebrow.

"That's right," said Matt, remembering his old comic book heroes. "And you still haven't answered the bloody question! Jesus, you're difficult to pin down! I wouldn't like to play you at chess."

"Chess?" Kate frowned. "I thought that was a board game where you try to kill your opponents king. What's that got to do with pinning me down?" she smiled. "You must be thinking of wrestling or something else."

Matt started to laugh. "Y'know, you should go on mastermind and your specialist subject should be changin' the fuckin' subject."

"Thanks," laughed Kate. "I'll take that as a compliment."

"Listen," said Matt. "Fair enough if you don't want to answer the question. I just thought maybe I could help out."

"What was the question again?" Kate giggled.

Matt threw his eyes to the heavens. "Do you fancy Dave? Would you like to get back together with him?"

"Right," Kate nodded. "And how do you think you can help?"

Matt was almost ready to give up. Kate seemed determined not to tell him anything, but he decided to persevere. "Well, if you want to get back with him, I'll help him get over his shyness and insecurity, because that's all that's stopping him from asking you out. And if you don't wanna get back together, I'll help you avoid getting caught in a tricky situation and at the same time, hopefully we can prevent Dave's feelings getting hurt."

"Right then," said Kate. "I'll tell you, but I don't know how you're so convinced he's about to ask me out."

"Trust me. I'll prove it to you."

"Ok, well basically I think Dave is a lovely guy and he does look a lot fitter and healthier, but I still don't really fancy him."

"Ok, fair enough," Matt nodded.

"So, what's the plan?" asked Kate.

Matt explained the plan and Kate agreed to go along with it. After a while the crowd started to empty out a bit, with people placing their bets for the next race. Kate left him on his own, reading his racing programme and pushed her way through the crowd to talk to Macker, Michelle and Stinger. A couple of minutes later, Matt subtly called Macker and Michelle over to have a look at the form, leaving Kate alone with Stinger. This part of the plan was to demonstrate to Kate that Dave was still very interested in her. Sure enough, within seconds of being left alone with Stinger, Kate noticed Dave leaving Sam and Jane and making his way over to Matt. This is exactly what Matt had predicted. He'd said that Dave would either go directly over to interrupt her and Stinger or get Matt to try and do it for him. The whole operation only took a couple of minutes, but before long Matt and Dave were both on their way over to separate Stinger and Kate. Not long after that, the third race started and Matt and Stinger went outside to watch it. Finally, Dave was alone with Kate. He'd waited long enough for this moment and even though he was incredibly nervous, he wasn't going to let it pass without asking her out to dinner. *This is it*, he thought.

This is it, thought Kate. *Matt was right!* She could tell that Dave had something on his mind and knew she had to act fast.

*****

Satan's Whiskers was a length ahead of the field when they crossed the finishing line. Unfortunately they had another circuit of the track to run, but the lads let out an ironic cheer anyway.

"I don't know about that," said Matt. "I'm not sure I like the fact that he's leading this early in the race."

"Don't worry about it," said Macker. "I was talkin' to Liam and seemingly Kevin has been told to keep him up front out of trouble. It's a bloody big field ye see."

"Fair enough," said Matt. "I just have a horrible feelin' he's gonna fall."

"Me too," muttered Shipsey.

"Will you two shut up?" shouted Macker. "Kevin's been told to ease him up going into hurdles…y'know…let him find his own stride."

"Which one's the favourite?"

American Pie said Shipsey, looking down at his programme. "He's number three…red jersey…yellow cap."

"There he is! He's in about fifth place."

American Pie had opened in the betting at 5/1 but at the off he was seven-to-two so there had been plenty of money put on him. As they entered the back straight he moved up from fifth to third and the noise of the crowd rose several decibels. A group of three blokes standing

224

right in front of the lads were roaring their heads off for *American Pie*, so the lads responded in kind.

"Come on *Satans Whiskers*!" Shipsey made sure to scream it right into their ears. The guy in the middle turned around and grinned at them.

"Ha! You have no chance," he sniggered.

With that, the lads realised that *Satan's Whiskers* wasn't the only one with a battle on his hands. All the way down the back straight they fought hard to drown out the roar of their enemy. Every time *Satan's Whiskers* approached a fence he slowed down to jump it carefully. In the process *American Pie* would catch up a length or two and their three rivals would get excited.

"Come on *American Pie*!"

Once he'd landed *Satan's Whiskers* would then pick up the pace again and re-establish his two length lead.

"Come on "Satan"!"

All the shouting was appearing to work, because with only two hurdles left to jump the two horses were about six lengths clear of the rest of the field. As "*Satan's Whiskers*" slowed to take the hurdle *American Pie* pulled up right beside him. The three strangers were jumping up and down screaming.

"Come on *American Pie*!"

But once more *Satan's Whiskers* proved faster over the flat surface and retook the lead.

"Come on Satan!"

As they approached the last hurdle he'd restored his two-length lead. Suddenly, Macker realised that there was a gap of ten lengths to the third placed horse and the implications of the final hurdle hit him.

"Jesus lads! If he jumps this last one we're goin' to fuckin' Cheltenham! Even if he only comes second we're goin' to fuckin' Cheltenham!"

"Fuck second!" shouted Shipsey. "We wanna beat this *American Pie* piece of shit!"

"Come on Satan!"

Satan's Whiskers didn't appear to be slowing down in his last few strides before the final hurdle. If anything he seemed to speed up and reach it at full pelt. The lads held their breath as he took off. Macker held his breath, closed his eyes, crossed his fingers and said two *Hail Marys* and an *Our Father"*

"Yessssssssssssssssssssssssssssssss!!!!!" *Satan's Whiskers* leapt magnificently over the hurdle and charged towards the finishing line leaving *American Pie* for dead. All the owners went wild and started hugging and kissing each other. It was as if Ireland had won the world cup. Not fully satisfied with their triumph on the racetrack, Shipsey wanted to ram home victory in the vocal warfare as well. He started singing...

> *"Bye bye Miss American Pie*
> *Drove my chevy to the levee but the levee was dry*
> *Satan's Whiskers is gonna win by a mile*
> *And we'll be in Cheltenham in a while*
> *We'll be in Cheltenham in a while"*

Cheltenham figured strongly in the banter and song that took place in the bar over the next few hours. "The Rocky Road to Cheltenham" and "It's a Long Way to Cheltnamary" became the adopted ballads of choice. The hot ports were going down sweetly and there were being toasts made to all and sundry.

> *"Up Satan's Whiskers!"*
> *"Up Cheltenham!"*
> *"Up Kevin Daly!"*
> *"Up Leopardstown!"*
> *"Up six to one!"*
> *"Up the hot ports!"*

It wasn't until the trainer Paddy Mulryan joined them for a quick drink that a slight dampner was put on things. He reminded everyone that it was a bit too soon to get carried away with ideas of Cheltenham. Although *Satan's Whiskers* was fine now he still had one more race to run before he would cross the Irish Sea and anything could go wrong. Paddy had earmarked a race in Down on the 8th of February that would be suitable. He then told them a story of a previous horse he'd had that injured himself in the horsebox on the way to Cheltenham. For a moment the mood fell sombre as the owners contemplated the possibility of *Satan's Whiskers* picking up an injury in his next race or even on the journey to Cheltenham. It was Shipsey who got the party going again, when he lifted his glass and roared, "Up Down!"

"Yeah! Up Down!" came the response.

"Up the 8th of Feb!"

"Yeah! Up the 8th of Feb!"

It was going to be a long night.

Towards the end of the night Dave and Matt had an alcohol fuelled heart to heart. Matt had not had a chance to find out from Kate how things had gone in her efforts to let Dave down gently, so he was glad when Dave started to spill the beans. Dave admitted that he was still crazy about Kate and had been planning to ask her out for New Years Eve.

"So what happened?" asked Matt, feigning slight surprise.

"Well, she must have read my mind," said Dave. "Before I could ask her out, she started telling me how *Stinger* had chatted her up and asked her out."

"Stinger asked her out?" gasped Matt.

"Yeah, that's what she told me!"

"What did she say?"

Dave frowned at Matt. "She said your friend Stinger has just asked me out."

"No, you plonker! What did she say to Stinger?"

"I don't know. She hadn't given him an answer. She said she wanted to ask my advice as a *Friend* what she should do. She made a real point of emphasizing the word *Friend*. That kinda hurt, but it made me realise that I was wasting my time asking her out."

"I see," said Matt. This hadn't quite being the plan he'd devised, but it seemed to have done the job and an embarrassing situation had been avoided. The only questionable part was had Stinger really asked Kate out or did she make it up?

"So, what was your advice to her about Stinger?" asked Matt.

"Well, I don't really know him that well, so I just said he's a decent bloke."

"A decent bloke?" Matt raised his eyebrows. "Did you not mention the cocaine?"

"No...Does he do cocaine?"

"I think so...He definitely smokes a load of hash."

"Really?"

"Yeah." Matt wasn't actually too sure about this. He'd known Stinger to smoke the odd joint in the past, but that was quite a few years ago. What he was pretty sure about was that Stinger and Kate were not a good match. He looked at Dave who had almost fully peeled the sponsor's logo off his beermat.

"So what do you reckon she said to Stinger in the end?"

"I dunno," said Dave dejectedly. "All I know is Kate's a special girl, but its time for me to move on. I've spent far too long fixated on someone who never really wanted to be more than a friend."

Chapter 26

The following morning Dave woke up in the knowledge that he was not going to get back together with Kate, but he was determined to approach the day with a positive outlook. The old Dave would have lounged around in bed for half the day listening to Coldplay, but the new Dave wasn't falling into that trap. The new Dave wasn't about to go into a prolonged state of paralysing heartache. No, the new Dave was going to look on the bright side...be positive...take affirmative action. The new Dave was going to have pop tarts for breakfast.

While munching through his tasty cereal snack, Dave thought back to the chat he'd had with Matt the night before. Matt had rightly pointed out that it had been as a result of the night with Helen that Dave had shaved his head and gone on the diet. Helen was the one who convinced him that if he lost weight and quit smoking he would feel better about himself. The new Dave may have spent all his time chasing Kate, but his origin was very much down to Helen. She was the one who'd been kind enough to really listen to what he had to say. The one who picked him up and restored some of his confidence...Oh, and the one who'd given him the best blowjob of his life in a cubicle in *The Endzone* nightclub. As he reminisced fondly about their university romance he decided to call her. *No, better still*, he thought. *I'll text her.*

He hadn't met Helen since the night of the cubicle incident and had only spoken to her a couple of times on the phone, but things were still pretty friendly between them. If he sent a text message, he could find out all he needed to know without putting his neck on the line. He could take his time, choose exactly the right words and avoid any awkward silences or the embarrassment of finding out that she'd just got married or moved to Peru. He put on CD number one of the "Party in the Park" compilation, while he designed the perfect text message. It wasn't until the end of CD number two that he was really happy with what he'd produced.

"Hey good looking! Need a date for New Years?"

It was straight and to the point, with a little edge of charm. Ok, Seamus Heaney didn't have too much to worry about, but Dave nodded to himself contently as his thumb hovered over the send button. He read the message another five times before deciding to replace the "g" in "looking" with an apostrophe. Macker and Michelle had arrived into the kitchen and beamed their "Hellos." They were somehow managing to combine the act of making coffee with a bout of light foreplay. Dave read his message one more time and pressed send.

Meanwhile in Naas, Co. Kildare, Kate was trying to deal with her own set of realities. As usual she'd been first out of bed and had gone to check on her mum. Her dad was snoring loudly in one single bed while her mum lay awake in the other, looking weary. This was the third morning in a row that she didn't look like she'd slept well. "Did he keep you up all night?" asked Kate, nodding towards her dad.

"If only," her mum whispered. She barely managed a smile. Kate could usually gage from this routine exchange just how her mum was feeling and she didn't look good. She was still suffering badly from the flu, which meant it was going to be another tough day. Normally she would struggle out of bed and get into the bath first thing in the morning. Her biggest singular complaint since she'd been diagnosed with lupus had been the aches and pains in her muscles and bones, and mornings were always the worst. The best way to soothe these was with warm water and she always felt better after her bath. But the last two days she hadn't felt well enough to get out of bed and she was now in quite a lot of pain. She did her best to put on a brave face when Kate brought her three hot water bottles and helped her take her medication. She always made a point of not complaining too much when asked how she felt, mainly because she didn't enjoy visits from the doctor, or worse still, visits to the hospital. But Kate always spent enough time with her to figure out just how bad she was and this was a bad day.

When her dad got up and started to get ready for work, Kate put the TV on for her mum. The bedroom TV was old and only really used when her mum was bed ridden. As usual it was tuned into The Nature Channel, her mum's favourite. Kate sat and chatted to her mum for a while as they watched a programme about a mother's role in the feeding habits of her offspring. The first part of the film showed a mother cheetah and how over a few months she raised her two kittens from suckling milk, to eating dead quarry and finally trained them to catch live prey. Kate held her mums hand as they watched the young cheetahs come of age. Nature programmes were easily her mum's favourite form of entertainment and always seemed to lift her spirits, but Kate couldn't watch when the focus of the second part of the programme changed to spiders. Kate loved nature programmes too, especially watching them with her mum, but she drew the line at spiders. Kate detested spiders. She continued to watch for a little while as an army load of spiderlings were being brought into the world by their mother. There were thousands of the tiny little things all blind and helpless. Kate didn't want to watch and was squirming in her chair holding her mum's hand. Then something awful happened. The day after their first moult the babies were ready to feed. The mother spider spun a huge web and started to trigger it in such a way as to guide her blind infants instinctively towards the middle of it. There waited their first meal. The mother had made the ultimate sacrifice. She'd given up her own life. She was still alive when her blind spiderlings unknowingly started to nibble away at her own flesh.

"Euuuuugggghhhhh." Kate held her hands over her eyes as she left the room to do some house chores.

As she was on her way downstairs the post flopped on to the hall floor. One particular envelope caught her eye. It was a card addressed to her. A late Christmas card was her first thought, but she didn't recognise the writing and the lime green envelope didn't look particularly Christmassy. Kate tore the envelope open and realised it wasn't a Christmas card, but a wedding invite. Nobody she knew was engaged! Rather than reading it, her eyes started to search frantically through the print for a name that she recognised.

Dave got a shock when his dressing gown started to vibrate. He'd just taken it off and slung it on the bathroom floor before jumping into the shower. It was only ten minutes since he'd texted Helen and he hadn't expected such a fast response. Now he was left with a few options. Option one: Enjoy his shower. Take his time. Dry himself. Get out and read the text. A sensible option, but it meant he wouldn't get to read the text for another five minutes. Would he really enjoy his shower that much without knowing what the text said? Option two: He quickly jumps out of the shower, grabs his phone and jumps back in. The only pitfall with this option is that he'd end up getting the floor all wet. Only the week before he'd had a go at Macker for leaving a pool of water on the bathroom floor. Finally, there was option three. He could stay in the bath and stretch a hand across the bathroom to reach his dressing gown pocket. He really wanted to read that text from the warmth of the shower. He'd only just got in and the water was perfect. The air outside it was freezing. He decided to go for option three and placed his knee on top of the side of the bath and held on to the shower pipe with his right hand. He was about six inches away from reaching with his left hand. The trajectory was all wrong. He was coming from too high an angle. To get lower down he placed both his knees in the bottom of the bath and stretched again. He took most of his weight on his lower belly, which was resting on the side of the bath. Painful, but definitely closer...only two more inches to go. There was some water dripping off his body onto the floor, but not as much as there would have been if he placed a hand outside the bath. Still, if he knew what he was in for he would have gladly placed a hand outside the bath and dealt with the consequence of a wet bathroom floor. He would have happily retiled the entire bathroom floor if he could have saved himself from what happen next. As he stretched nearer to the dressing gown his belly slipped on the side of the bath and he lurched forward. His pelvic region took the brunt of the blow, crashing into the hard ceramic surface. A split second later his left hand shot out to break the fall. He screamed in agony as a stream of water rolled down his wrist onto the cold bathroom floor.

"Mr and Mr James McCarthy are very pleased to invite "Kate McCann and Friend" to the after wedding party of their daughter Sarah to Mr. Paul Hennessy..."at this point Kate stopped reading and her heart stopped beating. The only man she'd ever really loved was getting married. Paul Hennessy, the man who she went out with for two years in university in Waterford. The man who was better at everything than all her other boyfriends. Talking, walking, smiling, laughing, lovemaking, even cooking. Paul Hennessy was going to be someone else's husband and it hurt. It started off hurting a little bit, but after Kate retreated to her bedroom and took out a photograph of her and her old flame it began to hurt a lot. It was one of those perfect photos that can only be taken when the subjects aren't aware. She could clearly remember the night it was taken. It was a warm June evening four and a half years earlier. She'd just finished her exams and all her college friends had gathered in the beer garden of their favourite Waterford pub. They sat outside drinking and laughing till closing time. One of her flatmates had taken a photograph of her and Paul with just the black night sky in the background. In it she was squeezing him tight and biting his ear. Paul had his eyes closed and his mouth open, lost somewhere between extacy and agony, but definitely closer to the former. That was another thing about Paul Hennessy. He had the best tasting ears in the world. Kate began to cry. How could a man with such good tasting ears leave her, go to Australia and cheat on her? How could he be getting married? Who the hell is Sarah McCarthy? Why did he invite her to the wedding?

Dave was still in his starting block position, knees inside the bath, hands and torso outside, when Macker came to the door. He'd heard the groans from the kitchen.

"You all right lad?"

Dave could only manage a low rumbling groan.

Macker put his lips closer to the door. "Dave, can you hear me?"

"Yeah," Dave moaned.

"What happened?"

"Slipped."

"You ok?"

"No."

"Need an ambulance?"

"No."

"Do you want me to help?"

"No."

"Ok, I'll be off then." Macker took a step away from the door and then remembered something. "Dave."

"What?"

"Don't get the floor all wet."

"Fuck off!"

Dave managed to clamber out of the bath, getting the floor very wet in the process. Standing was too painful so he sat down legs crossed on the cold bathroom floor.

"That's a good way to catch piles," his mum would have told him, but Dave wasn't too worried about piles right now. He was more concerned with the excruciating pain darting through his pelvic region.

Piles...my arse! He thought, neglecting to see the humour. *I'd gladly take a healthy dose of piles over this!*

He reached out for the dressing gown and took the phone from the pocket. He thought of his mums words again and slid the dressing gown under his bum, just in case.

The text from Helen read, "Maybe, but what about the girl from Kildare?"

With all that he had gone through, Dave had forgotten what he had said in his own text message, but he was sure he hadn't mentioned Kate. He had to go back and read it to try and put Helen's text into perspective.

"Hey good lookin'. Need a date for New Years?"

For a moment Dave didn't understand why Helen had mentioned Kate, but then he copped on. The last time he'd met Helen he spent the whole time talking about Kate. Even after Helen had given him the

232

blowjob of the century, he spent the rest of the night telling her how sad he was to have broken up with Kate. Dave held his hand to his head and cringed. He'd even asked Helen out at the end of the night when he was really drunk. Not the smoothest move he'd ever made, but then, he had a habit of doing stupid things when he was drunk around Helen. After one particularly heavy session, he'd fallen asleep in her bed only to wake up at 4am and piss in her linen basket. All things considered, she'd taken it unbelievably well. But that was Helen. She wasn't the type to go berserk over a few urine-stained garments. In fact, in all the time he'd known Helen, he only once remembered her getting really angry. That was the time her car got clamped outside a pub on D'Oilear Street. Needless to say, Dave was the one who'd parked it there and insisted it would be fine.

Dave realised that the next text he sent was crucial. From now on *Helen* had to be the one up on the pedastal, not Kate. He had to convey to Helen that she was the one he wanted and that if he got her back, he'd work hard to keep her. He had to convince her that he'd grown up a bit, but most of all he had to let her know that he was over Kate. He groaned as he got to his feet. He was still in a lot of pain, so he got back into the shower to warm the wounded area. This time it didn't take him long to come up with the perfect words, "What girl from Kildare?"

Meanwhile the girl from Kildare was lying on her bed drying her tears. As soon as she dried them, more started to flow. It had been a long time since she'd had a good cry and there were clearly plenty of tears waiting to be freed. She cried for Paul Hennessy, she cried for her mum, then she cried for herself. It had been two years since her mum was diagnosed with lupus. Two years since she moved back to Kildare and put her life on hold. She'd lost contact with most of the friends she'd made in University. She'd quit her Dublin job, which she enjoyed very much and her love life was non-existent. How was she going to meet someone to help her get over the fact that Paul Hennessy is getting married when she never goes out? In the last two years she'd had three boyfriends. Two brief encounters with local losers and the three months she went out with Dave, a man she should never have treated as anything more than a friend. Of course, Stinger had asked her out the previous day, but he wasn't exactly Paul Hennessy. Then there was the usual problem of when she does get involved in a relationship that she doesn't commit to it properly, because of her mum's illness. She took another look at the photograph in her hand. The girl biting Paul Hennessy's ear looked young and happy. Kate felt old and sad.

*****

Dave went out with Helen on New Years Eve and they had a great time. After having a few quiet drinks together they went on to a party being thrown by a mutual college friend. Helen was very impressed with how well Dave looked. Looks had never really been that important to her, but it was a pleasant surprise to see how much weight he'd lost since they'd last met. Dave made a point of giving her full credit for this. They spent the night in the company of many old friends and it very much felt like old times. They grew closer together over the course of January and by the time it came to take a trip to County Down to watch *Satan's Whiskers* fifth race, Helen agreed to go along. It was the 8th of February.

Kate's mum went into hospital in the middle of January. She was feverish, short of breath and had bad chest pains. The lupus was getting worse and had caused her lungs to become inflamed. At first, the doctors gave her more antibiotics, but they didn't work so they put her on steroids. These helped for a while, but gradually she started to get a cough. It was a dry unrelenting cough and it took a lot out of her. When Kate left the hospital at night she could still hear that cough in her ears all the way home. Her mum was diagnosed with chronic lupus pneumonitis. She still did her best to put on a brave face, but the lupus wasn't just eating away at her body. It was eating away at her spirit…her fight…her will to live.

And then she died. She was a week away from her fifty-third birthday. Kate was the only one by her side. It was the 8th of February.

Chapter   2 7

On the morning of the 8th of February Matt's phone rang. It was Shane McGowan. Or at least it was Shipsey's car stereo and on it Shane McGowan was belting out the lyrics to *Sally McLennane* as only *Shane McGowan* can do.

> *"I'm sad to say, I must be on me way*
> *So buy me beer and whiskey cos I'm goin' far away*
> *I'd like to think I'll be returnin' when I can*
> *To the greatest little boozer and to Sally*
> *McLennane"*

Shipsey and Macker were in the front of the car with Dave and Helen in the back. They said nothing, just held the phone up to the car stereo, but the message to Matt was clear.

"We're off to County Down to watch another fantastic victory by the irrepressible *"Satan's Whiskers"* and you're stuck in Dublin going to a christening…nah nah ne-nah nah."

Matt was not impressed. It was bad enough that he was missing out on all the fun and had to go to Sam's niece's christening, but now his nose was being rubbed in it. He could just about hear their laughter over the music.

"Bastards," he said and hung up.

Five minutes later his phone rang again. It was Freddy Mercury. This time he hung up without saying anything and started to get ready for the christening. Sam was in the bedroom standing in front of the mirror in a new suit. In January she had landed a well-paid contract with a prominent fashion company. As a coming on board gift they'd given her a whole wardrobe of expensive new clothes. She was trying on a very well-tailored, charcoal-coloured pants suit with an expensive white blouse. Matt was admiring her from the doorway. Even in all its formality the suit still showed off her knockout figure to its best. He couldn't take his eyes off her long legs and tight bum. He checked his watch, wandering if they had time for a quick shag. It had been a while.

"What do you think?" asked Sam, turning to face him.

"Huh?"

"What do you think?" she repeated, holding her palms out by her sides.

"Oh...yeah...great. You look the business."

"What do you mean?"

"Huh?" Matt frowned. What part of what he said did she not understand?

"Do you think it looks too businessy?"

Now how was Matt supposed to answer that? It was a business suit. Its whole reason for being was to look businessy and this one certainly did, but the tone of Sam's question clearly hinted at the fact that she didn't want to look businessy. To say this suit was not businessy would be like saying the rain is not rainy.

"Well," Matt hesitated..."It..."

"Forget it," said Sam, starting to take the suit jacket off.

"But it's a lovely suit," Matt offered.

"Don't patronise me!"

"I'm not patronising you. I think it's a very nice suit."

"You just said it's too businessy!"

"No I didn't! I didn't get a chance to finish what I was going to say."

"Oh!" Sam looked up accusingly. "What were you going to say then?"

Shit thought Matt. *Walked myself into that one.* "I was going to say that it's a very nice suit and you look great, but perhaps it looks a bit business-like."

"I suppose you want me to wear a short skirt or a dress!"

"I didn't say that," said Matt, imagining Sam in a very short skirt.

"I'm not wearing a skirt. It's freezing outside!"

Sam had removed her suit jacket and pants and was unbuttoning her blouse. Matt jumped onto the bed and stretched out on his stomach, placing his chin on his fist. He hadn't given up on the idea of sex.

"It's a bit cold in here too. Maybe we can warm things up," he said, patting the bed. Sam ignored him and started rummaging through her wardrobe for something else to wear. Matt dejectedly got to his feet and started to put on his suit. As he was doing up his tie, Sam looked him up and down.

"Is that what you're wearing?"

"What?"

"Are you wearing your work suit?"

"Yeah, why?"

"Is it not a bit *businessy?*"

Matt sighed and stopped doing up his tie. "I suppose it is a bit *businessy*, but I don't have anything else to wear and besides, I don't mind looking *businessy*."

"I see. So it's ok for you to look businessy, but not for me."

"I didn't say that! *You're* the one who has the problem with *you* looking businessy, not me!"

"So, why did you say my suit looks too business-like for a christening?"

"Look Sam." Matt was getting pretty fed up. "You asked me in the first place did you look businessy. Clearly that was not the look you desired and yet you were wearing a business suit. I merely pointed out the obvious fact that one of the side effects of wearing a business suit is that it looks business-like. Now, it's *your* niece's christening so nobody will give a shit what I wear, so I'm gonna wear my suit." Matt pointed to her suit on the bed. "I think that is a genuinely nice suit and you look great in it, but if you don't wanna wear a suit then don't wear a fucking suit! Pick out something else and stop carrying on like a four-year-old!"

That was the end of the argument. Sam continued to get ready in silence. The "store of gore" remained closed. She did not take the fact that they were fighting as her queue to remind him that he hadn't taken the bins out on Wednesday or he'd left an empty carton of milk in the fridge the previous week. She didn't bring up the fact that on New Years Eve he'd left her waiting in the cold for ten minutes or that by midnight he was almost too drunk to kiss her. It was a sweet unadulterated victory and Matt went to watch some TV quietly pleased with himself.

An hour later they were driving to the christening in silence. Sam was still sulking and Matt felt guilty. He began to wonder if he should apologise for shouting at her. It always seemed to work out this way when they fought. Even when he knew he was right, Matt was always the first one to break and offer out the olive branch. He was relieved when his mobile phone broke the silence. It was Shipsey again, this time to let him know that they'd stopped in Castlebellingham for a delicious pint of Guinness and were about to cross the border into Northern Ireland. Matt wished he was with them.

They met up with the rest of Sam's family outside Kilternan Church. Sam's niece, Noelle, was decked out in her christening outfit and everyone gathered around to admire her and take photos. When it came time to go inside and take their seats Matt's phone rang again. No doubt it would be Shipsey letting him know that they'd entered County Down or that they'd just seen a hedgehog at the side of the road. Matt took the phone out of his pocket and was about to switch it off when he saw Kate's name flashing in the screen.

"Hi Kate, how's it goin'?" He could tell straight away that she was crying. Her speech was slow and intermittant, being broken up by tears, sniffles and sobs.

"Matt...sorry...I need to...speak to my Dad...I couldn't get...through to his phone."

"Sorry Kate. I'm not with your dad. I'm in Dublin. What's wrong?"

Kate could barely catch her breath.

"It's...my...mum...she's...she's...gone."

"Oh no...Oh God Kate...I'm so sorry."

Kate was crying hard now and couldn't speak so Matt continued. "Where are you? Did you try to ring Macker?"

"Yeah...I couldn't...get him...either."

"They might be out of coverage. I'll try Shipsey and Dave. Where are you?"

"Naas...hospital."

"Who are you with?"

"I'm on my own." Kate started to sob hard again.

Matt made a quick decision. "Ok, I'm gonna drive over. Stay there."

"No...I don't wanna...stay here...I wanna...go home."

"Are you sure you're all right to drive?"

"Yeah."

"Ok, I'll meet you at your house. It'll take me about an hour to get there. I'll ring Macker, Shipsey and Dave on the way. When I get through, I'll get your dad to call you. What about your brother and sister?"

"I got through to my sister...she's gonna ring my brother...They're both on the west coast."

"I'm so sorry Kate. I'll get there as soon as I can. Be careful driving home .ok?"

"Ok...thanks Matt."

Matt went into the church and explained the situation to Sam.

"Who's Kate?" she asked.

Matt threw his eyes towards the church ceiling. "Macker's cousin. Y'know...the one who owns part of the horse. You've met her a couple of times. She used to go out with Dave."

"Oh yeah," Sam mused. "But I still don't get why you have to drive to Kildare."

"She's on her own. Her dad's in County Down, her sister's in Limerick and her brother's in Galway."

"Oh right...but can you not just stay for the christening...it's about to start."

Matt shook his head and left.

Not long into his drive he passed the entrance to Stepaside golf course and felt a lump in his throat. Five and a half years earlier, he had been about to tee off on the eighth hole when he got a call to tell him that his own mum had died. He felt a tremendous sadness rising up as the memory of that horrible day came flooding back. It was the most devastating day of his life and now poor Kate was going through the same. He didn't like the thought of Kate being on her own and applied more pressure to the accelerator at the same time as picking up his phone to try to get through to the lads.

After trying all three of his friends for twenty minutes, Matt eventually got through to Shipsey.

"Matt, how's it goin'?"

"Not good lad. I need to speak to Kate's dad. Is he with you?"

The lads had just caught up with Liam McCann at the racetrack bar and were settling down to a pint. Shipsey, Macker, Dave and Helen watched as the smile fell away from Liam's face and quickly made way for tears. The lads could tell exactly what had happened. It didn't need saying. Liam was Macker's uncle, he was Kate's father, but over the last year he'd become all their friends and it was clear that he'd just lost his best friend. It hurt to see the pain on his face. Macker began to cry too so Shipsey and Dave put an arm around each of his shoulders. In almost total silence they left their pints, walked to their cars and started driving back to Kildare.

Thirty-two minutes after hearing from Kate, Matt pulled up outside her house. He'd done the trip in record time, but not without a few close scrapes with oncoming traffic. It's not an easy road to overtake on, especially when you're on the phone. Kate had obviously heard him pull up and opened the front door as he was approaching the steps up to it. Her eyes were full of tears and they started to flow again when Matt took her into a hug. She held him tight and sobbed heavily as he softly rubbed her back.

"I'm so sorry Kate."

They maintained their embrace in the doorway for a good two

minutes before Kate finally led him into the living room. He'd been in this room before with Kate and her mum and her mad auntie Maeve, but this time the room felt empty...cold, bleak and empty. Matt sat down beside her on the couch and continued to rub her back.

"Is there anything I can do Kate? Do you need me to make any phone-calls or do you want me to get the fire going?"

"Yeah," said Kate, pointing towards the open fire, with tears rolling down both cheeks. As Matt sorted out the fire, Kate started to speak in fits and starts.

"I knew it would be today...I had a dream last night...I couldn't wake her...I knew when I woke up...she was going to...today was the day...Do you want a drink?"

"Eh...yeah," said Matt. "I'll get them. What do you want?"

"Whiskey and water...there's some in the kitchen."

Matt went to the kitchen and found an almost full bottle of Jameson. He was in the mood for one himself after his stressful car journey. He returned to the living room with two full glasses and got back to work on the fire as Kate told him everything that happened.

She visited her mum at ten o'clock that morning. Her dad had already been in the hospital since eight thirty and left for County Down shortly after Kate arrived. As usual he'd been reluctant to leave his wife, but had done so at her insistence.

"After my dad had left," sniffed Kate, "my mum just broke down. She started saying that she didn't feel strong enough to fight on and how it was hurting her to see me and my dad so upset. She said she wanted it to be over and would prefer it to happen before he got back for his evening visit."

Kate began to sob heavily again, her voice getting higher and higher, so Matt finished with the fire and went to console her.

"She started telling me...that I'd been...great...but it was...time for me to...get on with my life...Then she fell asleep."

At this point Kate couldn't speak through the tears. She was sitting sideways on the sofa crying into Matt's shoulder. Matt didn't know what to say. It was hurting him badly to see Kate so unhappy and all he wanted to do was reach inside her and scoop out a venomous portion of grief and consume it on her behalf. But the best he could do was rub her back and try to say the right thing.

"I'm so sorry Kate. I know I only met your mum once, but she was a really lovely woman."

Matt immediately felt guilty for talking about her mum using the past tense. Kate started to cry even more and he cursed himself for saying the wrong thing. He decided to stick to what he knew...pouring drinks, tending the fire and providing a shoulder to cry on.

After a while Matt went to top up their drinks as Kate dried her tears. When he returned she was crouched in front of the blazing fire, the tall flames lighting up her tear-stained face.

"Good fire" she said, without turning around.

"Thanks," said Matt, taking a sip from his glass and offering her the other one.

Kate stood up, took a sip and then looked at Matt confused.

"Why are you all dressed up?"

"What? Oh...I was at a christening."

"Oh Matt, I'm sorry. I didn't know. You shouldn't have come all the way out here."

"Don't be silly. I couldn't leave you on your own." Matt's mind flashed back again to the day *his* mum died. He took a little gulp of whiskey before continuing.

"I mean...it's your mum Kate...so...y'know...I had to come."

Kate could feel more tears building up. She'd been crying almost constantly for over two hours and was sure she'd dried herself out a couple of times, but each time it wasn't long before her eyes filled up again. She put her glass on the mantle piece and beckoned Matt towards her.

"I need that shoulder of yours again."

Matt placed his glass beside hers on the mantle piece and took her into another embrace, stroking her hair softly. And then something very unexpected happened. He started to cry. The first teardrop had rolled down his cheek before he realised it was happening. He felt silly and embarrassed and tried to pull himself together before Kate realised, but no matter how hard he tried he couldn't hold back the tears.

Kate's head was still nestled against Matt's shoulder when she began to sense that he was crying.

"Are you crying?"

"Just a bit," Matt sniffed.

"Why?"

"I don't know...it just hurts a lot to see you so upset...and then I started to think about the day my mum died...I'm sorry."

Kate lifted her head off his shoulder and pulled back to look at his face. Matt looked down and tried to smile at her through his tears.

"You're a beautiful man Matt, y'know that?"

Just as Matt was about to laugh, she reached up her mouth and kissed him on the lips.

In that instance Matt's head started to spin and his heart skipped a couple of beats. His lips were the only part of his body that seemed to know what to do. He returned Kate's soft kiss for a full four seconds before his head stopped spinning and he realised what he was doing. He pulled away and held her by the shoulders.

"Jesus Kate, I'm so sorry."

"Don't apologise" Kate diverted her eyes downward. "It's my fault."

"No, seriously Kate…I can't believe I did that. You have to forgive me."

"It's not your fault Matt. I kissed you."

"Ok, but I kissed you back…you caught me off guard…I'm sorry…I shouldn't have…y'know…but I really wasn't expecting that…I'm sorry."

"Matt, please stop apologising." Kate finally managed to look him in the eye and smile. "I might get the idea that you didn't enjoy it."

"No…I did enjoy it…it's just…well…y'know…well…em" After a long pause Matt held out his hands in a shrugging gesture. "Sorry Kate. I'm still in shock. I've forgotten how to speak."

They both chuckled nervously before Kate regained her composure.

"Listen Matt, you don't have to feel bad about this. I'm the one who kissed you. This is obviously not the right time, but I've wanted to kiss you for a while and when I saw your tears I…I know it's just been friendly flirting between us in the past, but…aghhhhhhhh!" Kate jumped backwards with a startled look in her eyes.

Matt jumped too with the fright. "*What*?"

"*Spider*!" Kate gasped. One hand was covering her mouth while the other was pointing out the offensive creature on the wall behind Matt. Matt sprung around fully expecting to see a tarantula bearing down on him. He was almost disappointed when it turned out to be a pea-sized dwarf spider. If this spider was a man, his surname would have been Thumb. Kate retreated quickly to the couch and tucked her knees into her chest.

"Are you ok?" Matt smiled.

"Yeah…sorry…I know I'm overreacting, but I've always hated spiders."

"Do you want me to get rid of it?"

"Yes please."

"Dead or alive?"

"Euuuugh dead…no wait a minute…alive."

"Ok," said Matt, looking around. "Have you got some paper or something?"

"Here, you can use this." Kate handed him a cream coloured card. Matt delicately scooped up the spider and headed for the front door. On his return he held up the card.

"What do you want me to do with this? It looks like a wedding invite."

Kate hesitated for a moment. It was a wedding invite. It was Paul Hennessy's wedding invite.

"You can throw it in the fire." She watched as the card quickly caught fire producing it's own bright flame. Then the flame began to diminish as the card distorted. Before long, all that was left was a few flimsy shards of black carbon.

A short while later the doorbell started to ring. The first to arrive were the next-door neighbours Mr. and Mrs. Keating. Not far behind were the parish priest and Kate's auntie Maeve. The Keatings went to the kitchen to make the tea and carve up some of the brown bread they'd brought while Fr. Gray and auntie Maeve sat on the couch, either side of Kate. As the two of them tried to out-religion each other Kate was caught painfully in the crossfire.

"She's with God now Kate…resting in peace."

"She's gone to a better place."

"In God's kingdom life will be eternal and full of interest."

"The souls of the just are in the hands of God and no torment shall touch them."

"To everything there is a season and a time to every purpose. A time to be born and a time to die."

With no sign of this religious ping-pong abating Matt decided it was time to leave.

At the same time Matt was getting up from his armchair, Kevin Daly was peeling himself off the muddy surface of Down Royal racetrack.

"Fuck, bollix, shite!"

He'd been in complete control of the race when *Satan's Whiskers* hit the second last hurdle. It wasn't enough contact to take the horse down, but Kevin hadn't been holding on tight enough with his heels and calves and popped sideways out of the saddle. He didn't like getting beaten at the best of times, but this was the worst possible way a jockey could lose. He slammed the shaft of his whip into his thigh.

"Fuck ye Kev…ye fuckin' eejit!"

He watched from a distance as *Satan's Whiskers* glided over the last hurdle. No longer carrying Kevin's eight stone he cruised away from the rest of the field to finish a good fifteen lengths ahead of the nearest horse.

"Fuck, bollix, shite!"

As Kevin made his way back to the jockey's enclosure he said a little prayer that his mistake wouldn't result in him not getting to ride *Satan's Whiskers* in Cheltenham.

"Heaven declares the glory of God. The skies proclaim his handiwork." Father Gray was doing his best to keep one ahead of auntie Maeve, but he didn't realise who he was dealing with. Auntie Maeve could beat God himself in a bible quoting competition.

"Love is as strong as death," she sighed. "Passion fierce as the grave. Many waters cannot quench love. Neither can the floods drown it."

Kate walked Matt to the door glad to get away from the biblical bombardment.

"Sorry I have to go Kate, but there's a big dinner on after the christening. I'll be killed if I miss it."

"That's ok. Thanks a million for coming out in the first place."

"Not at all...You gonna be ok?"

Kate smiled and nodded her head towards the living room. "Sure don't I have God on my side now."

Matt moved in and gave her a final hug.

"Listen Kate, about what happened earlier. I'm really so-"

"Please don't apologise again," Kate interrupted. "If you do I'll knee you in the balls."

"Ok, fair enough."

"You shouldn't feel bad about it anyway. You're a good guy Matt and you've got a lovely girlfriend. So don't worry, I'll try to control myself in future."

Matt kissed her on the side of the head and began to make his way back to Dublin.

Not long into his journey he started talking to himself and it wasn't just a case of private thoughts running through his mind. He was lecturing, preaching and debating out loud with hand gestures that a wartime politician would have been proud of. Fellow motorists would have been forgiven if they thought he was rehearsing for a Shakespearian play.

"What was that all about? I mean...what the fuck was I doing?

Ok, maybe she kissed me first, but I definitely kissed her back. I know it wasn't tongues or anything, but it lasted a good five seconds. It was a bloody good kiss too and fuck me she's a crackin' bird. I mean...a *really* sweet, funny, intelligent, beautiful girl, but the question is...do I really fancy her or was I just feeling sorry for her?

No I definitely fancy her. I always thought she was cute. It's got nothing to do with feeling sorry for her. I mean....of course I feel sorry for her. Her mum just died for Christ sake!

Oh my god! I can't believe I snogged Kate literally hours after her mum died! What the fuck was I doing?

Wait a minute, calm down. Lets try and think about this rationally. It wasn't really a snog. It was just a quick kiss, which *she* initiated. She might not even fancy me. It was probably just a build up of the days emotions. But then, she did say that she wanted to kiss me for a while...or something like that.

Why would she say that when she knows I'm with Sam? Wait a sec.....I'm getting' totally off the point here. It doesn't matter if Kate wants me or not. I'm goin' out with Sam and that's that.

But then again, I haven't exactly been having the time of my life with Sam recently. I mean it's not how it was a couple of years ago, but all relationships have their sticky patches.

So, is this just a sticky patch?

Fucked if I know! I mean we've had quite a few arguments lately including that stupid one this morning...but I still totally love her and that's the bottom line.

I wouldn't even be questioning my relationship with her if I hadn't just kissed Kate and that's a fact...but maybe it's not a bad thing if I *do* question it.

I mean...I've been with her nearly five years. There are plenty of *married* couples who've gone out for less time than that. Maybe she's not the one for me...Maybe Kate *is* the one for me...we get on great together and we've got plenty in common.

Hold on a sec...I'm not fuckin' thinkin' straight! Kate is just a friend. She used to out with Dave for God's sake!

This is not about Sam versus Kate. What I need to do is try to forget about Kate for a minute. Forget the kiss. Forget that there might be something there. Just wipe it out of my mind for a minute and take a real close look at what I have with Sam.

Do I wanna be with Sam? That's the question I have to answer.

Well...if I'm honest, I preferred it when we weren't living together. I mean...it was great at first, but all in all I think things were better when we lived apart. Maybe we just moved in together too soon...I mean...I wanted to leave it for a while. I only really did it to keep her happy.

It's like today...I would have preferred to have gone to the race instead of some crappy christening, but I went along with her so she wouldn't get upset. That doesn't sound too good. That makes me sound like a wimp...or it makes her sound like some sort of tyrant...which she is not But then again, we always tend to do things her way. I'm always the one who has to compromise. I go out of my way to make her happy...when does she do the same for me?

By the time he made it back to Dublin, Matt had given himself a headache. He was also getting some strange looks from other motorists so he decided he needed to talk to someone else. He pulled up outside Deansgrange cemetery and walked to his mother's graveside.

"Hi mum, hope they're lookin' after you up there. Sorry I haven't visited for a little while, but I've been really busy with all this house-moving lark. Anyway, I've just had a hell of a day and I've been thinking about you, and missing you a lot."

Chapter 28

Paddy Mulryan was excited. He hadn't been this excited about one of his horses ever before and he'd been training racehorses for twenty-three years. Although *Satan's Whiskers* jettisoned his jockey before the end of the race he came home from Down Royal unscathed and looking good. Unless something went wrong in the next month, Paddy would recommend to the owners that they run him in the Triumph Hurdle at Cheltenham in March. The Triumph Hurdle is one of the biggest races at the festival and would be full of top class horses, but Paddy felt that if everything went right for his horse he'd have a chance of finishing in the top three. He began to make a habit of dishing out special treatment to his favourite horse. *Satan's Whiskers* had a soft spot for pears. He found out by accident one day, when some of the yard hands were messing around, throwing pears at each other. On his way back to the stables from a gallop *Satan's Whiskers* bent down and snaffled one of the stray pears into his mouth. Paddy started to feed him the odd pear from the tree in his garden. They weren't great pears, but *Satan's Whiskers* loved them. As soon as it was clear that the horse was good enough for Cheltenham, Paddy started going one step further. *Satan's Whiskers* was the first horse he'd visit each morning. He'd check that he'd slept well and was looking healthy. He'd play with his ears a bit, which *Satan's Whiskers* loved, and then he'd feed him his treat. Three fresh juicy pears…and not just any old pears…not the small unripe ones from his own garden, but big tasty organic ones from McNally's green grocers in the village. If the other horses didn't know any better they'd think there was something funny going on between Paddy Mulryan and *Satan's Whiskers*.

Eileen McCann was buried on the 12th of February. It was a bitterly cold day, but that didn't stop a huge crowd turning out. The McCann's were there in strength of course and so were Eileen's family, the O'Mahony's. All the lads were there too, along with Jane who'd accompanied Shipsey. Kate cried from the first word of the ceremony to the final graveside prayer. Even her immediate family who were also in tears were desperately trying to console her. She was surrounded by people all day long, which meant that Matt didn't get a proper opportunity to talk to her, not that he would have known what to say.

Their contact was limited to a few consolatory words and the odd awkward glance, until it was time for him to leave.

"Sorry I have to go Kate, but I have a big day at work tomorrow and I shouldn't really be drinking anymore if I'm driving."

Kate reached out her arms for a hug. "Ok Matt, thanks for coming."

Matt kissed her on the side of her head. "Listen Kate, if you need anything, gimme a call."

"Ok, thanks."

"Anything at all…if you wanna chat or if even if you just wanna cry down the phone…don't hesitate."

"Ok, thanks Matt."

Kate closed the door behind him and the tears started flowing again.

Two nights later Kate and the remainder of her family were sitting at home in front of the TV. They were all dealing with the loss in their own individual ways. Beside Kate on the couch, her sister Aideen was reading up on some Logic for a philosophy exam. This was her second year taking philosophy and she still didn't understand what the hell logic had to do with it.

I mean…Descartes – "I think therefore I am" – fair enough Rene, whatever you say. Nietzsche – "Insanity in individuals is something rare, but in groups, parties, nations, epochs, it is the rule" – well said Friedrich, I think you might be onto something there. But Logic!! What the hell has logic got to do with philosophy?

There is more than one red car
All the blue cars run on petrol
Some of the non-blue cars run on diesel
Do some of the red cars run on petrol?
Logic is just silly…ok it's logical, but it's still feckin' silly!

Kate's brother, Neil was sitting on her other side feverishly sending sex texts to his new girlfriend. He'd started going out with a girl from college three weeks earlier and after two weeks of exhaustive courting she'd finally agreed to sleep with him. At nineteen years old, Neil didn't have much prior experience and was over the moon with his "conquest." He'd fancied Kelly Fitzpatrick from the first day they walked in as freshers and he couldn't wait to get back to Galway and pick up where he left off. In the meantime sex texting was the next best thing and he was going at it hammer and tongs.

Kate's dad was sitting in his usual armchair talking to the TV. There was a current affairs programme on about Northern Ireland, which was a subject that ran deep into the veins of Liam McCann. Ocassionally he would sit forward in his chair and splutter out an obscenity at the TV. This would usually happen when Ian Paisley was speaking.

"Feckin' Paisley...change the feckin' record...Reverend, my feckin arse!"

Kate was also looking at the TV, but she wasn't really watching it. Her mind was somewhere else and had been for hours. That morning she woke up and before she got out of bed she had a good long cry. That was the last time she'd cried. Maybe the tears had finally run out. For the first time in a very long time she began to look forward rather than back. She started to think of herself, rather than being immersed in the plight of her mother. It was time for her to think about what she would do next with her life. America was an option high on her list. She had a friend living in Florida who was doing quite well in real estate. Maybe she'd have a go at that or try to find some way to use her languages when she got there. Her thoughts were broken by the shrill ring of the doorbell. She scanned the other members of her family to see if any of them would offer to get it. Aideen was busy tutting into her Logic folder. Neil was giggling into his mobile phone and her dad was still grumbling at the TV.

Another neighbour, no doubt, thought Kate getting to her feet. The doorbell had been ringing regularly since word of her mum's passing got out. Friends and neighbours had been arriving from all directions brandishing consolatory offerings. Pastry goods were the order of the day and their kitchen was stacked high with homemade breads and buns.

"Better not be any more of those feckin' rock cakes," Kate groaned. "Why don't they bring something practical like McDonalds or sushi or a thirty-two" plasma screen." She opened the door and immediately took a step back with the shock.

It wasn't McDonalds or sushi or a widescreen TV...it was Matt Cullen with what appeared to be a breathtaking bunch of white roses.

"Hi," Matt smiled.

Kate was having difficulty speaking so Matt continued. "How are you?"

"I'm...eh...in shock, I think. What are you doing here?"

Matt held out the flowers. "I came to give you these."

"Why?"

"Cos it's Valentine's Day" said Matt, slowly reaching forward with the flowers. Kate was still reluctant to take them even though they were the most beautiful bunch of roses she'd ever seen.

"Do you not want them?" asked Matt, his arm still outstretched.

Kate was still hesitating, her hand on her forehead. "I do....I think...I mean...I'm sorry, but what are they supposed to say?"

Matt looked at the bouquet with a confused expression. His arm was getting tired. "They're supposed to say Happy Valentines Day."

"I see."

"Is that not good enough?"

"No, it is...I just thought...maybe you were going to say sorry again."

Matt shook his head and smiled at the same time. "Take the bloody flowers woman and givvus a hug."

Kate smiled and took the flowers. "White roses are my favourite. How'd you know?"

"I didn't," said Matt, taking her into a hug. "They were my mum's favourite."

They'd been holding each other for a couple of seconds when Kate asked, "what about Sam?"

"I think she preferred red ones."

"No you big dummy," Kate giggled. "Shouldn't you be with Sam?"

"We broke up."

"Well, in that case, come in."

Kate put the flowers in water while Matt said a quick hello to the rest of her family. She then led him into her bedroom for privacy. Kate sat on the bed while Matt nestled into the only chair. They made small talk for a while before Kate finally asked what was on her mind.

"I can't believe you're here. What happened?"

"Well I've been thinkin' about you all day...in fact I've been thinkin' about you all week. I had a match today and I played absolutely shite, cos I couldn't get you out of my mind. I wanted to call you when I broke up and I should have said something to you at your mum's funeral, but I didn't know what to say and I was worried it was all too soon...I mean...every time I looked at you there were tears rolling down your face, so I thought it was best to leave it for a while. And even *today*, it's probably too soon, but I couldn't hold back any more. So, I thought... *fuck it*, it's Valentine's Day, so I got in the car, flew down to the florist and hit the road for here. I said to myself if it doesn't feel like the right thing to do by the time I get to Naas, I can always just turn around, but I didn't...I couldn't wait to see you. I was panicking the whole way down." Matt smiled and shivered a little bit. "I still am now. I just hope I did the right thing."

Kate got up from the bed, walked to where Matt was sitting and kissed him on the forehead. "You did the right thing Matt. There should be more men like you in the world."

"Well, thanks."

Kate crashed back down onto the bed. "I still can't believe you broke up with Sam though. What happened?"

"Well," said Matt, trying to put it into a nutshell. "I'd have to put the blame for that on you and that kiss you gave me out by the fireside."

"That's it! One little kiss! If I had known that's all it would take, I would have kissed you months ago! How can one little kiss cause the downfall of a 4-year relationship? Was it *that* good?"

"Well, it was pretty good, but really it was just the catalyst that got me thinking. It's weird, but I don't think that I think very often...wait a minute that doesn't make sense. What I mean is I don't think I have a very good awareness of my happiness...y'know. I don't really question things...I just kinda plod along without really considering whether something is making me happy or not. I'm not sure if I'm making any sense here." Matt smiled at Kate and continued, "but *that kiss*, as brief and innocent as it was...that kiss got me thinking and when I left here I was literally talking to myself the whole way home. That's when I realised that I hadn't really been happy for a while and that things between me and Sam had no real balance." Matt paused for a moment.

"Have you ever heard the phrase *store of gore*?"

"No."

"I think it was something Shipsey made up, but basically his theory is that women have this ability to store in their memory every little thing that their partner did to annoy them. I mean everything, going back for years, and then, at the opportune moment, ie. In the middle of a dispute, they have the power and the presence of mind to delve into the *store of gore* and remind you about all the misdemeanours you performed in the past."

"I've never heard it been called the *store of gore*, but I get what you're talking about."

"Well anyway, Shipsey reckons that women are experts at keeping the store full of gore and that men are no good at it, but I actually found it quite easy and Sam didn't come out of it too well."

"Really?"

"Yeah, I mean...I don't think I need to go into all the details, but

Sam is pretty self-centred, everything always had to go her way. And since she got this new job…I mean…fair play to her, she's getting paid a load of money, but it's totally gone to her head. She was always high maintenance, but now she's high maintenance with a big ego and she's tetchy all the time, cos she's working under more pressure." Matt paused for a moment. All he really wanted to do was jump on the bed beside Kate and plant a firm kiss on her lips. "I don't wanna go on for ever," he continued, "but in the end it all came down to football."

"Football?"

"Yeah. After I left here last week I didn't drive straight home. I drove to my mum's grave. I stood there talking to her headstone for a while and then I remembered the football…When I was six I joined the local under-nine football team. My mum thought I was too small, but I cried until she let me go. She came to every match that season, home and away. She would always cheer me on and at half time she would come over and check that I was ok. If it was cold she'd warm up my hands in a pair of black woollen gloves she used to have." Matt felt his eyes welling up at this point. "Anyway before I start blubbing, I was standing by her graveside and I realised what should have been obvious for years. Sam was nothing like my mum. She wasn't in the habit of doing things for other people, even those closest to her. In four and a half years she didn't come to one of my football matches. Ok, fair enough…she had no interest in football, but it wasn't just that. She just wasn't a very giving person. She was only happy when things went her way and I always made sure things went her way. I think I was just blinded by her good looks, but not any more. I know now that I don't wanna be with someone like that. I wanna be with someone more like my mum….y'know…someone warm and kind as well as beautiful and fun to be with. I wanna be with you Kate."

Matt made his way over to the bed where Kate was grinning broadly through tear-filled eyes. For the first time in a very long time her tears were in the name of happiness. Then they kissed and this time it was for real. It was slow, but passionate and it was quite a while before Kate broke away.

"Do you remember the day I came to your cup final?"

"Yeah, that's right…last year."

"That's when I started fancying you," Kate admitted.

"Really? Was it the legs?"

"No, I mean…don't get me wrong…the legs are nice, but it was actually the way you stood up to one of your own players who was shouting at someone else for making a mistake."

"Wow, I can't say I remember that."

"Well I do and it was really sweet. You told the guy if he didn't have anything encouraging to say that he was to shut up."

Matt took Kate into a hug and kissed her on the cheek. Kate pulled back her head to look him in the eyes. "So, is it really over with Sam? What did you say to her? Was she mad."

"I told her I'd fallen for someone else. At first she laughed, but then I told her I was serious and she started to cry. So I put my arm around her and asked if she'd be ok and then she got angry. She elbowed me in the chest really hard and told me to get the fuck out. She actually kicked me out of my own house. It was quite funny really."

"So where are you staying?"

"Well, in the meantime, I've moved back in with my dad."

"Ah, poor baby," Kate sighed and moved in for another kiss.

The next few hours were a mixture of flirtatious chatter interspersed with passionate kissing. Matt successfully talked Kate out of any plans to go to America.

"You don't wanna go to Florida Kate. The humidity there is unbearable and then there's that swarm of killer bees, which are spreading their way up from South America. They've been spotted all over south Florida."

"I see," Kate smiled, "well I don't wanna be devoured by killer bees, do I? I suppose I could ring the language school in Dublin and see if I could get my old job back."

"That's a much better idea," Matt nodded and glanced at his watch. "Jaysis! Do you realise what time it is?"

Kate craned her neck to look at her bedside clock. "God, it's half twelve! How did that happen? I guess time flies when you're havin' fun."

"Yeah," Matt smiled and leaned in for another kiss. "I suppose I better be hittin' the road."

"You don't have to go."

"Really?"

"Yeah, you can stay the night. No funny business mind you, but I would like to fall asleep in your arms."

"Sounds good to me." Kate turned over with her back facing Matt and pulled his arm around her waist. Matt shimmied closer making sure the whole of the front of his body was in contact with the back of hers. His lips were nestled close to her ear as he stroked her hair. Kate let out a sigh of contentment.

"I still can't believe you're here Matt. I really didn't think this would happen."

"Really?"

"Yeah, I think I'd conditioned my body to deal with the fact that you were with someone else. I know there'd always been flirting between us, but it felt safe, cos you were with Sam. After a while I wanted it to happen more and I thought maybe there was a chance...y'know...maybe things weren't perfect between you two. I'd never seen her at any of the races, but then she turned up at Leopardstown looking stunning and you had your friend Stinger chatting me up. That's when I started to think it was never gonna happen."

"I didn't get Stinger to chat you up. I just thought that he probably would."

"How were you so sure?"

"Well, cos you're a babe I suppose."

"And you're a charmer."

"Did he really ask you out?"

"Yeah, he did."

"So why didn't you go out with him."

Kate smiled and pulled Matt's arm tigher around her. "I guess I was waiting for something better to come along."

Kate had just closed her eyes and was looking forward to the prospect of sweet dreams when Matt whispered in her ear. "Hey listen, I know you probably haven't thought about it, but are you gonna go to Cheltenham?"

"I don't know...you're right, I haven't thought about it, but I haven't really got any money."

"I'll give you the money Kate. We really need you there. Do you know that *Satan's Whiskers* has only won races when all six owners have been present."

"Really?"

"Yeah, I realised it the other night. He's run five races right. He won his first race here in Naas and then in Leopardstown at Christmas. Apart from that, he fell in Punchestown when Dave wasn't there, he came second in Listowel when your dad was missin' and then there was last weekend."

"I see, so what you're saying is, I owe it to *Satan's Whiskers* and my fellow syndicate members to show up at Cheltenham."

"Exactly."

"Well, with reasoning like that, how can I refuse?"

"Good girl," said Matt, squeezing her and planting a kiss on the back of her head.

Matt and Kate lay silent for a few minutes, both on the brink of sleep. There was just one more thing on Kate's mind.

"Matt?"

"Yeah."

"How's Dave?"

"He's great...Himself and Helen are getting' on really well. They went out for a romantic meal tonight and are talking about going on a skiing trip in April."

"That's great...Does he know you're here?"

"He doesn't know I'm here, but I did tell him what happened...I met him after I broke up with Sam and told him about our kiss. He was great about it. Do you know what he said?"

"What?"

"He said you were a special lass and that he'd be happy for both of us if we ended up together."

"Really? Ah, that's sweet. Dave is such a love. Sometimes I think I never should have finished up with him."

"Come here to me you," growled Matt, pinching Kate's bum and chomping down on her neck. Kate let out a squeal of delight, before turning to wrestle with him. For the first time in a very long time, she felt young.

Chapter 29

"Bing bong."

"We are now commencing our decent into Birmingham airport. Please ensure that your seatbelts are fastened, your seatbacks are upright and your tray tables are stowed away."

"Yey!! Woohoo!!"

This was not the first time the lads had cheered in their one and a half hour trip to Birmingham. They cheered on take off. They howled when the fasten seat belts sign went off and they really lost the run of themselves when the drinks trolley arrived. They still had a long coach journey from Birmingham airport to Cheltenham, but there was little that could dampen their spirits.

"Bing bong"

"We will be landing in Birmingham at nine fifteen pm, an hour after schedule. Please accept our sincerest apologies for this delay, which was caused by the late arrival of the incoming flight. It's currently raining heavily in Birmingham and the temperature has dropped to a chilly five degrees."

"Yehaarr!! Woohoo!! Yey!!"

Macker was the most excited of the bunch and could barely sit still. He was like a Mexican jumping bean under a powerful spotlight and had been jabbering in Shipsey's ear for the duration of the flight.

"Ship, I'm so excited, I think my head might pop off! I wonder if we'll get a chance to walk the course. I can't wait to see the hill. I've heard it's as steep as the sugar loaf. Do you want a whiskey? I might get myself one just to take the edge off. I hope there's a good atmosphere in our hotel. I'm sure there will be. I wonder will it be more Irish or English. Jaysis Ship! Imagine....tomorrow we're gonna be watchin' the Champion Hurdle live. And then the Queen Mother Chase on Wednesday, which is Paddy's day! Fuck! That's gonna be mental. I just hope I live through it all to make it to two o' clock on Thursday. Imagine, *our own horse* running in the Triumph Hurdle! I just hope my heart makes it. I'd be really pissed off if I died before two o'clock on Thursday." Macker looked up towards the fasten seat belt sign. "God, please don't take me before the end of the Triumph Hurdle. I'll gladly offer my soul up to you half an hour after the race, just not before or during it. That's all I ask lord."

"Macker."

"Yes big man."

"Shut up."

"Ok big man."

"Lads what'll we do if we win?" Macker managed to stay quiet for exactly nine seconds before opening up this question. Shipsey frowned down at him.

"What do you mean, what'll we do if we win?"

"What'll we do if *"Satan's Whiskers"* wins the bloody Triumph Hurdle?"

"We'll all shout Yey! and go and get really pissed. What the fuck do you think we'll do?"

"No, I mean with the money. What if he wins the first place prize money? Add that to all the bets we'll have on him and we could be takin' home about two hundred grand! And that's sterling! Jaysis, we could buy another ten race horses!"

"We could buy a pub down the country," offered Dave.

"We could buy a bookies," said Matt.

"We could buy a brothel," Shipsey grinned.

Kate leaned forward in her seat and slapped Shipsey lightly on the head "Excuuuse me."

"Sorry Kate." Shipsey turned around. "Just checkin' if you were still awake."

Kate was wide awake and enjoying the banter. She was sitting in the window seat behind Macker, Shipsey and Dave. To her left was Matt who was holding her hand and in the aisle seat her dad was snoring contently. Even though she'd only been going out with Matt for a month, her life had changed enormously in that time. She called the old school where she used to teach and they told her she could take over from another teacher who was resigning in June. She'd packed her bags and moved to Dublin two weeks earlier where she was staying with her friend Sally. Sally owned a two bedroom flat in Ringsend with her fiancé. They planned to marry in the autumn and were happy to receive a bit of extra income from Kate. As it happens Kate was spending most of her nights at Matt's new flat in Blackrock. In a short time the two of them had grown extremely close. Kate's move to Dublin seemed to accelerate the whole process and she was already becoming good friends with the other lad's girlfriends. The previous week all eight of them had gone out to dinner and on to a nightclub. It was one of those

257

nights that you don't want to end. She'd been sitting beside Helen and opposite Jane at dinner and hit it off really well with both of them. Michelle was sitting at the other end of the table so she didn't really get to speak to her until later in the night. But when they got to the nightclub Michelle grabbed her by the arm and led her to the dance-floor where they shook their booties for most of the night. By closing time she had all three of their phone numbers and was planning a girl's night out for when she returned from Cheltenham.

Matt was equally happy. He'd forgotten how much fun the beginning of a relationship could be. A few days before they'd gone to the cinema and snogged the face off each other. He never thought he'd be doing that again. But doing everything with Kate was more fun than it had been with Sam. They'd even gone on a brief shopping trip, which ended with the two of them in fits of laughter. He knew that one day the newness of the relationship would fade away, but there wasn't a single doubt in his mind that Kate would still be the one for him. When he broke up with Sam there was a niggling voice in the back of his head asking if he was doing the right thing. After a couple of wonderful weeks with Kate that voice had gone away for good. Dave had always said that Kate was special and Matt was really starting to get what he'd been talking about. Kate seemed to have more love to give than was possible for one person. She was generous and affectionate and generous with her affections. Twice that day when they'd been in Matt's local shopping centre she'd jumped out from behind him, grabbed him around the waist and given him a big sloppy kiss on the neck. Matt loved that. Later, when they were on their way to eat together, Matt bumped into his old neighbour from Killiney, Mr Dodd. Mr Dodd was sixty-five and lived alone. He had helped Matt and Sam lift a sofa into their living room when they were moving in. While Matt stood straight and tried to explain to Mr. Dodd why he was no longer his neighbour, Kate had her hand down the back of his jeans, pinching his bum. When they arrived back to Matt's flat it turned out that Kate had bought more stuff for him than for herself. She'd bought him a pair of slippers, a few games for his *Playstation* and a designer T-shirt. The designer T-shirt was way too tight, but Matt still wore it out that night with pride. Later, when they were walking home into a freezing wind he tried to put on a brave face, but as his lips turned purple and his slightly exposed tummy quivered with the chill factor, they were both forced to see the funny side. Thankfully when they arrived home Kate quickly stripped off to reveal the sexy lingerie he'd bought her. That heated things up in no time.

The coach trundled along into the black night. It had been a long journey, but Cheltenham was within striking distance now. As they passed a "Welcome to Cheltenham" sign three old fellas in the back of the coach burst into song. It was a song that had been written for the greatest ever Irish hurdler and it would be heard several more times over the next few days.

"It was in the year of '98
When Swan rode the six year old
It is thanks to JP and O'Brien
That the story would unfold
We've had Arkle, Imperial and Dawn Run
Donoli and Derrymoyle
But when he jumps the last
He won't be passed
Istabraq from Ballydoyle"

*****

Paddy Mulryan had arrived in Cheltenham two days earlier with *Satan's Whiskers* and a large sack of fresh juicy pears. He was staying with his friend and fellow trainer, Richard Simpson. *Satan's Whiskers* had gotten a little shaken up during the trip, but had settled down shortly after arriving at the Simpson yard. Paddy and Richard had become good friends over the years and Paddy would be returning the favour of Richard's hospitality the following month when two of the Simpson horses would be travelling across the Irish Sea to participate in the Punchestown festival. The two of them sat by the fireside sharing a few drams of whiskey and plenty of Cheltenham tales. Richard finished things up with the story of the year he trained a winner at Cheltenham. It was the last race on the final day and his horse was twenty-to-one. The field was huge, but the ground was very soft that year and Richard knew that his horse would go well in the mud. He put more than a few quid on the horse and roared him up the hill to win by half a length. It was the best day of his life. Of course he always told his wife that his wedding day was the best day of his life, but that was just to keep her happy. Paddy listened intently to his friend's story. Maybe in a few years time he'd be able to match it with one of his own. He shuffled off to bed at midnight to dream of what might be.

*****

Simeon Fatherington-Smythe was not impressed with the hotel he'd just checked in to. He was used to better than this. This hotel had a superiority complex if it felt fit enough to call itself a three star. The lobby was barely big enough to swing a cat in and the only decorative feature was a mangy fish aquarium with cloudy water. The sleeping quarters were far inferior to the ones he'd endured in his three years as a full-time resident at Greyfriars Hall, Oxford. In fact he would have been happier to spend the night in his old dorm back at Harrow. This would not do at all. He was used to better and he would be letting Tom Griffiths know all about it. That was if Tom Griffiths ever bloody well showed up. Simeon was a fund manager for the largest investment fund in the city, a highly responsible position that he had reached in his three short years out of university. Tom worked for one of the many banks that begged Simeon for business. Already that year Simeon had been taken on a golf trip to Peurto Banus, a Gambling spree to Vegas and a ski weekend in St. Anton. Each time the accommodation was at least four star and that's proper four star...not the kind of place that calls itself four star, because it serves peanuts at the bar and has a resident cat. Simeon stretched out on top of the uncomfortable single bed wondering what the hell he was doing in Cheltenham. He wasn't even in to national hunt racing. He loved flat racing. That was where the real money was. Flat racing was all about breeding and class. The Derby, The Oakes, Royal Ascot, he'd been to all of them many times over the years. His father and uncle were prominent investors in a well-known Arabian syndicate and he enjoyed moving in those circles. He liked caviar and champagne. Cheltenham was about burger-bars and Guinness, although maybe he could get a good curry. Simeon had a soft spot for curry. Ok, it wasn't exactly nouvelle cuisine, but since joining the city he had become addicted to it and the hotter it was the more he liked it. His favourite restaurant was the Raj and he'd paid them a quick visit before leaving for Cheltenham that evening. Tom Griffiths could start making things up to him by taking him to a good curry house. That's if Tom ever arrived. He'd phoned Simeon at the last minute to tell him he wouldn't be able to make it till the morning. Simeon chuckled ironically to himself. Here he was stuck in a dingy little room in a crappy hotel somewhere in the arse end of Cheltenham, on his own.

Oh well, he thought, scraping himself off the bed. *Might as well try to make the most of it. Maybe they'll have some nice port down in the bar.*

The bar downstairs was filling up fast with an enthusiastic racing crowd. The English were arriving in twos and threes...the Irish were piling in by the bus load. The only port they had behind the bar was produced in Australia.

Bloody typical! Thought Simeon, sitting down at the only remaining table and taking a sip. "Euugh." He screwed up his face in disgust. *I'm gonna kill Tom Griffiths!*

"How's it goin'? Do you mind if we join ye?"

Simeon realised he wasn't going to be able to keep the table to himself all night and ushered the strangers in. Macker said thanks and shook him by the hand.

"I'm Macker, this is my uncle Liam and my cousin Kate and this is Matt and Dave. There's one more with us, but he's up at the bar."

"Hi, I'm Simeon."

Simeon surveyed the motley crew that were filling the table around him. Kate caught his eye immediately. He'd always liked Irish girls and he'd often had success in chatting them up. They seemed intrigued by his floppy blonde hair, his posh accent and his good manners. Matt noticed that Simeon was smiling at Kate and made a point of putting his hand on her knee and grinning back at Simeon. Kate recognised it as an alpha-male moment, not too dissimilar to the one's she enjoyed in Wildlife programmes. She placed her hand on top of Matt's hand, thus declaring her undying love to her chosen steed and diffusing the situation. The sixth member of the group arrived back carrying six pints of *Guinness* in his bare hands. Well, in truth, five pints were clasped cosily into his shovel-like hands and the final one was pinned against his chest with his forearm. He seemed very proud of the feat despite losing much of the sixth pint down his shirt.

"Check it out lads...six pints!" said Shipsey, before easing them onto the table and taking his seat beside Simeon.

"Fair play to ye big man!" said Macker. "This is Simeon." Shipsey took Simeon's soft dainty hand into his large mitt. *"What's your name?"*

"Simeon."

"Simeon?"

"Yes, Simeon."

"What's your surname?"

"Fatherington-Smythe."

Shipsey smiled broadly and threw his arm around Simeon's shoulder pulling him tight into his beer-stained chest. "Jaysis lad," he announced confidently. "We're gonna have some fun with you."

261

It took a while for Simeon to get in tune with the Irish accents all around him. When he did begin to understand what was being said he found the conversation less than intriguing. Topics discussed included a horse called *Satan's Whiskers*, gambling, alcohol, toiletry habits, the capacity of the human bladder, the sex lives of walrus's, the sex lives of sea horses, toiletry habits, which jacks in a deck of cards only have one eye, which kings in a deck of cards only have one eye, where they might buy a deck of cards at half past eleven, toiletry habits, the best pub for Guinness, the worst pub for Guinness, toiletry habits and which is more painful...childbirth or shaving with a rusty blade and no shaving foam on a cold morning?

Simeon wasn't contributing much to the conversation. The four Dublin lads sitting around the table seemed to have a pretty full grasp on all the topics that were hit on.

"Anyway Simeon," said Shipsey, wiping some *Guinness* off his upper lip with the back of his sleeve. "What's your story? Tell us a little bit about yourself."

Simeon didn't know what to say. It wasn't that he didn't want to talk. He was in the mood for talking, having switched off the port and joined the lads in a couple of pints of Guinness. It was just that he didn't know what to say. He had no desire to tell them too much about his upbringing as it was clearly very different from their own. He'd had a few wild nights in university, but imagined they'd pale into insignificance when compared with the stories of four hardened drinkers from Dublin.

He shrugged his shoulders. "I don't know what to say. What would you like to know?"

"I dunno," Shipsey shrugged. "Anything....have you ever done something you've really regretted?"

And then it came to Simeon. He did have one funny story from his childhood that might appeal to this particular audience.

"Actually, I do have a regret," Simeon began. "It's kind of a long story though."

Shipsey patted him roughly on the back. "Let's hear it."

"Ok...well, when I was eight or nine our neighbours had these two cats. I can't remember what their real names were, but my brother and I called them *Fat Cat* and *Snot*. *Fat Cat*, as his name suggests was very fond of his food. I think he weighed between three and four stone. He didn't do much apart from eat and sleep, but we loved him. He had a very placid demeanour and loved being petted and tickled on his big belly. He was more like a dog really I suppose. He was way too fat to jump up on furniture or anything. Anyway *Snot* was a different kettle of fish. We called him *Snot*, because he seemed to have this endless stream of mucus flowing from his nostrils. *Snot* was a real pain in the neck. He was always getting snot on your clothes and on the furniture. He smelt funny too. I'm not saying *Fat Cat* didn't smell a bit, but he was nowhere near as bad as *Snot*. Anyway, one summer my brother and I got two rabbits. They were beautiful white ones and we kept them in a hutch in the garden. My brother's one was *Snowy* and I called mine *Bob*, but after a while we learned that *Bob* was actually a girl. I think *Snot* was the first one to figure that out."

Simeon paused to take a mouthful of Guinness while the Irish gang waited intently for what was coming.

"Anyway," Simeon smiled, *Snot* began to interfere with *Bob* on a regular basis."

"Wait a minute," Shipsey coughed. "The neighbours cat was shagging your rabbit?"

"Yes."

"*Snot* was fucking *Bob*?"

"Yes."

"So what do you get if you cross a cat with a rabbit...a cabbit?"

"I suppose so...or maybe a rat?"

"This is good stuff. Carry on."

"Ok, well, later in the summer, the neighbours went on holiday and they asked us to look after *Fat Cat* and *Snot*. It was a disaster. *Snot* just destroyed everything. There was snot all over the furniture, all over our clothes...everywhere. My brother's blankie that he'd had since he was baptized had slowly changed from a beautiful soft white to a horrible sticky green. And now that he was staying with us *Snot* was shagging *Bob* all the time. He found a way to get in through the top of the hutch and he'd spend the whole day in there, scaring *Snowy* and shagging *Bob*. It was disgusting. I had to wash the snot off *Bob's* back every night. So, in the end we decided we'd had enough. We wanted to get rid of *Snot* for good. My brother came up with the idea of leaving his food on the main road."

Kate held her hand up to her mouth. "No!"

"Yes, I know it's terrible," Simeon nodded. "But my brother was always a bit wild. I think because my dad spent so much time overseas trying to evade the taxman. Anyway, you've probably guessed the end already. *Fat Cat* was just a bit too fond of food for his own good. He was helping *Snot* eat his, when a Lexus came around the corner. *Snot* got out of the way, but *Fat Cat* was too slow."

"Oh no!" gasped Kate. "Was he killed?"

"Fraid so…*Fat Cat* became *Flat Cat*."

Simeon finally made it to bed at half four in the morning well and truly pissed. He'd tried to leave on several occasions earlier in the night, but the big guy with the shovel-hands and beer-stained shirt had been blocking his way and force-feeding him Guinness. He finally got past when Shipsey had to go to the toilet. He staggered up the stairs, leaving the Irish crowd to their sing-song. He woke up two hours later. The first thing he had to do was go to the toilet. The second thing he had to do was go to the toilet. The third thing he had to do was go to the toilet. He woke up again at seven thirty, sitting on the toilet bowl with his head resting against the sink. Somewhere inside his skull was a very small man…a very small man with a very big hammer. Simeon wondered what could have put him in such a state. A piping hot Curry and eleven pints of *Guinness*. That'll do the trick. As nice and friendly as the Irish crowd were, he decided to avoid them for the rest of the week.

Chapter 30

Macker lay wide-awake in bed at 6.45am. He'd only gone to bed an hour and a half earlier and hadn't slept a wink, but he still wasn't tired. It was the first day of racing at the Cheltenham festival and he was far too excited to be tired. He looked at his watch wandering if it was too early to ring his uncle. They'd agreed to go down to the racecourse together as soon as they woke up. They both wanted to check the place out before the crowd arrived. Macker had a shave and a shower. At seven o'clock he rang his uncle's room. Liam McCann was also wide-awake and happy to receive the call. At eight o'clock they pulled up outside the racecourse, which was already beginning to buzz. Their attention was immediately drawn to a crowd gathered on a grassy section just opposite the finishing post. When they got to the gathering they couldn't believe what they were seeing. It was a group of about forty Irish people saying mass. They were being led through their prayers by a Catholic priest with a bible in one of his outstretched hands and a racing badge in the other. The priest clearly had no scruples about asking God for a few special favours for his flock.

"Dear Lord, please see that all the Irish horses arrive home safely, but more importantly Lord, please see to it that they get to the finishing post at least two lengths ahead of their nearest English rivals."

To Macker's delight their badges entitled them to walk on the gallops. He finally got to find out what the famous Cheltenham hill was all about. He wasn't disappointed. Its no wonder the Cheltenham hill has determined the result of many a big race. On TV it doesn't look half as steep or as long as it actually is.

"It's unbelievable," said Macker, as they reached the finishing post and turned to look back down. They were both out of breath just from walking it. "Ok, it's not quite as steep as the sugar loaf, but you wouldn't fancy running up that…especially not with a small man on your back armed with a whip and a temper."

Next, they went inside to the hall of fame. Macker had a go on the mechanical horse before they settled down to watch some old videos of Arkle and Dawn Run. The hairs on the back of their necks were still standing up when they went back outside to admire the bronze statues of the same two magnificent horses. Next, they went back inside from the cold to have a look at the enclosures. The centaur was the most impressive one and by far the newest, having being completed only two months earlier. It had capacity for 3,000 people and the plan was to use it for a lot more than just horse racing. The bar on the upper level was massive and was named *The Istabraq Bar*. Macker and his uncle agreed that they would share a few pints in there before the week was over.

From 11.00 onwards the crowds started to arrive in earnest. Liam and Macker watched as they flooded through the turnstiles by the busload. By 12.30 the whole racecourse was bursting at the seams. By the start of the first race the seams had well and truly burst. The first race was won by an English horse and was greeted with a mighty roar. The second race was won by an Irish horse and was greeted with mass hysteria. All of a sudden Irish Tricolours were being pulled out of back pockets and draped around necks. Strangers were gladly kissing other strangers so long as they had an Irish accent. The Paddys were happy and Cheltenham 2004 was officially declared open. By the end of the day there were five English winners and two Irish. As they made their way up to the Istabraq bar Macker turned to his uncle.

"We'll get them tomorrow Uncle Liam. Paddy's day tomorrow. They don't have a fuckin'chance."

By 9pm Simeon Fatherington-Smythe and Tom Griffiths had run out of things to say to each other. Apart from work they had little in common and they were both sick of talking about work.

"Let's go lap dancing," said Tom, "or the real thing if you want? I know where to go."

"What do you mean by the real thing?" frowned Simeon, hoping that his guess was wrong.

"Y'know," winked Tom, "brass."

"No thanks. Not for me."

"Well…lap dancing then?"

"Yeah, ok." Simeon was disappointed that Tom hadn't come up with something a bit more imaginative. *You can take the broker out of the city, but you can't take the city out of the broker.* Simeon wasn't a big fan of lap dancing. It was all an exercise in frustration as far as he was concerned. He was ok with the part where the sexy woman takes her clothes off and dances erotically in front of him. That was fine, but he had a problem with the part where he has to keep his hands behind his back at all times and if he so much as brushes off the girl with his little finger, he'll get thrown out on his ear by some steroid riddled bouncer. He agreed to go, as it meant he wouldn't have to worry about talking to Tom and at the same time he could work up some serious expenses on the account of his unimaginative broker.

Tom Griffiths hated lap dancing. He'd been plying his trade in the city for fifteen years and lap-dancing clubs had gone beyond clichéd. He possibly enjoyed the first ten or fifteen visits, but after that the novelty wore off. Nonetheless it was his job to entertain clients and lap dancing always seemed to keep them happy, especially the young go-getters like Simeon. Tom and Simeon eventually arrived back to the hotel at half three in the morning. It had been a marathon session of handing over money vouchers to beautiful naked women and both were tired, frustrated and ready for bed. Simeon was mulling over the idea of having a wank when he heard his name being called.

"Hey Simeon! Yo Simbo! Over here Sim Card!"

He turned around in trepidation. He recognised the Dublin accents. Macker, Shipsey and Dave were beckoning him over to their table.

"How's it goin' lad? Where have you been?"

"Hi guys...oh just some lap dancing bar in the town...This is Tom."

"Lap dancing?" Shipsey frowned. "What are you goin' lap dancing for?"

"Well...to look at semi-naked women I suppose."

"I never really saw the point in lap-dancing...I mean...did you get to touch or shag any of them?"

"No."

"Did you get a big stiffy?"

"Sorry?"

"Did you become sexually aroused at any point?" Shipsey asked this question in his best posh accent.

"I suppose so," Simeon shrugged.

"Well what's the point in that? You blow a load of cash to give yourself a big boner and then you're not even allowed to touch any of them! You're actually paying money to become sexually frustrated!"

"You know what?" Simeon nodded. "You're dead right."

"I know I'm right...see...us Irish believe in value for money. Take Guinness for example. It's the most nutritious alcoholic beverage in the world. There's eatin' and drinkin' in it. You could survive on Guinness alone for days...ok...you'd probably spend most of your time on the toilet, but you wouldn't die or anything. Shipsey frowned and looked up to the ceiling. "Actually you know what? I don't think I've taken a dump since we left Dublin."

"Me neither!" gasped Macker. "Must be all the travelling."

"What's travelling got to do with takin' a shit?"

"I think it's like...cos you're sittin' down all the time, you don't need to take a shit."

Shipsey shook his head. "That doesn't make any sense! You *have* to sit down to take a shit! How could a lot of sitting down stop you from wanting to shit?"

At this point Simeon made a gesture to leave. Shipsey grabbed him by the arm.

"Ah no, you'll have a quick pint and a game of cards." Shipsey forced a full pint into Simeon's hand. "Here, you have this one. I haven't quite finished my last one."

Shipsey and Tom had a brief argument about who would buy the next round. Tom backed down under the threat of physical violence. They all sat down and Macker started dealing.

"We've just invented a new game. Have you ever played Indian poker?"

"Is that the one where you put one card in the middle of your forehead without looking at it and then bet on who has the highest?"

"That's the one. And have you ever played three card brag?"

"That's just three cards each....best poker hand."

"Exactly, well we're playing three card Indian brag."

Macker had just finished dealing them three cards each. "So, don't look at those...just spread 'em out and stick 'em on your forehead."

Simeon and Tom spent the next two hours with a Guinness in one hand and the other hand pinned to their foreheads. By the time they waddled upstairs to their room Simeon had lost £40 and Tom had lost £175. Tom was not used to spending his own cash, never mind losing it at poker. Simeon was chuckling to himself as he walked away from Tom's door. *Try putting that down to expenses.*

*****

Half way through the St. Patrick's Day race card Shipsey finally needed to go for a number two. He darted into the nearest cubicle he could find. He wanted to go quickly as he had a big interest in the next race. There was an Irish horse in it called *Liathroidi Mora* ("Big Balls" in Irish). It was being ridden by Shipsey's favourite jockey, Mick Fitzgerald. Shipsey had won some money on *Rough Quest* when Mick Fitzgerald drove him home to win the 1996 Grand National. The Cork man became famous for what he said in the post race interview. Shipsey nearly fell off his seat laughing when Fitzgerald caught the usually unflappable Des Lynam off guard by telling him on Live TV that winning the Grand National was better than sex. Shipsey was only halfway through his business when the race started. "Shit!" The good thing was that the racecourse commentary was being pumped into the toilets. He decided to take his time and enjoy two pleasures at once.

Simeon Fatherington-Smythe burst through the door and made his way quickly to the cubicles. They were all occupied. *Shit! Why did I have curry again? I might have been ok if I'd avoided being accosted by those mad Irishmen and their never-ending supply of Guinness.*

Suddenly he could hear a voice coming from inside one of the cubicles. It started off softly.

"Come on Micky Fitz. Come on, you can do it. Get up there!"

Over time the voice became more and more urgent.

"Come on Micky Fitz! Get up yeboyo! Come on Mickey! Get your fuckin' finger out!"

Then the voice was joined by another one coming from the adjoining cubicle.

"Come on Big Balls! You can do it!

"Come on Micky Fitz! Show them why!"

Simeon was doubled over with the pain, his head resting between the two speaking cubicles.

"That's it Big Balls! Drive it home!"

"Come on Micky! Get stuck in there wee fella!"

"Keep goin' Big Balls! Get up there!"

"Yes Mickey Fitz! Come on! Ride him hard! Drive him home. That's it! Good Lad!"

"Come on Big Balls! Push hard! Keep goin' till that fucker begs for mercy!"

"Come on Micky Fitz!"

"Come on Big Balls!"

"Come on Micky!"

"Come on Big Balls!"

"Yes Micky! You fuckin' beauty!"

"Yes Big Balls! You fuckin' good thing!"

With that, there were two flushes and both cubicle doors swung open. The occupants immediately hugged each other and began to share details of how much they had won on the horse and why they had backed it. Simeon tried to ease his way into the first cubicle without being spotted.

"Oi! Sim Card! Is that you?"

Simeon turned around and Shipsey took him into a bear hug.

"Had a few bob on that Irish one there. How you gettin' on?"

Simeon was in too much pain to make polite conversation. "Not too good actually. I really need to…y'know…go. I'll talk to you later."

"Say no more Sim Card. When ye gotta go, ye gotta go. I'll seeya tonight…Oh! you might *not* wanna use that one though."

Simeon turned his head to where Shipsey was pointing. The smell emanating from the cubicle was foul, but with the other cubicles already taken he had no other option.

"I'll take my chances."

"Fair enough. You have fun in there. I know I did."

Simeon's next encounter with the gang from Dublin was no more pleasant. He arrived back to the Hotel at 2am and they were even more drunk than usual. The St. Patrick's Day decorations, which had been decorating the Hotel walls and ceilings were now being worn as costume jewellery by the Irish residents. The bar floor was seeped in *Guinness*. The sing-song was louder, but less coherent than the previous night. Macker was the first to spot Simeon and roared at him to come and join them. He forced a pint of Guinness into Simeon's hand and held him tightly around the shoulder.

"Camear timmy Shimeen me Sasnach friend. Do you know wha day t'day ish?"

"St. Patrick's Day?"

"Thash righ. God yer acshent ish verry niche. I'd say ye wur brough up well."

"I suppose I was."

"Good, -hic- me too. Now…do ye know wha day Tamara ish?"

"Thursday?"

"Yeah, ok, but wha race do we have on a tchursdy?"

"The Gold Cup?"

"Now Shimeen, I'm gonna shay shumtin' to ye now an a wan ye to take it d'righ way ok?"

"Ok."

"Fuck the Gold Cup! Yearme Shimeen? Fuck the Gold Cup! Cos Tamara are hoss is runnin' in the Tri –hic- Triumph Hurdle. An ye know wha?"

"What?"

Heesh gonna fuckin' winnit!"

"I didn't know you had a horse. What's he called?"

"Heesh cald *Shatan's Whishkers* an heesh the besht hoss ever.

"So you think he has a good chance?"

"Were ye not lishtnin' timmy Shimeen. Heesh gonna fuckin' winnit! Heesh de besht hoss over fences by a mile."

"You mean hurdles."

"Thash whaya shed…heesh de besht hoss over hur hur –hic- liddle fences by a mile."

*****

Liam McCann was the first of *Satan's Whiskers* owners to wake up on the day of the big race. Since his wife passed away he'd gotten himself in the habit of talking to her instead of saying prayers. Why would he want to talk to *God* when the woman he loved for thirty years and missed terribly was sitting right next to him?

"Hi Eils. Hope you're being looked after up there love. Me and the kids are fine. You took a little piece of each of our hearts with you and things will never be as good without you, but I know you'd want us all to try and be happy, so that's what we're doing. I wish you were here today love. Me and Kate are in Cheltenham to watch your favourite horse run in a big race. Kate seems really happy. She still cries for you, but she's with one of the Dublin fellas now and the two of them are having a good time together. Matt is the lad's name. I don't know if you met him, but he's Michael's best friend and Michael tells me that he's never seen Matt as happy, which is good. Neil and Aideen are back in College and have promised me they'll do their best. Don't know what else to say love. I seem to be saying the same things all the time, but y'know I do this as much for myself as for you. They say people who talk out loud in a room by themselves are insane, but I do this to keep myself sane. I just miss you so much and I wish you could be here love, but I know you're still with us all and will be smiling down on us today."

Paddy Mulryan woke up at seven on the dot. He'd gotten himself into a routine since arriving at Richard Simpson's yard. It was built around giving *Satan's Whiskers* two run outs, one at 8am and the other at two on the dot. The morning one would be brisk, but not over the top. The one that commenced at two was all business. He would get the jockey to take him to 95% and run him for two miles and two furlongs finishing on the steepest part of the gallops. The Triumph Hurdle was only two miles one furlong, but Paddy knew that *Satan's Whiskers* would need that bit extra, because running against twenty-five other horses on a track like Cheltenham is a lot more demanding than running on the gallops. Today *Satan's Whiskers* would be fed his usual quantity of pears and do his normal morning work out. The routine would be broken at 11.30 when he would be loaded into his box and driven the short distance to the racecourse. This would be a crucial part of the day and Paddy knew he could tell a lot from how *Satan's Whiskers* responded to being loaded up. If the horse trotted happily into the box it was a good sign. Paddy would put his racing saddle on his back just to let *Satan's Whiskers* know that there was a serious work ahead and it commenced at 2pm.

When Kate opened her eyes Matt was gazing into them, his face only inches from hers. "What are you starin' at ye Jackeen?"

"I was starin' at you my sweet country lass. You look even more beautiful when you're sleeping than you do awake."

Kate poked two fingers towards her open mouth as if to make herself sick "Euuuugh."

Matt rolled onto his back and chuckled. "Oh…well that's just bloody charming! Can't even pay me bird a compliment."

"Who says I'm your bird?"

Matt poked his thumb firmly into his chest. "I says."

"Oh, ok then." Kate smiled and draped her arm over Matt's torso. She rested her right hand on his left shoulder and her lips next to his right ear. After a couple of moments silence, she spoke.

"Matt."

"Yes bird."

"You know I'm falling in love with you."

"Really?" Matt frowned and turned to face Kate. "Well that's a bit disappointing."

Kate's heart sank. "Why?"

"Well I'm already *there* and you're only *falling*, Matt smiled. "What are you doing falling so slowly…cut your bleedin' parachute woman and get on with it!"

Kate laughed and threw her right leg around Matt's waist. As she straddled him she pinned down both his arms. She started kissing every part of his face except his lips. "You big bastard. Were you planning on telling me at any point?"

"I wasn't sure if you'd believe me and anyway I like to do most of my correspondence by e-mail and you don't have an address."

Matt was moving his head from side to side trying to catch Kate on the lips.

"Lips please, lips!"

Kate kissed him on the cheek, the forehead and the nose.

"Lips, lips, please, quickly lips!"

"Not until you say it!"

"Say what?"

Kate started biting into his ear.

"Ok ok! Kate, I think you're a really great lass and I'd like to see you again some time."

Kate swung her right leg up and positioned it between Matt's legs. "Say it ye feckin' Jackeen!"

Matt could feel her knee resting beneath his scrotum. "Ok ok, mercy mercy!"

Kate slid her knee back down the sheets, preparing it for forward motion.

"I'll do it Cullen! Don't tempt me."

Before she could let fly, Matt overpowered her. In a second he had Kate on her back and he was on top. He smiled down on her beautiful face. "I love you Kate."

Kate tried to keep a straight face, but a powerful smile was spreading across it.

"Well Matt, I really like you too."

Liam McCann was on his way to breakfast, when he heard his daughter's screams. He was about to burst in the door, but something made him stop. These were not the screams of someone being attacked. This was the sound of his eldest daughter trying to catch her breath from being tickled.

"Ok ok, I love you too Matt Cullen. I love you too."

Liam smiled and shook his head at the same time. He hadn't given the go ahead for Matt to spend the night in Kate's room, but what the heck, for the first time in a long time his favourite child was really happy.

Macker was the last of *Satan's Whiskers* owners to wake up. His room was unbearably bright as he had been too drunk to close the curtains the previous night. "Fuck! What time is it?" He leapt out of bed and stood upright with one sharp jerk of his body…a move that didn't go down well with his head. He concentrated hard on his watch.

"Five to fucking three!" His screams could be heard at the far end of the hotel. "No! Please God, no! Don't do this to me you fucking bastard!"

He stared at his watch for another five seconds and collapsed onto the bed clutching his heart.

"Quarter past eleven. Oh thank you God… thank you *so* much… and sorry about the language big man. Won't happen again."

This was not the sort of day that Macker wanted to piss God off.

He clambered to his feet again, holding his head together between his two hands. He turned on the shower and got in, making sure to bring his two little friends with him.

"Come on *paracetymol*, come on *neurofen*. Let's get to work boys."

By twelve thirty he was at the racecourse checking out the early prices for the Triumph Hurdle. *Satan's Whiskers* was quoted at fourteen-to-one. There was a clear favourite named "Barnackle Army" who had won all five of his previous races. He was nine-to-two, which was a very short price for a field of twenty-six novices.

At one o' clock the owners gathered around Paddy Mulryan to hear his thoughts.

"He's in excellent shape guys. He gotta little bit shaken up on the way over, but that's nearly a week ago now and he's settled down nicely since. He's been workin' well and he's fitter than ever. I've been givin' him plenty of stamina training cos this is a tough old track. He knows he's here to do a job. I could sense it in him when I led him out of the box when we arrived. He doesn't seem bothered by the crowd at all and trust me there'll be at least half a dozen horses in this field that will be."

"So whadya reckon' Paddy?" asked Liam. "Is he good enough for a place?"

"I think he is Liam, but there's a few horses in this race that I haven't seen. It's a big old field so you need a bit of luck. I've told Kevin that unless they go off at a stupid pace that he's to try and keep him in the top six and stay out of trouble. There'll be plenty of argy bargy in the middle of the field. That favourite is a bloody good four-year old, as good as I've seen in a while. He's trained by that fella from Norfolk who has done very well the last two days. I've told Kevin to keep an eye out for him. If he's on form, I'm not sure ours is good enough to beat him, but at fourteen-to-one, each way looks like a good bet."

Macker badly needed to go to the loo. The excitement was getting too much for him and he couldn't control his bladder. In the hour leading up to the race, he handed money over to eight different bookies and made nine dribbling deposits in various different toilets. He'd only twice smoked marijuana in his life and hadn't really enjoyed it, but he'd gladly wolf down a big cake of it now just to calm his nerves.

"And the Triumph Hurdle 2004 is...off!"

"Oh Jesus Lads! I think my hearts gonna stop!" Macker grabbed Kate's hand. "Kate, please hold my hand and help me make it through this!"

Kate squeezed her cousin's hand. "Relax Michael, you'll be fine."

"Twenty six runners and riders and they're all trying to get a good position…Plenty of bumping and barging, the hallmark of all Triumph Hurdles. The field is spreading out a bit now as they all try to get a gook look at the first hurdle. The three in front are *Internet Queen*, *Roll out the Dole* and *The Mighty Ike*. A short gap back to the field, which is being headed by *Bouncing Check* on the inside of *Tomohawk* and *Be my Lady*. They take the first hurdle and the leaders are over it safely. Contact in the middle of the field, but they get away with it. "Fujiwara Fire" did not land well and looks like he might be pulled up. One race too many for him this week."

"Where is he lads? Can anyone see him?"

"That might be him about five from the back."

"Still *Internet Queen*, *Roll out the dole* and *The Mighty Ike* setting a pretty hot pace here. A gap back to "*Tomohawk*," *Be my Lady* next is *Double top finish* and *The Tailor Quigley* followed by *Hoover it up*, *Slan Abhaile* and *Tony Two Stools*. The favourite, *Barnackle Army* is travelling well in mid division. Slightly detatched from the back are *That's my Lipstick* and *Randalstown Lad*. As they approach the second here in front of the stands, the leaders are over it safely. *Bouncing Check* has hit that one hard and unseated Kenny Kane. Kenny's on the inside of the track and the field have avoided him. He looks ok, but *Bouncing Check* is still on the move and may cause problems for anyone stuck behind."

"Where the fuck is he lads?"

"There's too many of them! Can't see a thing. He must be somewhere in the middle of that big bunch. I don't think that's him towards the back."

"The rest are over it, but we're now down to twenty four in with a shout of the 2004 Triumph Hurdle. They head out around the top bend into the back straight with *The Mighty Ike* now taking up the lead on the outside of *Tomohawk*. *Little Black Number* is coming up to join *Be my Lady* and *Internet Queen* who's getting a few reminders. A length to *The Tailor Quigley* *Tony Two Stools* and just behind those two. Then it's *Roll out the dole* being joined by *Glaswegian Buoy* and *Pantafelino*. Next is *Let's Get Mullered* and *Mistic Toffee* Half a length behind is *Fantalanny* on the inside. On the outside is the favourite *Barnackle Army* and in between is…*Satan's Whiskers*

"Yey! Wahoo! Come on Satan you good thing!"

"The leaders take the third. A bit of a mistake from *Tomohawk*, but he survives. *Little Black Number* flies over it and joins *The Mighty Ike* up front. Oh! And there's a faller *Internet Queen* is down and *Pantafelino* has been badly hampered by the loose horse. The rest of the field get over it safely, but there's a few at the back that don't look like it'll be their day. Beginning to spread out a bit down the back straight. Freddy Simmons asking Barnackle Army to get closer to the front and he responds positively."

"Come on Satan! Stay with him! Come on Kevin Daly!"

"Also going well are *Glaswegian Buoy* and *The Hot Stepper who's* tracking the favourite."

The Hot Stepper? Didn't we race him before?"

"That's right! He won that race in Punchestown...
remember...when our one fell."

"*Barnackle Army* is moving through the field now and lands over the fourth only three lengths behind *Little Black Number*. Vying for second are *Tomohawk* and *The Tailor Quigley*. *Be my Lady* is moving backwards and about to be passed by *Glaswegian Boy* and *Mistic Toffee*. Then it's *Barnackle Army* who's cruising up on the outside of *Fantalanny* and *The Mighty Ike*, who looks spent already. "Behind the favourite we have *The Hot Stepper* and *Let's get Mullered* just ahead of *Satan's Whiskers*.

"Come on Satan! Keep goin' lad! Stay with them!

Little Black Number leads them over the halfway mark, but there are still plenty in with a shout. *The Tailor Quigley* is on the outside of the leader. Then it's *Tomohawk* being challenged by *Glaswegian Boy* and *Mistic Toffee*. *Barnackle Army* has these in their sights, as they take the fifth hurdle. *The Tailor Quigley* jumps it best and lands in the lead from *Little Black Number*. A gap to *Mistic Toffee* and *Tomohawk*, then *Glaswegian Boy*, half a length to *Barnackle Army* who's still travelling well and don't count out *The Hot Stepper* or *Satan's Whiskers*."

"Come on Satan you fuckin' good thing!"

"The field starts to make its way into that big looping final bend and with only three hurdles left to jump it's all up for grabs. *The Tailor Quigley* and *Little Black Number* will be first to meet the next hurdle. They get over it safely, as do...oh no! *Tomohawk* has fallen. He slipped on landing and horse and jockey went down. *Mistic Toffee* has jumped it well though and looks strong, as does *Barnackle Army*. *Glaswegian Buoy* is starting to fade and looks like he'll be passed by *The Hot Stepper* and *Satan's Whiskers*."

"Come on Satan!"

"Jesus lads! We're still in with a chance here!"

"Around the top of the final bend and it's still *The Tailor Quigley* and *Little Black Number*. *Mistic Toffee* is starting to put them under pressure on the outside, while *Barnackle Army* sits in behind them. A length and a half to *The hot Stepper* and *Satan's Whiskers* who have moved past the fading *Glaswegian Buoy*.

"Jesus lads, he's in fifth! Come on Satan! Come on Kevin! Bring him home lad!"

"Only half a mile left now, but it's the toughest half mile you'll find. *Mistic Toffee* looks like he has every chance, as does *Barnackle Army* who's looking for a gap. *The Tailor Quigley* and *Little Black Number* aren't showing him any room so he's gonna have to go the long way round. *Mistic Toffee* hits the front and will be first to have a go at the second last. He's over it, but *Barnackle Army* has absolutely belted over that one and moved from fourth to second. *The Hot Stepper* and *Satan's Whiskers* are still stride for stride and will have to go round the outside of *Little Black Number*. *The Tailor Quigley* did not jump that well and has lost ground. Now we're down to the nitty gritty in the Triumph Hurdle. Who has enough in the tank to get them up that hill. Well *Barnackle Army* certainly looks the real deal. He's swooped up on *Mistic Toffee* and looks like a winner all over. There's a gap of about three lengths back to *The Hot Stepper* and *Satan's Whiskers*.

"Jesus! Come on Satan! Stay on your feet lad! We could be on for a place here boys!"

Barnackle Army has blasted past *Mistic Toffee* and left him in a cloud of dust as he approaches the last, the favourite is looking good...No! I spoke too soon! He's down! *Barnackle Army* is down! He seemed to get too close to that hurdle and Horse and Jockey are down!

Mistic Toffe jumps it and looks like he's just been handed the Triumph Hurdle on a plate. *The Hot Stepper* and *Satan's Whiskers* both get over it and all of a sudden are battling for second."

At this point Paddy Mulryan let out a booming roar. "Come on Whiskey! You can catch him! He won't make it up that hill!"

"*Satan's Whiskers* is starting to look like he can win the battle for second. Kevin Daly's working hard on him now."

"Come on Kevin!   Come on Satan!"

Macker was squeezing Kate's hand so tight it had gone numb with the pain, but she didn't care. She was jumping up and down screaming, her heart thumping inside her chest.

"Come on *Satan's Whiskers*! Come on Kevin!"

"*Satan's Whiskers* has moved into second, but has he got a chance of catching *Mistic Toffee*? The gap is closing, but *Mistic Toffee* looks like holding on…Only two lengths between them now and about a hundred and fifty yards left. *Satan's Whiskers* is closing on *Mistic Toffee*."

"Come on Satan you fuckin' good thing!"

"Coming up to the line and this is gonna be close. *Satan's Whiskers* is closing with every stride.

"Come on *Satan Whiskers*!"

"They flash across the line and it's very close! *Satan's Whiskers* may just have got up."

"Yessssssssss!!!!"

"Did he win it?"

"He fuckin' won it!!!!"

"How d'ye know?"

"Look at Kevin Daly! He'd got his fuckin' whip in the air!"

"Yessssssssss!!!!"

*****

The scenes from the winner's encloseure were shown on the RTE news that night. While the BBC concentrated more on the winner of the Gold Cup and the misfortune of *Barnackle Army*, RTE were showing pictures of the celebrations of *Satan's Whiskers* contacts. First they showed a shot of Kate hugging and kissing *Satan's Whiskers* head, then they showed Shipsey picking Kevin Daly clean off the ground and kissing him squarely on the lips. Then there was a very brief interview with Macker when he was asked why he called the horse *Satan's Whiskers*. Macker was crying and shaking his head.

"I can't fuckin' remember!" The RTE censors had bleeped out the curse word.

Lastly there was a slightly more extensive interview with Liam McCann.

"Liam McCann, owner of *Satan's Whiskers*, how does that feel?"

"Well…I only own half the horse…If it wasn't for my Nephew Michael and his friends from Dublin…and my daughter Kate we never could have afforded him…It feels absolutely fantastic! I'm over the moon. I only wish my wife Eileen coulda been here to share it, but she passed away last month…I had a word with her this morning though and it seemed to do the trick."

Liam's voice was starting to crack a bit so the interviewer tried to change course.

"A big party tonight then Liam?"

278

"Oh yeah, the whole week has been a big party really and I'm sure we'll down another few pints tonight"

"Lastly Liam...anything to say about the favourite *Barnackle Army* who fell at the last. He seemed to have the race won?"

"I couldn't give a flying...ffiddle about "Barnackle Army," but I would like to say a big thanks to my friend Paddy Mulryan who prepared *Satan's Whiskers* to perfection and to Kevin Daly who gave him one hell of a ride."

The camera then got a good shot of Macker, Shipsey, Dave, Matt, Kate and Kevin Daly with their arms around each other dancing around in a circle. In the background Paddy Mulryan was playing with *Satan's Whiskers* ears and feeding him a pear.

Chapter 31

Shipsey got to work on the song as soon as they were on the road back to the hotel.

"Lads, what rhymes with *Born*?"

"What?"

"What rhymes with *Born*? I'm gonna write a song to immortalise this day."

"Oh, excellent! let's see....corn, torn, morn, worn, forlorn, thorn, scorn, horn, porn

"Ok, ok, that's enough."

Shortly after they got back to the Hotel he'd completed four verses and he showed them to Matt.

"That's fuckin' brilliant! It's like *Spancil Hill*!"

"Exactly, it's supposed to be sung to the tune of *Spancil Hill*."

"Well get up and fuckin' sing it then!"

Matt jumped up to make an announcement. "All right folks, Shipsey's gonna sing a song about today, so a bit of cuinas." (Irish for Silence)

Shipsey got to his feet and began nervously.

> *"It was on the 18th day of March, the day after Paddy was born*
> *A horse from county Kildare, stole Treballion's corn*
> *Kate and all the lads, were screaming from the stands*
> *So Satan cocked his ears and grew to twenty hands!"*

There were cheers and shouts from all around the bar. Matt stood up with his arms outstretched. "Hold on! Three more verses, three more verses!"

Shipsey continued and gave it everything he had.

> *"Kevin Daly cracked his whip saying, "Satan we've got them beat"*
> *He flew past "Barnackle Army," who couldn't get back on his feet*
> *"You're better than "Mistic Toffe" roared trainer Paddy Mulryan*

And Satan proved them both right, by getting first to the line

If I live to be a hundred, I'll never forget this day
When he entered the winner's enclosure, the crowd they did
say
He looked like he was beaten, he looked like he would die
But Satan you better believe it, God was on your side.

And now we've got the Triumph and next year we'll have the
Champ
The English might as well pack up their bags, the Paddy's are
settin' up camp.
In the year twenty twenty "Satan's Whiskers" will still have
the heart
To give those Limeys a hiding, like we did back in Stuttgart.

"Yeay! More, more! Aris, aris!"

The song would be sung another twenty times before the night was over. Each time more and more people joined in, until half the bar seemed to know it off by heart.

At 5am Liam was knackered and decided it was time for bed. He gave Kate a kiss good night and turned to go. Just as he was leaving, Shipsey started to sing his song again. Liam wasn't much of a singer, but he enjoyed listening to the song and decided to hang around for one more performance. It seemed to get better and better each time. Kate was singing with her eyes closed. She had one arm around Matt's shoulder and the other around Dave's. Shipsey and Macker were also shoulder to shoulder, leading the whole pub through the verses. Suddenly someone else popped his head between them, grabbed them tightly around the shoulders and joined in the final verse.

"And now we've got the Triumph and next year we'll have the
Champ
The English might as well pack up their bags, the Paddy's are
settin' up camp.
In the year twenty twenty "Satan's Whiskers" will still have
the heart
To give those Limeys a hiding, like we did back in Stuttgart."

Liam looked closely at the drunken intruder who was swaying from side to side between Shipsey and Macker. He definitely looked familiar. His hair seemed to be drenched in sweat and his shirt was certainly soaked in Guinness, but he had a nice voice and looked like he was having a very good time indeed. Finally it clicked. Liam turned to go to bed happy that he'd indentified the young man. He was no stranger...he was Simeon Fatherington-Smythe.

Chapter 32

"Right lads," said Macker. "We all done?"

"Yeah, what now?"

"Now we're gonna have to show them to each other in case any of them match."

They all slid their pieces of paper into the middle of the table. Each piece of paper had three investment ideas written on it.

"Jaysis Dave! Could you have written them any bigger?"

"Yeah Dave, that's not fair you'll have to redo them."

"What?"

"They're too bloody big! That gives you an unfair advantage."

Dave tutted and started re-writing his ideas.

"Ah for fucks Shipsey!" Macker groaned. "We're not buying a bleedin' brothel!"

"We are if it comes out of the hat. Anyway, you've got *Dry Cleaners* written down. What the fuck do we want with a dry cleaners?"

"Who put *Car Park* down?"

"That'd be me said Matt. Do you know how much it costs to park in town these days? Those car park owners are rakin' it in!"

"Right, myself and Matt both have *Pub*, so one of us will have to change it. Matt, do you have any back up ideas?"

"I do, as it happens." Matt took his piece of paper, scribbled out the word *Pub* and replaced it with *Lingerie shop*.

"Nice one!" said Shipsey. "Right, what now?"

"Now we pass them all to our left, then each person chooses the one they think is best and puts it in the hat." Macker had brought a shiny black top hat especially for the occasion. He'd retreated it from the attic in his mum's house. It had belonged to her grandfather, but was still in very good nick. The other lads had been very impressed when he showed up with it. Macker passed his list to Shipsey, Shipsey passed his to Matt, Matt to Dave and Dave to Macker. There were a total of twelve ideas to choose from, some of which were another racehorse, a pub, a car park, a betting shop, a dry cleaners, a brothel, a video shop, a restaurant, a lingerie shop and a cruise around the world. They each tore off a piece of paper, rolled it up and threw it into the top hat.

"Ah Dave, roll it up tighter than that!"

"Yeah Dave, stop tryin' to cheat."

Dave tutted, but took his piece of paper back out, balled it up tightly and chucked it back in.

"Right," said Macker, picking up the hat. "I'll give it a good shake and then we pick one out and stick to it, ok?"

"Ok, Who gets to pick it?"

"I'll do it," said Matt. "I'm the oldest."

"I'm the youngest," countered Macker. "I'll do it."

"Well, I'm the biggest," said Shipsey. "I'll go."

"Well, I'm clearly the best lookin'," said Dave and they all laughed.

Then Shipsey took the konch out of his pocket.

"I'd been saving this for later, but why don't we let this little baby decide?"

"Fair enough…wait a minute…who gets to spin it?"

"It's my spin," said Shipsey.

Matt shook his head. "No, I don't like the way you spin it."

"What?"

"You've got a dodgy spin."

"Tough shit, I earned this konch, so it's my spin."

"Not for this it's not. It's your spin for the next konch task. This is completely different. We'll decide who spins by doing seventh head."

"That sounds fair," said Macker, taking a coin out of his pocket.

"What the fuck is seventh head?" asked Dave.

"Ah ye must remember seventh head. We go around in a circle tossing coins. Each time a head shows that counts as one. Whoever tosses the seventh head wins."

"Right ok," Dave nodded and took a coin out of his pocket. "Hold on…wins what?"

"Well, in this case he wins the right to spin the konch, which will decide who picks out of the hat."

"Clockwise or anti-clockwise?"

"What?"

"Do we go around in a clockwise or an anti-clockwise circle?"

"Clockwise you spoon! When is anything ever done anti-clockwise?"

"Well, there's the racetrack in Leopardstown," offered Shipsey.

"And the one in Cheltenham," Macker added

"Water washing down a drain."

"Opening a bottle."

"Ok ok," said Matt, "but not fucking seventh head! Seventh head goes clockwise and always has, now can we *please* get on with it."

"Right, who goes first?"

"What?"

"Who tosses their coin first, ye see, I think there's an advantage going later."

"Are you fucking serious?"

"Yeah."

"Well I think it's better to go earlier," said Macker. "So I don't mind going first."

"Well I wanna go first as well," said Matt.

"Me too," Shipsey added.

Dave sighed and leaned back in his chair. "Why don't you just toss a coin for who goes first?"

Matt scowled at Dave. "How the fuck do you toss a coin between three people?"

"I don't know. You could do like…a round robin or something."

Shipsey grabbed the top hat, holding it close to his chest. "Lads, this is getting' a bit fuckin' ridiculous. We're gonna have a round robin tournament of coin tossing between three of us which will decide who tosses the first coin in seventh head, which in turn will decide who spins the poxy konch, which will decide who picks the bleedin' piece of paper out of the hat, which could very well shape the rest of our lives! It's just as well all our birds are out together tonight or they'd all leave us."

While they were laughing, Shipsey closed his eyes tight and started to shake the hat above his head. "I'm goin' for it!"

The laughter stopped. "What?"

"I'm fuckin' goin' for it. I'm just gonna pick one out and that's that. Come on, you know I'm no good at cheating."

"Yeah, fuck it. Go ahead," said Matt. "All agreed?"

"Yeah, go on."

"Ok, here we go." Shipsey opened his eyes and started to unravel the little piece of paper. There was a collective intake of breath.

"Oh my God!"

"What? What is it?"

"Oh lads, I think we should go again."

"Why? What the fuck is it?"

Shipsey took another look at the piece of paper to check that he wasn't seeing things

"Who the fuck picked this?"